CW00448376

WHOM GODS DESTROY

A NOVEL OF ANCIENT ROME

SERTORIUS SCROLLS
BOOK FOUR

VINCENT B. DAVIS II

THIRTEENTH PRESS

Dedicated to Andre Majors.

You were my friend, my brother, my partner-in-crime. Rest in Paradise, my friend, you earned it.

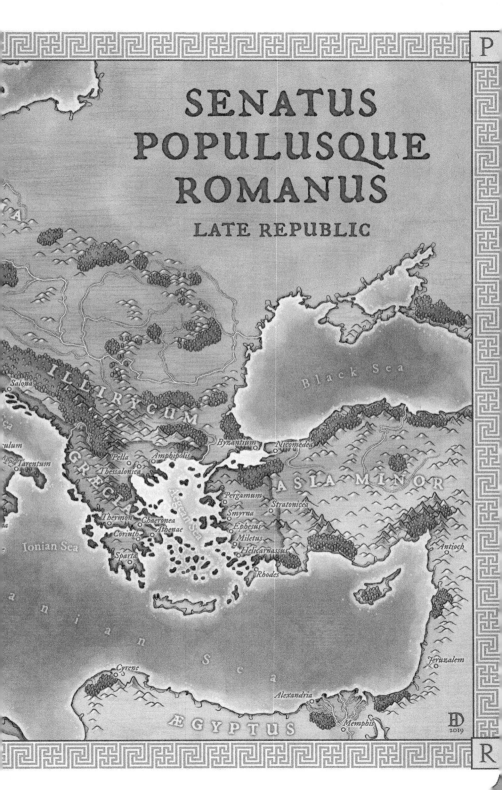

SENATUS POPULUSQUE ROMANUS

LATE REPUBLIC

Black Sea

ILLYRICUM

Salona

GRÆCIA

ASIA MINOR

Byzantium   Nicomedea

Pella   Amphipolis

Tarentum   Thessalonica

Pergamum   Stratonicea

Smyrna

Thermon   Chaeronea   Ephesus

Corinth   Athenae   Miletus

Aegean Sea   Helicarnassus

Ionian Sea

Sparta

Antioch

Rhodes

Cyrene

Jerusalem

Alexandria

ÆGYPTUS   Memphis

Sea

READING ORDER

To enhance your reading experience, scan the QR code below to *Join the Legion!* You'll receive free downloadable companion materials like:

- High-resolution maps
- Family trees
- Free eBooks
- Glossary
- And more!

PART I

SCROLL I

THE KNIFE CUT DEEP, and the victim made no sound of resistance with his dying breath. Blood seeped out and ran through the cracks of the marble altar. Torchlight flickered in the wind and illuminated the priest's hands while they worked.

I gestured for the men to stand fast and I moved forward, pulling my cloak under my chin and bracing myself against the strength of a gust.

"What does it look like?" I asked the haruspex.

His hands were slippery with blood as he meticulously peeled apart the liver, inspecting it for signs of the gods' will.

"What do you think?" He nodded toward the grey clouds in the distance covering the midday sun. I looked up anticipating the flash of Jupiter's lightening or a crack of thunder.

I peered over the priest's shoulder, as if I might be able to spot some imperfection in the slaughtered lamb, but it just looked like a dead animal to me.

He turned to me and gravely shook his head.

"The gods' will is uncertain, except for one thing: you must not sail tomorrow. Neptune forbids it."

"The liver tells you that?"

He analyzed me with baleful eyes. "Correct, legate. A storm

will come upon you, Triton's scourge will pull your men to their doom and dash your ships upon the rocks."

I didn't need a priest to tell me a storm was coming. The dark clouds moved swiftly and the nip in the breeze that always proceeded rain showers. The farmers would be pleased, to be certain, because the winter had been dry. But no one would envy those on the water.

"I'll relay the message to the commander. Gratitude." I bowed to the priest and turned to leave, but he grabbed my wrist with his blood-soaked hands before I could descend from the altar.

"Your commander… Didius, right?"

"Proconsul Titus Didius is our commanding officer, yes." I freed myself from his grasp, painfully aware of the warm blood now running over my fingers.

"He is a prideful man. A good Roman, but a prideful one. Do not let his pride become hubris. Do not let his *dignitas* bring all of your men to their doom. You *must* not sail."

"What should I tell him?" I asked, frustrated. He was my superior after all. If he wanted to depart for Greece, then—gods be damned—we would. "Should I tell him he'll lose his entire army if we do? Is there some sacrifice we can perform to appease the gods? I cannot return to him empty handed with only orders to remain idle."

He shook his head, disappointed. "There is no sacrifice he can make, and he will not lose his entire army. The propitiation will be who is lost on the way. Tell your general he can sail if he wants to, but only if he's willing to accept the loss he'll sustain. The blood will be on his hands." He lifted his own to illustrate his point.

I found Didius on the Field of Mars. Until then our interactions had been limited. He wasn't a general like Marius—one whom you could approach with anything you deemed necessary. Didius expected the chain-of-command to be followed to the letter, and even as a legate I wasn't to interrupt him unbidden. Didius seemed pleased to have a distinguished veteran on his staff but he made it clear we wouldn't be friends.

At least on this occasion, though, he'd requested my presence.

He walked through the neat rows of his legion's tents with parchment in hand, trailed by two slaves. I'd never seen a man write and walk at the same time, but Didius had a complete inability to sit still. He bore the parchment on a block of wood and signed each page, handing them over his shoulder for one of them to take.

I hurried up behind them. The aroma of leather so common to Roman camps filled my lungs, putting me at ease, but only slightly.

"Legate Sertorius, what does the priest say?" he said without looking up.

I snapped to attention and offered a salute regardless. "Sir, the haruspicy were not good. The omens say we must not sail for Greece or we will experience great losses at sea. There will be storms."

He chuckled to himself and looked at the foreboding sky. "The gods truly speak to them, don't they? The priests are so enlightened." He shook his head. "Do the men know of the results?"

"Those with me at the altar of Mars may have overheard, but I haven't announced anything yet. I wanted you to know first and seek your instructions."

"You were right to do so." He continued walking with long strides I had difficulty replicating. "We will not inform the men. Let this burden be mine and yours alone. No need to arouse the fears of the simpleminded rank and file."

"Don't tell them, Proconsul?" I paced alongside him to see his expression.

Didius finally stopped walking and handed off his parchment. He approached me and crossed his arms. Rumor had it he was a champion wrestler in his youth, and it wasn't difficult to believe. His forearms were thick and sinewy, his chest broad. He stood a head taller than me. He was an imposing presence with his stature alone, but the coldness of his grey eyes could stun men into submission.

"Legate, I do not believe in the gods, omens, or auspices. I especially don't believe the gods—if they existed—would speak through the liver of a slaughtered lamb. And here I am. The first of my line to be made Consul, a triumphant general in every command I've ever had. If there are gods out there, legate, they leave me alone. I'll not remain in Rome a day longer than we have planned, regardless of what some half-blind dim-witted priest has to say about it."

I expected as much, but his candor in blaspheming the gods stunned me. I imagine there were plenty of men amongst Rome's elite who felt the same way, but very few would be so bold as to speak it into existence.

"Understood, Proconsul," I replied.

I thought I heard a crack of thunder in the distance. Judging from the craning heads of the legionaries around us, I knew I wasn't the only one.

"It's near war season, and I intend to make it to Greece by the Kalends of March." He resumed his walk, thrusting out a hand for his documents.

"Is this not a peacetime campaign, sir?" I asked. Of course it was, but I already knew it was erroneous to assume anything with my new commander.

"For now. We expect no trouble with the Greeks. They've been beaten into submission for some time now. But I've worked too hard to secure the wealthy province of Greece to return home without a triumph, so at some point we will have to find 5,000 men to kill."

"On a peacetime mission?" I did not question what he meant about working hard to secure his province... they were supposed to be drawn by lot. He twisted his neck to pop it, poorly restraining his irritation at my insolence.

"Correct, legate. My last command was in Macedonia. There we found a tribe of reprobates who needed to be wiped from Gaia's earth. Now they are rotting on the fields of Pella and I am a triumphator. I will not be returning to Rome with less than I did last time." Didius stopped again and met my eye. "Your job as my legate is to find the right men to kill."

I inhaled deeply and pursed my lips. He waited for me to acknowledge so I gave him a nod.

"I'm glad we have an understanding. You and your ships will depart from Ostia at first light tomorrow." He crossed his arms. "It's inappropriate for the general to travel with his men, so I will be leaving from Brundisium as soon as my carriage can bear me there. In my stead will be my son, Publius. You will look after him for me, won't you?"

"Certainly, Proconsul."

"Good. He's received his position as military tribune by his own merit. On this campaign I will regard him as an officer of the legion rather than my heir. He'll have to earn everything for himself, as I did. But everything I do is for that boy. I push so far because one day he'll be duty bound to outdo me. In the meantime, I need good officers like yourself to teach him all he needs to know."

This was the first compliment he'd given me, and I did not take it lightly. "I understand, Proconsul. You are a good father. I try to be one myself. If we're indeed at peace in Greece I'd like to bring my wife and son for a time, if you'd permit it." He peered at me through the corner of his eyes and gave an all-knowing smile, the first sign of humanity I'd sensed in him.

"Our families can be our undoing. Remember this legate:

Agamemnon conquered Troy because he was willing to sacrifice his own daughter for victory, even though she was innocent. Priam saw Troy burn beneath him because he refused to sacrifice his son, even though he'd been wrong." He shook his head. "Remember this if you ever become a commander yourself. You must remain cold and pragmatic. It's best for your legions, your career, and indeed even your family."

We walked to a campfire where several Mules were sitting around eating their evening meal. When they saw him, they sprang to attention and saluted, but he paid them no mind, still continuing to sign his name on document after document. Eventually he extended his hand, to which a legionary quickly passed a cup of water.

Drinking deeply, he lifted one of the documents and passed it to me.

"The commission for the men you're bringing on this campaign. Who are they?"

The document had the names L. Hirtuleius, Gn. Herennius, Au. Insteius, and Sp. Insteius listed, along with their ranks.

"Tribune Lucius Hirtuleius is one of the finest officers I've served with. He served with distinction in the war against the Cimbri and Teutones." I neglected to tell him we were childhood friends. "First Spear Centurion Gaius Herennius is a veteran of over twenty years, also serving with bravery and distinction in the war against the Cimbri. He will be invaluable in training up the new recruits."

"And the other two? The Sabine twins."

I hesitated and considered how honest I'd like to be. Aulus and Spurius Insteius grew up with Lucius and me. We'd been inseparable, the four of us. We all studied under the same tutor and played the same games. In the years since I departed for Rome, they'd both served as local magistrates in our hometown of Nursia, but neither had touched a sword. "Old friends."

He cocked an eyebrow. "And that's it?"

"Correct, sir. They are good men and will become good offi-

cers. Serving Rome has left me with little time for companion-
ship, so I've been forced to bring my companions with me." He
locked his eyes with mine, and I refused to look away until he
cracked a smile.

Didius poured some of the water into his hand and rubbed it
over the close-cropped, white-gold hair on his head. "Most of
my officers are selling positions to the highest bidder, so I can't
fault you for bringing along a few men your trust. As long as
you understand you're responsible for them." He pointed at me.

"Absolutely, sir... certainly."

"Hand it here, then. I'll sign it." He scribbled his signature
and passed it off to his slave. "Go and reconvene with your
legion. If anyone asks about the haruspicy tell them the results
were favorable."

My heart sank. "Duty demands I not lie, sir," I said as confi-
dently as I could manage.

He rolled his eyes and shook his head. "Then cough and look
the other direction or something. But you will be sailing tomorrow, along with all your men. You'll carry them kicking and
screaming onto the ship if you have to, but at first light oars will
be slicing through the wake. Understood?"

"Understood, Proconsul."

"Dismissed, legate."

That evening I took Arrea to the roof, bringing two chairs and an
amphora of wine. We sat at the edge of the terrace and looked
out over the city. Torchlight illuminated the temple steps at the
base of the hill. A gentle breeze caused them to flicker.

We sat in comfortable silence, my hand outstretched and
holding on to hers. There was only one thing on our minds—my
departure the next morning.

"Can I refill your cup, dove?" I asked.

"Still nursing it." She swirled her cup around to prove it.

"The roses are already blooming. Perhaps summer will come earlier than we expected," I said, inspecting the flowerpots Arrea had planted on the roof a few weeks prior.

She released my hand, tucked her knees to her chest, and wrapped her arms around them.

"Do you need another blanket?"

"How long do you think you'll be gone?"

The moonlight shimmered in her eyes as they peered into mine. Her hair was wild from an evening of packing and preparing for my departure, but she looked as beautiful as the day I married her. I found my gaze fixated on her lips, and I wondered how I would manage to be away from them for so long. All my ambitions and dreams seemed foolish and meaningless when I looked at her. Was it worth it, to be gone from her for so long?

I inhaled deep and long and reminded myself why I accepted the command in the first place. "I don't know. It could be a year or it could be ten. I expect the former. Greece has been free of conflict for years."

She shuddered at the thought. "Ten years... Gavius will be nearly the age you are now when you return."

"As I've said, dove—"

"I knew what to expect when I married you, Quintus. You don't need to explain yourself to me." She stood and walked to the balustrade. "I just worry."

"About what? You can speak plainly." I put down my cup of wine.

"We've worked so hard to get you *home*. And I worry when you return again the campaign will come with you. I dread the anger and the drinking and—"

"I know. Trust me, Arrea, I know." I stood and wrapped my arms around her waist. "I fear it too. But I'm not going to let that happen. What sorrows have I to drown out, eh?" I pinched her side to make her smile. "I'm married to a lovely woman, have great companions to keep me company, a good son to live after me. Fortuna has blessed me. And I will not allow my soul to be taken again."

She spun and threw her arms around my neck. "Oh, Quintus. I will miss you."

I closed my eye and inhaled the scent of her hair.

I put a finger on her chin and raised it to look at me. She cupped her hands around my face before I whispered, "I will remember the way you are right now and remember this moment until I return to you."

"You must come home, Quintus. I need you. Do you hear me?"

"Yes."

"No, I mean it Quintus. No heroics. Do nothing you'll have to carry back with you. Go and serve and then come back to me safely, the man you are now. Because I love the man you are right now."

"I vow it, Arrea."

"I have something." She revealed a leather pouch and handed it to me. Within was a gold signet ring, bearing the image of an eagle. I knew it well. My eyes shimmered.

"Your mother told me to give it to you before you leave. She said it's been yours since your father died but … she's been holding onto it all this time."

"Do you know what this is?"

"A signet ring, right?"

"Yes, but it's much more than that." I turned it over in my fingers, the torchlight glistening on its polished edges. "Years ago my ancestral tribe fought the Romans. When we lost the war, the Romans were so impressed by our bravery and courage they immediately decided to strike an alliance and make us part of their Republic." I lost myself for a moment while I tested the fit. It fixed perfectly on my finger, as it had my father's. It'd always seemed so large when I was a boy and I was amazed it fit me now.

"What does that have to do with the ring?"

"The Roman general gave this ring to my ancestor as a token of peace and friendship. It's likely worth more than this home."

"That's amazing, Quintus. I had no notion it was so important," she said, but I knew she couldn't understand how much it meant to me. No one could, save perhaps my mother. "You can use it to seal every letter you send home."

"I will. Thank you, Arrea." I leaned down until my lips meet hers.

And because Mercury, god of mischief, loves ruining moments such as this, Gavius and Apollonius came pounding up the stairs behind us.

"I can't sleep, pater," Gavius said, his voice deepening every day. If he was anything like his father and me, he would be growing his first chin hair soon.

"I tried to stop him," Apollonius said. "He demanded to talk with you."

Gavius and I had grown much closer over the past two years, since Arrea and I had married. As a boy he had clung to Arrea, but the older he became, the more he relied on me.

"Join us." I released Arrea and waved them toward us. I poured a little bit of wine into a cup and handed it to Gavius. "What seems to be causing you insomnia?"

"It's the moonlight. It's too bright," he said, taking a tiny sip as he wasn't fond of the taste yet. I hoped that would remain the case.

"Master Gavius," Apollonius said, hands akimbo on his hips, "I've told you to shutter that window at night. That should do the trick."

A father's intuition told me the moon wasn't the cause. He was dreading tomorrow.

"Come here, lad." I pulled Gavius between Arrea and me.

"Apollonius, grab yourself a cup too. Tonight is a night for celebration."

"What's to celebrate?" Gavius said. "The Quirinalia isn't until next week."

Watching a child grow up is incredible. In each word, in every movement, I could see shades of others. He had Titus's pragmatic and serious demeanor, and perhaps his mother's sadness. He had Arrea's gentle spirit and resolve, and he shared my sense of humor and good looks—or at least I told myself that. It brought me joy to hear him repeating terms or phrases he'd picked up from me.

"Tonight is special, because it's your last night as a boy. Tomorrow you become a man," I said, retrieving my cup of wine.

"I've not dawned my *toga virilis,* father. Have you drunk too much?"

Arrea's furtive laugh hung in the air.

"The toga virilis is just a symbol of manhood. But many boys become men before their time because the Fates demanded it. And this is such a time." Everyone looked at me skeptically. "Tomorrow I am departing for Greece, and your grouchy old tutor Apollonius will be accompanying me. So tomorrow you will be the pater of this house. You'll have to protect your mother—"

"And listen to her as well." Arrea smirked.

"Well, yes. Certainly. Listening to women is part of manhood." I leaned closer to him. "Believe me."

Arrea jabbed me in the ribs.

"At times you may even have to answer to your father's clients," Apollonius added. Gavius' eyes widened at this.

"He's right," I said. "And you'll have to visit your grandmother in Nursia to ensure she doesn't become lonely. Oh, and work with my horse!"

"I'll do it, pater," Gavius said, straightening his shoulders.

"Well, then raise your cups." I lifted my own. "To Gavius!" They echoed it and drank from their cups.

I would miss this moment when I was in Greece.

I ruffled his hair. "Now, go sleep, and give your mother and me some privacy."

He scrunched his face but allowed Apollonius to lead him back into the Domus.

"He's so much like you," Arrea said.

"Hopefully some time apart will make him more like you then. If you had been born a man, you'd already be Consul," I said playfully, but her smile faded.

"Let's hope it's not too long apart."

I put my arm around her, and we stood in silence, staring out over the city as the temple's torches were extinguished one at a time.

SCROLL II

WE APPROACHED the Ostian docks while it was still dark. A single fire from the lighthouse illuminated our path and the ships awaiting us.

"You will write to us soon, won't you?" Arrea asked, both of her soft hands around mine.

"Of course, my dove. You have my word."

"And you'll be safe?"

"I have Apollonius here to protect me." I gestured to my friend and freed slave who winked at Arrea and little Gavius. He hadn't said much on our walk to the docks, probably more nervous for the trip back to his homeland than I'd previously realized.

"Good morning," Lucius Hirtuleius approached, rubbing his eyes warily.

"A good day for a sea voyage," I said while he kissed Arrea on either cheek.

"Much too early to be awake, if you ask me. But if I'm forced to be up, we might as well be sailing the *Mare Nostrum*."

I hadn't told Lucius about the haruspicy. As traditional and superstitious as any Roman, the truth would haunt him.

"Which one is yours, pater?" Gavius asked, fascinated by the vessels and their sails flapping in the early-morning wind.

"If you're legate Sertorius, it's this one here," an old sailor said, joining us.

"That's me," I replied, extending my hand, "and you are?"

"Captain Municius. This is my vessel," he said. He had a rather rugged handsomeness until he smiled, revealing rotten teeth.

"How do the waters look, Captain?" Arrea asked.

"This is my wife, Arrea," I said.

"I'm pleased to meet the man who will be keeping my husband safe," she said with a curtsey.

"Aye. I'll do that. The waters will be choppy, so prepare for the ride. But we'll make it there just fine. I've sailed on the first day of war season for nigh on thirty years and haven't lost a vessel yet. I'll get him there, ma'am." He bowed his head and kissed her hand. She leaned toward him and whispered something to his ear. It must have been quite funny, as his laughter rang out and cut through the still morning air.

"Care to explain?" I asked my mischievous bride.

The captain lifted his hands in mock surrender and stepped away.

"I told him you have a deathly fear of the water, my love." She grinned.

I shook my head and chuckled. I would miss her dearly. "Let him find out when I'm emptying my stomach in the sea for two weeks. No need to spoil the surprise."

Bells sounded throughout the bay.

"First to board! First to board!"

"I'm afraid that's us, dove." I leaned in and kissed her lips, savoring the taste. "I will see you again soon."

"You swear it?"

"On the Fires of Vesta."

I turned then to Gavius and pulled him into my embrace. He'd grown like a weed since Arrea and I had wed. I no longer needed to kneel to his height or pick him up. I figured he would be as tall as myself by the time I returned.

"Goodbye, pater," he said.

Gavius was Titus' son, stubborn and tough. He did his best to send me off in front of my men with the most stoic and respectful goodbye he could muster, but I could see the shimmer of tears in his eyes. "Goodbye, my boy." I kissed his head and ruffled his hair. "The next time I depart for campaign I imagine you'll be riding out alongside me," I said and his face shone with pride.

"First to board!"

"We can hear, you old bastard," Lucius grumbled as he tightened his horse-hair plumed helmet and tried to blink his eyes awake.

"Lucius, I'm afraid you're becoming an old man before my eyes," I said and Apollonius chuckled.

"I'm afraid you've been an old man since we were children."

"You may be right," I said.

We fell into line with the rest of the men who were previously identified as the first to board. We would sail the ocean on *quinqueremes*, which could each hold four hundred and twenty men. After you included three hundred rowers and twenty deck crewmen, there's only enough room for about one hundred soldiers. The legion under my command had 4,000 fresh recruits, so you can do the mathematics to determine the great quantities of boats our expedition would require. Only three boats could line up abreast in the harbor, and we piled up on the ramp to Municius' vessel in the center.

"We'll have to name her," Lucius said.

"Who? I'm afraid you've lost me," Apollonius said.

"The ship. Every ship must have a name."

"I think I'll call her the *Medusa*," I said while we inched closer.

"Why? Because she'll petrify our enemies?" Lucius asked.

"No. Because she petrifies me."

"I don't care what I have to do to get to Greece. My first chance to win some glory for myself," he said. He was Tribune Laticlavius for the seventeenth legion, as the fourth under my command already had one enlisted. There would certainly be a chance for glory, but I'm not sure why he'd want it.

"Glory isn't worth it, *amicus*, I assure you."

He shook his head. "That's easy for you to say." I noticed something different in his eyes, something I'd never noticed before. "You've already achieved it. Perhaps I'll say the same when I have some glory of my own, but before that I must acquire some."

I was about to reply when a shout from the docks diverted our attention. "Don't forget us, you bastards!"

Too dark to see the men piling up behind us, I already knew who it was—my boyhood companions, the Insteius twins, characteristically late.

I tried to conceal my grin and looked up at the sun which just now peaked over the ocean in the east. "I was afraid we'd have to sail without you." I shook my head in mock disappointment.

"Spurius here took me to the wrong dock. We boarded and were halfway to Sicily before we realized it was an old fisherman's vessel," Aulus said breathing heavily as Lucius and I both pulled them into an embrace.

"Well, I'm glad you made it back in time, comrades. Greece wouldn't be the same without you," Lucius replied, perking up for the first time that morning.

"You're right. Greece will *never* be the same after Aulus gets ahold of it." Spurius laughed, the love he had for his twin brother evident in the look they exchanged.

"They call Sertorius... sorry, Legate Sertorius... the Hero of the North. Well, by Juno's tits they'll call me the Hero of the East." He beat his fist against his breastplate. Since I had last seen them I had fought in several battles, embarked on a perilous espionage mission, became a senator, lost my brother and a host of other friends, and seen Rome on the brink of destruction. After everything it's remarkably refreshing to see some things hadn't changed.

The line thinned out before us and we could finally step onto the vessel which was to be our home for the next two or three weeks. The boat bobbed up and down with the gentle morning current, and already my heart raced. I held onto the railing. I wasn't cut out for long sea voyages, not after my near-death experience as a child. The trek would be long, especially with the priest's warnings ringing in my mind.

Triton's scourge will pull your men to their doom and dash your ships upon the rocks.

Three days on the sea and I still hadn't adjusted. I was quartered in a small room with some of the other officers, and unfortunately sleeping on the upper loft. The wood creaked with every big wave the rowers hit, and I bounced along with them.

I threw a straw pillow over my head to force myself back to sleep, but eventually gave up. Bile began rising in my throat so I hurried to the deck.

Surprisingly the sun had already burst upon the horizon, reflecting right to the ship like a paved road to Olympus. The cool, crisp, life-giving air filled my lungs and settled my stomach.

"Good morning, legate!" Aulus shouted with an exaggerated salute from the port side of the ship.

"I see you've risen before me, gentlemen. I can respect that," I said, approaching the twins.

"Risen? How can one rise if one never set?" Spurius asked, raising a finger to his lip like a contemplative philosopher.

"Lucius' feet were stinking up the entire room. It was unbearable." Aulus scrunched his face.

It was remarkable how two men could look identical, and yet somehow totally different. Sometimes I thought I imagined it, but everyone else seemed to agree. The features of their faces were almost identical, the short light hair atop their heads the same. And yet, Spurius was the more handsome of the two. More serious and more respectful, too, but Aulus always had better luck with the opposite sex. Why? Because he kept them laughing.

"You're right, Aulus," I said. "The last three days have been the longest of my life."

"It will all be worth it when we arrive." Aulus rubbed his hands together and licked his lips. "In all my days I've never been with a Greek girl."

"So you've been with a woman of any kind now, Aulus?" I asked, knowing the answer already from our childhood adventures.

Aulus burst into laughter, irritating some of the groggy deck crewmen.

"Here's old Quintus. He gets married and thinks he's every woman's Apollo. Remember how nervous girls use to make him, Spurius? 'S-s-say how are you today, L-licinia?'" he mimicked.

"Not every woman's Apollo, just one woman's Apollo. You little bastard." I gave him a punch in the ribs and he feigned agony.

"I wonder how Balbina will feel about your gallivanting with Greek girls?" Spurius asked his brother with a raised eyebrow. I often forgot they were married. Strange that two men so integral to my life were married to girls I'd never even met.

"We discussed it before we left," Aulus said. "She has two rules. The first is that I shall not sleep with another woman of equal station. Second, that I don't lie with anyone younger or more beautiful than her." We shook our heads. "You really mean to tell me you don't plan on enjoying any Achaian cunny? We may be gone a long time."

"It would break the heart of my Cassia,"Spuruis said. "I don't even lie with our slaves."

"My wife is a Celt, I remind you," I said. "She's liable to track me down and geld me if she caught wind of it." My heart sank as I remembered the sweet face of my Arrea.

Aulus cracked his mischievous smile and nudged Spurius. "He's finally found a woman who doesn't make him nervous, that's what it is. 'E-e-xcuse me, A-a-phrodite, how much for a r-romp?'"

The laughter made my stomach churn again, so I hurried away. I knew if I threw up in front of them I'd never hear the end of it. I made my way to starboard and pretended to be contemplative when really I was heaving overboard. Luckily, I hadn't eaten in so long there wasn't much for me to offer the sea. Then again, if I did, perhaps I'd find some relief. When I stopped heaving, I noticed a young legionnaire quietly sitting close by.

"I apologize. I'm sure that wasn't pleasant," I said, but he didn't look up. A knife in his hand, he whittled away at a block of wood. "What are you working on there?"

"A dog," he said, cheerfully. "I think I'll make several of them to sell in Greece. If I make enough perhaps I could buy a real dog. Do you think they have dogs in Greece?" he said, as if to himself. His voice wasn't high-pitched by any means, but I could tell it belonged to a young man.

When he looked up, this appeared to be the case. I didn't spot any stubble on his chin, nor wrinkle or sunspot. I assumed he was at least my height, but thin as a *pilum*. I guessed he was no more than sixteen.

I smiled as if he were joking, but he didn't appear to be. He wanted an answer.

"Oh, yes. Certainly. I'm sure they have dogs. But what would you want to do with one in the legion?"

He returned his attention to the block of wood. "You know… maybe we could train him and he could be a real legionnaire."

I could tell he wasn't speaking in jest. "Well," I said, sitting beside him, "what would you do if our enemy hurt this dog?"

I saw rage pass before his eyes for an instant.

"I wouldn't like it."

"What is your name, soldier?"

"Castor."

"What about your full name?"

He seemed confused for a moment then nodded. "I told the registrar my first name was Gaius... cause that's everyone's name. But I've only ever been called Castor. My parents died of the fever when I young and I only remember hearing them call me 'boy'." A wide smile split his face. "Everyone called me Castor because I had a dog named Pollux who went everywhere with me! But he died last winter." As quickly as the smile appeared, it vanished.

"I'm sorry to hear about your Pollux. I have a horse named Sura, and I'll be bearded and ash-covered for a month or more when she rides to Hades."

His eyes spread wide, and he jumped to his feet and to attention. "I'm sorry, sir," he said, obviously not noticing my crest. "I didn't know you were an officer."

"At ease, at ease. Sit. We're all equals when we sail on Neptune's waters." It wasn't really true, but for some reason I wanted to continue our conversation.

He sat again, but seemed less comfortable than previously, and returned to his whittling.

Some squawking galls took turns diving to the water, bobbing for fish. I wondered how they could fly so far away from land.

The waters were calm. Aristocrats would have paid fortunes to have a toga as blue as the sea beneath us. I thought of the bad omens and wondered if Didius was right. Even I wasn't trembling when I glanced over the railing, which says a lot.

"Well, Castor, besides dogs what do you like?"

"Pigs," he replied, quickly. "Sometimes Pollux and I would

go to the Boarium forum and play with the pigs until the shop-keepers would make us leave. Sometimes they'd let us sleep there to ward off thieves."

My heart sank. "You're homeless?"

His face twisted in confusion. "The drill instructors said the legion is my home now. Will we not have somewhere to stay in Greece?"

Young Castor was clearly simple but talking with him seemed to calm me. He had wet, green eyes—the most curious and unassuming I'd ever seen. Not a drop of deception in them.

"Yes. Of course we will." Something flashed before my eye in the water. "Look!" I spun him around and pointed to the distance.

His face lit up. "Those are some big fish!"

"Dolphins. They say Neptune's chariot is sometimes pulled by them. He must favor us!"

They took turns leaping as if taking part in a choreographed dance. We watched until they faded into the horizon.

My smile faded. Red clouds ascended like smoke from a fire.

I knew very little about the sea, but I heard tales about red clouds in the morning since I was a child. Some called it 'Triton's Scourge.' I swallowed hard and gritted my teeth. I had stood tall on the battlefield with ten thousand barbarians howling for my blood. I wouldn't panic in the face of a storm. I wasn't going to die on this ship. The priest was wrong. I'd make it back to my wife and son. "Captain Municius!" I shouted.

"I just spotted it," he said as he came to my side. "I hope you're ready, Legate. We're about to go to war with the gods."

SCROLL III

"WE'RE TOO FAR OUT. We won't be able to beach until after the storm has hit us. See how swiftly it's moving toward us?" the captain had said, and he was right.

The cadence drummer increased his tempo to double time, sending the vessel churning through the choppy waters for hours, but still no sign of land.

"If we can't reach land then what shall we do?" I had asked, maintaining my composure only by the silent prayers I was saying.

"We'll have to ride it. We'll have to sail straight into Neptune's wrath."

The winds picked up violently as we grew nearer to the storm. The air became heavy with moisture, and even with my one good eye I could see a wall of rain in the distance.

I ordered a formation on the stern of the deck.

"Alright, lads. Listen up. We're going to be riding into a storm. Braver men than I have turned and run or fallen to their knees or on their swords. But we aren't going to. Are we?" I asked. They shook their heads. "Lift your voices!"

"No!" they shouted.

"That's right. This is the stuff of legend. If Homer were alive today, he'd tell a tale of our journey. With the courage of Odysseus we'll meet this storm. We'll follow in our ancestor Aeneas's footsteps and prove our worth to the gods!"

They brandished their swords and beat them against their shields like the storm was an enemy army in full array across from us.

I asked the captain to convey his instructions. My rank meant nothing now. Neptune's wrath—if that's what it was—does not discriminate. The captain instructed us to remain in the bowels of the ship and spread out to keep weight distributed evenly. There was nothing else for fighting men to do.

"And wear your helmets, lads. You'll need them," he said.

We broke formation and hurried down into the lower levels one man at a time.

"Let's bring some wine," Aulus said when we reached our quarters. "If I'm going to die, I'll not do it sober."

"You'll be spewing it all over us within the hour!" Lucius shouted.

"It'd be a shame to waste the wine. But then I'll drink some more."

Apollonius was the only one of us who didn't scurry around frantically.

"Are you not afraid, my friend?"

He smiled and sat on the edge of his cot.

"Aristotle tells us of a certain river creature which is born and dies each day."

I exchanged a confused glance with Lucius.

"Simply tragic. Were I a playwright I'd tell this fascinating tale," Aulus said.

"Leave off," Spurius said, "he isn't finished."

Apollonius looked up and met my eye. "Wouldn't it be strange to us, ridiculous even, that one of these creatures would feel cursed to die in the morning, or that another would feel blessed to die in the evening? What difference does it make? It's trivial. And that's what our life is, Quintus. A whisper, a blink of the eye. I've lived well and you men have too. It makes no difference if we die today or tomorrow."

The ship jerked and it sent all of us crashing into whatever was nearest.

"Well, gentlemen," Aulus teased, "I think the old man's finally gone mad."

"By the gods, Apollonius, if you can teach me half your wisdom and fortitude, I would conquer all of Gaul." I leaned over and kissed his head. "But for now, let's get as low as possible. I'll live into the evening if it's possible."

"I think I'd prefer it, too." He smiled.

We gathered what little we needed and hunkered down along the wooden planks of the port side wall. For what seemed like hours, we linked our arms together and held as fast as we could as the ship bounced and spun from side to side. Several times I thought we would flip. Water began spilling in from the deck above us, a trickle at first but soon a steady pour.

"Pass me the wine, will you?" Lucius said when the water reached his sandals.

"Better to die drunk I say," Aulus replied as he struggled to pass it along.

"Nobody is dying," I said, "comrades. I'll swim to Neptune's palace and fight him myself to save you."

"Hard to imagine you even swimming in a bathtub," Aulus said. It wasn't far from the truth, and we needed the laughter.

The dark—which had been almost pitch black after the torches were doused—was now illuminated from above by lightning bolts. Even from the belly of the ship and over the waves crashing into the ship we could hear the crack of thunder.

"It seems we've pissed off more than just Neptune," Aulus said.

The ship bounced and for a moment felt almost suspended before we crashed down hard, sending all of us on top of one another.

"You should have sacrificed more pigeons, Lucius," I said.

For a moment he snarled but his laughter rang out above the roaring waves and booming thunder.

The water reached my hips. I laid back and said a prayer. My mind scrambled. Not focusing on any god in particular, visions flashed before my eyes of all the good things I'd promise to do if I lived.

In my fear I imagined the sensation of drowning, as I once experienced it as a child. The gasping, clawing, straining. Water filling the lungs, the chest tightening, the limbs growing numb.

Apollonius patted my chest. "You stopped breathing."

"I'm still here, old man," I said, my voice now as shaky as my legs were.

I heard harried shouts from somewhere above us.

"What's happening?" Spurius asked. "What's happening."

The thunder and rushing water seemed to quiet enough for us to hear the voices from above.

"The rowers are dying from exhaustion! Others double over with cramps. We're going to die!" someone shouted from above.

Aulus lowered his head and swore. "Hand me back the wine if you don't mind, Lucius."

"We are not dying here!" I shouted, struggling to my feet. The water reached my ankles now, our personal effects submerged. "Let's go. Now." I helped Apollonius to his feet. "Move!" I grabbed onto the ladder and hoisted myself up first.

We hurried onto the rowing floor and strained to see the rowers' faces. Endless rows of benches awaited us in the shadows, and indeed some of them contained men slumped over, or on the floor beside them.

I sprinted to one closest to me and thrust him aside. I grabbed the oar. At first I followed the speed of the rower beside me, but eventually pushed harder to relieve him. "Row, you bastards! Row!" I shouted, cutting my oar through the violent sea.

Land was the most beautiful thing I'd ever seen. Aphrodite herself must have come down to earth taking on the form of a beach. I sifted sand through my fingers and thanked whichever god would listen for delivering us through the storm.

I have no notion how long we rowed. Perhaps an hour, perhaps all night. Either way, the sun was breaking by the time our vessels reached the shoreline and I was utterly spent. Once I made it to the sand, I found myself unable to rise. Perhaps because of how precious I found the earth beneath me.

The deep blue water became teal at the shoreline like stitched embroidery on the hem of a tunic. The early morning sun sparkled along the calm waves. I saw no sign of the treacherous storm, except for the debris which came in with each tide.

I found the atmosphere on the island interesting. On the one hand, some of the soldiers were singing songs, drinking wine, and telling exaggerated tales about their bravery during the storm. On the other, men silently and somberly helped down the bodies of the dead from the deck and laid them in a row with a blanket over each of them.

"Legate Sertorius!" a gruff voice called from the shoreline. I turned to find my old centurion, Gnaeus Herennius.

"I'm grateful to see you." I took his hand. We'd both been in Rome preparing for departure for nigh on six months, but I'd hardly seen him. He trained with the men of course, which I envied. Most of my time was spent signing provisioning documents, attending logistics meetings, and doing other bureaucratic duties.

"I thought we were all going to drown," he said.

"I knew we'd make it."

He grinned and shook his head. "You lie, but I appreciate it. I haven't had the chance to thank you for bringing me on this campaign. I had no notion you'd even remember me after you returned to Rome, let alone give me a commission." He placed a hand on my shoulder.

"They say the fool is an orphan but the wise man has many fathers. If there is any wisdom in me, Herennius, I must admit you're one of those fathers. I'm honored to have you serving in my legion."

"You flatter me, I think, but I am honored to be here."

"How long have you been here? What's the damage?"

He scratched at the stubble of his grey beard and considered it. "If my numbers are right … and don't bet on it by the way … we're only missing three vessels. Most of the ones here lost a rower or two to exhaustion during the storm, but otherwise I'd say fortuna has favored us."

"*Only* three? That's a lot of men." I closed my eye and rubbed my head, trying to forget the priest's warnings.

"Don't worry, legate. I talked with each and every one of those captains before we left. They're as experienced with the sea as I am in battle. They'll make it."

"I hope you're right."

"I bet you're famished," he said. "Come then, let's get some porridge."

"Without being on that damned boat I might even be able to keep it down."

We both filled a clay bowl with porridge and settled in around a hastily built but roaring fire. Warmth had never felt better, but I still shivered from the damp of my clothes. Apollonius joined us as well, and I forced him to wrap up in a cloak and fill a bowl for himself, despite his resistance.

"Tell me," I said between mouthfuls, "how are the men? I'm assuming you've had a chance to assess them."

"Aye. They're a lousy bunch of degenerates," he said to my surprise, until he smiled. "And I rather like them. Perhaps I'm becoming soft in my old age." He took a pull of wine and ignored the drops rolling down his chin.

"I doubt it," I said.

"I mean it! I used to run them ragged. Now, I hardly raise my voice at them. It's tough on the throat, yelling so often." He chuckled.

"I'd say these men just survived the worst thing that'll happen to them on this campaign," Apollonius said, "If they can endure this, a peacetime mission in the center of philosophy and wisdom should be nothing."

Herennius handed me the wine skin, and I gratefully accepted it. Apollonius shot me a curious look.

"What? Afraid I'll get drunk and gloomy as I used to?" I asked with a raised brow. The deaths of Saturninus and Glaucia and the departure of Marius had been catalysts which allowed me to grow into my own man. I was once contemplative and filled with sorrow, haunted by my past. Now I was a senator and a legate, with the family I'd always desired. Too much was going right to be downcast.

Smiling, Apollonius said, "I was simply going to ask for a drink."

"Legate Sertorius," a man said from behind me.

I turned and didn't recognize him, but saw he wore the crest of a legate on his breastplate. "Yes, I am he." I stood and extended a hand, which he ignored.

"It's unseemly for you to dine with slaves and those beneath your rank." He looked over my shoulder at Herennius with scorn. "You should be seated with me. We have things to discuss."

I passed the skin of wine to Apollonius. I took a moment to size up the man and now recognized him as Paullus, legate of the seventeenth legion. He was an aristocrat, certainly. An aging one too, trying desperately and failing to cover up his baldness with a few wisps of hair remaining to him. "What have we to talk about?" I asked.

Frowning, he said again, "You should be eating with your equals."

I nodded and picked up my bowl of porridge. For a moment his shoulders relaxed as he anticipated my submission. Instead, I turned and walked to a gathering of Mules and sat beside them, ensuring to smile at him over my shoulder as I did so. I had not worked to achieve this rank to be told what to do by men of equal rank, even if they were of superior birth. They were not my men; these Mules were my men. "Soldiers," I said, gesturing for them to remain seated and eating. "How are you recovering?"

"Satiated and ready for sleep, legate," one of them said with an urban accent.

"I'm glad to hear it. We'll be back on the sea tomorrow, I'm certain, but hopefully the storms are behind us," I said. Over the young soldier's shoulder I saw Castor sitting by himself and stirring his porridge meticulously. He appeared to be humming a tune to himself.

"Now what we really need is to—"

"Why isn't young Castor eating with the rest of you?" I asked.

"Who?" one of the Mules replied, turning to see him. "Oh, that's pig boy. He's an odd one, legate. A bit peculiar, if you catch my meaning."

Castor must have made the mistake of telling his fellow soldiers he slept in pigsties before joining the Colors. Legionaries were known for many things, but empathy wasn't one of them.

"Castor, join us." I waved him over. Some of the Mules exhaled and exchanged a glance, but when one of them made the mistake of meeting my eye I shamed him into silence.

He seemed reluctant, debating whether or not to comply, but eventually came and sat beside me on the sand.

"Have you all seen Castor's woodwork?" I said. "It's quite impressive."

He smirked and pulled out the rough etching from the pouch at his side.

"The water made it expand. It looked better before."

"I rather like it now. With a few fine touches, you might be able to make it into a lion instead of a dog. Actually, you mentioned selling it. How much would you like for it?"

His eyes widened. "Well, I'm not finished with it yet."

"Don't worry. I'll make a down payment for now, and we'll decide on a final price when it's completed." I took out a few denarii from a bull scrotum pouch still filled with water and passed them to Castor.

He was as proud as if he were holding his first child.

"You know, soldiers…" I lingered until everyone was waiting with anticipation, "we will be quartering with Greek civilians, two soldiers per home. The man you'll be stationed with will be decided by lot." I could see disappointment in their downcast eyes, but continued, "There may be a time when you are forced to fight for your lives in battle. You'll be responsible for the life of the man beside you, and he will be responsible for yours."

One of the Mules rubbed the back of his neck and another sifted sand through his fingers.

"And he likely won't be your best friend, or the one with whom you have the most in common, or the one whom favors the same god as you, or the one whom hailed from the same part of Italy." I stood. "Two weeks after our arrival you will be tested by the centurions on how well you know the man with whom you're quartering. I want you to know everything from their favorite color to the name of their first pet. I suggest you begin learning about one another now."

I waited for a salute and then departed. I wasn't certain I'd remember to actually have them tested, but the desired effect would be the same. When I turned, I saw men running to the shoreline. Another vessel was appearing in the distance. My heart leapt and I sprinted down and waded into the water. Even from a distance I could see the quinquereme was as damaged as any of those already on the beach, and it seemed to be lower in the water that it should've been.

We guided them in and helped secure the damaged ship onto the beach and tied it down with massive stakes.

The crewmen let down the rope ladder, and one by one they descended. They passed us by without saying much, looking like they had seen a gorgon.

I spotted who I believed was the ship's captain and hurried to his side. "Captain, what's the report?"

"We suffered a loss, legate," he said. His eyes were pink and wet, and he stared off in the way men often do after battle.

"How many?"

"Just one,"

I exhaled with relief and nearly kissed the man. But I could see the fear in his eyes was unabated. "Who did we lose?"

"The son of Titus Didius."

SCROLL IV

No more songs were sung, no more tales told. Wine stopped flowing, and jokes ceased. We built up a pyre and placed the bodies of the few men who died upon it.

Publius Didius had fallen overboard, swallowed up by Neptune's waters, so we couldn't give him a proper burial. The best we could do was place his shield on the pyre with the rest of the fallen. We lit it ablaze and watched in silence.

"You're the only one who knows Didius well. How will he react?" Lucius asked the following morning while we prepared to depart.

"I don't know him well enough to be certain," I said, "but if I had to guess, I'd say the world will feel his wrath."

The crewmen patched up the ship where there were damages and ensured the vessels' bellies were de-barnacled. And then we set off, leaving the ashes of our men scattered with wine on the beach.

"Were proper sacrifices made to ensure our safe passage?" Spurius asked Aulus, Lucius and me once we were back on the water. "We don't want to fight another storm. I'm afraid we couldn't bear it."

The sails rippled above and the deck beneath us shook with the repetitive beat of the pace-drummer below.

"We sacrificed thirteen good men in the storm," I said. "We'll have to pray this will suffice." I leaned on the rail and stared out over the wine-dark sea.

"I've already made a vow," Lucius said, before suddenly glaring at me, "and before you say anything—yes—it's pigeons. I've vowed to sacrifice twelve upon our arrival. I'd suggest you gentlemen make a vow as well, and perhaps the gods will spare us."

"I'll not argue if it gets us there alive." I smiled and raised my arms in mock surrender.

"How mighty our gods are to spare us for a few pigeons," Aulus said. "Do they really need them so desperately? I'm sure there are a few hundred rotting birds in the forum right now if it'd help."

"Keep it up, Aulus," Lucius grumbled. "Anger Neptune again and this time he'll not fail to swallow us all."

Castor approached, his head down and shoulders bent. Several of the Mules whom I sat with the night prior were across from us on the port side of the ship, but I assumed Castor joined us because they would not include him. I wondered if I was his only friend in the legion. I certainly had taken a liking to him. Perhaps he reminded me of an older Gavius, or even a shade of myself. More likely, he was something like what I might have been if tragedy and war hadn't stolen the twilight of my youth.

"Castor, how are you feeling? Glad to be back on the water?" I said before realizing how stupid the statement was.

"Yes," he said, the irony lost to him.

"You approach your superiors without a salute?" Aulus asked. I knew him well enough to see he was joking, but sometimes his humor was lost to others.

Castor looked at Aulus defiantly. "We're all equals when we sail Neptune's waters." He quoted me almost verbatim, which amused me and Aulus.

"Castor, I outrank the both of them." I gestured to the Insteius twins. "If they give you any trouble, let me know and I'll make them stand on their heads or something."

"I jest, lad." Aulus smiled and clapped Castor's shoulder.

"What awaits you on the other side of the legion, soldier?" Spurius asked. Castor stared back blankly, so Spurius clarified, "What do you want to do after you retire from service?"

"I'd like a family. A wife and children. And animals. A lot of different animals."

"A fine dream for any Roman," Spurius said.

"Children…" Aulus shook his head. "I'd like to have some as well, but first my wife would have to couple with me."

"Your wife doesn't lie with you?" I asked, grinning and awaiting the conclusion of the inevitable joke to follow.

"Rarely. It's my gods' given right to force her, of course. But then it would be her gods' given right to talk of her feelings until my ears bleed afterward. Better to live as a eunuch."

We all laughed, save Castor who didn't quite understand the joke.

"I have a child," I said.

Castor turned to me with a sparkle in his eye. "You do?"

"That's right. His name is Gavius. He'll be taller and stronger than me one day, and it will be my joy to watch it."

"I still haven't met the little bastard," Aulus quipped. "If he's anything like Titus was as a child I'd have to imagine him a young Hercules."

"Quintus!" Apollonius shouted.

I turned to find several men gathered by the prow. "What is it?" I asked, running to him.

He pointed.

In the water beneath us, now floating to the side of the ship, was a body.

Was it Publius Didius? I squinted my eye for clarity. No, it was not a man. But a woman. A child, actually. A small girl.

"Neptune's balls, what is that all the way out here?" Captain Municius asked from my side.

"It's a child," I said, looking to find land or another ship, but none was in sight.

"Impossible. A corpse maybe," he said, already losing interest.

I leaned over the railing and strained my eye as much as I could. The clouds above us must have shifted, as the sun suddenly illuminated the waters where the girl clung to a piece of driftwood.

Most of the men were losing interest too. A body wasn't nearly as interesting as loot for the taking.

Just before I turned away myself, the little girl turned her head to us, her blue eyes shimmering in the sunlight. A tiny hand stretched out toward us.

"Shift the sail! Shift the sail! She's alive!" I shouted.

I'd never been more proud of the men under my command. They reacted immediately, each to their station, to ensure we saved that little girl.

A rope ladder was thrown down off the edge and Lucius—gentle soul he is—nearly jumped overboard to be the first to scamper down it. He wrapped his burly forearms around her waist and pulled her to his chest, using his one free hand to hoist himself up.

The men cried out and cheered when Lucius' blond head appeared above the ledge.

"We got her," he said.

Lucius placed her at the base of the mast. She was still clutching to that piece of driftwood, unable to believe she was finally safe. I could see her arms and legs were turning as blue as the ocean, so I ripped off my cloak, tearing it in the process.

"You're safe now," I said, and tucked it in around her.

She was shaking violently, both from the cold and her fear, as her eyes darted around the strange faces before her.

Now that the pitiful child was safely secured, the men stopped cheering and seemed to lose interest.

"What do we do now?" one asked.

They lost interest, that is, until I said, "Good work, men. I'll have a discussion with the quaestor upon our arrival and see to it each of you receives five denarii for your bravery!" A chorus of cheers sounded out. "And also for all the men of the crew!" The wood beneath us quaked as the rowers must have overheard. "And ten for the captain." I shot Municius a wink, which is terribly ineffective for someone with one eye.

I turned again to the frightened child. She had long raven hair, straight and stiff from the cold. Her eyes were so blue they were almost violet, and atop them were lashes so long and curled women in Rome would have paid a fortune for them. Freckles were sprinkled along the suntanned skin of her cheeks.

Looking at her tightened my chest. Something told me she was precious and sacred and should be protected at all costs, the same inexplicable phenomena that made men and women protect children for eons.

"You don't need to be afraid," Spurius said kneeling beside her.

"She's freezing," Lucius ordered one of our men. "Go and get a torch."

"We need to put it by her feet," Apollonius said gravely, pinching her toes and receiving no reaction. He rolled up my cloak to analyze the state of her legs, and for the first time we saw the rusty iron shackles connecting them. We exchanged a glance and he hurried to cover them again.

"Can you tell us what happened to you, girl?" Municius asked, leaning on the mast above her.

She continued to tremble, but her eyes finally settled on my face. I worried my missing eye might scare her, so I covered it up with my hand and smiled. Her shoulders seemed to relax.

"It's all right," I said

"My ship wrecked in the storms," she said in Greek.

"What in Hades does that mean?" Municius asked.

"She said her ship wrecked. She's lucky to have survived. This piece of wood is the only thing that stood between her and the River Styx." I reached forward, slowly and deliberately to ensure I didn't frighten her. I pulled away the wood and she tucked my cloak to her chin.

"She said a shipwreck?" Municius asked. His face changed somehow, as if it'd been drained of something vital.

"Yes. Surprising?" Apollonius said before I could. "After those storms I'd say there were many shipwrecks."

He stepped away.

"We're going to get you warm and into some dry clothes," I said as Lucius held the torch as close to her flesh as he could manage without harming her. "And then we'll get you something to eat and drink. You're safe."

"She's cursed," Captain Municius said when he returned.

"What?" I looked over my shoulder.

"Her ship wrecked. Neptune has cursed her."

I could see the shadows and hear the footsteps of several men approaching.

"Preposterous. We were in the same storm," Aulus said shoving his way to the forefront. I nodded to reaffirm him.

"But our ship didn't sink, did it?" one of the Mules said. "That's the difference. Neptune spared us. He didn't spare the ship of this little girl."

My breath quickened and I felt a tremor develop somewhere in my core. I didn't want to follow their logic to its inevitable conclusion.

"Her ship wasn't spared, but she was. Does this count for nothing?" Apollonius pleaded.

"She wouldn't have been spared if we didn't interfere. We're assisting a cursed girl," another man said.

I sprang to my feet. "And what are you suggesting?"

"We need to give her back to Neptune, lad," Captain Municius said quietly, contritely as if we had no other choice. Several of the Mules nodded. All the pride I so recently felt in my men was replaced by anger. He turned to the rest of the men. "I've been a captain a long time, lads. Neptune is a cruel but predictable god. Do as he commands and we make it to Greece alive. If you disobey him, we will drown before we arrive—I've seen it many times over."

An anger I hadn't felt in years—one repressed by sadness and turmoil—erupted like a flame. It enveloped and controlled my entire body. The rage centered deep in my belly. My fists clenched without intention and my eye blinked rapidly as if it would somehow alter what was before me. A tremor developed which wouldn't go away until I hurt someone.

And it took all the strength within me to avoid doing so.

"You want to send a little girl to her death?" I said, hoping she couldn't understand Latin.

"We don't want to, legate! It's our responsibility," the Captain shouted, and others joined him.

My jaw twitched. I breathed heavily through my nose, trying to remind myself, *you are a legate, you are a legate.* In an attempt to stave off my anger, I spun toward the child. "Where are your parents at, girl?" Asking a risk for sure, but after seeing the shackles I had enough context to guess.

"Dead," she replied in Greek.

I exhaled. Gods forgive me for saying so. "See? This girl is an orphan. In an attempt to appease one god, you threaten to anger the other. Aren't the stranger and the needy sent by Jupiter to test us? And he who fails these, are they not enemies of the god of gods? Doesn't Hesiod write that the man who harms the supplicant, the stranger, and the *orphan* is hated by Zeus?" I implored them with all the rhetorical prowess I'd acquired in the senate.

Their faces were blank at the reference, but I could see many were beginning to waiver. They looked to the captain. Even he seemed to consider what I said.

"Even Jupiter has no power here," the captain finally said. "Neptune rules the sea. And his orders are law, above everything else."

The men seemed to be divided now. In the midst of them all I spotted Castor. He watched me with those curious eyes, waiting to see what kind of man I was. I was determined to show him, along with all my ancestors above. I spent my life trying to determine what it was to be a good man. Now it was time to be one. No more second guessing, no more thoughts. Instinct took over.

I'd tried to be tactful. Now only power could be wielded. "This is all irrelevant. I am a legate. This girl is now my property. I am in charge here. The girl doesn't go overboard."

"Not on this ship. I am captain of this ship, Legate," Municius shouted, the veins in his neck flaring. If he were any younger or any stronger, he would have hit me. Rather than step away, I moved in to meet him, looking down on his toothless snarl.

"I don't care if we're on the sea, on Mount Olympus, or deep in Tartarus. I make the rules," I said, locking my one eye with his. He might have been right, but in the moment I didn't care.

The Captain went slack jawed, appalled and disgusted. "Impudent welp! In all my years I've never been talked to like this on my own ship."

"I'd say this is the first time you're trying to murder a child on your ship as well," Aulus said as he, Spurius, and Lucius hurried to stand beside me. "Correct, Captain?"

"He can punish us later! It won't matter if we don't make it to Greece alive," a soldiers shouted.

"We don't want to kill her, we just want to leave her where

we found her. If Zeus wants to save her, he still can! If Poseidon wants to spare her, he still can!" another echoed.

"You dishonor Neptune!" I roared without even preparing what I was to say. The rage took over. "You think you honor him by throwing this little girl to the sea. All that stood between her and death was a little plank of wood. Do you really think so little of the sea god you believe he couldn't kill a small girl clinging to a piece of wood?"

A good point, perhaps, and one which might have swayed them earlier. But their minds were made up. Municius had convinced them. Many of them young and afraid of their first campaign in the Legion—even more terrified of another storm—they were easily swayed.

"We have to put her back, legate," one shouted.

That strange intuition which springs up in your mind before a catastrophe appeared to me then. Lucius and the twins began to advance alongside me in defense of the girl, but I held out my hands for them to wait. "Silence!" I bellowed as if I was twice my own size, and to my surprise they actually listened. "There is only one solution here without our blood filling the sea around us. Single combat. One on one. Who will face me to decide the fate of this little girl?" I looked at the source of this argument for the first time since it began and was relieved to see she was confused. Frightened, perhaps, by our volume, but confused. I said, mockingly, "If Neptune is on your side and the sea is his domain, of course you will be victorious. He will guide your hand." The stoic in me was absent, and for good reason. He wouldn't have the answers to solve this problem.

No takers stepped forward. Most eyes were downcast.

I continued, "You will not receive punishment if you defeat me. A legate—a senator even—soft and spoiled, who amongst you cannot say you have trained to the point where you can defeat a man who hasn't lifted a sword in years?" I asked. Still, no one stepped forth. I raised my arms to the heavens above us and evoked with the same voice which allowed me to command an audience from the rostra. "By Orcus, Dis, and Proserpina I vow that the man who defeats me will not only be spared judgement, but will be awarded a crown for having saved his comrades from the wrath of the gods! My own officers will attest." I turned to Lucius and the twins, who stared at me wide-eyed. Eventually they nodded.

Finally, a man stepped forward from the crowds.

"I'm sorry, sir. I mean you no disrespect," he said. I could tell from his accent he was a farming lad from somewhere far outside the city. "I have to make it to Greece alive. I have a daughter. A little girl like her. I have to make it back home to her safely." I stared until he met my gaze, gulls squawking in the distance, the ship rocking beneath us. He couldn't maintain it for long. He stared at the worn wood of the quinquereme and strained his head to swallow from a dry throat.

He was brave enough to fight me—he was the only one to step forward after all—but was he ashamed to fight his military superior, or to send a child to her inevitable demise?

Standing well over six feet tall, if I remember correctly, he was a giant by all accounts. I had noticed him in formation previously, it was impossible not to do so. If I guessed correctly, he was wearing the largest *lorica* size our armorers constructed, yet it still seemed too small for him.

"An honorable explanation, even if you are a sniveling coward for desiring to murder a child to save yourselves." A true statement, perhaps, but I would've never said this with a clear mind. In this moment though, reason escaped me. I cared only about defending the girl and hurting whoever tried to stop me.

"Legate, I mean no—"

"Raise your sword," I said.

He slid the blade from its sheath and held it how he'd been taught in training. His size alone could defeat me. The legion taught us many adages, and one of them was "reach always wins"—to encourage the men to stab rather than slash, but it applied equally to men with arms much longer than their opponents.

He moved himself into fighting position, and I pulled out my gladius. The weight of it in my arm filled me with ecstasy. It'd been too long.

I lowered my stance and tucked the blade at my side, ready to strike. We circled each other as those gathered stepped back to allow us room.

He inhaled and tried to summon up courage. He stepped in. He remained rigid, like a soldier in a phalanx formation. He moved with his upper body, as most recruits do. Veterans know you win battles with your feet. He feigned to the left and then stabbed to the right. I swung my sword and batted his away. We rotated further. Then he swung overhead, which I blocked and stepped to the side. I might have been able to strike at his midsection then, but I wasn't ready for the fight to be over yet.

Whatever the reason for the shame he had felt, it evaporated now. His eyes were now animalistic, as I'm sure mine were.

He stabbed again, as I predicted. I parried and swung my left fist into his face. He flew to the side, blood flinging from his lips. But he recovered quickly.

Some of the men cheered. Most, however, watched intensely, believing whoever won must be correct and have the favor of the gods.

I had no idea who the gods favored. Nor did I care. I was going to win because I was a superior fighter. And if the gods favored those who desired to kill children, I'd rather not serve them anyhow.

He slashed from the right, which I blocked, but I was too caught up in my thoughts to see the fist which hammered my face from the left.

For a moment my vision flashed black and white, and I could taste the iron of blood. Some of the men cheered. My vision was hazy but I managed to see Lucius inching forward in my peripherals. "Don't!" I shouted. And he must have complied, for the battle continued.

I had been hit many times before and afterward too, but few times had one hit rendered me seeing three of the enemy before me. Instinct prevailed and saved me as I met his sword and carried it with mine to the right before pushing forward and stabbing into his breastplate. It didn't go deep, only enough to draw blood. He rotated his shoulder to make sure he had full motion—which he did—but otherwise didn't respond to the pain.

In fact, it seemed to invigorate him.

We circled each other further, and as soon as my back was to the ledge, he charged.

He led with the point of his sword, stabbing for the killer blow at my throat.

I stepped to the side and dropped my sword. With my right hand I grabbed his sword arm, with the other I latched onto the back of his neck. I sent him toppling over the ledge, only holding him up by his arm.

Terror replaced the rage in his eyes. "Please, legate!" he shouted.

"If the girl goes overboard you do, too. What say you?"

"Please!" he cried out. "I was wrong, don't let go."

My grasp was slipping but I held as tight as I could manage. I turned to the rest. "What say *you*?"

"Pull him up," they all agreed.

I did, and he thrashed against the wall of the ship until he could cling to the ledge. "Is there no one else?" I asked. I scanned their faces. "Anyone?" Nothing. "Any *two* of you?" I reiterated. No response. "That's what I suspected. I'm a legate not a god! Even you yourself don't believe your fears or you would act against me."

For a moment—the anger now dissipated—I felt ashamed. Since I had become a political figure in Rome, I had acted nothing like this. Was I wrong to do so? Had I shamed my

Republic or my rank? I took a quick look at the shivering girl there by the mast and all of those doubts fled.

"Line up in formation. Port side," I bellowed. "Officers in front!"

They complied and moved much quicker than they ever had before.

Once they were aligned, I strolled before them, inspecting every face as I tried to collect my breath. "Let this be a lesson to you, men. This is what happens when we act out of fear. Innocent people die." I waited as long as I could, analyzing each man and giving them a chance to offer objections if they had them.

None were offered.

"All right then. Break your fast and go eat, all of you," I said, and they were happy to comply. "Except you." I pointed my sword toward the brave man I had fought. "You bring your portion to the girl," I said, and he nodded vigorously.

I thought I was being merciful, and rational even, given the circumstances. But who knows? If a storm came and sank us all, I would have been cursed forever as a blasphemer.

Maybe I was.

After the men were dismissed, I turned back to Apollonius, Lucius, and the twins. They all seemed relieved. I also think they were proud of me, perhaps even surprised. Then my eyes drifted to the girl who was at the center of it all. Her tremor had lessened, but she was still shivering and alone.

That reconfirmed everything. I'd do anything to protect her.

SCROLL V

THANKFULLY THE GIRL fell asleep after the ordeal, none the wiser to the danger she'd been in. And she must have been exhausted too, for she slept until we docked on Cythera that night.

No one ever mentioned what happened again. Shame filled the eyes of the men who passed me, and when given the chance I would mention their bravery in rescuing the child and leave out what followed.

As the ladders were thrown down, we all lined up to descend to the beaches. I took her hand and led the way. A few of the men tried to speak to her, but she only looked back blankly.

"Don't worry, I speak your tongue," I said.

She looked at me with a sparkle in her blue eyes. "You're Greek?"

"No, but I was taught Greek, and I enjoy speaking it a great deal. The best part is we can talk and none of them will be able to understand us." Probably true too, with the exception of a few officers.

When we reached the ledge, she peered over it before shrinking back.

"Don't worry. See him at the bottom?" I pointed and she

strained to see. She nodded while I pointed at Lucius. "He jumped in the water to save you. If you slip, he'll catch you."

Lucius didn't speak a word of Greek and stared back at us with a cocked brow.

She took my hand and I helped her over the ledge, and fortunately she made it to the bottom without relying on Lucius' reflexes to catch her.

"Get her to the fires. I'll get you both something to eat," I said. He saluted and complied.

The moon that night was as large as the sun. Stars were out too, and the sky was clear enough that we could spot the constellation Orion.

I waited for Apollonius when I reached the bottom. He wasn't nearly as old as I accused him of being, but he wasn't exactly known for his coordination or balance.

"That was special, Quintus. What you did," he said, his eyes wet.

"Any honorable man in my position would do the same."

"I don't think so, my friend," he said. "That girl... she... she..." He began to weep and I placed a hand on his shoulder. "She reminds me so much of Anaiah. It would have killed me to see..."

I kissed his head and smiled to stop his tears. "My friend, we are almost to Greece. To Athens, where she was taken from you. She was the first thought in my mind when Caepio showed up and told me of this campaign. I'll do everything in my power to find her."

His tears dried but his face hardened. "Do not say it. Please. I dare not hope it."

We said nothing more until we were balancing bowls of porridge in our arms and handing them out around the fire.

"Here you go." I passed a bowl to the child, who studied it at first, but then gorged herself the way Lucius was known to do on the Saturnalia.

"How long do you think you were out there?" Lucius said.

"She can't speak Latin," I said, before translating. She shrugged in response and continued to feast.

We ate in uncomfortable silence for a while, not sure of what to say or do next.

"What is your name?" I asked.

"Kirrha," she said, her voice soft, delicate, and perhaps hoarse from going so long without water.

"A pretty name," Apollonius said.

The men at another fire began chanting a drinking song.

She looked at me, her eyes wide.

"Oh, yes. He can speak Greek too," I said.

"Where were you from?" he asked.

She took her time to respond, ensuring her food was swallowed before speaking. "I was born in Piraeus. My ancestors were from Corinth." I arched a brow. Her first sentence she'd strung together, and for the first time I noticed her endearing lisp. Despite this, I could tell she was intelligent for her age.

"Corinth," Apollonius said, impressed. "I've heard it was once the most beautiful city on the Aegean."

"My family was enslaved when the Romans destroyed it," she said, without malice or anger, as matter-of-fact as if she was speaking of the weather.

I lowered my gaze and fidgeted. Half a century had passed since Rome razed Corinth, and still the tales were told with trembles. Every building alight, a thousand years of history gone up in smoke. They said every man was slain and every woman and child was sold. I exchanged a look with Lucius and Apollonius as we tried to determine what to say next.

She continued without prompting. "Everyone says I'm a slave. Dolios said we were slaves and our mom was a slave. He says mother and father are our owners, but it's not true."

"Would you like some more?" I asked when she scraped together the last bits of porridge on her spoon. I handed it off to a mule and nodded for him to fill it, which he hastened to do, several of the ashamed men assisting. "Let's get closer to the fire."

"Who is Dolios?" Apollonius asked.

"My older brother. He was the smartest boy in Piraeus. He knew Latin and was going to teach me, but he was taken too. So were Mother and Father." She wiggled her toes in the sand, likely thankful she could feel them again.

There was so much I wanted to know. Who were her parents? Where were they taken? And by whom? But I decided it could wait. I didn't want her to feel as if we were interrogating her. She seemed at ease but she was a little girl and might frighten easily. I leaned back and enjoyed the crackling of the fire, humming along to the song of some men down the beach from us.

Kirrha broke the silence. "You are Romans?"

"Yes, we are," I said, curious how she might respond.

"My parents were Romans."

I translated for Lucius, who squinted and shook his head. Not possible.

"I... well. Do you think maybe they just... looked like Romans?" Apollonius asked as carefully as he could.

"No. They were Roman citizens."

That couldn't be the case. If her parents were Roman citizens, they couldn't be sold into slavery. This would be a catastrophe the Republic had never seen before.

She turned to me, satiated at last, and analyzed my face. She no longer appeared skeptical or frightened, but perhaps now irritated we didn't seem to believe her. "There were other Romans on our ship too."

I swallowed hard. "This can't be the case, Kirrha. Romans cannot be sold into slavery."

"Yes they were."

I couldn't believe everything I heard from the mouth of a traumatized child, but if what she said was true than I... well, I didn't know what I'd have to do. "How can you be certain?"

She shrugged. "Because they spoke your tongue. And they wore armor just like yours."

SCROLL VI

FORTUNATELY THERE WERE NO MORE storms. We sailed into the Port of Piraeus without so much as another drop of rain. When we spotted the harbor, we all ran to the prow to drink it in. The Ostian docks were nothing more than a wharf compared to the bustling Athenian port of Piraeus.

Our excitement was stalled while we waited in line for most of the morning, vessels of all kinds stacked as far as the eye could see. The sails of every foreign nation imaginable rippled in the wind, and the voices of a thousand different languages rose to greet them. Most were small trading ships, coming with wares from all across the Mediterranean, but there were transport ships too, and the luxuriously gilded boats of emissaries and distinguished individuals.

Our captain barked orders as the rowers slowly shifted the ship parallel with the docks and eased us toward them. The harbor master complained that military vessels weren't permitted in this harbor, but there wasn't anything to stop us from getting off the damned *Medusa*. I convinced him our soldiers had more coin than sense, were poor at managing it, and would likely spend on every trinket in sight. All true and eventually even he relented.

We met under a pergola flanked by massive statues of historic Athenians and marble columns. Travelers eyed us suspiciously as the men packed into formation, shoulder to shoulder.

"We're the first to dock," I said, "and the rest will be quick on our heels."

"Not bad for a one-eyed seasick legate!" Aulus shouted from behind the ranks, the men stifling their laughter.

"It'll take several hours for the rest of them to disembark and the captains to sign their manifests. So I'm giving you liberty until ninth hour." They started to murmur so I raised my voice. "At this time, I want you all in formation outside the Piraean gate for inspection. Enjoy yourselves, but not too much." I gestured the act of drinking and dismissed them.

The men rounded up with their companions and discussed what they would do with a few hours to themselves. Apollonius, holding Kirrha's hand, joined me.

"Not quite like our previous campaigns," I said to Apollonius.

"Thank Jehovah for that," he said.

So this was to be my home for the foreseeable future. The mountains were tall and green in the distance beyond the city, and even when we had stepped away, the sea salt lingered in the air and clang to our lips. The tunic under my armor dampened and stuck to my skin, absent the sea winds for the first time in a while. But the heat was better than seasickness, I vow it.

"I never thought I'd be paid to stroll around Greece!" Aulus was jubilant as he and his brother approached.

"Nor shall you. I'm docking a day's pay for insulting me during formation," I said.

His jaw dropped and he was in shock until he realized I was joking. "A pox on you, Sertorius." He smiled.

"What are you boys going to do?"

"Set ourselves up with something good to drink," Lucius chimed in. "The wine from Chios is said to make Falernian grape taste like soldier's piss."

"Very good, and very expensive," Apollonius said.

"We're officers! We can afford it. You'll join us won't you, Sertorius?" Spurius asked.

I gestured to Kirrha. "I think we'll stroll the market, but I appreciate your offer."

"I'll bring a vial back for you. Let's go." Aulus clapped my shoulder and set off, expecting the others to follow him.

"Are you happy to be back in Greece?" I asked Kirrha as we approached a woman selling bright flowers in ceramic vases. She said nothing but seemed to scrutinized the crowd for faces she'd recognize.

I pulled Kirrha closer as we followed Apollonius to the *emporion*. Sailors and shipowners were perusing the various shops, thick crowds centered around the most unique displays. Grooves were worn into the cobblestone beneath us, and I wondered how many legends of old had walked these streets throughout time. Athens had created democracy when Rome was still sleeping in huts, after all.

"This is the only place in Attika allowing international trade," Apollonius said. "You'd better buy now if there's something you have an eye on."

We passed through rows of grain carts. Bread baked in ovens behind them, the smell enticing and the heat warming our skin. Vegetable vendors called out to us and displayed the ripeness of their imported turnips and local grapes.

"Are you hungry?" I asked both, feeling my own stomach grumble at the sight.

Kirrha looked uninterested.

"We can buy bread and vegetables anywhere," Apollonius said, tapping his temple, "but figs from Rhodes and almonds from Thasos are only found here. My mother would bring me here as a boy just to acquire them."

"Let your nose guide you then, and we'll all share in the delight."

I paid for a few delicacies and sat on a stone curb to eat.

Beside us a young man played a lyre and a woman sang with rich vibrato.

"What do you think?" I asked Kirrha with a mouthful.

"I eat these a lot," she said thoughtfully.

We continued our journey through rows of kiosks where fishermen were displaying their day's catch and shouting about its freshness, the smell pungent enough to indicate otherwise. I ignored the urge to purchase a new sword as we passed a blacksmith rotating a bronze blade over a red coals.

We passed through a throng of Egyptian tourists led by a local guide holding up an ostrich feather to remain visible.

"I feel as if I've walked back into the forum," I said.

Kirrha reached over, wrapped her tiny hand around mine, and squeezed tight.

Just before we exited the emporion to receive a little breathing room, a shopkeeper began shouting at Kirrha. For a moment I wondered if it was someone who knew her, but instead it was just a matted-haired old woman trying to peddle her wares.

"You like? You like?" she asked, extending a terra-cotta doll and shaking it to move the arms and legs.

Kirrha studied the doll with interest, but without hope.

I stopped. "Do you want this?"

She looked up at me, her mouth open. She couldn't bring herself to ask, but I took that as a yes.

"How much?" I asked the shopkeeper.

"Six denarii."

We both knew it was too much. "You're a thief," I said. "Two denarii."

"Five." She snapped her fingers and held out her hand, expecting my compliance. It was the same game merchants played in the forum. I could have continued to play it too, but I wanted to see the girl smile more than I wanted to save a few denarii.

The shopkeeper tested the weight of the coins I passed her, and—finding it to her satisfaction—handed Kirrha the doll.

Her eyes shimmered but she couldn't find any words. She stared at it in amazement as we exited the emporion.

I was about to ask her what she would name it when I saw several men shouting from a platform just before the road to Athens proper. The crowd was packed in before it and watched a slave master display a woman for sale by spreading her lips to reveal the condition of her teeth.

"Fifty!" one watcher shouted.

"One hundred and fifty," said another.

The man pulled down her tunic and cupped her breast. "Plump, supple, and still time to grow."

Kirrha looked down as a winning bid was announced and the girl was delivered to her new owner. Several young men were pulled from cages and pushed onto the stage.

I still doubted the veracity of Kirrha's claim, but I couldn't help but wonder if any of the men and women being sold were Roman. Regardless, this was likely the very place Apollonius and his niece were bartered off and separated years before.

"Let's leave this place. Now," I said.

"I agree," Apollonius said.

We led Kirrha away, going nowhere in particular.

"So this is your home?" I asked to which she nodded. "Would you like to show us where you lived?"

She seemed to consider it; then her eyes lit up. "Maybe Mother, Father, and Dolios survived and made it back too!" she shouted.

No longer clinging to my hand, she ran through the crowds as quickly as her tiny legs could carry her. We exited the denser part of the city and into the slums closer to the water. I could tell she knew the way well.

Soon I was greeted by the foul smell of death. I covered my nose with my sleeve, and found Apollonius was doing the same.

Kirrha ran ahead, her arms pumping in step with her feet. "It's right over here!" she hollered back and waved us on.

The smell seemed to be emanating from the mounds of dead insects and shellfish. Her family must have been dyers then, using these tiny *murex* to collect the purple dye for which aristocrats paid fortunes. And it must have taken a lot of the little buggers too, if one could judge by the size of the mounds.

She ran directly to a brick shack covered in chipping blue and white plaster. It had a shingled roof, well worn from age and exposure to the sea salt. Kirrha went to enter rather than knock. It was locked. "Perhaps they are afraid the bad men will return. They'll be so pleased to see me," she said as we joined her by the door. She knocked several times, and as we continued to wait, my heart began to sink. Kirrha would experience their deaths all over again if they weren't here.

"By the Furies, what is it?" a man called from the side of the house. He seemed to be irritated at the disturbance, and nothing in his demeanor changed when he saw Kirrha's face. She stepped back.

I sensed something. I approached the man. "Is this your home?"

"Yes, and who asks?" he said, struggling to shift his excessive weight.

I examined him and deliberated about how to respond. He was an older man, and I couldn't sense any violence in his eyes. He'd been scraping the skin from a hide stretched across a tanner's rack, and beside him several other pelts were soaking in a basin filled with water and urine. He was a tanner, not a slaver. But I still decided to proceed with caution. "I had business with the owner of this home."

His brows furrowed and he nodded. "And when did this 'business' originate? I just bought this home on auction not a fortnight ago."

"Some time before that I believe," I said, hanging my head.

He frowned and dabbed at his forehead with a rag.

"I'm sorry, Roman. But they're gone."

I turned to find Kirrha sobbing into Apollonius' tunic as he rubbed her back. "Do you recall what happened to them?"

"It's my understanding they were enslaved. Sold off and had their property taken. I hate to profit off of someone's misery, you see, but the deal was too good to pass up, and I needed a place to tan outside the city limits... because of the smell."

"Do you know anything about them?"

He noticed Kirrha weeping behind me and watched curiously. "How did you know them again? The owners of the home."

"As I've said, we had business to conduct. What do you know of them?" I stepped into his line of sight.

He seemed to debate how to respond and inhaled deeply. "Good folks, from all who knew them. A bit haughty by nature perhaps, for cloth dyers at least. He was head of the dyers' guild actually, if my memory hasn't abandoned me."

"And they were Roman citizens?"

"I've never met a Greek named Gaius Scribonius, so I'd say so. Why? You know him from across the sea?"

I exhaled as my mind raced from the implications. "Yes, something like that." I began to turn away but stopped. "So... I want to make sure I'm perfectly clear... these were Roman citizens who were enslaved?"

At length he nodded. "I would assume so. Why? What has this to do with me?"

"Roman citizens cannot be enslaved. It's against the law."

"Is it?" He seemed surprised. "Lots of men around here are breaking the law then." He shifted his considerable weight uncomfortably, wondering if he had said too much. "If you'll excuse me. I should resume my work."

I accepted his hand half-heartedly before returning to Apollonius and Kirrha. I knelt and inched closer to conceal her from prying eyes.

"What are we to do? Presumably some of these locals know

her. Perhaps they would take her in?" Apollonius asked in Latin. "This is her home..." He supported her weight and continued to sooth her by stroking her hair.

"That's the problem. If..." I didn't want her to overhear anything she might understand. Apollonius pulled her closer and placed his hand over her ears. I whispered, "If the wrong individuals find out she's survived, she could be in danger. I don't know how any of this is possible, but we must find out. In the meantime, we cannot put her at risk."

Apollonius nodded and slowly pulled her away from him. She rubbed at her swollen eyes with the back of her hand, lips quivering. "Kirrha, would you like to come with Quintus and me for a while? Or do you want to stay here with someone you know?"

She clutched the new doll to her chest and considered it for a moment before pointing at us.

"It's settled then. We'll go together," I said.

At least until we found out who was responsible for this. And when I did find out—I vowed to Orcus—they would all die.

SCROLL VII

WE MADE it to the Piraean gate just in time for formation. The twins and Lucius came running behind us, Aulus weighed down by several trinkets.

"Aulus," I asked, "what in Jupiter's name is all that?"

He sat down a leather satchel and raised a red-figure vase and a blue cloak hemmed in gold fabric. "Items I might need on campaign." He shrugged.

I laughed. "And what use have you with an ornamental vase?"

"You know ... put grain in it or oil ... or something."

"It's the wine, Quintus," Lucius said. "Fool wanted to buy everything he could find."

The smile faded from my face as I spotted the glistening silver cuirass of a commander in the distance. He was seated in a backless chair in front of the formation, waiting for stragglers to show up. The Legate Paullus stood at his flank, but Didius appeared so cavalier I knew the news of his son's death hadn't reached him yet.

"Excuse me for a moment, comrades," I said. My legs felt like they were weighted down with bags of sand as they bore me to the commander. Could a man deliver worse news than the death of a child? I imagined someone telling me something happened to Gavius. I would call the man a liar and a deceiver, and I'd threaten him with violence. Who could blame a father for such a reaction?

As usual, he was working diligently on a stack of scrolls.

"It's nothing but paperwork, Sertorius. Don't let anyone tell you different," he said without looking up. "Every little boy wants to be Consul. You'd only have to explain the reality of it all to scare him into something more practical."

"Sir." I snapped to attention and saluted.

"How was your journey? It took you longer than expected," he said.

"We were caught in some storms, Proconsul."

He chuckled and finally looked up at me. "Storms, and yet it appears we've survived after all. Your priests were incorrect."

The irony—once he found out—would be palpable.

"Where are the rest of the men?" he said. "I'll have them scourged if they got drunk, my son included."

"Sir," I said, stalling for time.

He set down his scrolls and stood. "Where are the rest of the men, legate?"

"We experienced casualties on the journey."

His jaw flexed and he inhaled, preparing himself for what he was about to hear.

"And where is my son? Where is Publius?"

"We should talk privately, Proconsul." I hung my head.

"I'm a Roman, legate. Just spit it out."

"He was lost at sea, sir."

He crept back and collapsed into his chair. Slumped over. I saw his knuckles whiten as he squeezed the armrests of the chair. He straightened then and met my gaze. If there were tears in his eyes, I could not see them. "How many did we lose in total?"

"A few dozen. No more."

He smiled ruefully. "How ironic it is the commander's son would be amongst the very few losses."

"I thought the same thing. I spoke with the captain and it appears nothing could have been done. He braved the deck to support the tearing sails, and a wave sent him over the edge." I rubbed my neck, "I'm sorry, sir."

He cleared his throat, still wringing the armrest so tight it was moments away from splintering. But when he spoke, his voice was calm. "A good death in any case. All a father could ask for." He blinked rapidly and cleared his throat again. Then he released his grip and leaned forward, glaring into my eye. "I asked you to look after him."

"I... t-here was nothing I could—"

"I jest," he said, but the flash of rage was genuine. "My wife is too old to bear me another child. I'll have to find another." He turned to his slave. "Prepare a letter to my brother. He'll need to find a suitable bride."

"Yes, dominus," the slave said.

Didius turned back to me. "Leave me with my thoughts for a moment."

"Certainly, sir." I saluted and about-faced.

"No, wait. No. I've already put out orders. Legate Paullus can put them out to the men. You come with me," he said, standing.

"Where are we going, sir?"

"To speak with the incumbent governor. The men have arrived so it's time for him to leave. And perhaps he can point to the five thousand men we need to kill." He smiled and looked up at the azure sky. "It's funny isn't it? Agamemnon and Priam? I guess we know which I am now. Come then."

He set off into Athens, and I followed.

"Come, come! Join me. Will you take some wine?" the incumbent governor shouted as we entered the megaron. Typically a banquet hall, Governor Atius had clearly turned this into his living space for the duration of his term.

He was seated at a long table overflowing with Greek delicacies but other diners were absent.

"Thank you for your offer. I'll not, though," Didius said.

Despite the governor's clutter, the megaron was stunning. Garland clang from marble columns of ruby red and coral. Beneath Atius' table and couches were checkered white and black tile, polished to reflect the torchlight. The walls contained a stunning depiction of Hades stealing Persephone, her mother weeping on the other side.

"Join me at the table at least, won't you?" he said.

Didius considered it but eventually sat across from the governor, and I did as well.

He appraised us as he gnawed on a cut of dark meat. His hair was fading but rust colored, as were the wisps of facial hair on his neck. Excess flesh bulged over the edges of his breastplate. If it was the one he'd worn since taking command of Greece, he'd certainly expanded in that time.

"This is a good province, Didius. I tell you. No damned plebs barking at you, no senate meetings, nor long-winded speeches from magistrates who enjoy hearing their own words. Ha! I'm not sure how I'll readjust to Rome!" He took a gulp of wine.

"I'm certain you'll manage, Atius," Didius said. He was a proper and fastidious man, even at the worst of times, and had difficulty concealing his disgust.

"Oh, you're right. I'll tell you how too. An enormous Domus on a hill outside the public eye. I can afford it now after all."

Didius exhaled. "You've found your time here lucrative then?"

"Gaia's womb, yes! It's been a wonderful year. The Greeks are submissive as a temple whore. Hard to imagine them standing up to the Persians or conquering Troy. They'll give you no trouble. Collect your taxes and consider your stay a long holiday." He burped into his hand and excused himself. Several Greek slaves came to refill his cup and collect empty plates and errant scraps of food.

"And this is where you've stayed? In this great hall?" Didius asked.

He nodded. "And you can too. Let the men sleep in camps outside the city walls. We didn't strive for position to continue roughing it in the elements, nay?"

Didius, clearly irritated, finally poured himself a cup of wine.

"The men won't be staying in camp. We'll be quartering with the locals," he said, eyes locked on Atius, inviting him to a challenge.

"Queer idea, if you ask me."

"I didn't ask you, actually. The Greeks housing the men will also be responsible for providing a single meal each day. That alone makes it worthwhile."

"Not sure they'll be pleased," Atius said, puffing out his cheeks.

"You said they were submissive. They'll get used to it. Besides, it will save hundreds of thousands of denarii over the course of my campaign."

Atius' eyebrow raised at the word 'campaign', but then he burst into laughter. "More money for you, aye? Wish I'd thought of it!" He rocked himself to his feet and gestured for us to follow him to the couches. He plopped down and reclined, but Didius remained on his feet so I did as well.

"We shall not stay much longer. We only wanted to ask a few questions about the province," Didius said, crossing his arms.

"Such as?"

"Anything you'd like to share would be useful. What do we need to know, and who?"

"There's only one thing you need to know about governing Greece: talk to Timoxenos." He cupped his hands behind his head.

"Care to elaborate?" Didius said.

"You'll understand when you meet him. Do whatever he asks and your term in Greece will be smooth as a eunuch's legs." He smirked.

"Very well. If there is nothing else you wish to share then—"

"Do you," I stepped forward, "know anything about Roman citizens being enslaved here in Greece?"

Atius sprang up and fidgeted, the smile finally gone from his face.

"Hush, legate. Can't you see your betters are discussing?" He looked to Didius for support.

My commander looked at me with a mixture of confusion and irritation, but I leaned closer and whispered, "I'll explain more later, but this might be our best lead to finding an enemy for your triumph, Proconsul."

"Go on, Atius," he said.

The governor stood and waddled toward us, no sign of joviality or humor in his eyes. "Neither I nor any of my men have anything to do with it. Or know anything about it." He turned and scowled at me, "And it would be wise if you inquired no further about it."

SCROLL VIII

AFTER BEING DISMISSED BY DIDIUS, I received the name and location of the family I'd be quartering with. Apollonius, Kirrha, and I made our way to the ceramics district, beneath the temple of their patron god, Hephaestus. Didius himself was going to be staying in the large home of the state priest near the acropolis and I'm sure the other officers were staying in grander homes as well, but I wanted to bear the same conditions as my men, even if those conditions were much more lax than anything we'd experienced at war. This was something I learned from Marius.

We hadn't even made it to the agora before a cool rain poured down in sheets of gray, the skies darkening above us. Puddles formed almost immediately and a slush of mud covered the stone. The homes here were shabby but constructed well, built to withstand rainstorms like this but perhaps not much else.

"Can you be certain which one it is?" Apollonius said, holding his cloak above his head and blinking water droplets from his lashes.

"The quaestor said there's a shop on the lower level, facing south. Is that south?" I said. We looked up and found it difficult to locate the sun behind angry clouds.

"That's south," Kirrha corrected me, "back toward home."

A wooden door opened behind us and a short burly man peered out, a hand shielding his face from the rain. "You the Roman legate?"

"Yes, Legate Quintus Sertorius," I said, praying this was the man I was looking for.

"Come in then, you're soaked through." He waved us in.

We hurried to oblige but stopped to unstrap our sandals before entering. I'm sure they were prepared for typical Roman arrogance from their guests, but I was determined to prove this was still their home and I would respect it as such.

"My name is Niarchos. It's a pleasure to meet you." He bowed. I shook his hand and found them rough and callused, a thin veneer of clay permanently glued to them. He belonged to a certain class of hard-working craftsmen my father admired, and perhaps would have chosen for me if given the choice.

"This is Apollonius," I said, "my friend and aide."

"And who is this?" A woman gestured to Kirrha and hurried to us with towels in hand.

"Yes… she was… well, the situation… she'll be staying with us for a while, with your permission," I said.

"Of course. The presence of a child is always a blessing." The woman beamed.

"This is Anthea, my wife," Niarchos said.

"It's a pleasure, ma'am." I kissed her hand.

"We've prepared a meal for you, if you're hungry." The potter gestured to a table with a few simple bowls of porridge and figs, as well as some bread I was unfamiliar with.

"No, no. I thank you. But if you'll show us to our rooms we will—"

The potter shuffled and clicked his tongue. "Of course. However, you should know…" He smiled. "It is considered rude to refuse the meal of a Greek."

"Then we'll eat the whole table, won't we?" I ignored my almond and fig-bloated belly and prepared to join them. I sat and gestured for Kirrha to join me, but she only stared at the ground, her eyes glazed over. "The girl has had a very long journey. Is there any way we can lay her down to rest before we dine?"

"We understand." Anthea smiled. "Just follow me."

"I'll lay her down, Sertorius," Apollonius said as the two of them followed her to a second floor.

"I thank you for your hospitality, Niarchos," I said when he slid a bowl to me.

"You Romans could have demanded it at sword point I suppose, so I appreciate being asked by your commander. It's no trouble, anyhow. We're simple craftsmen, you see, and it's just the two of us. Aphrodite never blessed us with child."

"Thank you regardless. We came across the girl clutching to a piece of driftwood during our voyage to Greece. I didn't know what else to do but bring her with me until an opportunity presents itself."

"You're a fine man." Niarchos poured me a cup of wine from a decorative black-figure amphora. Looked like one of the finer pieces in the home, and I have no doubt he'd crafted it himself.

"Well, it's complicated further by the loss of her family. From what I gather, her brother and her parents ... or owners ... were on the same ship, and none of them were lucky enough to survive. I'm sure I'll be occupied with my military duties but—"

"Say no more of it. We'll look after her as long as you need. I'll teach her to mold and perhaps she can help me in my shop."

Apollonius and Anthea returned and joined us. We managed to devour the rest of the food but continued to sit together for several hours after Kirrha fell asleep. We spoke of Greek life, customs, and traditions, which thrilled Apollonius. We discussed Greek history and literature, the potters surprising me with the extent of their knowledge. But more than anything, we discussed the current situation in Athens. I didn't want to ask him about the enslavement, not yet, but I searched for other clues which might help me in my search.

As the wine flowed freely, I reclined on the couch and

seemed to take the first exhale since I set foot on the *Medusa*. I probably filled my cup a time or two more than I ought, but I needed it.

"Well, I think we'll retire," Niarchos said. "Potters rise with the sun, and I'll bet soldiers do too." He stood and stretched.

"You're correct. I shall soon follow you," I said. They departed but left the half-full amphora.

Apollonius guessed correctly I wasn't ready for sleep.

"What am I supposed to do, my old friend?" I asked. My belly was warm and my vision swirled but my mind was working clearly.

"About what specifically?" He already knew the answer but he always made sure to clarify.

"No one will believe me if I tell them what's happening. And no one is willing to share information about what's behind it. Do you really think it's possible? Roman citizens disappearing in the streets?"

"I suppose it is, but it would take bold men to do it."

"That's what I'm afraid of."

"Quintus…" He leaned forward and tapped a finger to his lip as he did before saying something I wouldn't like. "Is there any chance you *want* to find something? Perhaps you're anticipating a war because you've never worn that armor without one, and you think finding it early will make enduring it bearable?"

His comments irritated me so I looked away and took a larger pull of my wine. "You heard what the man said just the same as me. I want to make it back to my wife and son. I don't want insurrection. I don't want to chase gorgons in the night."

"Of course, of course. I just mean… well, you know what I mean." His voice was gentle and I knew it only carried the weight of his concern for me.

My expression softened and I turned to him again. "You may be right, Apollonius. I don't know. Perhaps you are right," I said, "And if I did discover anything definitive it would throw a peaceful land into chaos. I think I just need to sleep."

He patted his knees and stood. "I agree. Let's get some rest while we can."

"Go on ahead." I saw the concern in his eyes. "Go ahead. I just need a moment to myself," I reassured him. At length he departed, so I poured another cup.

I walked barefoot on the dirt road, searching on all sides for someone friendly to show me the way. No one appeared.

Rays of sunlight poured around dead tree branches but offered no warmth. There was no breeze. I could hear nothing. Silence is deafening when you've heard only noise for so long. We pay no mind to the movements of critters and insects, or the rustle of leaves, but when they cease we take notice.

My mouth was as dry as an old leather sandal, and I tried to cry out but couldn't. The trees seemed to enclose around me. My lungs expanded but yet I felt no air enter.

I tried to quicken my pace, but my legs refused to move any faster. Ahead I noticed a bubbling spring. Something deep within me groaned. The water was as clear as the August sky, and appeared tastier than the gods' ambrosia.

I knelt to drink but recoiled when I heard the faint cry of a babe in the distance. I swiveled each direction but found nothing. The sun had all but faded, the tallest branches of the barren trees now hidden in shroud.

"Hello? Anyone!" I managed to say, my voice faint.

There was no response.

I turned back to the water and tried to scoop some to my lips, but my palms came up dry. I heard the creaking of a tree branch above me. I lifted my gaze until I saw the dead feet of a woman dangling from a noose.

I fell back and scurried away. Everything remained still

around me save the woman who swayed slowly from side to side.

"What is it, child?" the woman asked.

"Mother?" I cried, eye wide with fear. I searched the face and realized I did not know her. The flesh of her body was rotting but her face was smooth as silk and white as snow. I did not know her.

Her eyes opened. Colorless and emotionless they watched me.

"What do you need to know?" she asked, her lips not moving and her voice enveloping me from all directions.

"I don't know where I am," I said.

"You've asked me no questions, Quintus," her hypnotic voice resounded.

"Who am I looking for?" I asked, reaching up to touch her feet as if in prayer.

"You already know the answer."

"I don't! I'm lost and alone. I can find no one. I don't know how I got here."

"You know how you got here, Quintus Sertorius. And you know where you are going. You know this from your first breath to your last. And you know who you're looking for, but not where to find them."

"Please, tell me where to find them," I begged. I kissed her purple feet, freezing against my lips.

"The one who sees all, and yet is seen by none."

"The gods?"

"You will play your part and the gods will play theirs. They are watching," she said. Her swaying quickened.

"If not the gods then who?" I cried. "Please tell me."

"I will not tell you what you've been told before. What you already know."

I shook my head. "I don't understand."

Her eyes remained vacant and her lips still, but she began to shout at me.

"Quintus! Quintus! Quintus!"

My eye split open and a sea of reality flooded over me, the woman's voice becoming that of my friend. I was in a bed. Apollonius stood over me.

"Quintus, a messenger has arrived for you." He pat my face until I appeared to register. I was in Greece, in the home of Niarchos the potter.

"I was dreaming," I said, mostly to myself.

"Must have been some dream. What of?"

"Making love to my wife. Third time tonight," I said.

"Spare me the details," he said. "A messenger from Didius has arrived and is waiting at the door." He didn't seem to discern anything unusual for once.

"What? Who? Why didn't you tell me?" I pounced to my feet and began putting on my armor.

"What do you think I've been doing?" he asked, helping me slip into my lorica and tie my bracers.

I hurried to the envoy, who to my chagrin carried a torch because dawn had not yet broken.

"Legate." He saluted. "Proconsul Titus Didius requests your presence." He was a smooth-faced young man, likely the son of a senator.

"It isn't even light out." I clenched my jaw.

"My apologies, sir... your first campaign under Proconsul Didius?"

"Yes."

"He rises early, sir. And he doesn't like to rise alone. He requests your presence at the western gate in one hour."

"May I ask why?" My nostrils flared.

"He never says." The envoy saluted and departed.

Didius was saddled on his horse with one hand gently holding the reins, the other on his hip. As always, Didius spoke before I could address him. "Timoxenos has invited us to break bread."

"Who?" I asked, giving a salute I knew wouldn't be returned.

"Timoxenos. The man Governor Atius mentioned to us." He pointed to a riderless stallion beside him.

"But who is he?" I took the reins and pounced onto the steed, grateful for the chance to ride again but uncertain of the destination.

"I don't know. And I don't care, at least yet," he said. "Atius seemed confident this man is someone we should know. I wouldn't generally listen to a word the fool says, but this smells of truth. I know where he lives. It's hard to miss. Let's make our formal introductions."

He pushed his horse to a trot and I followed, his guard trailing behind us. He led us down a dirt path surrounded on all sides by blossoming trees, the fragrance sweet. The winds strengthened as we sped up. I wasn't thirsty, and my lungs filled with air, but I wondered if we would discover the hanging woman at the end of our ride, and I would still be dreaming.

We rode on until the sun had nearly reached its apex. We passed by families on their way to the Athenian markets, to visit their ancestral graves, or to see one of Aristophanes' plays reenacted.

When we arrived, I thought we were taking a detour to visit a small city. We cut off the main road once we reached Megaris onto a dirt path. It led to a singular building so far away it was difficult to see. Two heavily armed guards remained fixed as statues as we passed between them.

The path was flanked on one side by olive trees as tall and far as the eye could see, and on the other by every fruit I'd ever seen and some I hadn't. The mansion at the end of the long stretch of road was so large and grand it would have appeared more natural on the acropolis than on a dirt path in Megaris.

I could hear cattle in the distance, and such an outrageous

number of dogs roamed toward us for a moment. I wondered again if I was dreaming. "This is it?" I asked, craning my head to see the top of the home, where a marble statue of Apollo and Aphrodite rested at the zenith.

"If it isn't, I say we forget Timoxenos and meet whoever lives here," Didius said, equally as impressed. He waited until one of his guards crouched by his horse, then used the man's back as a stool to step down.

The massive doors swung open with the labor of two slaves. A single man and woman exited and swaggered toward us, hand in hand. They smiled from ear to ear and walked with a careless gait. The man was average height at best, and had no discernible physical characteristics suggesting greatness. His hair was longer than most, oiled back and curled at the bottom, so pale it was almost white. He had a neatly trimmed beard, the height of fashion at the time if I remember correctly. Not young, perhaps, but there wasn't a wrinkle or blemish to be found on him. He glistened like the sun god himself with gold necklaces, torques and armbands, and earrings inset with emeralds.

"Great Romans! How good of you to come on such short notice. I am humbled and honored to greet you here. My name is Timoxenos, and I welcome you." He bowed low before approaching and embracing us. Afterward, he stepped past us and greeted each of Didius' guard with the same deference.

"With all the flowers blooming here I would think Aphrodite herself must have strode this land," one of the guards said.

Timoxenos smiled and reached again for the hand of his wife. "Indeed she has. This is my wife and dear friend Phaidra, queen of this house," he said.

Her cheeks blushed as she bowed. Her copious bracelets jingled with her every movement. Her hair was as red as her complexion, styled and curled to perfection.

Didius hesitated but was eventually wise enough to kiss the hand of the lady, and I did as well.

"We thank you for your hospitality, Timoxenos." Didius crossed and uncrossed his arms.

"My friends call me Timo, and you are my friends! I would suffer greatly if you had arrived in my homeland without a formal welcome. I have prepared a traditional Greek meal for you, if you'd like to join me." He led us back to his home, and to my disappointment he led us up a stairwell to the roof rather than give us a tour of what lie within. "It's so lovely this time of year, we'll take our meal on the shade of our balcony if it pleases you," he said, leading the way.

"It... pleases me," Didius grumbled.

Garlands draped the rooftops. A sheer white cloth wrapped around a pergola and fluttered in the breeze. Couches had been prepared for us in advance, and enough for all of Didius' guard as well. Their eyes glistened. No one of such stature had ever given them a place at their table.

"Please, sit. We shall feed you the best Greece has to offer," Timo said, taking a seat beside his wife.

Everyone was too stunned to say anything, so we took our seats in silence. Too many servants to count appeared from all around us, gilded decorative plates and amphorae in hand.

"The black vintage is from Smyrna, the same wine the Greek heroes drank in the *Iliad*, if you remember. If you prefer something sweeter, the white Psythias wine is for you." He watched us, pleased as we accepted his gifts gratefully.

"You fancy yourself a connoisseur then?" Didius asked.

"I considered myself a vintner at one time, but I failed miserably," Timo said. "Now, I just consider myself a drinker. I import the good wines and just grow what I can manage." He flashed a charming smile and leaned back on his wife's bosom. "Like these olives, for instance. Just plucked this morning."

Didius wasn't known for conversation, so he ignored him and moved on to the point, "What do you do, Timoxenos? Who exactly are you?" he asked, setting aside the wine offered to him.

"Who am I?" He considered it thoughtfully. "What a complex

question. I'm not certain any of us could truly ascertain the answer. And even if we knew, could we communicate it properly?"

"Your occupation then," Didius snapped.

"Retired, if you'd like me to answer honestly," he said, a panting dog appearing at his side. "I spend my time here. King of my own little kingdom. This month, I play with my dogs and spend time with my wife. Next month, I'll oversee the harvest." He pet the friendly mutt beside him.

"You must have acquired this wealth somehow," Didius said.

"Indeed." Timo nodded and sat up. "My father was a famous sculptor in Argos. They say men of every nation would come to have him sculpt their image. When he died, he left me a small fortune. Now, as a young man, of course, I considered squandering it all on temple prostitutes, wine, and the games. Instead, I decided to do something that'd pay dividends for the short remainder of my time here on earth: I bought an army."

"You bought an army?" Didius arched a brow.

"A few small bands of mercenaries at first. Then I lent them out and used the return to hire more. Now I have an army." He sat on the edge of his seat and fixed his attention entirely on Didius. "And that's why it is in your best interest to work with me."

"In what capacity?" I asked.

"Allow me to keep all of Greece in line for you," he said. "I receive ten percent of the taxes, and I will ensure all of Greece complies with your every whim and command."

"I have my own army, Timoxenos. Two legions at full capacity. I do not require outside support to keep your countrymen in line." Didius' grey eyes were cold as the two remained transfixed on one another.

"I do believe you are wrong, my dear Roman. You see, if men of the Colors are seen beating Greek peasants in the street, it will incite unrest. The Greeks do not want to fight the Romans, you see, but we were a proud people once and we can only take so much. The trick is to offer Greece the guise of sovereignty. It's how you avoid a war here. Allow my men to do what the Romans should not, and your time here will be much easier," he said. "I assure you."

"And why should I work with you?" Didius asked, the food in his lap growing cold.

"Because every Roman governor for thirty years has worked with Timo," Phaidra said. "And for thirty years he's ensured no conflict has broken out between Rome and Greece."

For a moment, I expected Timo to reprimand her for speaking out of turn. Instead he smiled and nodded.

"Nonsense. You would have been little more than a child thirty years ago." Didius shook his head.

Timo looked over his shoulder at his wife and the two of them smirked. "You attempt to flatter, methinks, but I'll be fifty-seven next month. I can almost remember when Corinth was burned. And the Roman governors since have been intelligent enough to work with me. I have Greece's best interests at heart, and their best interest is to avoid war with Rome. Rome's best interest is to avoid war with Greece." He leaned back and gave a toothy grin. "Everyone wins."

Didius finally picked up his wine and drank deeply.

Silence continued until one of the dogs decided to break it. He raised his wet, black nose which wiggled black and forth as he sniffed for something interesting. Whatever the mutt was looking for he found it in Didius' direction.

My Proconsul started inching back, sensing what was happening before the dog even reached him. The dog's tail wagged more the farther Didius moved away.

"What is he doing?" Didius asked.

"Who?" Timo asked, partaking of his wine.

"The dog. Why is he approaching me?"

"I think he likes you, general," I said, concealing my laughter.

In a moment of anticlimax, the dog simply licked his knee.

"You know, commander, those licks are actually quite valuable," Timo said. "I call him Hippocrates because... well, I was stabbed long ago. A man with an army is often the target of such events it seems. I would have died there in the street if this little man hadn't come to me." Timo scratched behind the dog's floppy ear. "When the priests of Asklepios arrived they said there must have been a healing salve in the saliva of the dog. Since then, I give a home to every stray dog I find. But Hippocrates is the only one who sleeps in my room. Isn't that right, Hippo?" The dog spun around and returned to his master with a wag of the tail.

"You want ten percent of our taxes? For the entire province of Greece?" Didius said.

To my surprise, he seemed to be considering the offer.

"Correct, barely covering the cost of paying my men. Of course, the more you tax the more work I'll have to do to keep civil unrest at a minimum." Timo reclined and ran his fingers through his wife's red hair. "If war breaks out you stand to lose a lot more than ten percent."

Didius tapped his fingers against his cup of wine as he took another sip. "Deal."

"Splendid!" Timo clapped his hands, stood, and gave Didius a kiss on either cheek. "I believe we're going to be the best of friends. I've a special gift for each of you to celebrate this momentous occasion, if you'll give me just a moment." He gave his wife a passionate kiss before departing.

"I need to use the latrine." I stood before I could reconsider it. I didn't know why, but I trusted Timo. Perhaps I was under the spell of his charm. Perhaps I was better equipped to spot good men after seeing so few over the years. Either way, I trusted I could ask him a question and receive an honest answer. I descended the stairs to the main floor and nearly lost myself in the maze of marble columns and busts of the gods, but Timo spotted me from a distance.

Unalarmed by my intrusion, he approached. "Good. Perhaps

you can help me," he said. He waved for me to follow him, but then turned and extended his hand. "I do apologize. I don't believe I recall your name."

"It's Quintus, sir. Quintus Sertorius, legate of the Fourth Legion."

"It's a pleasure to meet you, Quintus Sertorius. I have a treat for each of you, but none will benefit more profoundly than yourself." He received a bundle from one of his servants and extended it to me.

Within was an luxurious purple toga, the softest I've ever felt. I had a newfound respect for the purple dye as well, after seeing the painstaking process by which it was made. "I... don't know what to say. Thank you, sir."

He smiled. "The rest will get one too, but it's fitted to show off these muscles of yours. You'll break the hearts of every maiden in Greece."

"I've a wife at home, so I'll avoid that as much as possible," I said, smiling from ear to ear.

"Keep it for her, then. She'll think she's married Adonis when you return to her. But in the meantime, don't deprive the ladies of Greece from something to look at, or they'll be forced to coo over old men like me or your commander." He squeezed my shoulder. "Come. You can help ensure I bring enough."

I followed him to an open courtyard in the center of the home, reminiscent of a Roman peristylium. Several dogs of varying shapes and sizes chased each other, and butterflies fluttered in the air. Chickens pecked errantly at seed spread on the tiled floor. In the center was an altar dedicated to the protector of the home, Zeus Herkeios, with burnt vegetables and sweet cakes on it.

Several purple fabrics were stretched over looms and completed togas were folded neatly on a table beside them. Not even at a senator's symposium had I seen so much expensive cloth.

"Does Phaidra do the weaving?" I approached the loom.

"Gods, no! She can't cook, clean, or weave." He cracked a wide smile. "But she loves me. And I love her." He counted out a few of the complete togas and handed them to me.

"I've heard men call their wives many things before, but never *friend*. That's what you called her before. How have you managed to stay so happy for so long?"

"I married for love, that's why. I had everything on Gaia's earth I could desire. Everything except my Helen of Troy. I saw her as a child and put a curse on her that would one day make her fall in love with me."

"And it worked, gods be damned," Phaidra said, appearing at the doorway. "Your guests grow restless. Come now."

"Yes, my queen," he said with a bow. "How many more do we need?"

"Two I believe," I said. A servant came and took them from us both and proceeded up to the balcony. I stopped him before he could do the same. "If I may, I actually have a question for you, Timoxenos."

"Of course. What can Timo do for you?"

"I was wondering if you've heard anything about Romans being enslaved here in Greece," I said. "I've only been here a few days and I've heard and seen strange things. I'm concerned for the welfare of our citizens."

He inhaled, furrowed his brow, and nodded. For a moment I feared he would respond the way Atius and the tanner had. "I do not know much, Roman. I do know if I am overheard talking about it my life could be at risk." The comment was especially shocking because Timo owned his own army.

For the first time I believed it all. Every suspicion I had was turning out to be more than paranoia. "I have no desire to put you in harm's way, Timo. I only need to know if this is true. And if it is, I must do something about it."

He seemed to consider whether he should say what he was about to. Eventually, he gave in but lowered his voice. "It is true.

They aren't isolated circumstances, either. Romans are disappearing in the night… men and women of good standing, too."

Sudden onset nausea and vertigo overcame me. It took all my strength to remain on my feet.

"I—"

"But listen to me. You cannot do anything preemptively—not even discuss this with your commander," he said, drawing near. "Lives are on the line. Greek *and* Roman lives. I will be in Athens for the Great Panathenaia festival in two months. Come to me then and we will discuss things in more detail, and more privately. Until then, listen with two ears and watch with your one eye, but do not speak at all." He winked and slapped my shoulder.

Timo was jovial and grand again by the time we reached the balcony. But he was right about one thing: I couldn't speak at all.

SCROLL IX

―――――――

FOR THE FIRST time since Ostia some sense of normalcy was established. Didius formed a redundant but useful training schedule with my aid. We managed to hang on to a modicum of legionary discipline by requiring every man to muster on the fields of Attica before sunrise. We ran sword drills, defensive formations, response to ambush, and missile training until at least one or two of the men had fainted from the heat of exertion. Didius had us rolling boulders, boxing, and throwing javelin as often as possible, watching it all as he paced the length of the training field with his arms crossed.

In the evenings, I dined with my gracious hosts. Niarchos fed us well, and I imagined he spent more than he ought on a potter's wages, but he refused any form of payment when I offered. In the evenings he taught Kirrha the basics of pottery design. She delighted in the wet clay gliding through her fingers when Niarchos spun the potter's wheel. After we had cleaned up the mess this inevitably created, Anthea would bring out her harp. She attempted to teach Kirrha this as well, but we soon learned Kirrha had played the instrument since she was old enough to walk. Soon the student became the master, and we all marveled at the spectacle.

Despite this, I did as Timo suggested and kept my ears pinned back and my eye open. I was determined to find out who was responsible for the abduction of my people. But as the weeks turned to months I wondered if I had made it all up. Perhaps it was all part of the same dream that led me to a speaking dead woman hanging from a tree.

I told Apollonius of the dream, and he refused to say definitively if it had any meaning. Dreams can tell us things, instruct us, but sometimes they were just dreams. Regardless, her words echoed perpetually in my mind, taking on a new meaning each time.

Nothing noteworthy happened until a meeting of the officers the day before the Panathenaia festival. We met at the home where Didius was quartered, which belonged to a stately old priest.

"Let me see you, child," the priest said when I entered, his voice low and gravelly. I stepped closer, and found he had a different meaning of 'see'. His leathery hands touched my face and explored the contours. "My name is Kallias, priest of Poseidon. It's an honor to meet you."

He reminded me of someone, but I couldn't determine who. He had a calming presence though, and I would have rather stayed and talked with this priest than meet with the officers. "My name is Quintus Sertorius. It's an honor. I have great respect for the priests," I said, thinking back to the priest of Asklepius who encouraged me years before.

He paused when he reached my eye patch. "It appears we have at least one thing in common, Quintus Sertorius," the old man said with a smile, his vacant eyes staring past me.

"It appears so. Have I arrived at the right time? I was told we were meeting governor Didius here."

"Yes, I will show you to him. Will you assist an old man?" he said. I took his hand and led as he slowly shuffled through his corridors to the courtyard.

Every adornment and trapping within the home revealed the

image of some god or another, some ancient tale or another. It wasn't luxurious, by any means, especially not compared with a home like Timoxenos'. The place seemed a rather odd choice for Didius to stay, but he told me previously, 'It's the safest place in Athens. If we do stir up trouble, the people are less likely to attack the home of a state priest than anywhere.'

Several of the other officers—including Lucius and the twins —were already gathered. They watched over Didius' shoulders as he moved terra-cotta figurines around a map of Athens.

"I'll leave you to it then. Gods keep you, child," the priest said as he departed, to my disappointment.

"Legate Paullus, report," the Proconsul said without looking up.

"Two down with flux, one missing," he said.

Didius glared over his shoulder. "What did you say?"

"One missing, sir."

Didius' open hands slowly transformed into fists. "If he does not report by fourth hour tomorrow, or if he hasn't been captured or killed, I want him scourged and crucified for desertion." He looked to each of us to ensure we understood. He must have noticed me wringing my hands together, so he said, "Legate, I know Roman citizens can't be crucified without trial. He gave up his citizenship the moment he swore his oath."

He had a habit of reading my mind, and my thoughts irritated him. I was relieved he couldn't see the look on Aulus' face behind him. The twins had never been exposed to this type of severity.

"Proconsul… he… he's a good lad," Paullus said, "I've sent a detachment to find him. He's probably just gone off and drunk too much wine, sir." Paullus lowered his head.

"And how will we ensure others don't do the same if we do not offer swift and complete punishment?" Didius said. "My order is not up for debate. Legate Sertorius, report."

"Two down from flux. One from training injury," I said.

"Any missing?" he asked.

"No, Proconsul."

"Good." He continued to move pieces around the map, placing one at each gate and intersection. From the number of them, I concluded they represented cohorts. "We need both legions at full capacity tomorrow. We need two cohorts in Piraeus, another two on watch by the postern gate, one on the Acropolis, one in the agora—"

"I'll take the agora with the First Cohort," I said.

He shook his head and smirked. "You want the agora? Do you have any idea what chaos awaits you during a festival like this?"

"Certainly. I want to be where I'm needed most." I didn't actually, but our rigorous training had prevented me from visiting the one thing in Athens I desired most to see: the Stoa. My father's philosophy was born here.

"So be it." He flicked his wrist at me. "Actually, this reminds me. You need a new shield-bearer, legate. That damned Jew of yours looks like he's going to faint every time he carries your shield in training."

Paullus laughed, thankful the attention was off him. I gritted my teeth. "If you require I have another personal attendant—"

"For your military tasks." Didius sneered. "Yes I do."

"Then I will choose legionary Castor of third cohort, sixth century," I said.

The First Spear Centurion of Paullus' legion guffawed and slapped his leg. "Queer choice, legate. He's quite possibly the stupidest little shit-worm I've ever trained."

"Sometimes it takes the discerning eyes of a legate to realize the potential of young soldiers." I glowered at him until he frowned and lowered his gaze.

"So be it. You can give him a pay increase if you like, but it's coming out of your wages," Didius said.

"I'll do that."

"Legate Paullus, I want you and your first Cohort on the Acropolis then. Tribune Hirtuleius can lead a cohort at the postern gate. And you two," he pointed to Spurius and Aulus, "can take the two cohorts to Piraeus. I expect there to be trouble there, all the foreigners shipping in and out."

Spurius smiled and Aulus' eyes widened. They hadn't been required to lead in any capacity thus far, and from the looks of it Aulus wasn't thrilled with the opportunity.

"Affirmative, Proconsul," Spurius said, straightening.

Didius quickly assigned the rest of the cohorts and their respective leaders to various gates and checkpoints throughout the city and immediately outside of it. When he finished, he straightened. "There can be no civil unrest. Do you understand? None. If there are rabble rousers, aggressive athletes, or belligerent fans, you have only to report it to Timoxenos' men. They will take care of it and we won't be held responsible. There can be no civil unrest. Do I make myself clear?"

We all nodded, although I wondered how much of it we'd actually control.

"Good. After the festival, I want a century from the Nineteenth Legion to travel with Timoxenos back to his home. Legate Sertorius, you'll take that Herennius fellow and go yourself if you wish."

"As you wish, Proconsul," I said, trying not to reveal how pleased I was to have a chance to talk with Timoxenos further.

"You'll be transporting his payment back with him and I won't allow anything to happen to it. I'm not paying it twice," he said.

"I would be careful not to keep written accounts of this payment, Proconsul," Legate Paullus said, still flushed from the conversation about his missing soldier. "The senate would question the legality of such a—"

Didius slammed his fists on the table. "Generals can hire mercenaries. And that's what he is. A mercenary!" He bellowed. "He will be compensated when I want him to be compensated, and he'll be discarded when I want him to be discarded."

With no apparent reason for his anger, I wondered if something had happened before my arrival, but from the wide eyes of Lucius and the twins I decided they were just as stunned as I was. Ignoring my fear of his wrath. "The Proconsul is right. But I am surprised you want to work with him, sir... if it's true you desire to earn a triumph in battle."

He looked up at me. I tried to read what his eyes were saying, but I could not determine. His eyes were bloodshot and pink-rimmed, the crows-feet on either side more pronounced. He'd never looked so human, so old. "I am biding my time. I need to determine which god has cursed me."

The room seemed to collectively gulp. No one wanted to ask, but eventually I did. "What do you mean, sir?"

He waved his hand around and shook his head at me. "The god who took my son. Whichever god gave those bad omens. I need to determine which god it was. Until then I'm paralyzed." He looked to each of us again, searching for any objection. We all dropped our heads and stared at the floor. "And when I deal with whatever god that may be, we will be ready to strike."

I took note that Didius said 'deal with' rather than appease.

"Strike, sir?" Aulus asked, careful to not meet the general's gaze when he turned to him.

"Our men are weak. They need to spill some blood so they can be ready when the next horde of barbarians come howling for us. Yes, tribune. Strike. Someone will die by the tips of our swords. If no good candidates present themselves, perhaps Timoxenos and his petty band of reprobates will do."

No one dared to speak up, but I prayed he spoke in jest. Greece would be thrown into chaos if something happened to Timo or his men.

"Tomorrow every Greek in this city will be drunk, and we'll be responsible for maintaining order. I'm going to sleep. I suggest you gentlemen do the same."

I expected the hordes of people. I didn't anticipate the livestock. Every Athenian descendant from across the Mediterranean had sailed to Attika. And each of them brought a sacrifice for Athena. Centurion Herennius, Castor, and I pointed out animals of every size and shape, each adorned with garlands, laurels, and a colorful tapestries. An outsider would have thought the pigs, oxen, and goats were the ones celebrating.

The smell of baking sweet cakes mixed with the stench of livestock feces. All around us the Athenians danced and swayed to the lyres and harps playing throughout the agora. Couples leaned up against walls and kissed.

"This isn't as bad as I imagined," Herennius said, relaxing his shoulders.

"Give it a few more hours, friend," I said. "When the wine starts flowing this whole city will be in chaos."

We strolled through the marketplace in loose ranks, four abreast and ten deep. We narrowly fit through the slim paths between the stalls pedaling their wares to drunken visitors. Castor walked at the front with the Centurion and me as my new shield bearer. Although, one must admit he seemed to be struggling just to carry his own shield, still not filling out the armor, its weight a strain on his thin frame.

Centurion Herennius leaned toward me and whispered, "And if you want to partake in this wine, I'll look the other way." He winked.

I laughed and shook my head. "I wouldn't expect it of you, centurion. But I appreciate your offer."

"I mean it! I served a tour in Thrace some years back. Whenever we would have a moment to ourselves, we'd all drink together," he said. "Whoever was the most sober got the highest rank. We passed around the officer's crest like we did the wine, and before I knew it there was a First Spear wearing the crestless helm of a recruit."

"No. You can't mean it." I laughed. "Really?"

A dancing man stumbled into me. He jumped back and ran off when he saw our armor.

Herennius raised his hand to take the oath. "On Jupiter's stone."

"If I did drink, these Mules would be sure to join me." I gestured to the legionaries behind me. "They'd be off bedding merchant's wives and gambling away their rations on dice throws by the end of the watch."

He chuckled. "You may be right."

A small wrestling bout broke out between a few stalls a few hundred feet ahead of us. Nothing too serious, probably over the hand of a duplicitous lover if I had to guess. But it caused a disturbance regardless.

I caught the eye of one of their associates and shouted, "You stop it or I will."

They quickly wrapped up the dueling drunks and pulled them apart, allowing us to continue our march.

A burly legionary with crooked teeth shouted from behind us, "This must be agonizing for you, aye, Castor? All your friends," he pointed to the pigs, "marching to their deaths." He maintained a feigned seriousness but several of the men behind us burst into laughter.

I threw up a fist to signal for a halt. I turned to the legionary and squared up to him.

"Your name?"

"Rufus, legate," he said, a glimmer in his eye which indicated he still found it very funny.

"I have need of something." I fished out a few coins from the pouch on my belt and handed it to him. "That stall there. It's selling bread, isn't it?"

"Yes?" he said with a raised eyebrow, his companions cackling as they anticipated his punishment.

"Go and purchase a loaf for me. But I want you to crawl along the ground. Crawl to that merchant and buy the bread with your face on the stone."

His jaw dropped as his eyes darted back and forth between Herennius and myself.

"I'm sorry, legate. ... I was only—"

"No need to explain, lad. This isn't a punishment," I said. "I just want bread. And I want you to purchase it. From the ground."

When he saw Herennius was now laughing with the rest of us and wouldn't be of any assistance, he slowly lowered himself to the ground, eyes fixed on the soot and animal dung awaiting him.

It made for quite a spectacle, watching a legionary crawl twenty paces to purchase a loaf of bread. The Athenians scratched their heads, stupefied.

"You didn't have to do that, sir," Castor said, his face still blushed from the insult.

"Truly, I just wanted the bread," I said, loud enough for the rest of the men to hear.

It might seem cruel to someone who hasn't served. But the embarrassment would ensure the legionaries wouldn't insult others so flagrantly. When enough time passed, he'd find the humor in it. Then he'd at least have one legion story to tell his family that he wouldn't be too haunted to tell.

Rufus returned and snapped to attention in front of me, holding the bread aloof like he was delivering a precious letter. "Your bread, legate."

I took the dirty bread but let him keep the remaining coins. I split the loaf and threw it into the paths of a few pigs. "Job well done, soldier." I clapped him on the shoulder and gestured for him to return to formation.

Signaling for us to continue our march, Herennius bit his knuckle to keep from laughing. "These Greeks look like they've been asked an intricate riddle."

"If they only knew the nonsense intrinsic to wearing this uniform," I said. "Wait, is that the Stoa up ahead?" I craned to see over the procession before us.

"I wouldn't know, legate. Not much for philosophy," Herennius said. "At this rate we'll be there by tomorrow evening." He shook his head at the slow crowds before us.

"I like riddles," Castor said.

"Oh, you do?" I asked.

"Ilithyia used to tell the best riddles," he said as if we knew her. "Would you like to hear one?"

"I'll leave it to you, legate. They make my head hurt," Herennius said.

"What month has twenty-eight days?" Castor asked.

"Well, that's not a riddle, boy. That's just a question. Well, there's June... and Sextilis..." Herennius pondered it.

I thought about the twelve months all but one had over twenty-eight days. It wasn't a very good riddle, if I'd ever heard one.

"Februarius," Herennius concluded.

"All of them," Castor said with a boyish grin.

"Ah! I see what you've done. Very clever." I smiled.

"No... Some of the months have thirty days? And others still have thirty-one?" Herennius said.

"Give the centurion just a moment to consider it, Castor." I chuckled.

He scrunched his face until the moment of realization. "Ah. I understand. Clever. Let's have another then, one not full of trickery."

"I'm not sure you understand the point of riddles, friend," I said.

"I shave every day but my beard stays the same," Castor said. "What am I?"

"Out of regulation," Herennius said. "No, a babyface. You can't grow anything?"

"No. That's not it!" Castor said, eagerly.

"A Gaul. Hairy bastards," I said.

"A barber!" Castor said, more animated than usual.

"Clever." I said. "Very clever."

We marched on as Castor thought over a few more riddles. As dancers were forced to step out of our path I heard, "These are Athenian games, not Roman!"

I said to the men, "As long as it's just words, we keep marching."

"Roman dogs!" others shouted.

They were drunk, I told myself. Timoxenos' men would take care of it regardless. They knew their limits, and they didn't *actually* desire to test Rome.

We approached the Stoa on our right, and as the crowds slowly migrated on, I could see inside clearly.

I called for a halt, surprised at the simplicity of the building. A rectangular building with simple Doric columns and chipping paint on the walls. There were innumerable buildings just like it in Rome, and probably throughout Greece. But my eyes welled up regardless.

To think centuries before, men just like my father gathered here to talk about finding meaning in a tragic world. If not for the words spoken by those columns, I wouldn't have made it back from Arausio. I couldn't have endured the Cimbri camp. And I wouldn't have survived my first year in the senate.

"Legate?" I felt Castor turn to me, but I couldn't break my gaze.

There was nothing within but a few benches and a beggar shaking an empty bowl toward the crowd. But I believe I could still hear the echoes: *Man conquers the world by conquering himself.*

I thought of my father, my brother, and all the men I'd lost. That's what they had taught me, and because of their teaching I was able to endure life without them. I blinked the tear from my eye and forced a smile. "I have a riddle, Castor."

"And I'll bet I can answer it," he said.

"Who is 'the one who can see all, but is seen by none'?" I asked, not really expecting an answer.

He thought of it for a moment, and I began to inform him I didn't know the answer either. But first his eyes widened, and he pointed to the old beggar leaned up against the stoa columns. "Him!"

The beggar spoke to those passing him by, offering his sad story and asking for help. No one listened.

My hands felt numb and the hair raised on my arms.

"Was I right?" he asked.

"I believe you were, Castor," I said. "Herennius, take watch for a moment."

"Take a break, lads. Remain within eyeshot," he shouted.

I cantered over to the beggar and slipped the coin purse from my belt. He didn't notice me until I was at his side, and he jumped when he saw me.

"I've done nothing wrong, sir! Nothing wrong, sir!" He shuffled away but I took off my helm and took a knee beside him.

"I'm just here to give you something." I jingled the coins in my hand.

"Athena bless you!" he said, holding out the bowl and bowing his head low.

"Where do you hail from?" I asked, placing a coin within the bowl. Even if the dream meant something and Castor was correct in his guess, I didn't know what to ask the man.

"Here, sir. Here!" He pointed to the earth beneath us.

"Athens?"

"Right here. It's all I can ever remember," he said.

I couldn't determine whether he meant Greece, Athens, or perhaps even the columns of the Stoa itself. "Were you born a free man?" I asked.

People began to notice him now, probably expecting to see him dragged off and punished for begging on the day of a festival.

"I was and still am." He straightened. "Patrobos of the Erechthesis tribe."

"It's a pleasure to meet you, Patrobos. My name is Quintus Sertorius." I shook his hand.

His smiled revealed rotting teeth. "All Romans are named Quintus, aren't they?"

"Most of us, at least." I looked over my shoulder to ensure the men were behaving and found most of them watching me. "I have a question for you, Patrobos. Have you seen any Roman citizens—probably named Quintus—who've been enslaved or gone missing?"

I placed two more coins in his bowl, but he caught my hand and pushed it back.

"You've already done enough, Quintus from Rome." His pride was kindled since he spoke his name, and he appeared almost a different man than the wretch who crawled away from me. "A few Romans used to bring me coins, but they don't any longer. I don't know what happened to them. But if it's to do with slavery, Hyrkanos of Achaia will know if it. Not a slave is sold in this city without his knowing."

I took a deep breath. Hyrkanos. Nothing definitive, but I had a name.

"Do you know where this Hyrkanos is?"

Patrobos spoke with an even but gravelly tone. "He works from the base of the Areopagus—Ares' Hill."

"Are you certain I can't give you something else for your aid?"

"Don't need it." He shook his bowl. "With this I'll eat and drink with the rest of Athens tonight. The gods will give me what I need tomorrow."

"It's been a pleasure to meet you, Patrobos. Perhaps we'll cross paths again before I leave."

He reached out and took my hand. "If you cross paths with Hyrkanos... kill him. I've friends he sold for a pittance. He's a wretch." He didn't release me until I nodded.

"What was that about?" Herennius asked.

I bit my thumbnail and recirculated the name Hyrkanos through my mind. "Herennius, if I thought there was someone here who posed a threat to Rome, would I be right to stop them?"

"Who? That old bag?" He chuckled until he realized I was serious. "Proconsul says we should report to the mercenaries, right?"

I considered it. But could Timoxenos be trusted? What if he was involved? Even if he wasn't, wouldn't fear preclude him from acting?

"It's something only Rome can handle."

He searched my eye for more information. Not finding it, he clasped my shoulder. "I know you, legate. I trust your judgement. If you believe we need to act for the good of Rome, we should."

I didn't trust my own judgement—not really—but I was honored nonetheless.

"Thank you, centurion."

"Legate." He could see I was conflicted and waited until I met his gaze. "Trust your instincts. Rome has asked you to act in her best interests. You know how to do so."

"And the men would follow?" I asked.

He smiled. "Into Pluto's arse."

They didn't know why, but they listened when I ordered them into tight formation. Herennius took the lead and shouted orders for anyone in front of us to make way. We quickened the pace and dancers and drinkers jumped out of our path.

"Where again?" Herennius asked over his shoulder.

"It's a big rock beneath the Acropolis," I said, knowing he

wouldn't recall the name. He nodded and shouted at partygoers again.

My heart raced but I felt weightless, my chest tingling and stomach fluttering. A sensation often preceding battle. I relished it. I became more aware of the gladius bouncing at my hip. The ache in the heels of my feet disappeared. My shoulder bore the weight of my lorica easily. I had craved this. Action. I was done listening and waiting.

Torches began to light on the side of the streets. I could tell more wine was being consumed the further the sun set as the cheers of festivities engulfed us from all sides.

I feared something might happen in the agora, and I'd be held responsible. But I no longer cared. I wanted to see this Hyrkanos as much as I wanted to see Arrea. I wanted answers.

Herennius signaled for a halt as we reached the foot of the massive limestone hill. "This it?"

"This is Ares' Hill." I scanned the area and found only one building fitting Patrobos' description.

Two guards were placed before it, and they looked like the kind of scum one would expect to make a living in slavery.

Some of the men whispered behind me about what we were doing. Castor was as perplexed as the rest of them but was mostly struggling to catch his breath.

"Legionaries," I said, turning to them. "those within this building have threatened Rome. I cannot disclose any more information. But will you go with me?"

"Yes, legate!" They slammed their shields into the ground, frightening the locals.

"If they lay down their arms, we'll simply talk to them. If a blade is drawn on us, we'll draw first blood. Understood?"

They stamped their shields again.

I stepped off.

"On the legate, lads!" Herennius shouted and lifted his shield, in his element as much as ever.

As we neared, the guards scurried to their feet and grabbed at the hilts of their swords.

"What's yer business?" one shouted.

A murder of crows burst from the hilltop above us, causing everyone to jump.

"Stand down," I said in Greek.

Their eyes darted about as they counted our numbers.

"You've got the wrong place," the other guard said. "We operate legally and all that." His Greek was no better than mine.

"I don't think so. Open the doors."

"Not gonna happen. We's told no one can enter during the festival."

"I am Rome, boy," I said, squaring to the man and close enough to feel his breath.

The guard looked for help from his friend, his lips quivering.

"Don't try it." I gestured to the other, sensing his grip was tightening on a sword hilt, although I could not see it with my bad eye.

"We just can't let you go in," the other pleaded.

"You've no need to fear your employer. He will be the one afraid."

The guard stuttered "But, sir, Hyrka... he's gone to the festival. He should—"

I lost my patience and threw the one man aside. I lifted my leg and kicked the door in. The ground beneath me shook as the men rushed to my side.

"Two ranks, stand guard," Herennius said.

"Hyrkanos! Show your face!" I shouted. What if he ran a legitimate—although seedy—business, and had nothing to do with the disappearing Romans? Didius would be furious. The thought flashed before my mind, but I quickly disregarded it. Too late now. "Hyrkanos!"

I lowered my head to continue into the dark building. A tomb-like stench filled my nostrils. On either side of the hallway were caged rooms, and I could make out shadowy figures on the floor within. No one spoke, but some moaned, and I heard the buzzing of flies.

Herennius and I approached one of the cages and peered within. What little light was available to us illuminated several boney, naked bodies, huddled together. Water dripped incessantly from the ceiling. A mound of human excrement lay at the opposite side of the room.

This wasn't anything like the cages of the slave markets, which were kept relatively clean. These wretched creatures were not the well-fed and bathed slaves of the market, trying to catch the best price. This was the underbelly of the world, the closest we can come to Hades this side of the River Styx.

"What if I told you this was happening to Romans?" I said to Herennius.

He stared back blankly, trying to determine if this was another riddle. "Are they?" he said, his eyes widening.

"I don't know. But I have reason to believe the same thing is happening to Roman citizens."

The veins in his neck bulged. "Hyrkanos!" he roared.

Two more guards appeared and charged down the dark hallway. They didn't have enough time to assess the situation. One drew a sword on me, but even with the darkness and one eye I could see it coming.

I grabbed his arm and cracked my knee into his sternum. I tossed him aside as my men pounced to restrain him.

The next hesitated, but I didn't. I drew my blade and slapped his from his hand, then sent my elbow into his nose. I grabbed his arm and twisted it until he fell back. "Where is Hyrkanos?" I asked through gritted teeth.

"Who are you?" I twisted his arm until he grimaced. "He isn't here!"

My heart sank but I tightened my grip. "I don't believe you."

"I'm right here, you barbarians!" A voice shouted from behind us.

I turned to see a dark figure in the doorway behind my men.

"Let him through," I said.

The men parted on either side but maintained a grip on their swords and watched his every step.

He swaggered through the opening, stopping to look each of my men up and down. "What has Hyrkanos done to deserve such disrespect?"

His voice didn't belong to a Greek. A Cilician perhaps? A Thracian?

"Let's talk, you and I," I said.

"That'll cost you. My time is expensive," he said, swaying from whatever drink was in his hand. I flashed just enough of my gladius for him to see the shine in the dim light. "I guess I don't really have a choice then, do I?" He moved on past me and gestured for us to follow.

"Herennius and Castor, on me," I said. "The rest, stand by and keep your sandals on their necks." I pointed to the groaning slavers on the floor.

I needed Herennius to come for protection. I wanted Castor so I didn't do anything I'd regret.

Hyrkanos led us to an open corridor and lit two lamps, illuminating several tables overflowing with empty cups and spilled wine.

"Wine?" he offered, pouring himself a cup. We said nothing, "Girl? You Romans like our girls."

"It's of Romans I want to speak," I said, standing over him rather than sitting alongside him at the table.

"One might have assumed." He drank freely.

"I was told every slave exchanged in Athens goes through you," I said. "Is it true?"

He smiled and gave a slight nod.

I exhaled. "And how long have you served in this capacity?"

He poured another cup and offered it to Herennius and Castor, but I held out my hand to stop the transfer.

"I've been the lion atop the hill for... ten years now," he said, "under the auspices of Rome I might add."

"Oh, I'm sure," I said. He shrugged.

Rage boiled up in my gut like water over a furnace. I thought about what I might ask him but all I wanted to do was smash his teeth into the table before him.

"What is it you wish to ask, Roman? I'd like to continue the festivities," he said.

My mind froze as I consider the question, until he faked a yawn. "My friend Apollonius and his niece Anaiah were enslaved in Athens less than ten years ago. Do you know of them?"

The room was silent accept for Hyrkanos slurping and my heavy breathing through flared nostrils. I saw the shadows of Herennius and Castor shifting uncomfortably.

"I've enslaved many uncles and many nieces," he said. "Many Apollonius' and many Anaiah's. I apologize, Roman. If that's why you're here, you'll find no answers from me." He swept his thin black hair behind his ear and shook his head with feigned contrition.

I stepped closer. "His father was named Yulios and he was indebted to opiate peddlers."

He let his head back and clutched his belly. The laughter he omitted was piercing.

"Now this fool I remember! A businessman like myself has his hand in many enterprises. He purchased my product and he owed me a fortune. I took his son and granddaughter in payment. Even still I never made back what he owed me."

My eye wouldn't stop blinking and my vision tunneled. If I hadn't felt the quiet gaze of Castor behind me, I would have buried my gladius in his neck.

"Where is the girl?" I said. He took a sip and shrugged. I brandished my gladius and sat it on the table beside him.

"Oh! Now I remember. The girl. We sold her for a few barrels of grain to the sanctuary of Delphi, to be some sort of nymph of Apollo," he said. "Who knows what they do with children there. If it had been up to me, I would have held on to her for a while.

Give her enough time to grow some tits and she would've sold for double, even tri—"

I threw a right cross into his jaw. He flew back and off his chair but collected himself and returned to his seat as if nothing happened. His split lips creased into a smile and he dabbed the blood from his teeth.

"Hit me all you'd like, Roman. But you know I don't act alone. I take orders from someone above me, just like you."

"The same who orders you to enslave Romans?"

He wagged a finger at me. "Now, now. You know I can't speak about that. They would kill me."

"I will kill you if you don't." I picked up my sword and placed the tip under his chin. Castor gasped and Herennius grabbed his arm to restrain him.

He shook his head. "No you won't. See, I know you. You have orders and answer to someone *just like I do*. You cannot kill me."

I considered plunging the sword through his soft throat, but eventually slammed it back down on the table.

He smiled triumphantly.

I grabbed him by the throat. "Tell me this then: does Timoxenos have anything to do with this? Even a nod of the head will do."

He laughed and spit blood from his chin onto my hand.

"No, Roman," he said. "They don't like Timoxenos very much."

PART II

SCROLL X

I WAS SUMMONED before Didius the next day. When I arrived at the priest's home, I found none of Didius' usual attendants. Only Herennius was present, and I immediately knew word of our incident had spread before I could draw up a formal report.

I joined Herennius at attention before the Proconsul, who was leaned up against a column and wringing his hands together.

"Do you know why you are here?" he asked, hardly above a whisper.

"Sir, I—"

"Do not even speak!" Didius bellowed, storming toward us. His eyes darted rapidly between Herennius and myself, considering which to chastise first. "You... well, I don't know whether to call you fools or traitors. Do you know what you have done?"

I struggled to swallow and shook my head.

"We do not, sir," Herennius said for us both.

"You abandoned your damned post. Two rival athletic clubs fought in the agora and several shops burned to the ground." My knees weakened. "Do you understand the trouble this will cause me?" He labored to control his breath and I was certain he was about to strike me. The gentle old priest Kallias squirmed behind him, and I believe his presence was the only thing that stayed Didius' hand.

"Proconsul, if I could only—"

He held up his hand to stop me. "I don't give a brass obol for your explanation, legate. I'm inclined to have you whipped before the legion." He turned to Herennius and squared up to him. "Despite your experience and seniority, I'm inclined to say you were simply following the orders of a rebellious legate." He turned and glowered at me. "But you. You knew better. I've wasted hours explaining to you the delicacy of this mission and you seek to jeopardize everything! Now... what have you to say for yourself?" His voice calmed but his nostrils continued to flare.

"I have it on good authority that Romans are being enslaved here in Greece, Proconsul. I felt it was in Rome's best interest to—"

"And why shouldn't Romans be enslaved? We enslave others, don't we? Reminds us that we still exist in the wilderness, that danger lurks around every corner. That's what is wrong with the Republic, Sertorius," he shouted, spittle flying from his lips. "We feel too safe, we feel protected by status, wealth, and connections. That's what I know that the rest don't. There will always be someone stronger lurking in the shadows, waiting to take what we've acquired." He seemed to forget we were there.

I shifted my weight and did all I could to hide my shock. He could have been tried for treason himself just for uttering something like that. His words were usually calculated and measured, but he now roared without restraint.

He rolled his eyes at me. "Of course we'll do something to stop it if this is true. But what is this 'good authority' you speak of? Where is this ring of spies you've acquired?" He glanced around the room, hoping to find them.

I bit my lip and considered whether or not to tell the truth.

My father's guidance eventually prevailed. "I learned it from a beggar, sir."

Didius stared back blankly until he doubled over with laughter. "Truly, legate, I had no idea you were so humorous." He dabbed a tear from his eye. "I'll be sure to find you a position in the theater upon our return to Rome." His face hardened and his eyes became sinister. "Because you'll never serve in the legion again if you speak the truth."

I'd been handling this the best I could but was beginning to lose my patience. I was aware of the mistake I made in abandoning the agora, but I wasn't used to being mocked so. "I've time in espionage, Proconsul, if you recall," I said, wringing my hands behind my back. "I understand how to gather intelligence, and I've been doing so since the moment we arrived. The beggar was simply the man who pointed me to a likely culprit."

"And when you found this slaver, this… Hyrkanos… did you find hordes of the good and faithful citizens he's reportedly stolen?"

"He said as much with his own mouth," Herennius said.

For the first time the indignation in Didius' eyes was replaced with a shred of belief. "And if any of this is true, you should have come to me." His fury returned. "We could have strategized and planned and taken a whole damned legion down upon them!"

"I know I was wrong, Proconsul," I said. "I humbly request your pardon."

He shook his head like a disappointed father and turned to Kallias. "Bring me some water. I'm boiling like a hot spring."

"Permission to speak, sir?" Herennius said.

Didius considered it and nodded.

"I don't know if the slaves we found there were Roman or not. But if there is even a single Roman being treated like this… something must be done."

He spoke with enough conviction that Didius nodded, slumped onto a bench, and exhaled deeply. "Looks like we won't be going home in October after all. Good work, Sertorius." He smirked.

I lowered my gaze.

He gulped from the water as Kallias smiled at the two of us, offering his silent sympathies. Didius set aside the cup and turned his attention back to us. "I'm docking a week's pay from the both of you. It will pay the merchants who lost their stores. Any objections?"

We said nothing.

"Good. And let me make myself clear," he said, waiting for eye contact. "If I sense even a shred of insubordination again, I'll have you both stripped of rank and assigned to latrine duty for the remainder of our term."

"Yes, Proconsul," we said in unison.

"Now we understand each other. The two of you will begin to regain my trust by escorting Timoxenos back to his villa. And if I hear so much as a word about Roman slaves without you presenting one in shackles, I'll sell the both of you to slavers myself."

"Understood, Proconsul," I said, deflating.

"Now get out of my sight." He flicked his wrist and turned back to Kallias.

We waited for Timoxenos outside the western gate as the sun set and darkness crept over the hills.

"Why would he want to travel at night?" Castor asked from beside my horse, tugging anxiously at his chainmail.

"Because we can avoid the traffic, my boy!" The voice which could only belong to Timoxenos sounded in the distance, followed by the footsteps of his armed guard. "That, and I don't think anyone will give us any trouble. We've got more blades than a field of grass." His horse clopped to my side and he extended his hand.

"Sorry I wasn't able to meet you last night, Timoxenos. I…"

"Timoxenos hears everything, lad. I know what happened, and you have no need to explain yourself to me," he said. "Shall we begin? I'm ready to sleep off this bloody hangover."

Herennius took the front and led our men out before us.

"Is Phaidra not accompanying us?" I asked.

"She stayed home. It's quite remarkable really. For one so bejeweled as my love, you'd think she'd enjoy the pomp and spectacle of a festival. But alas, she prefers moonlight wine drinking and peach picking." He grinned at the thought of her.

My mind flooded with questions I wanted to ask but I also recalled Didius' warning. I decided to remain quiet about that topic—for now. "So tell me how you enjoyed the festival."

"Shh!" Timoxenos said, holding out his arm, "You hear that?"

I stopped and listened closely to the rustle of the leaves on either side of the road. I awaited bandits and my eye played tricks on me in the form of imaginary spears flying through the darkness. I whispered, "I hear nothing."

"Cicadas." His white teeth shined in the moonlight. "Can't you hear their song? They're out late this year. That means we're on the brink of resurrection, spiritual awakening. That's what my father used to say, anyways." He was almost giddy.

"My father used to say the cicadas were once human, transformed by the muses into creatures that spend their entire lives singing," I said, somewhat uninterested.

"And what a blessing that was. We all have a song to sing don't we, Roman?" he asked. He placed one hand on his hip and tightened his grip on the reins with the other. "I believe we need to talk discretely. Isn't that correct?"

I exhaled with relief.

"I'd very much like that, Timo."

"Let's ride on ahead then." He quickened his steed to a trot, forcing the legion ranks to part before us.

"Uhh, sir... what are you doing?" Herennius reached out to stop us.

"Getting a little fresh air," Timo said.

"We should maintain the front. For protection."

Timo pulled back his cloak to reveal an ornamental bronze blade on his hip.

"This is all the protection I need. Besides, this fine specimen here could fight off the worst Greece has to offer." He pointed to me and winked. Herennius shook his head but protested no further.

We moved out of earshot and slowed to a trot. I waited for him to initiate conversation, and he took his time.

He looked up at the night sky, his eyes bewildered with the light of the stars. "The gods speak to us in many strange ways, don't they? Insects, constellations, the entrails of animals, the flight of birds..." He lost himself in thought.

"If I were a god I might pick different means. Or perhaps I'd be more direct and speak my orders outright."

He chuckled. "Imagine an officer giving orders to his legion by the flight of birds. I'd say Rome would have trouble conquering the world were that the case." I smiled and tried to reply, but he spoke first. "I believe that the gods orchestrated our meeting. After all these years you're the first Roman who's shown the slightest interest in uncovering what lies beneath the peaceful veneer of Attika."

"You're saying other Romans have known?"

He shrugged. "One cannot know for certain. But I must assume they knew *something*. Sometimes it's easier leaving to the shadows what lives in the shadows. It takes a brave man indeed to take a light to the darkness, knowing a gorgon might be there waiting for him," he said. "Have you heard the name Cerberus before?" As soon as the word escaped him he craned his head in all directions to ensure no one listened.

I raised an eyebrow. "The three-headed dog that guards

Hades?" I was under the impression that everyone knew the tales of Cerberus.

He shook his head. "I'd be much less concerned about a deformed hound." He turned to me. I could feel the intensity of his gaze even in the darkness. "That is your enemy. Cerberus. You'll hear the name whispered in taverns and scribbled on buildings in the agora, but no one speaks of them openly. I know not whether this Cerberus is a man or an organization or a militia... but they are the enemies you seek."

The chill of sweat developed on the nape of my neck. "Cerberus is enslaving Romans?"

He exhaled. "I believe you're stuck on the idea of a few disappearing men. It appears to be more sinister than that, I'm afraid."

I tried to speak but my dry tongue clung to the roof of my mouth.

"From all I gather they are bent on Rome's destruction. Operating in the shadows to villainous ends."

"How do you know this?" I asked, resisting the idea the same as Didius had previously. This was the stuff of tragic plays in the forum, not reality.

"Timo knows all, remember? I've received menacing letters, threatening to end my life for assisting Romans. Each has been stamped with the seal of the three-headed beast."

"This could be children," I said. "Or petulant zealots."

"Some of my men are known to enjoy the pleasures of less than reputable establishments as well. And they report to me the whispers they hear. Cerberus has plans larger than the disappearance of a few merchants and cattle drovers. They're making alliances. They're seeking out Rome's enemies across the Mediterranean. From the Pillars of Heracles to the sand dunes of Parthia."

"They'd find no shortage of enemies, I'm certain. But truly, how much havoc can be wreaked by a few rebels in the shadows?" he asked.

He turned his gaze to the stars once more as the hypnotic chant of the cicadas seemed to heighten. "Wasn't it rebels in the shadows that freed Rome from her kings?"

"If you are so frightened of them, why would you continue to work with us?" I asked, feeling anger rising in me for no apparent reason.

"The length of life's thread is already determined. The Fates decided long ago when each would be severed." He formed a knife with his hand and cut through the imaginary cord. "Even Zeus bows to their dictates. If he does, then so should Timo."

I said nothing but looked up to analyze the stars Timo found so interesting.

"But I'll say this," he said, interrupting my contemplation. "Timo is afraid of nothing. But Cerberus makes me shake in my sandals. If that tells you nothing, my words will not convince you either."

"Thank you, Timo."

"Do not thank me, my boy. I might have just cost you your life."

SCROLL XI

I DID as any reasonable man would. When I returned, I immediately consulted my advisors. Apollonius led me to a tavern he vowed was the finest in Attika, and Lucius soon joined us.

Some of the tavern patrons sang drinking songs, the others played knuckle bones. I made sure to notice each of them. I assessed their clothing, their speech, their eyes. The level of intoxication was important too, because I needed to know how closely they might be listening in. Timoxenos's words made me paranoid, so I couldn't be too certain.

"So much intrigue I feel like you're planning to go spy on some barbarians again," Lucius said with a smile as he sat down beside us, three cups of wine balanced in his hands.

"No intrigue. I just want to talk," I said, half-honestly.

"Well, that's a shame," he said. "I'm beginning to grow bored of this campaign."

"Bored? How could you be bored?" Aulus appeared in the doorway and clapped each of us on the shoulder. "We have friends, time enough for wine and song, and no women to give us a fuss. Speaking of women… Apollonius, does this tavern have any… you know." Aulus' grin was glowing as he joined us.

"No, it does not. This is not that type of establishment, Aulus. And if I had known you were coming I would have chosen somewhere less reputable," Apollonius said, a poorly concealed smirk giving him away.

"Where is your brother, Aulus?" I asked. "Is he not joining us also?"

Aulus looked between myself, Lucius, and Apollonius. He furrowed his brow and leaned on the edge of the table. His eyes watered. "You aren't serious?"

I was utterly perplexed.

"Yes? Yes. Is he joining us or not?"

He crossed his arms and cleared his throat. I believe his lips quivered. "Quintus," he whispered, "Spurius has been dead for three years."

The room seemed to shrink around me. I nearly fell from my chair.

Then he burst into laughter. "You turned redder than a Nursian turnip! You see that, Lucius? Old man? His other eye nearly burst out of his head!" Aulus bellowed as I punched at his rib cage. "He'll be here any time. Busy writing a letter to his precious wife, as usual."

I didn't find the joke funny until my heartbeat slowed, and by that time Spurius had joined us and bought another round of wine for the table.

"Gentlemen, there are a few things we need to talk about before we get too drunk," I said, interrupting the jokes and storytelling that had already begun.

"You bastard. You speak of me and I know it," Aulus said as he wiped a bead of wine from his chin.

"I'm serious," I said.

He sobered and ran a hand through his golden hair. "Sorry, legate. Proceed," he said, and for once I believed him to be serious.

"First, I have some news for my dear friend, Apollonius." All eyes turned to my Greek friend as his breathing quickened.

Hope filled his eyes, but he had hoped for so long there was doubt there also. I prepared myself for the tears that were sure to come. "Apollonius, I know where Anaiah is. The slaver Hyrkanos gave us a location. We're going to bring her back, my friend."

We each stood to clap him on the shoulder and kissed his head as he attempted to process it.

His lips parted as if he would speak, but he said nothing. His eyes stared blankly at the wine-stained table before us, not with relief and joy but with confusion as if he'd be posed with a riddle. "Where?" he managed to say, barely audible over the roars of applause at a good dice roll in the back of the tavern.

"Delphi. And the moment I have a day's leave I'll be riding there myself to bring her home. And you can come with me." I lifted my cup, and everyone did the same. Except Apollonius.

"Hyrkanos was his name. He is who enslaved us," he said, almost to himself. He tapped a trembling finger against his lip, deep in thought.

"Then we have every reason to trust this intelligence," I said, disappointed in his response.

"But that's been years now. She could have been sold again. Or the owners could have moved. Or she could have..."

They patted his shoulder again, but this time more out of sympathy than excitement. I thought about pressing on the matter, but I decided to give him a moment to process it. I believed it in my heart we would find her. I wouldn't stop until we did. His faith in that was irrelevant. All that mattered was her freedom and their reunion.

"The rest of what we need to discuss cannot leave this table." I scooted closer.

Lucius said, "Excellent, we have some intrigue after all." He licked his lips.

"I mean it. It could cost lives. Namely our own," I said as he acknowledged his understanding. "There is an organization here in Greece that is working in some manifestation to bring about

Rome's destruction." I ensured my voice was only loud enough for the table to hear.

They deferred to one another to respond, but none of them seemed to want to.

Lucius conceded and said, "Quintus, I would assume there are groups of fools all throughout the Republic that seek our downfall."

And for a moment I imagined sitting in their seats and hearing about this. I couldn't blame them for thinking I was losing my wits. The doubt ran through my own mind for a moment as well. Was this just the hidden scars of too long at war? No. I hadn't dreamt it all. This wasn't like the lady and the tree.

"That's the problem, Lucius," I said. "Independently they can do nothing, but if they can all unite forces they can pose a real threat to Rome."

"How could they expect to do so?" Spurius said, doing his best to not patronize me.

"I don't know the answer to that any more than you do. But I've spoken with individuals who know more than we do. And this shadow enemy calls themselves... Cerberus." Again I realized how outlandish it all must seem.

"Cerberus?" Aulus said, but I cut him off by gesturing frantically for him to keep his voice down.

"Yes. They are responsible for Roman citizens in Greece being enslaved. I was told specifically that they're making alliances with enemies of Rome from Spain to Parthia." I sighed. They weren't believing me. "If rebellions were to strike up across the Republic, we would be powerless to stop them all."

I leaned back in my chair and allowed an uncomfortable silence to settle in. Each of them considered my words, save Apollonius who hadn't heard a word since we spoke of his niece.

"Quintus." Lucius placed a hand on my arm. I could tell he was struggling to say something uncomfortable. "I know nothing of which you speak. Grand conspiracy is above my level of intelligence. I'm a simple soldier. Show me an enemy and I'll conquer him, point and I'll go. I know nothing of this, but I trust your judgement. If you believe all that you say, I do too."

"That's right," Aulus said.

"Just tell us what to do," Spurius said.

I choked up with relief. Why should I have ever doubted them? But then I was left with the uncomfortable question: *what do we do*? And to be honest, I hadn't really considered the answer. As long as Didius refused to believe me, our capacity to act was limited.

"Sertorius?" Lucius asked, reminding me how long they'd been waiting on my response.

"Yes…" I stalled for time. How does one fight a faceless enemy? One that does not wear a uniform, or have a flag? "We keep our sword arm strong, and at the ready. We remain vigilant. And we keep our eyes and ears open. Nothing can go unnoticed. And when the time is right… we strike."

SCROLL XII

BEFORE WE KNEW it the October Horse was upon us and the war season was over. We would have begun packing our things and preparing for the voyage back to Rome, but Didius was able to convince the Senate and People of Rome to vote for us to stay. Despite his doubt, and despite my desires to return home, he used the murmurs of sedition as reason enough for our campaign to continue.

If only Arrea knew it was my own doing that kept me from returning to her. I could imagine the famous fury of a Gallic woman would have been on full display.

About this time that I received my first letter from her. To my surprise, correspondence was far slower to reach us in Greece than when I'd been in Gaul, as letters have a habit of disappearing as they cross the sea.

"I imagine this is from a loved one. It's scented with perfume," Niarchos said, peaking into my quarters and extending the folded scroll. The smile on his face revealed he understood my anxiety, and quickly departed so I could read it in private.

· · ·

My dearest husband,

Nearly a year has passed since you left us. Occasionally it feels as if you've been gone a lifetime. Occasionally it feels as if you just left my side.

Our bed remains cold without you beside me, despite the festering heat of city life, which I am still unaccustomed.

Your son is growing like a wheat stalk in spring, and I swear it he looks more like you each day. It's as if the gods knew he would be yours one day and ensured he looked the part. His smile reminds me of yours, enough to keep the image of your face fresh in my mind. But it becomes more blurred each day. O, how I long for your return.

Rhea is visiting often, and we've been visiting her. She continues to teach me the basics of reading and writing. I still have much to learn, so it is by her hand that this letter is written.

Quintus—this line is from your mother—I insist that you write me soon. I am your mother. You know, the one from whom you came. I am creating a list of chores for you upon your return, and each day I don't receive a letter, the list grows longer. I jest, but I miss you dearly, my boy.

Your mother is convinced that your loyal steed, Sura, misses you more than any of us. She has been pouting and cranky since the day you left and refuses to listen to anyone. And yes, we know she's deaf. Still, she'll only obey Gavius and we must assume his resemblance to you is the only reason why. I believe you'll have to let Sura sleep in the Domus for a few weeks after your return to make it up to her.

Rome is quiet without you, my love. Rome is quiet in general, if you can believe it. Every few weeks a new trial is brought against the former associates of Saturninus and Glaucia, and generally the accused are being persecuted and exiled. A few have been executed. I know this must sadden you but assume you would want to know.

There is so much else I would say to you, husband. Some of which would be inappropriate for your mother's hand to write. So I will finish and seal this now. Please, write me soon. Visit soon. Come home soon.

Your dove,
Arrea

On the back, Gavius attempted to write something as well, and to my surprise it was legible even with the numerous mistakes:

Father,

I am keeping mother and ~~grandmat~~ grandmother safe. You would be proud. When they don't have me helping around the home or grand-mother's farm, I train with your bow and your old sword. I am becoming quite proficient. Perhaps next war season I could visit you. If I could prove my ~~meda~~ mettle and my prowess in battle, perhaps the legions would ask me to stay on?

Otherwise, I need you to return soon. Too many women around, not enough men. It's not good for a young man. I even miss old ~~Appalo~~ Apollonius and his constant blathering. If I'm forced to keep my present company for much longer I'm afraid I'll begin plucking a lyre and wearing a wig.

For the Republic,
Gavius Sertorius, son of Quintus Sertorius

Not until I rolled up the scroll and set it aside that I realized I was weeping. I could hear every word as if Arrea's gentle voice whispered it in my ears. I could see Gavius as clearly as the crisp, cool morning when I taught him how to properly draw back his bow.

The scrolls did indeed smell like Arrea's perfume. The scent filled me with warmth and longing. My stomach churned and turmoil enveloped my mind. The conspiracy I was pursuing was keeping me from them. But it was for them that I did it all. What if these enemies of Rome were successful, and something happened to my family? I couldn't allow it. Even if it meant I never saw them again.

"Quintus?" Niarchos peered in again. I quickly dried my eye. "I apologize. I've been called for *heliast* duty, a homicide case that will certainly result in conviction."

"That sounds like a great honor," I said, ensuring my voice was deep and didn't crack.

"Not really. Every citizen can be called to serve in the jury. And it costs me a day's work." He shook his head. "Regardless, is there anything you need before I leave?"

"No, no. I'm quite all right." I followed him into the courtyard where Apollonius was seated and reading over some old writings or another.

He'd attended the Libraries of Aristotle a few months prior and was ecstatic to borrow some of the writings he once transcribed. Today was his Sabbath day, which meant he would be in that exact spot for the rest of the day. So far, he'd said nothing about his niece.

Kirrha and Anthea were whispering and giggling with one another as they worked delicately on a loom.

"Well, I best be off then." Niarchos departed and left me standing awkwardly in the middle of them all.

I approached the altar to Zeus Herkeios in the center of the garden and knelt before it. "I greet this day with gratitude for my life and the many blessings therein." I broke off a piece of honey cake and rotated it over a candle until it caught fire. It filled the room with a sweet smell like incense as I continued my prayer.

"Quintus, I apologize again…" Niarchos said, reappearing.

"Have you missed us so much already?" Anthea jested, but she quickly sobered when she saw the stern Roman behind her husband.

"He met me at the door. He needs to speak with you."

I recognized the man as one of Didius' attendants. He was the sort of man who never smiled, but I knew immediately from the dark circles under his eyes and the flushed color of his face that something was wrong. "What has happened?"

He saluted. "I've been sent to collect you. Proconsul Titus Didius requests your presence immediately."

"On what business?"

"I'm not at liberty to say, sir," he said through clenched teeth.

"The Proconsul instructed me to muster on the fields for training this morning. If he has other intentions for my day, I need to know; so I can pass along instructions to my centurions," I said. In reality I wanted to prepare myself for the whipping Didius had promised me if that was my fate.

He exhaled and his eyes glanced at each member present in the room, who all looked away and pretended they weren't listening.

"To be forthright, sir. I don't entirely know myself. A woman arrived at Kallias' residence this morn. She was crying and hysterical. I do not know why, or who she is. But she requested you specifically by name."

I felt everyone's gaze slowly shift toward me. Nodding, I said, "Let me grab my sword."

I could hear crying as soon as I entered the priest's home. I followed the sound to the garden, where I found Didius with his head bowed, rubbing at his temples. I assumed he wasn't the type given to consoling a hysterical woman.

Behind him, Kallias held onto the weeping woman. She wore the black cloak of mourning, with the hood pulled low over her eyes.

"Sir." I saluted. Didius simply stepped aside and gestured to the crying woman.

I knelt and waited for her to turn to me, and at first I didn't recognize her. Phaidra's red hair was gone, only patches of stubble remained between scrapes and cuts. The veins of her eyes were like red spiderwebs, all reaching out and clinging to the shimmering iris. Her black makeup was smeared and ran down her face with the stream of her tears.

"Phaidra, what has happened?" I said.

At the sound of my voice, she burst into tears again. Kallias released her and she threw herself into my arms. "They t... t... took my Timo!" she sobbed.

I wrapped my arms around her and pulled her head to my chest. I struggled for words and to remain composed myself. "Get her some water," I said to anyone listening.

Didius said, "She won't drink. She won't eat. She won't sleep. She says she'll die before she satiates herself while her husband is missing and alone." He exhaled deeply.

"Phaidra, look at me." I pulled her chin up delicately. "We need you to tell us everything that's happened. We need you to stay strong and think clearly about the details. And then we will do everything we can to find him."

She stifled further sobs and straightened, remembering the grace and nobility she radiated when we first met. "We received a menacing letter. I opened it first and panicked when I saw it, but Timo said we had received the like before. It said he would be sacrificed to Hades for betraying his people." The memory sent her spiraling into her own thoughts.

"Go on," I said.

"There were three fingerprints in black ink. He said it was of no concern, probably someone his men roughed up... but he then went missing."

"See?" Didius said. "Missing. Are you certain he hasn't gone hunting? Visiting a relative? Tending to a mistress?"

Her sad eyes became menacing when she looked up at Didius. I saw then that the mosaic beneath her depicted Persephone being kidnapped to Hades. Something about that struck me.

"In twenty-seven years of marriage he has slept in my arms every night. He has never left without telling me."

"Where was he when he disappeared?" I asked.

She finally accepted a cup of water from Kallias and drank as one who finds a stream in the desert. "He was in the andron, the men's quarters. My servants were preparing me for sleep when a crash came from across the villa. Women are not permitted to enter the andron of course, but the noise startled us so much my servants and I ran to find him. He was gone."

"Any broken doors? Any blood? Weapons?" Behind her, Didius rolled his eyes and tapped his foot.

"Nothing. But our guards were missing. And they never go missing. They must have scurried off and allowed someone to enter quietly."

Didius swallowed hard then and said nothing more.

His voice soothing to all of us, Kallias said, "That doesn't explain what happened to your hair, my child."

Tears pooled in the corners of her eyes and slowly rolled down her ashen cheeks. "I cut it all off and sacrificed it to Hermes, along with the wings of all our chickens... 'god of thieves, if you can steal my husband, can you steal him back?'" she recited while I rubbed her back.

"Where are the rest of your husband's men?" Didius asked.

"Gone. Scurried off like rabbits the moment news of my husband's disappearance spread."

Didius' eyes shot open and he swore underneath his breath. Now he was panicked.

"Legate Sertorius, you must ride out to Timoxenos' house immediately. Search for anything the lady might have missed. Use your training and find this man. Understood?"

I slowly released Phaidra back into Kallias' arms and stood. "Certainly, sir. I'll take Tribune Hirtuleius with me—"

"No!" he barked. "No... with Timoxenos' men gone we'll need to pull tighter security here. Take that simple shield bearer of yours and nothing more. Any more would slow you down."

I considered his response carefully, then nodded. "Phaidra, if he is still alive I will bring him home to you. I swear on Jupiter's black stone," I said. Perhaps I should have chosen my words more carefully. At the mere implication that he might be dead she fell apart again. I hurried to the exit.

"Legate, if I may have a moment." Kallias hurried to me with the help of a cane made of olive tree wood.

"Yes, sir."

There was a slight tremor in his hands and face, but I assumed that might have been a permanent fixture of his old age. He raised a leathery hand to scratch at his forehead as he chose his words carefully. "I've spoken with some of the other priests. The auguries and auspices haven't been this bleak in over a century, they say. I'm afraid something bigger than the disappearance of one man might be afoot, no matter how important the man. The gods are angry with us."

I considered asking if he knew about Cerberus, but there was no guile about him, no intrigue. He was a simple old priest who believed in the gods' signs. "I'm inclined to agree," I said. "What should I do?"

"Go and go quickly. But be careful and keep your sword ready. I do not like you going alone when there are miscreants about."

"We shall stay off the main road." I smiled and patted his shoulder. "I will return."

He kissed me on either cheek. "I will sacrifice to Athena and Poseidon that you do."

SCROLL XIII

TIMOXENOS' home was usually bustling, but now we found it empty. No guards watched the road; no slaves tended the fields. The only sound was that of a smoldering fire, smoke still wafting from it.

It seems Phaidra spared nothing in her sacrifice to Hermes. An altar wouldn't suffice, so a bonfire before the doors of her very house contained the charred remains of wheat, vegetables, fruit, and the wings of her fowl. And her silken red hair.

Castor said, "I've never seen a home this big. It's just your friend that lives here?" He craned his head and peered up at the statues atop the villa.

"The man we are looking for, yes. He and his wife. But they have many servants and guards as well," I said.

"Where are they then?"

"I'm wondering the same thing." I held my tunic up to keep the smoke from my nose.

"Perhaps they went searching for him?" Castor said.

I nodded but knew in my heart they'd deserted. With Timoxenos gone and Phaidra unstable, this must have seemed like a perfect opportunity to run. She wasn't likely to chase them down while her husband remained gone, and their private force was unlikely to do anything about it, either.

Or they feared the bad men might return and take them as well.

We entered the home, an eerie silence hanging over the high walls.

"Hello? Is anyone here?" I shouted.

"We're friendly!" Castor joined me. We heard nothing. "Should we split up, legate?"

"No, I think it's best if we stay together. I need your protection," I said. He beamed and blushed, although I was more concerned for his safety than my own.

"What are we looking for?"

Both of us jumped with a start when we heard a rumble upstairs. In one motion I grabbed the hilt of my gladius and positioned it atop my shield. Castor watched me and carefully did the same.

The patter of paws on mosaic floors reverberated.

I exhaled and hung my head. "It's just the dogs."

Timo's favorite mutts ran down the steps like legionaries in formation. They encircled us and greeted us with wagging tails and licks.

Castor knelt and basked in their affection, happier than a man in Elysium.

"So you are the only ones who haven't left? Loyal beasts, and truly a friend to man," I said.

"This one looks like my old Pollux!" he said, scratching behind the dog's ears.

"I think he likes you. Perhaps they were siblings?"

"If I ever became rich, I would have this many dogs. Or maybe more."

I gestured for him to follow me up the stairs. The andron was the best place to start since that's the last place Timo was seen. "Is that right, Castor? What else would you have?"

He whistled and patted his leg for the dogs to follow us as he considered his answer. "Children. As many children as dogs. Olives and grapes. I don't know how to grow all that, but I'd learn. Pigs too. Maybe some chickens, and a house that's warm in the winter and cold in the summer!" He became more excited as he imagined it.

I smiled. "I believe you'll need a wife for some of that, my friend."

"Yes. A wife that really loves me. I was in love once. Did you know that?"

We reached the top of the stairs and made for the men's quarters—a a square room with couches lining the walls in a U shape. It was notably more cluttered than the rest of the home, with grand chalices and amphorae of wine littering the room.

"I did not know that. Tell me about her," I said, kneeling to inspect the concrete for any signs of confrontation.

"Well, I don't remember her name. She was older than me and had yellow hair. My friend Cassius gave me a few coins that morning and I used that to pay her. She said she gave me a price she didn't give to anyone else." He smiled. "She fell asleep beside me and I knew she loved me from how safe she felt. At least I think it was love. Maybe when I get home I'll marry her."

"I think that's a fine plan, Castor," I said, although of course it wasn't. I found twine on the floor and coiled it around my hand, inspecting it for blood. There was nothing. I tested its strength and decided it was certainly strong enough to restrain a man if tied properly.

Another clamor sounded downstairs, and I turned to find that the dogs had followed us, anxious for human affection.

"Do you think they have more pups?" Castor lit up.

"No, I don't. Quiet now." I pulled him farther into the room and knelt.

The entrance door opened. Footsteps echoed through the empty house.

"When we find the bitch, I want the first go at 'er," a rough male voice said.

"What gives you the right?"

"Because I was the first to mention it."

"Ridiculous. We'll roll dice for it," another said.

I closed my eye and focused all my energy on what I could hear. If they had been quiet and careful before, they certainly were taking a different tact to abduction now.

Castor whispered, his voice cracking, "Legate?"

I ignored him and tried to count. There were three of them. No, four. How many more could be waiting outside? I inhaled slowly and calmed myself. The faster my heart beat the more present and controlled I felt. "Castor," I whispered, "I need you to do exactly as I do and follow my direction. Understand?"

"Who are these men?" he said, a familiar tremor developing in his limbs. His helm had fallen to the side awkwardly, blocking part of his vision.

"I believe they're the men who took Timoxenos. We need to be quiet." I strained to hear again and could sense they had split off, searching different rooms.

Footsteps—perhaps a single pair—drew near. I turned to Castor and placed a finger to my lips. I moved toward the doorway and crouched beside it. Castor followed with one hand on his hilt and the other covering his mouth as if there was no other way to cease his panting.

The dogs, perceiving that others were joining us, took off out of the room and in all directions. I held out my arm to ensure Castor didn't follow them.

Within moments, I heard one of the dogs yelp. Then more.

"Stupid mutt!"

"How many of these beasts did this fool have? I'm going to roast them up if they snap at me," another shouted.

"Focus on the bitch. You can return to kicking dogs afterwards." They laughed.

I turned to Castor and shook my head. To my surprise his fear had transformed into rage.

"Oh, Phaidra! We have a gift for you," a man close to the andron shouted.

"Four gifts, and mine's the largest," another said, farther away. They all laughed, and I knew that the closest was about to enter.

I pulled the pugio dagger from my calf and tucked myself as close as I could to the wall.

A fat man in a conical helm entered, not but a few feet from my face. He couldn't be bothered to look around. He walked past us, toward an amphora he was hoping might have another drop, if I had to guess.

I broke from the wall and crept up behind him. In one swift motion I covered his mouth with one hand and thrust the dagger into his chest with the other. His teeth sank into the soft flesh of my palm and I did all I could to remain silent. I wedged the pugio free and stabbed again, and a third time.

He fell limp in my arms, and I braced to keep his rotund body from crashing into the floor.

"The longer we have to look, the rougher we're going to be with you!"

"Don't worry, my peach. You're coming with us either way."

They continued to shout from all over the house as I nodded for Castor to follow close behind me. His sword was drawn and at the ready.

We crept as quietly as we could back to the stairway. From there I could see a beam of light pouring in from the other side of the villa. Someone was searching the balcony. Two left in the house.

We moved slow to avoid alerting them, but every step seemed louder than the last.

One of the dogs began to snarl downstairs.

"Ouch! This bastard mutt bit me!" one man yelled.

I knew his location then—in the courtyard.

"Kill him and move on then. Stop your bellyaching," another

shouted from the back, where I imagined the kitchen might have been.

The barking ceased, was replaced with whimpering, then silence.

"I'm bleedin' something fierce," the man in the courtyard said.

We made it to the bottom of the steps with several of growling dogs surrounding us. They couldn't distinguish friend from foe.

I stretched out to them as slowly as I could manage. One smelt me and was pacified. The others were not. The hair on their backs raised up like a legionaries' plume and vicious barks erupted from them.

"Damnit I said to kill them!"

"It's not me," the other cried, and then both intruders silenced. Sandals stomped toward us from multiple directions.

We froze, but it was too late. One of them entered first, slack-jawed and stunned to find a Roman there instead of a helpless woman.

I sent my dagger spinning at him. It wedged into his throat as he collapsed beneath a statue of Phaidra as Aphrodite, flailing his legs like an he had Apollo's curse.

Something struck me and I almost lost my senses.

"Legate!" Castor cried and I looked down to find the feathers of an arrow suspended from my breastplate and caught sight of an archer beside two ornate busts of Apollo in the distance.

I lifted my shield. "Get to the horses!" I shouted, running toward the assailant. My breathing was wheezy, but my limbs were still strong. If I was bleeding out, I still had time. Time enough to at least ensure the boy made it out alive.

An arrow wedged into the shield. My enemy then threw down his shield and I heard steel sliding from a scabbard.

"Legate!" Castor bellowed.

"Do as I say!" I shouted.

I ducked behind my shield and charged until it crashed into

the assailant. He stepped back and tried to swing overhand. I lifted up and blocked it with the shield and grabbed his throat with my right hand. I cracked his head back into one of the busts, sending it shattering to the ground. I squeezed as tight as I could, the bones of his neck cracking under the pressure. He beat against the shield with depleting strength. I cast him to the ground, released the shield, and struggled to draw the gladius from my hip. The angle wasn't right and I couldn't bring it free, but I continued to tighten my grip on his throat.

He reached up with near death's desperation and jammed his thumb into my only eye. Unable to stop myself, I cried out as I felt for my shield again. I lifted it up and crashed it into his temple. Then again.

His force was dwindling. Mine was expanding. I cracked the shield into his face again. I wedged myself free of his grip and grabbed hold of the shield with both hands and then with a final roar I sent the shield into his face one last time. One of his eyes bulged out, but both of them were empty as they looked back at me, and blood poured from several places. He was dead.

I rolled to my back and tried to catch my breath. But the last of them was already upon me. Before I could even register it, one thrust his great sword down upon me. As if the gods took over and controlled my limbs, I snagged my gladius free in an instant and batted the sword away.

He recoiled but came back again quickly, careful not to give me time enough to collect my balance.

I held my sword out enough to block it, but the pain in my ribs was beginning to reverberate. He straightened and poised to strike again. I lifted my blade horizontally but knew I could no longer hold off his assault. I closed my eyes and for a moment I saw the Nursian fields and my family there upon it. The man gasped and when I looked up again the tip of a gladius was piercing through the man's sternum.

He grimaced, blood gurgling from his throat. He fell to the side, revealing Castor there behind him.

"Legate, are you all right?" he asked, suddenly more panicked than he'd ever been. He reached to help me up.

"We must go!" I sprang to my feet and pushed him toward the exit.

"My sword. I could not wedge it free," he cried.

"We'll get a new one," I shouted as we reached the exit. He'd brought the horses to the front, where they pawed nervously and shook their heads against the reins.

I reached down for the arrow and broke off the end of it before grabbing onto my steed's mane and hoisting myself up. I managed to shout '*lead!*' despite the lack of breath in my lungs.

Castor took off and I kicked my horse into following after him, not knowing what would be following behind us.

SCROLL XIV

THE ARROW HADN'T PIERCED my flesh. My breastplate and the chainmail beneath it served their purpose, but the force was still enough to keep me doubled over in pain. I couldn't be certain, but I assumed I was purple and blue. I clutched the wound with one hand and the reins with the other. We rode and we rode fast, driving shepherds and their bleating sheep running off the path.

We dashed under trees and through thorny thickets, but my mind reexamined the attack at Timoxenos' over and over again, remembering certain details I'd at first forgotten, and perhaps inventing others. Killing these men was different than combat. There was a personal element which sometimes escapes you on the battlefield. The animosity in their eyes, the sour stench of their breath hot on my flesh. Were these the men that drove Kirrha's family into slavery? Those who plotted to bring Rome to her knees?

With no time to waste, we passed the stables and made straight for the priest's home, where we hoped to find Didius.

He and Phaidra were still there, along with Kallias and a few other officers. They jumped with a start when we burst into the courtyard, faces covered in soot from the hard riding. Phaidra's eyes lit up when she saw us, but then I slowly watched her heart break again as she realized her husband was not with us, and we did not bring good tidings.

Didius jumped to his feet. "What's happened?"

"We were attacked." I bent over and placed my hands on my knees, trying to catch my breath. There was still a wheeze present I was unaccustomed to.

"On the road? Or in the home of Timoxenos?" Legate Paullus asked. He ran his meaty fingers through the plume of his helm.

"In the home of Timoxenos," I said. "They returned for Phaidra."

"In what condition did you find the home? Did you learn anything?" Didius said. I could tell he'd become wine drunk as he'd been forced to listen to Phaidra's mourning.

"Abandoned," I said, peaking to see how Phaidra reacted. She didn't. "There was twine strong enough for binding a man, but nothing else. We could not search for long. Four assailants arrived shortly after we did."

Didius slumped back to the bench and snapped for another cup of wine. "Phaidra, did your husband have any enemies? Anyone that would want to see you both disappear?"

"Of course he did." She lifted her pink-rimmed eyes. "Anyone who owns a private army has enemies. But *none* of them would have the courage or ability to take him, let alone come back for his love," she said.

"Was there perhaps something your husband kept from you? A gambling problem perhaps?"

"Sir, if I may…" I said.

"Timoxenos didn't gamble," she said through gritted teeth. "Even if he had enough money to do so carelessly."

Didius rolled his eyes. "What is it, Legate Sertorius?"

"I believe this is more than personal animosity. Anyone in Greece knows that Timoxenos works with the Roman authorities here," I said. "This is a direct attack on the dignitas of the Republic."

"*Gerrae*! How could you come to that conclusion?" Legate

Paullus bellowed. "Proconsul, he's clearly injured and not thinking clearly." I could see the doubt in his eyes. He didn't want to believe me, but he did.

"Let him speak, Paullus. I've doubted Legate Sertorius in the past, and perhaps I was wrong to do so," he said. "Speak."

"Timoxenos confided in me when I escorted him home. He told me of a... well, I don't know what to call them—"

"Spit it out, man!" Paullus shouted.

"A cult. They call themselves Cerberus and are devoted to destroying Rome. They've been enslaving our citizens, and gods only know what they've done with them and what other schemes they have planned."

Paullus laughed, but Didius remained as still and cold as a statue. Phaidra did nothing. Kallias leaned over and rubbed his eyes, shocked but equal parts broken.

"Why would they do this?" the priest said emphatically, trying to convince himself. "Rome has been good to us. They cannot be sons of Greece."

"I do not know, sir. All I know is that they're here. Operating in the heart of Greece."

Didius leaned back and tapped a finger rapidly against his cup. For a moment I spotted hunger in his eyes, the look which comes when a man is presented with an opportunity for glory. "One thing is for certain," the Proconsul said, "this province is not as safe as we thought. We can no longer quarter with civilians in the city. It's too dangerous."

"I vow that no harm will befall you in my home," the old priest said.

Didius said, "I'm afraid prayers would be unable to stop them." He realized he'd come off ruder than he'd meant. "You'll remain my advisor and confidant while I'm in Greece, but I can no longer stay here, my friend."

His voice fragile and gravelly, Kallias said, "I understand."

"What time is formation in the morning?" Didius asked, although I was certain he knew.

"Second hour," Paullus said.

"Good. You'll put out the news then."

"You won't be present?" Paullus asked.

"No." Didius shook his head. "I have business with the Oracle of Delphi. I won't be waiting. I'll be departing with my guard before the end of fourth watch." He scanned our faces to ensure we understood. "Have the men construct a proper fortress two miles from the western gate. Give them time enough to gather their belongings in the evening. Tomorrow we become a real legion again."

"Yes, Proconsul," Legate Paullus said, despite sulking.

"In the evening I want the officers to meet and discuss how and where to devote resources to searching for these rebels..." He looked at me and I nodded to Phaidra. "And Timoxenos. I'll ratify whatever orders you prepare upon my return if they suit me."

"We're going to war with a faceless shadow," Paullus said to himself.

"Sertorius." Didius approached, suddenly sober and threatening. I met his gaze and realized he wasn't blinking, "If you are wrong and I'm made to look like a fool..."

"Understood, sir," I said, not keen on hearing the rest of his threat.

He gestured to my side. "Get your wound dressed," he said. "I'm going to need you at full strength. This is your war now, Legate Sertorius. You'll be leading from the frontlines, whatever that may mean."

"I thought you Roman men were supposed to be tough," Niarchos said with a furtive grin while I winced.

"I think he's plenty tough. He has a cracked rib," Anthea said as she dabbed at the wound with a willow-soaked rag. "This should help numb the pain, but you'll feel it tomorrow."

"I'm feeling it now." I bit my knuckle and laid my head back on the courtyard couch.

"Will he be all right?" Kirrha asked.

Her little lisp warmed me. "I'll be fine, my child. Just a scratch."

Apollonius brought me a cup of wine and slowly tipped it back for me to drink.

Kirrha said, "I don't understand why anyone would want to be a soldier." She frowned and shook her head. "They know they'll die eventually."

I chuckled and reached to take her hand. "Have you ever seen a sad pig?" Anthea leaned me up and lifted my arms to wrap a bandage around me.

"No," Kirrha said.

"That's because there are none," I said. "They live a life destined for the slaughter, and yet each trots along as happy as a man in love. Because *they've* never been slaughtered before."

She smiled. "That's silly. Why not be a poet or something safe?" She sat on the couch beside me and cautiously eyed the bandages.

"I should like that very much." I chuckled. "But I'm not afraid to die. I polished Charon's denarii long ago. When it is my time, I'll be ready." Although I wasn't certain I meant it. "Soldiers like me fight to ensure little girls like you get to grow old and have children of your own."

She played with the hem of her tunic and then leaned over to peck a kiss at my cheek. "Thank you then."

I smiled and pinched her cheek. "I would fight in a thousand battles and die a thousand deaths to protect you."

"What about Apollonius? And Anthea? And Niarchos?" she said. Everyone laughed except Kirrha who studied me.

"I've already fought in several battles to protect Apollonius. Why do you think he follows me everywhere I go? He owes a life debt to me." I smirked at my old friend who rolled his eyes.

"That's not quite how I remember it, Quintus," he said.

"There. All patched up," Anthea said as she cut the cloth and tied it off. "I believe the broken rib is causing the wheeze."

"What is your prognosis then, doctor Anthea?" I said to which Kirrha giggled.

"I had an uncle in Rhodes who had a similar injury. Fell off his horse," she said, "Asclepius will make you whole in time. But you must restrict your training. If you move too much you're liable to come apart like an old sack of wine."

"Thank you, Anthea."

As silence descended on us I had the chance to let everyone know I'd no longer be quartering with them. But I couldn't bring myself to do it. I'd come to take great comfort in their company. They had become a second family to me as I was away from my own. And I would miss Kirrha dearly. I could still visit on occasion, certainly, but it would not be the same. So instead I said, "Well, if it's rest I need I shall begin my recovery with a good night's sleep."

"I'm inclined to do the same," Niarchos said. "Although I should be rested enough from sleeping during *heliast* duty today. Who knew a murder trial could be so dreadfully boring?"

"I'm sure you'll be back to forming clay soon enough," Apollonius said, rubbing the weariness from his eyes.

"We're doing just fine without him, aren't we Anthea?" Kirrha said to our humor.

I kissed them each and made for my assigned room, unable to remove my hand from the wound. I untied my *caligae,* noticing the muck covering my feet for the first time. I didn't care. I ignored them and laid back, not bothering to change from my soldier's tunic to something more appropriate for sleep. I was exhausted and didn't feel like standing or kneeling, so I said a prayer to my ancestral gods there from my hay-packed mattress.

Despite the fatigue of my body, my mind raced from one thought to another. Here I dwelled on the fight at Timoxenos' home; there I brooded over Didius' words and what the future might entail.

There's no telling how many hours I laid there, still as a statue, with my mind running faster than a charioteer in the Circus Maximus. At one point I all but gave up on acquiring any meaningful sleep, but then the familiar sound of battle filled my ears. The same dream recurred to me most nights; only rarely would Hypnos allow me to have no dreams at all.

It was Vercellae I believe. Perhaps Arausio. The wind whistled inside my helm as I led the cavalry charge at the barbarian flank. The clash of iron echoed then, and the cries of battle rose to greet it. Torches roared through the air as they crashed into buildings, lighting everything ablaze.

My eyes shot open. The noise still continued. I pounced to my feet and struggled to retie my sandals.

Apollonius rushed into my room.

"I hear it, I hear it," I said.

"What is happening?"

"We're under attack," I said. "Get my shield."

"By who?" he cried.

"I'll soon find out." I threw the chainmail over my head and struggled to get my arms through.

"Wait, you cannot fight. You surely don't mean to fight?" He stepped away with my shield.

"Who will then? You? Niarchos?" I met his gaze. He was trembling, I was not. He knew I wouldn't be swayed. "This is who I am, Apollonius. I am a Legate of the Roman Republic. Injured or not I must rally the men."

"I won't let you, Quintus." He hid the shield behind his back.

"We are losing time!" I roared. He tried to summon enough courage to defy me, but I quickly added, "I am going out there, my friend. I can either go with my shield or without. Your choice."

He complied and hurried to the courtyard to find the others stirring there as well.

"Quintus! What is happening?" Niarchos asked, as if I knew.

"We're under attack. I must rally my men." I buckled my helm. "Niarchos, Apollonius, arm yourselves and guard this home with your life. Anthea, take Kirrha and hide under a bed or crawl into the cellar."

They all sounded off with questions but I ignored them and burst from the home.

Flames illuminated the streets. I could make out unarmed Romans running through the streets, but they each fell as soon as I could spot them.

Was this a nightmare? Perhaps I was living out the Battle of Burdigala from the perspective of the besieged. Such a dream was not foreign to me.

An arrow whizzed by me and struck the stone so close to my face that a chip of stone hit my cheek.

I lifted my shield, no longer feeling the pain in my side. "Romans! Legionaries! Rally to me!" I bellowed, unsure if I could be heard over the tumult. I laid my sword against the top of my shield and squared up toward a gang of assailants in the distance. They heard my cry and turned to me, bloodlust in their eyes.

"Romans!" Someone else bellowed, and the cry was repeated by others in the darkness. While keeping the enemy in my sight, I tried to peer around to spot any of my allies. Nothing.

The rebels approached. Some wore Corinthian helms, others conical. Some held the long spears of a Macedonian phalanx and others axes and clubs. I spotted some with the plumed helmets of a Roman, but they didn't move like legionaries. They had taken them from the dead.

Two assailants sprinted toward me.

I whispered and rushed in. "Father, protect me."

An axe flashed through the air. I caught it with my shield and kicked its wielder in the knee. The other tried to circle me, but I spun in his direction and brought my gladius down on his spear, splintering it before it could reach me.

My face jolted back as an elbow crashed into my nose. I stepped back and centered myself as the two men crumbled before me, crying out and struggling to reach the *pila* wedged in their backs.

"Romans, on me!" I shouted, the iron taste of blood settling on my lips. Two or three men gathered at my side, still struggling to don their armor.

"Legate, who are these men?" one cried.

"It doesn't matter," I said while we formed our shields into a wall. A few more legionaries fell into formation behind us.

"What are we going to do?" a legionary from the third cohort asked.

I remained vigilant as I considered the answer. What were we to do in an assault like this? We were spread out across the city with no centralized point to protect. Should we make it to the walls and seal the gate, or were all of the attackers already within? Should we fight toward Didius in the northern part of the city? Rally at our training grounds? Protect the district of the city in which we were quartered?

What we did was mostly irrelevant. More important was that I spoke definitively and with confidence, that they trusted I was prepared for this moment. "We must reach the high grounds. From the Temple of Hephaestus, legionaries from around the city can spot us." The idea seemed to be given to me from somewhere else. I thanked my father, in case he'd been the source.

The temple was close by, and we moved toward the foothills beneath it as quickly as formation would allow. Sprinting feet were heard from the right—enemy archers running through the alley. They dropped to a knee.

"Shields right!" I roared just in time for our shields to meet the brunt of the shafts. One man was struck in the shin. "Do any of you have *pila*?" I asked as a few assented. "Let them fly now."

The front ranks ducked as the spears whistled through the

air. A few of the archers crumbled and the others ducked into the shadows of the surrounding buildings.

"Forward!" I shouted as we reached the long path to the temple. We stepped over slaughtered livestock, sheep still bleating as they squirmed under the weight of arrows.

A woman holding a swaddled babe to her breast sprinted past us.

"Get indoors!" I shouted. Her home was likely one of the many ablaze. But to remain on the streets was a death warrant.

Along the path I spotted three enemies standing around a single Roman. He remained in position with his shield fixed at the ready, but they swarmed him. He moaned when pierced from all sides. As he fell I noticed he held the standard of the first cohort, the flag falling with him.

I pointed at them with my gladius and we shifted our march. "Step away from the standard," I said. "Now."

The rebels shot me toothless grins and one stomped it into the mud.

I broke from formation toward them, and my men followed. I leapt in the air and stabbed down into the chest of a poorly armored giant. Another slashed at my face. I jumped back but the tip sliced through my cheek just beneath my good eye. My men pounced and before I could see straight, his arm was missing and a blade was wedged in his belly. "Protect the standard!" I shouted, ignoring the sting of my flesh.

"Protect the standard!" they echoed as one of them picked it up and hoisted it into the air.

We reached the temple, and from that great height we could see fires burning around the city. The cries of thousands rang out from all directions.

"Gods below," the legionary at my right said.

The defense towers rang out when someone sounded the alarm. It wasn't the guards, that's for certain. They would've done so immediately if they weren't already dead or in league with the enemy to begin with.

144 | WHOM GODS DESTROY

"Stay in line. Stay in formation," I shouted. I pulled them back and we planted ourselves under the temple's columns. The new standard bearer continued to wave the muddy flag as high as he could. In the darkness, figures could be spotted running toward us.

"Here they come!" one of the men said.

"No, they're Roman!" I held up my arm to halt their assault.

"Legate! Legate!" a voice cried out, and even in the darkness I knew it was my shield bearer.

"I'm here, Castor," I shouted.

He hurried to us, the fire reflecting in the wetness of his eyes. "I was afraid they'd got you."

"Fall into line."

A legionary in a wolf pelt, the mark of a horn-blower, stumbled up the steps toward us as he blew into his *cornu* with all his might. We cheered, hoping enough soldiers would now be able to find us.

He pitched forward and crashed on top of his instrument. We swore, noticing the three arrows jutting out from his shoulder blades.

At the base of the hill shadowy figures began to form up. They did not rush to join us. The enemy. And They could smell our blood.

Even in the shroud of darkness I could see they outnumbered us three to one. "Jupiter!" I lifted my gladius.

"Optimus," the men answered, half-heartedly.

"Jupiter!" I raised my voice.

"Maximus!" Now they joined me.

"Jupiter!"

"Optimus!"

If this was to be our final stand, we would take the bastards down with us. As I continued the war cry with increasing tempo, I looked for anything we could use to block their path. Large stones, wooden pallets, statues... nothing was in sight but pottery. Hephaestus was the god of the forge, after all.

We would have to meet them. But another thought struck me like an arrow. These vases were filled with offerings: oil, pitch, unwatered wine… all flammable.

"Men, grab those vases! Go on, break formation," I shouted. "You two, grab those torches."

They took off toward the temple entrance, despite their confusion.

The rebels at the foot of the hill began their ascent.

"Light them, light them," I cried and my men began to understand.

Within moments there were little fires burning in pots all around us. The men didn't wait for orders now. They placed the burning pottery on their shoulders and launched them down the path. The vases shattered and flames erupted.

"Put it out, put it out!" voices cried out in Greek.

But the rebels continued to charge.

"More," I shouted as pots flew past me.

A ring of fire was beginning to surround us, and through the flames I could see the rebels hesitate.

Only a few were brave enough to charge through.

"Forward!" The men formed around me as we charged to meet the aggressors.

They were big brutes with bigger spears. If there'd been a wall of them we would've been in trouble with no way to flank them.

One of the spears pierced through the shield of the man to my left, gliding on into his sternum. The legionary screamed. I severed the spear and released my shield to grab the broken end and pull the assailant toward us. Unwilling to loosen his grip, he was swallowed up with flame-glistening swords.

Beyond the flames there was fighting. Rebels were flailing and crying out from puncture wounds as well as the burns.

I spotted the shimmering of a silver eagle lifted high above the tumult.

"Roma victrix!" I bellowed and lifted my gladius. As the

flames slowly burned out we rushed forward and crashed against the retreating rebels. Only a few squeezed out from amongst us and sprinted away in whatever direction they could.

"By the gods I never thought it would be so good to see your ugly mug," centurion Herennius said, his white teeth contrasting with the scarlet blood dripping over his face.

I clapped the back of his neck and kissed his cheek. Men on either side of the two formations broke rank and embraced their companions on the other side.

"Where is Didius? The Insteius twins? Hirtuleius?" I asked and his smile faded.

"Not spotted them yet, legate."

"What of Legate Paullus?" one of the men asked when I failed to do so.

"No word yet."

"Then it's up to us to deal with the rebels," I said.

They looked at me with confusion.

"I believe we've already done that, legate," Herennius said.

I raised my sword and pointed at rebels fleeing in the distance.

"This isn't over yet."

SCROLL XV

WE FOUND them hiding behind street merchant carts, in wagons of hay, or by temple altars praying for deliverance. Thirty or so were rounded up and brought to an open courtyard before the postern gate. We encircled them and kept our swords poised unless any of them attempted a feat of bravery.

Herennius pointed to two and a few legionaries dragged them to us.

One of the captured rebels cried, "Please, I don't know anything. I'm just a pig farmer." A legionary bound his feet.

The fires had been extinguished but the early-morning moon was bright and full enough to illuminate their glistening sweat.

"Pig farmers don't burn down cities," Herennius said.

I turned to the next who seemed totally oblivious to the arrow in his thigh. "What of you? Are you willing to cooperate?"

"A pox on you, Roman dog," he with a snarl, hocking and spitting at my feet.

"What did he say?" Herennius bashed the rebel's nose in with the hilt of his gladius. The rebel fell back unconscious. His friend squirmed when Herennius lifted his sword again.

"Please don't hurt me. Please." Drool dripped from his lips.

"Where are the rest of you? Where did you come from?" I asked.

Herennius lowered the blade instead and placed the tip on the man's throat.

"I don't know where they're all from or what they want... I was ordered!"

I nodded to the centurion and he pushed the blade forward just enough to break the skin.

"We were in Corinth! That's where we gathered. The ruins of Corinth. That's all I know."

"Did he say Corinth?" one of my men asked.

I said, "He did."

"Who ordered the attack?" Herennius asked and I translated. "Who commands you?"

"I don't know," he cried. Herennius lifted his blade and the captive raised his bound hands. "Please have mercy! They called themselves Cerberus. That's all I know! Take me to an altar and I'll swear on the lives of my ancestors." Trembling he turned to his fellow captives, wondering what they'd do when he uttered that name. They were in little position to retaliate even if they desired to do so.

Enunciating carefully as if that would make the man understand Latin, Herennius said, "Do not fear them, rebel. Fear us."

"What is Cerberus? Or who is Cerberus?" I asked.

He shook his head and tears ripped from his eyes. He couldn't lift his voice; so he mouthed again, "I do not know."

"He says he doesn't know who commands him. Isn't that strange? Soldiers who know not who they follow?" I crossed my arms and turned to Herennius.

"I say we crucify them one by one until someone summons up the courage to speak," Herennius said, eyes never leaving the weeping captive.

I knelt beside the captive and waited patiently for his tears to dry. Eventually he met my eye. "What is your name?"

"P.. Par... Parmenion, lord," he said.

"Parmenion. Is that what we should do with you? Should we crucify you until you tell us what we need to know?"

He violently shook his head. "I will tell you everything I know. Everything!"

"Was any member of this Cerberus here tonight?"

He struggled to swallow and again shook his head. "No. I was contacted months ago and was told to remain ready to get back at the Romans. I thought it was like a guild, you see... I didn't know..."

"On with it," I said.

"I think they were going to muster a large army and bring the fight to Rome, but they didn't have time." His breath caught in his lungs.

"Slow your breath and you'll slow the beating of your heart."

"Word spread that the Romans in the city would be fortifying tomorrow. This was our last chance. We marched under a man called Dexipos. He serves Cerberus loyally."

I relayed the message to Herennius.

"Ask him where Dexipos is now," Herennius said, knuckles whitening around the hilt of his sword.

"Beside me, sire," the captive said, his head hanging in shame.

Dexipos was just beginning to stir.

"You two." I pointed at two legionaries behind me. "Take this rebel to the megaron. We shall share words when we're done."

"Done with what, Legate?" one asked, afraid they'd miss something. I didn't reply but stared until they departed, dragging the limp body of Dexipos with them.

"This is your last opportunity to speak, young Parmenion," I said. "Whether you live to see the sun or not depends on the next words out of your mouth. Answer wisely."

"Anything. I beg of you, anything at all!"

I allowed silence to linger for a moment, and when I spoke I articulated myself carefully, "Where is Cerberus?"

He hyperventilated. He shuffled to his back and tried in vain to squirm away but I restrained him easily.

"Wrong answer, Parmenion."

"No! I don't know where they are. They don't tell any of us! They say they'll be revealed at the right time. They're an Archon, a Polemarch, and a—"

"A what?"

"I don't know what the other is! I swear it, on the life of my firstborn, I swear it."

"You said before you did not know Cerberus," I said. "You changed your mind."

"I can't think rightly, sire," he said. "I'm afraid." He looked down at the dark pool of urine puddling up underneath him.

"Apparently Cerberus really has three heads. One is an Archon, another a Polemarch," I said to Herennius.

"What about the third?" he asked.

"No word yet."

"Well, are there any other antiquated defunct positions of Greek authority we should be aware of?" Herennius clenched his teeth.

"That's enough, Parmenion. I thank you." I pushed to my feet.

"What are we going to do with them?" Castor asked. Until then I hadn't realized he stood right behind me.

"I am thinking." I bowed my head and rubbed at my throbbing temples. I considered every possibility imaginable, and I couldn't summon one up that didn't result in their deaths. They killed too many Romans. If I let even a single man go free, I might be tried for treason.

"Legate," Herennius said, noticing my apprehension. "they should be made an example of. We must crucify them along the road to Athens. A testament against all who defy Rome." Herennius placed a hand on my shoulder. "I don't relish the work anymore than you do, but it's necessary."

"We cannot kill them. They are unarmed," Castor told Herennius.

"They were armed. That's what matters," the centurion said. "Boy, I like you. I do. But you do not belong in this conversation."

"Silence." I took a few paces away and felt the wind in my hair, my cloak flapping at my back. I could wait for Legate Paullus. Perhaps he was still among the survivors somewhere in the city. I knew for certain Paullus would order their crucifixions. A shred of naivety struck me, and I considered leaving them all here while I consulted Apollonius.

He wouldn't have offered a direct answer, of course. Instead he would provide me with a story or an anecdote on the nature of forgiveness and redemption.

I could always wait for Didius. No... it could be days before his return and there wasn't a brig large enough to contain these rebels in all of Attika. No, I had to be decisive. I had to convince the men I knew what I was doing. "Every captive is of fighting age," I said, the wind carrying my voice across the courtyard. "They understood what they were doing when they marched into Athens with torches and swords. They lifted their hand against not just this legion but all of Rome."

Some of the men lifted their swords and roared their approval, blood lust in the eyes of some, and the tears of mourning in others.

"These men butchered our brothers. The loss of life is still being calculated. And they threatened their own kinsmen—the Greek people under our protection." My voice was shaky like a reed in this wind, but I hoped no one was close enough to hear it. I clasped my hands behind my back so no one could see them shaking. "Their lives are forfeit."

I heard Castor gasp behind me and my heart sank.

"They must be put to death by the sword," I said. Some of the captives began crying. "But we've received the information we seek. We shall give them clean deaths, more than what they have given many of our brothers. Their bodies will be put on display for other renegades to witness. After a fortnight their families can collect their bodies and dispose of them as they see fit. Except for Parmenion. I have other plans for him."

No one cheered now. Too lenient for some, and too bloody for others. In that moment I did not envy Didius' position. I didn't want to be a general. I hoped I never had to make this decision again. I raised my fist and dropped it. The circle of legionaries enclosed around the captives as swords sang from their scabbards.

Every impulse within told me to turn around. I gave the command; I didn't have to take part in its execution. I could walk away, divert my gaze even. But many of these young men had never tasted battle before this night, and I couldn't ask them to spill blood I wasn't willing to spill.

I brandished my gladius and stepped forward with the rest of the men.

"On your knees or standing?" I asked the first man I came to as the screams of resisters rose all around us.

"I'll die standing, Roman," he said, struggling to his feet.

I placed my sword above his navel and he met my eyes with neither hatred or fear. I rammed it through the soft flesh of his belly as he collapsed into my arms and embraced me. His lifeblood spilled from his lips onto my shoulder when I wedged the blade deeper, slicing through sinew and organ to the bones of his back.

The words of my wife rang in my ears as loud and clear as if she were standing beside me: *"Do nothing you'll have to carry back with you. Go and serve and then come back to me safely, the man you are now. Because I love the man you are right now."*

I cast the words from my mind, but they continued to echo as I laid the dying man down and moved on to the next.

SCROLL XVI

WE GATHERED outside the gates decorating the road with the bodies of the dead when we heard the stamp of soldiers approaching. As if we didn't believe the gods could be so cruel, no one formed up or grabbed their shields. We turned toward the noise and waited for the soldiers to appear.

Lucius was at the front, a few hundred scraggly legionaries trailing him.

"I see you fared as well as we did." Lucius craned his head to view all of the pikes and the fallen strewn upon them.

"Brother, I feared I lost you." I set down my helmet and rushed to him. I wrapped my arms around him in an embrace, careful not to stain his cloak with the blood of my hands. Rather than avoiding the same, Lucius grabbed my neck with dripping palms and kissed me on either cheek.

"The gods favor us today!" Lucius roared and the men behind him cheered. Most of the legionaries behind me did not, but then again they were occupied with distasteful work.

"Where did you go?" I said. "We searched the city for survivors and found none."

Spurius jumped between us and clapped me on the back.

"Lucius rallied us near the north-eastern gate," he said. "We held off an attack and followed the invaders toward Marathon."

"Spurius, thank the gods." I kissed his cheek.

"Oh don't worry, Aulus is fine too," the other Insteius twin said, shuffling his way between us. He wore a smile, but none of the usual humor lay behind it. His skin was drained of all color like the corpses behind me. Beads of sweat dripped from his brow despite the morning chill.

"I was praying for both of you, you bastard," I said.

Herennius wiped his bloody hands on an even bloodier rag and joined us. "What became of the rebels you followed?"

"Those we didn't defeat in battle took their own lives," Spurius said. "Is that the same fate these received?" He pointed to the limp bodies.

"Some of them," I said. "The rest we had to execute."

"Grisly business," Lucius said. "That's certain. But it had to be done." Lucius placed a hand on my shoulder.

Silence flooded over us while we watched the legionaries struggle to hoist the limp corpses onto the spears.

Aulus doubled over, placed his hands on his knees, and wretched.

"The next time we're to be attacked in the night," he said, "remind me not to drink dark wine prior." Something in his eyes told me it wasn't the drink that ailed him.

I caught Lucius staring past me, so I followed his gaze toward the gate. There my shield bearer sat, his legs tucked to his chest and his head buried in his arms.

"Isn't that your man, Quintus?" Lucius asked. "Was he injured?"

"In a manner of speaking." I turned to the rest of the men. "Keep moving, ladies. Next we must construct a proper fort, then we can get grub in our bellies and wine in our hands."

This did little to motivate them, but I hadn't expected it to.

"Allow us to help," Spurius said, grim but resolute.

Lucius gestured for his men to follow. Aulus stood back still trying to catch his breath. I didn't ask him to join. If I didn't feel it was necessary, I wouldn't have joined either.

The sun was rust colored and creeping to the horizon by the time we finished setting up camp. They hadn't used their entrenching tools since we arrived, and it showed. Construction took hours. At first it looked like the Cimbri camp—out of line and disorderly. To the dismay of our weary soldiers, we had to deconstruct a time or two and begin again. But if there was ever a time when discipline mattered, it was now, a lesson Gaius Marius taught me well.

Lucius and I oversaw the construction of the most pitiful praetorium a Roman camp had ever seen. It would be Didius' headquarters upon his arrival, and he would no doubt be displeased with its austere and basic design, free of all the trappings generally associated with a man of his rank and authority. But we decided something was better than nothing.

As the camp layout finally passed our quality inspection, the men were allowed to downgrade their gear and break bread. Most of them were too tired to be bothered with eating, instead crawling into their tents and greeting the coming night with blaring snores.

Those who did attempt to eat huddled around their tent campfires and yelled instructions at one another, all forgetting the basics of legionary cooking while being pampered in Greek quarters.

But of us officers, rest would come later. We had more work to do. I ordered a meeting in the praetorium so that we might discuss strategy for the next few days. Didius' trek was to Phokis, and he was unlikely to return for a few days. He was likely still enjoying his quiet time in the green hills of Mount

Parnassus' eastern slopes, knowing nothing about the attack. It would be another day at the earliest before our envoys would reach him, even with the fastest horses in the legion assigned to them.

"What are your orders then, general?" Aulus asked me, no longer green in the face.

"Hush, man. Didius overhears that and I'll be hanging from a pike with the rebels." I chuckled but meant it.

Lucius asked, "What's the report on the scouts?"

Spurius said, "Four *contubernia* have been sent out in each cardinal direction. They've been given landmarks to designate their sectors of watch." He was beginning to look every part the officer and talked like it too.

"And our messengers?" Lucius asked.

"Two have been sent to Epirus," I said. "Didius should receive word soon."

Lucius nodded. "I guess that's all we can do for now. Except wait."

"I'm not sure waiting is the best idea," Spurius said, growing into his position of authority. Lucius cocked an eyebrow but also smirked with pride.

"What would you suggest?" Lucius asked, but Spurius looked to me, assuming I felt the same.

"The surviving rebels... we need to question them further. We need to know everything," I said. "We'll need hot irons and whips. They'll need to be tortured." I looked over my shoulder to ensure Castor hadn't joined us as he usually did. Fortunately this time he hadn't.

"I suppose you're right." Lucius exhaled.

I pointed to the two guards at the entrance of the tent. "You two. Go and retrieve a few rebels. Bring them shackled."

"How many do we have?" Aulus asked. The lump in his throat bob up and down as he struggled to swallow.

"Only a few. A man called Parmenion who is inclined to

speak with us, and a few of the treacherous gate guards were captured as well," I said.

"And I suppose you mean to torture them right here?" Aulus asked, trying to smile as he often did, but for once it was not infectious. "Seems beneath a man of your stature."

"I'll give them a chance to talk first," I said. "We'll treat them like civilized free men until we have no other choice. Then they'll suffer whatever is necessary to get them to talk. This has happened because our enemies perceive Rome as fat, lazy, and weak. We must quash the notion immediately." No one objected.

The two guards entered the praetorium and tossed two rebels to the ground between us.

I pointed to a single wooden post holding up the center of the tent. "Chain them."

Parmenion looked up at me as if I were Hades himself.

The guards hoisted the rebels' shackled wrists and chained them on either side of the post.

"I'm sorry you've decided to waste your freedom," I said. "In another life we might have protected you from threats abroad. We might have celebrated festivals with you and drunk wine together." I crouched and looked into the eyes of the captured gate guard.

Parmenion needed no further intimidation, though I doubted he knew much else.

"This is the path you have chosen," I said. "Now the path will lead to its inevitable conclusion. The Fates have prepared two threads for you. Either you die, or you cooperate. And the choice is yours."

The gate guard met my eye and swallowed. He was afraid. I could see that by his rapid blinking. But he was also brave.

"What is your name?" I asked.

He bowed his head. "Craterous."

"How long have you served as gate guard to this city?" Lucius asked behind me.

"Four years." I could hear his breath, controlled and

deliberate.

"And how long have you been cooperating with Cerberus?" Lucius asked. "How long have you conspired to betray your people?"

I turned to him and shook my head as softly as I could. He exhaled and stepped back.

"Not long. Not but a few months, perhaps."

"And will you tell us all you know, Craterous?" I asked, still measuring him up.

He hung his head. "I'm afraid to do that, sir."

"You should be afraid of us, Craterous. You are in shackles before me," I said. "Your life is forfeit with the flick of my wrist. But if you tell us all you know, I'll guarantee your life."

Parmenion shouted from the other side of the column. "I'll tell you everything!"

I lifted a hand and Spurius silenced him.

"I'm not afraid for myself, lord," Craterous said, "but my family."

"You're afraid for your family?"

"Yes, sire."

I stretched out my arm and the legionary tossed me the shackle key. I held it before Craterous, close enough to smell the iron.

"If you tell me everything you know, I will free you and I will guarantee the safety of your family."

His eyes stared through me as he weighed out his options. What was to second guess? How could they have so much power over this man that he fears them more than someone with a knife at his throat?

"What do you wish to know, sir?" he said. Tears welled in his eyes, probably wondering if he'd just damned his loved ones.

"Tell me the story. From the beginning. How did you come to work with these rebels they call Cerberus?" I said.

He tried to speak but struggled, smacking his lips together a few times and trying to moisten them.

"Bring him some wine."

"Can I have some as well, please?" Parmenion asked.

"Thank you." Craterous rested his head back against the column after a few gulps.

"Please continue." I snapped my fingers, and a chair was brought to me. I sat before him and listened intently.

"Messengers came to me. Said they'd been watching me. Said I was a faithful son of Greece." He paused but I waited in the silence for him to continue. "And they said all true sons of Greece were rising up against our oppressors. They said the Republic was decaying. Corrupted, bloated, and gorging on itself. Now was the time to rise up and fight. The envoy said there were tribes and kings from every corner of the earth who vowed by sacred oath to destroy Rome."

I didn't try to process it all now. I turned and nodded toward parchment for someone to take notes. "Go on,"

"At first I told them to go bugger their mothers. They smiled in reply. Then… then…" Tears streamed down his ashen cheeks. "They began to name each of my children. They knew my house was in the ceramic district, and that my bedroom window faced south. They knew where my wife bought our grain. They didn't need to say anything else…"

I considered what to say next, so I gave him a moment to collect himself.

"I knew if I didn't help them they would butcher my family… they would end my line," he said. His tears began afresh and this time his lips quivered and his voice cracked. "My boy is only four months of this life, sire."

"So… to save your family you would sacrifice every family in Athens?" Lucius said, and I knew him well enough to notice the rage behind his stoic face.

Craterous hung his head in shame. He knew he'd done wrong.

"Thank you, Craterous. I have a family as well. I can imagine nothing I wouldn't do to protect them."

"He's a coward, Quintus," Herennius said. "His words mean nothing."

I cleared my throat. "So to protect your family you offered to open the gates?"

He nodded. "Aye. They said I'd be called upon whenever the time was right. They said there'd be a few days' notice to get my family out of the city. But they came suddenly and said the time-line has changed. I was instructed to mark my door with black paint and they'd be spared."

"And were they?" I asked.

He gulped. "I don't know, lord."

"What else did they tell you?" Spurius asked. "What else were you promised? Are there more impending attacks?"

"I believe this was the first of many. I was an outsider to them and entrusted with no more information than that. But their goal is to push Rome out of Greece, and to ultimate to topple the grand city itself."

"I can't listen to this much longer," Herennius said.

"Is there anything else you can tell us, Craterous?" I asked.

He shook his head. "Sadly I'm of no more use to you." He breathed a bit easier despite the shackles still round his wrists.

"I say we torture him to find out what he's not inclined to share," Lucius said.

"We promised him life, dear tribune," Aulus said as if he didn't care.

I could feel Lucius glaring at my back. "Yes. We promised him life. But the Legate said nothing about torture."

"Back in Rome a confession isn't considered legal unless torture is involved," Herennius added.

Craterous said nothing, resigned to fate.

Light burst into the tent as the flaps opened. An injured man entered, and for a moment I didn't recognize him.

"Oh, don't all of you salute me at once." If not for the fury in his eyes and the bulging veins of his throat I might not have recognized my commander.

We all stood and saluted, wide-eyed and stunned silent.

A scarlet cloth was wrapped around his biceps and dried blood stained his face. He unbuckled his helmet and ripped off his cloak. He looked every part the rank-and-file soldier, save the patrician gait natural to him. He paced to a bowl of water in the back of the room and splashed it on his face. "Who are these?" He pointed to the captives and dried his face.

I said, "Rebels. We were attacked in the—"

"Yes, yes, I know all about it."

Spurius said, "Sir, how are you—"

"Attacked on the road," the commander said. "I knew immediately when I saw those bastards running down the mountain that the city had been attacked."

"How many?" Lucius asked.

"Enough. Half my guard killed instantly… I barely made it out with my life."

"What of Phaidra?" I stiffened.

"Dead," he replied without pause. My jaw dropped. "She practically threw herself at them. Perhaps she believed they'd take her to Timoxenos. Perhaps she missed a man's touch. Either way they set upon her with sword and club instantly. Her screams didn't last long."

Herennius asked, "Are you injured badly?"

Didius looked down and analyzed the cloth concealing his wound. "I'll live," he said before turning to me, his eyes cold as ice. "Unfortunately for you."

I didn't take his meaning, but he approached Craterous too quick for me to consider it. He pulled a dagger from its sheath on his calf.

"We've promised him life for cooperation, Proconsul," I said.

He lunged at me so quickly I feared for a moment I was his intended victim. "And who gave you the right to make decisions of life and death? Who gave you the right to spare traitors?"

Everyone looked away. I stared ahead. Satisfied with my silence he turned again to Craterous and jammed the dagger between his ribs. He buried his forehead in Craterous' and gritted his teeth. "There will be no burial for you, traitor." Didius spit. "No coins for Cheron. You'll walk in darkness for all eternity with no one to mourn your name."

Parmenion wept on the other side of the post.

Didius pulled out his dagger and Craterous slumped to the side. Fresh blood dotted the commander's freshly cleaned face. He pointed to Parmenion. "What of this one? Have you promised him life?" Didius asked me.

"Not yet," I said.

He stepped forward and placed the dagger against Parmenion's throat. But then stood. "No. Come, Legate. You will carry out his sentence of death." He extended the dagger.

"Sir," I said, "if you might just explain your hostility toward me—"

"Do it!"

I took the dagger and knelt before Parmenion. I placed the blade against his throat, as he wept and squirmed. Barely audible he moaned for his mother.

"Go ahead, Legate," Didius said over me. "Prove your loyalty to Rome."

I pressed the blade further against his skin, but then jumped to my feet.

"If this is some sort of test, Proconsul, I'll not play along," I said. "To do so would be to suggest that I'm not above suspicion. My loyalty to Rome has never been questioned, and I'm uncertain why it is so now."

He shrugged and ripped the dagger from my hand. In the same motion he sliced through Parmenion's throat, silencing his cries. He dried the blade on his stained cape, the praetorium silent save the blood dripping from the captive's throat.

"Clean this up. I'll not have corpses in my praetorium." Didius grabbed someone else's cup of wine and drained it. "Do not plan on getting sleep tonight, men. We'll plan throughout the night, and tomorrow we go to war."

SCROLL XVII

We had a few hours to ourselves while Didius bathed and tended to his wounds. Herennius found me sitting with the horses outside the Veterenarium and brought me some porridge.

I took a few bites and enjoyed the warmth, but otherwise had no appetite.

"Perhaps we should share a cup of wine before the officer's meeting?" he said.

I considered it but shook my head. "I'll need to think clearly. Didius seems to hold me accountable for everything that's happened," I said. "I've searched the corners of my mind for a reason why and have come up empty."

He knew it was true, so he didn't reply. He'd seen the outburst. Everyone had.

Herennius inhaled deeply and released it as a sigh. "The Proconsul believes the gods have cursed him … and they say, 'whom the gods destroy, they first make mad.'" He didn't offer to elaborate, and I didn't ask. "I'm going to ensure everyone knows how bravely you rallied a defense," he said, patting my arm. "I vow it."

"I'd rather everyone forget I was there at all. I've tired of achieving glory; it's meaningless to me now. They called me

'Hero of the North', and what has it got me but trouble?" I realized I was sulking and being difficult. Herennius wasn't responsible for the attack or Didius' anger. I exhaled and clapped him on the back.

"If you've grown bored of glory, I fear you'll be disappointed. Something tells me you'll achieve much more."

"What does that mean?" I asked.

"Come now, I can see the officer's rallying. We should arrive early to avoid provoking the gorgon's wrath." He stood and offered me a hand.

We found Didius' headquarters to be well-lit with fresh torches, and some of his affectations were now stationed throughout. A table was placed in the center with a wine-stained map of Greece and Macedonia atop it.

The Proconsul was different from the bewildered, blood-soaked man who killed the two prisoners just hours before. In his officer's regalia and gold-lined black cuirass, he was also free of other men's blood and his own wounds were stitched tight.

"Legate Sertorius, a word," he said, and walked to the back of the tent. All eyes fell to me as I lowered my head and took a deep breath.

I passed Lucius and the twins as if I were heading to the Tarpeian Rock for execution, eyes forward and resigned to my fate.

He snatched an amphora from a servant's hand and poured two cups of wine himself. "Will you drink with me?"

"Ah, no, sir. That's quite all right. When I drink wine this late—"

"I insist." He held out the cup until I accepted it. He lifted his own and clanked it against mine when I did the same. "To survival."

"To survival," I repeated less enthusiastically.

He analyzed me for a moment, leaving me wondering what plans he had in store for me. Instead he placed a hand on my shoulder and said. "I would like to retract my words to you this evening. You bore the brunt of aggression that was not your own." He cleared his throat and tightened his grip. "It takes a lot for a man of my stature to apologize. I insist that you accept."

"I do accept, Proconsul," I said, "though I don't understand."

He tapped my cup of wine to ensure I was drinking at an equal rate.

"It all seemed to work out a bit too well for you."

"I don't take your meaning, sir," I said, my stomach churning.

"I'd barely made it back to Attika before I heard about Sertorius' glorious defense. You'd have thought Quintus Sertorius was general of the whole legion by the rumors spread," he said, swirling his wine. "Then there was the death of a man you obviously detested—and admittedly I did too—leaving you the unquestioned second-in-command of the legion."

"Wait? Who? Paullus?"

"Dead. Confirmed. Found him burnt to a crisp, still nestled in his bed if I understand correctly," he said with a chuckle and a shrug.

"I didn't know…" I imagined what those final moments must have felt like.

"Well, now that you do, you can understand my suspicions. I was the only man in your way to ultimate power here in Greece, and I nearly died on the road." His eyes turned menacing for a moment. "And I thought, 'how smart this Sertorius is.' He pushed for the war and somehow ensured there was a dagger at the throat of any man who threatens his ascension to power. You were a few inches away from being the most powerful man in Greece." He lifted his arm and measured the distance between the wound and his heart.

The tent was silent behind me. I could say nothing and maintained his gaze.

Then he smiled and pat my face. "But I was hazy from the blood loss and hard riding. I wasn't thinking clearly." He wrapped his arm around me and turned to the room. "Quintus

Sertorius is a faithful son of the Republic and I'll kill any man who denies it."

His sudden amicability was somehow as concerning as his rage.

"So," Didius said, "as our first order of business tonight, I'd like to announce that the entire fourth legion has voted unanimously to give you the Grass Crown for saving your legion." He clapped and everyone else joined him.

My mouth hung open like a trout as Herennius and the twins came to embrace me. Lucius stood behind and clapped half-heartedly.

"This is the highest honor bestowed on a Roman officer. Congratulations, boy," Didius said.

"I... do not know what to say, Proconsul. I do not believe I deserve this. I'm not certain I can accept." I stole a glance at Lucius and I could see the disappointment in his eyes.

"It's not yours to accept or deny," Didius said. "The men have chosen for you."

"But there were others who acted with bravery to the salvation of their men," I said. "Tribune Lucius Hirtuleius led a contingent on a counter-offensive, tracking down several of the retreating rebels."

"And yet it is your name on the lips of every legionnaire." He clapped again, and more forcefully now.

A few soldiers rushed in behind me and knelt with bowed heads, extending a crown of grass, wheat, and fading flowers. Didius waited until I placed it on my head.

I desired to sulk into the shadows if the praetorium torchlight allowed for any.

"Now, let's settle in and discuss our stratagem." Didius rubbed his hands together and approached the map. "What intelligence have we collected from the captives?"

I wanted to mention we could have achieved far more if he hadn't slaughtered them too quickly. But I did not. "Cerberus is led by three men. One is an archon, another is a polemarch. We are uncertain about the other."

"Forgive me," Didius addressed the room. "My history is a little hazy. I was under the impression these positions were retired when we squashed the last revolution in Greece?"

"That is true," Spurius said. "These men must be claiming their ancient positions of authority to give themselves some form of weight or legitimacy."

Didius nodded, satisfied with the answer. "I would do the same were I them. What else?"

"These attackers rallied in the ruins of Corinth. Perhaps this site was of geographical necessity, or to avoid the prying eyes of citizens," I said. "It's also possible this was a symbolic location, to remind the men of Rome's destruction of Corinth in the past."

He smiled. "I'd like to remind them of this as well. Perhaps they would mind their place if their memories were sharper. What else?" We looked from man to man, there wasn't a lot else we could offer.

Lucius cleared his throat. "Proconsul, some of the men we hunted down and killed wore bronze armor. They say… they say that the best bronze armor comes from Argos. So… perhaps they were from Argos. Or knew someone from there." He swallowed and awaited Didius' response.

The Proconsul looked around the room, gauging our response to this, but ultimately ignored him.

"So, if no one has anything else to share, I will now report what intelligence I've managed to gather," he said. "The torture detachment with the sixteenth legion was successful in squeezing out some information from a few rebels before they were drained of their lifeblood."

He picked up two terracotta figures in the form of soldiers. We moved closer to see the demonstration.

"The rebels indicate that one of the leaders operates in Laconia, perhaps from Sparta. The other from Attika, probably here in Athens. Just as your source reports, Legate Sertorius, the third is an enigma." He placed one figurine over Sparta in the south; the other on Athens in the east.

"What is required of us, Proconsul?" Lucius asked, stepping forward.

"The first thing we need to do," he reached for his wine and took a long pull, "is figure out which god has cursed us." When no one replied, he continued, "The gods hate cowards, yes? And these rebels are irrefutably cowards. Yet they were able to breach our walls and slaughter not only our men but also the people we're entrusted to protect. The gods must be offended."

"I thought you didn't believe in the gods, Proconsul?" I said without thinking.

He inhaled deeply and cracked his knuckles and neck. "I said they have not thus far intervened against me. Now they have. They stole my son from me, if you'll recall. Then they threaten to take away my legion. If it wasn't for your glorious defense they might have." I said nothing in reply, so he continued. "To determine the will of the gods, there is only one place we can go. The Oracle of Delphi."

Everyone nodded.

I said, "The fourth legion has several priests, whom we could—"

"No." Didius lifted his hand. "I want you to go." He pointed at me.

"Me, sir?" I asked. Despite my desire to retrieve Apollonius' niece, abandoning my legion for a trek through hostile territory didn't appeal to me.

"That's right. The legion's most pious and respected man," Didius said with another sip.

"Couldn't the priests—"

"The gods detest priests. Most of the time at least. How many priests have been immortalized as heroes of the gods? None that I can recall. The gods love men of action. Jason, Achilles, Ajax… Sertorius." He gestured to me.

"I'll go if you order it, Proconsul." I hung my head, but I could feel Lucius' eyes piercing through me.

"Of course, you will. Otherwise, I'll strip you of rank and have you crucified," he said quickly and continued as if he hadn't. "We'll need to split the forces. Athens must remain our priority, especially in its weakened state. But if it's true that the enemy operates in Laconia we cannot allow them to expand unmitigated."

"I'd like to volunteer to lead the Sixteenth to Laconia." Lucius squared up with Didius.

I watched to see if he'd look in my direction but he did not.

"Is that right?" Didius asked, considering it. "Well, as *tribune laticlavius* you are the most senior officer of the sixteenth now that Paullus is dead. Very well. The fourth will remain in Attika and the Sixteenth will go south."

"Thank you, sir. I will serve honorably." Lucius banged his fist against his breastplate.

I lost interest in the rest of the discussion. I couldn't wrap my head around why Lucius would leave my side willingly. And that damned crown was beginning to itch me awfully.

Something Didius said later regained my attention. "These attackers appear to be little more than poor farmers, merchants, and sheepherders who were indebted to this cult in some way. But from what the torture detachment managed to learn, they seem to have a real army."

"Where would they hide such an army? We have eyes all over Greece," Spurius asked.

Aulus nodded beside him but otherwise seemed absent.

"That is a good question, tribune. I feel certain they've trained up men and leant them out to the Hellenist neighbors in the east. Their men have probably been serving as mercenaries for the Seleucids, the Ptolemies… they'll come home battle-hardened and well-equipped if that's the case."

We all contemplated in silence what it might be like to go up against a true phalanx wall like our ancestors had when conquering Greece. There was glory to be earned, and I could tell by their eyes that some found this intriguing. Aulus, I believe, shared my sentiment: dread.

"Proconsul, I have a request… if I may?" Lucius said.

Didius shrugged. "Go on then."

"The sixteenth lost a lot of good men. I need officers to accompany me. I'd like to borrow these two men from the fourth to serve alongside me." He held his arm out to the Insteius twins.

Again Didius clasped his hands behind his back and shrugged, then looked to me with a smirk. "They're your officers, legate. Do you acquiesce?"

I struggled to swallow and locked eyes with Lucius. I found no emotion there, none of the familiarity I'd known since I was a boy. My voice weak, I said, "If it will help the good Tribune, certainly."

"No more laxity and half-measures," Didius said. "We'll rest tonight and then tomorrow we go to war. Tribune Hirtuleius, you'll leave at first light."

"Excellent, sir."

We were dismissed and Lucius immediately made for the exit. I hurried behind him and grabbed his wrist.

"What are you doing? We've always served best at one another's side…"

His eyes locked onto my crown and he smiled sadly. He shook his head. "You know, you've always been blessed, Sertorius. When we were children the girls favored you. Our tutors applauded you. You understood things I couldn't. You held sway over people with your charm and the power of your words—"

"Lucius, what does this—"

He held up a hand. "And I've watched you over the years. At times you've doubted that the gods even exist. Other times you've ignored them as if they didn't. You've mocked me for making proper sacrifices."

"I spoke in jest, friend. Where is this coming from?" I pleaded.

He frowned. "That's not the point and you know it. I've spent my entire life doing everything right. Following the instruction of my forebears, of our gods, of our trainers and officers," he said. "I make the proper sacrifices and yet it's you the gods love. I share the same scars as you and yet the men cry your name. You are truly blessed, Sertorius."

"I've not asked for any of this."

"I know." He scratched at his forehead and exhaled. "I know. And that almost makes it worse." He rubbed at the back of his neck, then met my gaze. "There is no sunlight for the rest of us beneath your shadow." He patted my shoulder and turned to leave.

I found no proper words. I didn't know if I was ashamed, angry, disheartened, or all of them. I remained in place as I watched him depart, knowing it might be awhile before we saw each other again. I walked back to my tent and sat down on a log outside it. The sun was beginning to creep up beneath the mountain fog, a pale blue glow in the sky.

It had been over two days since I'd last slept, since I'd last had a meal, since I'd last thought of my family. I hadn't even been able to check on Apollonius or Kirrha.

I was too hungry to eat and too exhausted to sleep. It was remarkable how much two days could change. Everything else in the world had faded, its existence in question. I was already back on the battlefield, and again the only real thing was war.

SCROLL XVIII

I KEPT myself busy after the battle. I staged the corpses, built the fortifications, held meetings—enough distance to distract me from the reality of what had happened. With no other objectives to steal my attention: I quickly remembered how wretched a city can appear after it is sieged.

Apollonius, Niarchos, and I walked through the streets together, looking for ways we could help the citizens.

Carts were stationed at random intervals, and they were already overflowing with the bodies and body parts of the fallen. Trampled babies lifeless and stiff like terracotta dolls lay just out of the reach of their mother's cold arms. Livestock carcasses littered the streets, most of them nothing more than a wisp of fur and guts, unrecognizable.

Always a stark reminder, this made me hate war and all the destruction it brought. But it also reminded me why we fought. To avoid tragedies such as this.

We continued rebuilding for a few weeks until Didius tired of my presence and determined it was time I made my pilgrimage to Delphi.

The one reprieve to this was the thought of reuniting Apollonius with his niece, Anaiah. I thought he'd be thrilled at the prospect of making the journey and returning with his only remaining family. Again I misjudged my old friend.

"There's no sense in abandoning one child who needs me to search for another I'm unlikely to ever find," he said, gesturing to Kirrha.

Since the moment I'd met Apollonius, he'd thought of little else than rescuing Anaiah. I dwelled constantly on his reasoning and found no satisfying conclusion. I didn't try to convince him. Instead, I asked for a physical description and how I might recognize her. He reluctantly described her golden hair, dark complexion, and brown eyes.

"Is there anything I might say to her that'd convince her you're with me?" I said before my departure.

He considered it thoughtfully. "Tell her she's the moon and the stars, my light in the darkness." He looked away to avoid tears. Then I left.

A carriage was prepared for me outside the gates. When I arrived, friendly old Kallias was seated there on it.

"Good day, young Roman. I hope you don't mind some company," he said as I crawled up.

"Not at all, though I'll need to write a letter or two as we travel," I said, kissing his cheek. "I've found so little time to write to my wife."

"You'll learn this when you're my age, my boy. The gentle lull of a carriage puts any old man to sleep."

When our bags were secured in the back, the legionary whipped the two horses to a trot and we set off.

The priest said little but smiled and nodded to all passing travelers and admired the trees and flowers of the field.

I broke the silence. "So why have you decided to make the trek to Delphi?"

"It's been many years since I've made the journey, and I've longed for it deeply. Before the Pythia I am no longer a priest but just a man, reverently beseeching the gods. It is a humbling experience, one that connects us with all those that came before and all that come afterwards."

I nodded and wondered if I'd feel the same. I'd consulted very few prophetesses before and hadn't ever enjoyed the experience as much as one might expect. "Do you mind if I ask another question?"

He turned to me and smiled. "Anything, my child."

"Did Didius ask you to come to keep an eye on me?" I watched for a flicker of the eyes or twitch of the lips—anything that might give the truth away.

Instead, he nodded and placed a hand on my knee. "Your Proconsul is a very broken man, even if he doesn't look it."

I assumed that was my confirmation.

"He certainly doesn't look it."

"I've felt his heart breaking every night since news of his son's death arrived. He's afraid of everything… grasping and desperate to hold onto what he has left."

"I can understand this," I said. "Although I beg the gods for an explanation as to why he doubts me."

"There is no explanation, my child. When the fortifications of your life seem to collapse, there's no one above suspicion," Kallias said. "The gods will speak cool and balm through the heat of his pain in time, and he will greet you with the same trust and admiration I know he truly feels for you."

"I hope you're right."

He smiled, his faded eyes scanning over the careworn features of my face in a way that calmed me.

"For what it's worth, I am not here to spy on you. I've accompanied you for the pleasant conversation and to see a beautiful city I've not seen in a very long time."

"Thank you, Kallias."

He returned his gaze to the lush greenery on the side of the road, and I pulled out parchment and a stylus.

I was about to begin my letter when I exhaled. "Since you are perhaps the wisest man I know, I have a question of the heart for you."

"Those I can answer."

"I'm afraid I've lost my friend Lucius."

"That doesn't sound like a question."

"He's angry with me... he says he has no opportunity while 'in my shadow.' Whatever that means." I picked at the leather threads of my *balteus*. "I've never once stolen an opportunity from him."

"Have you ever stepped aside to deliberately offer him one?" he asked. "Sometimes that's necessary for others to shine in whatever capacity they're able."

I exhaled and shook my head. "I don't mind discovering when I'm wrong," I said. "but I truly detest when someone else does it for me." We laughed. "I'm afraid it's too late though. Lucius is moving south and may not be back for some time."

He patted my knee. "You can be reunited upon his return. Perhaps he'll have his own glory then."

The faint smile on my face disappeared as I looked at him. "That's if we both make it out of this alive."

He didn't reply. Kallias had a lifetime of experience and wisdom concerning matters of the heart, but no experience at all with matters of war.

"I have another question, if you don't mind."

"Of course."

"I have a dear friend who's lost someone he loves. To slavery, not death. She is said to be in Delphi. I invited him along to find her, to restore her to his arms... and yet he refuses to come. There is no hope in his eyes when I speak of her. And yet I know his love overflows. How can this be?"

He nodded, knowing already his response. "No, Sertorius. It's not that he hopes too little, but that he hopes too much. The hearth of his heart is kept burning by this hope. Once it's extinguished, he's afraid his life force will fade with it. And he might be right." He stopped and looked to the horizon.

I knew he wasn't finished so I only nodded.

"Since the moment his loved one disappeared, he's likely known how impossible it would be to retrieve her. Even with the opportunity to reunite, pursuing such an end and returning empty-handed would drain his hope of all substance. In this moment, he is praying with the entire essence of his being that you return with his girl. But if you do not, at least he will have one farther step he can take to restore her."

I sighed. "It seems cowardly to me."

"Nay." He shook his head. "To hope against all reason and wisdom is the very heart of bravery."

At length I nodded. "I guess it's up to me to find her then."

He smiled and patted my knee again. "It's up to us. I will help you. There is nothing that does an old man more good than to witness the love of those who will live on after him."

I thought of ways I might thank him but found nothing sufficient. Before long he dozed off as he anticipated, his head slumped over on my shoulder.

I grinned and moved as carefully as I could to begin my letter.

Dear Arrea,

Not a day has passed that I haven't cried out in longing for your touch. The nightmares I've grown accustomed to have given way to visions of your face, as even the horrors of my past cannot overcome the power of my love for you.

The soldier's life is often one without comfort or reprieve. I can think of only this one: love. With it there is warmth. With it the suns shines through whatever darkness besets my path. You can feel it too, if you try. It resonates from within and manifests itself in the deepest, truest part of us. Even from so far apart, you keep my fire burning.

· · ·

I looked over my shoulder to ensure Kallias wasn't overlooking. He was fast asleep. I smiled. It wouldn't do my reputation as a warrior any good for word of my sappy poetry to get out.

With love time slows to a halt. The hour keeper holds no weight. The time and distance between us means nothing when our love burns so strong. The tragedy outside our door is still present, but one can no longer hear the tumult of it. It can wait.

I paused and sighed. I needed to tell her of the attack on Athens before she heard the newsreaders crying it in the streets, although I doubted my letter could make it in time. I also didn't want to worry her though—a fine line soldiers have walked since the beginning of time.

There was a small rebellion here in Greece. A few miscreants with clubs and torches, nothing we couldn't handle. Don't let the newsreaders concern you. I thought of our family and nothing else as we rallied a resistance. We quashed it easily and are stamping out any remaining insurrection as we speak. I hope and long to be home soon, and I believe with swift action we can achieve that.

I felt the guilt of dishonesty in that moment, but I ignored it and continued.

Hello, Gavius. And hello, mother. I miss both of you dearly. Mother, please dote on Sura as much as possible. Although a simple mare she has the heart of a human, and I have spoiled her with affection since the moment I purchased her in Gaul. If you can spare them, give her peaches when you're able. This will quickly endear you to her, and you'll soon be her best companion—at least until my return!

Gavius, I am thrilled to hear how you've grown. You have no idea the immense pride a father feels to know his son has become a man, even in his absence. More than this even, my heart is gladdened by the kind of man you've become. Good, noble, and honest. Your grandfather rejoices with the gods when he hears your prayers. When the timing is right, perhaps I will invite you here. I've no doubt you could impress the entire legion with your prowess and strength. I'm afraid they would strip me of rank and give it to you! My hope is that there will be no need to bring you to this foreign place, though, as I'd like to return to our home and our horses before my hair fades any further.

All of you, take heart and know that the gods guide my sword as they guide my hand as I write this letter. Their protection watches over me as they answer your prayers, as I hope they comfort you as they answer mine.

I will return to you soon. And when I do, it will feel as if no time has passed at all. Then I'll make up to you for all we've missed during my time away.

Gods protect and guide you until the moment of our reunion,

Quintus Sertorius, Legatus Legio IV

I rolled up the parchment and delicately returned it to my satchel. I sat back and listened closely to the gentle clop of the horse hooves on the paved road to Phokis. I put aside thoughts of Lucius, Apollonius, Didius, and the rebellion. I closed my eye and dwelled on Arrea's face. Soon I was fast asleep like Kallias, and dreaming a little easier than I generally might.

SCROLL XIX

I'M sure many have wondered over the centuries how one place could be considered the religious center of the world. But after one glance at Delphi they'd no longer ask why.

We passed underneath two massive cauldrons atop twirled columns as we climbed to the zenith where the oracle resided in the temple of Apollo. Ancient cypress trees hemmed our path. On all sides massive mountains of lush green protected us. Some called Delphi the "navel of the world", and now it was easy to understand why.

Dogs roamed free but neither barked nor gave chase, as if even they could sense the sacred in the air. Some of the finest gold goblets and jewelry cluttered the temple steps, free for anyone to steal, but no one seemed to do so. It was a wonder Delphi hadn't been plundered before, by either Greeks or Romans. It made my eye water to think that even brigands, mercenaries, conquerers, and the impoverished had one place considered too precious to defile. If only we considered the rest of Gaia's earth in the same manner.

"Is it how you remember, Kallias?" I asked when our driver pulled the horses to a stop and offered us a hand down.

He nodded. "Precisely. Once this place enters the mind's eye, it's unlikely to ever leave—especially when you can see no better than I can. They say some part of your spirit will forever remain in this temple once you enter."

"I should hope all of my spirit will be returning with me to Athens, but I wouldn't mind to have this sight fixed in my mind." I peered around, lost in the view. The trees seemed to stand still. Zephyr's wind had fallen silent the moment we entered Delphi.

"You should see the Pythia first. If I have time, I'll go after you," he said.

"Are you certain?" I said. "I have many more winters to consult the oracle. I'm not certain you have as long."

He laughed and patted my arm. "Who lives longer: the old priest, or the young soldier? It's a question to which even the philosophers would have no answer to," he said. "Yes, go on ahead. I'd like to walk these old roads once again, perhaps for the last time." He unstrapped his sandals and wiggled his toes in between the rocks and sand. "To stand before the Pythia is to stand before the gods. A great honor. But you can feel their presence anywhere, if you dare to try."

"For your wisdom, Kallias, I'd give up my command and everything I own," I said. "I'll meet you outside the temple of Athena Pronaia if we can't find one another."

"In the meantime, I'll be asking for the whereabouts of the child you seek." He smiled.

"I thank you, priest." I bowed my head.

"And what was her name again?"

"Anaiah."

"A beautiful name. I've faith the gods will restore her to you."

I felt the same tinge of resistance I knew Apollonius had. Unlikely, but I nodded and ascended the steps to Apollo's temple.

"Why have you come?" A man with a cane asked from the entrance, dark paint on his eyelids.

"To consult the Pythia," I said.

He exhaled. "Yes. Of course. But why? Every man who comes to this temple seeks her guidance, but not every man deserves it."

I cleared my throat. "I'm the commanding officer of a Roman legion. I've been sent by my commander to seek guidance from the Pythia. We fear we have offended the gods and need answers as to how we should proceed."

"There's no doubt you've offended the gods," he said. "The gods abhor your dominance and violence, your molestation of the Greek people."

I sighed. "That may be true. We seek to make amends with both the gods and with the Greek people, if only the Pythia will guide us."

The dark-eyed man studied me for some time, but eventually nodded. "Do you swear to honor our maxims?" he asked, pointing to etchings on the temple exterior.

Three lines were inscribed there. They were not decorated, gilded, or inset with jewels. I wondered how long they'd been there and how many men had repeated them before me.

"I do."

"Then repeat them."

"Know thyself. Seek nothing in excess. Surety brings ruin."

"Now you may enter. But first, you must pay for the laurel branches and the black ram which must be sacrificed."

I guessed at the cost in my head and wondered how many men and women made the pilgrimage to Delphi only to be turned away from the Pythia for lack of coin. "How much?" I asked, pulling out my coin purse and sifted through. I cautiously glanced over my shoulder to ensure no one was watching, I'd brought more than I was likely to need.

Rather than giving me an amount he reached out and counted through the coins with black-painted fingernails. Satisfied, he snapped and the great doors to Apollo's hall were pulled back by two strong men. "May you find the answers you seek," he said as I passed him.

Despite the daylight from the door behind me, the temple was almost pitch black. I was forced to wait for my eye to adjust. Dim lights beneath me showed a staircase descending to a lower level. It wasn't until I began the descent that I noticed the heavily armed guards standing in the shadows on either side of me.

Before the Pythia was even into view the stench of burning oleander filled my lungs, almost knocking me back.

Rather than the brightly gilded and heavily adorned throne room I expected, the Pythia sat in an empty room on a covered tripod cauldron. Beneath her was an open chasm, vapors rising from it.

Rather than a wise old woman I found a beautiful young girl, not more than a few years into womanhood. She didn't seem to notice me, undisturbed and uninterested in my presence. She shook bay leaves to waft the vapor to her and she inhaled deeply. She seemed to sway from side to side, but perhaps because of the fumes.

When she spoke, her voice was like that of the gods—deep and powerful—encompassing the room and arising from no one place in particular. "Who now greets me? The one covered in the blood of his countrymen."

I took off my helm and knelt on the cold rock beneath her. "I have never shed the blood of my countrymen, Pythia." I felt my heartbeat quicken as I gazed upon her. How many kings had knelt before her in this very spot? Agamemnon and Leonidas might have felt the chill of this stone on the flesh of their knees as well.

"No. No, not yet." She lifted her gaze, revealing deep black pools for eyes, no iris to speak of.

"I come seeking your wisdom."

"You come seeking answers." She changed the pattern of the bay leaves, inhaled, and tilted her head back.

"Yes. I do. I ask for many."

"You do not know the answers you should seek, nor the questions you should ask. Yet you will ask regardless."

I inched backward, afraid the fumes were getting to my head.

"Have we offended the gods?" I asked, although I wasn't certain I wanted to know the answer.

"All have."

"Is this why the gods have allowed us to be attacked? Allowed our men to die in flames while they sleep?"

"Apollo tells me your great punishment is that the gods have left you to your own devices. The world will feel cold without their embrace. The malevolence of others will devour your children." She gasped as if she saw a powerful vision, then moaned.

"Is there one in particular god we need to propitiate?"

"All."

I grunted. Was this Apollo's prophecy or the groaning of an intoxicated child? I felt shame for the thought, and I sensed she'd heard it, for her eyes opened wider and brighter and stared right through me. "What can be done to appease them?"

"Nothing but the willful shedding of innocent blood beneath the mighty shield of Athena can stay the gods' wrath."

"A sheep or ram? Or a white bull?"

Her voice suddenly became frail and distant, she said, "A man."

"The Romans do not practice human sacrifice."

"Nor do the Greeks. But the gods require what they may."

From all the tales I'd read, Apollo's Pythia always spoke in riddles. I hoped this was such an instant, otherwise I'd wasted my time in consulting her.

She seemed lost in her haze, and I considered leaving. Before I could stand, I asked, "Will Cerberus win?"

She gasped for air, her chest heaved rapidly, and she flung her long dark hair from side to side. She fell still. "In a manner of speaking."

It felt as if my blood began to boil and my face flushed. "I'm sorry but I cannot believe you."

"Neither would they," she said.

I noticed how white my knuckles were becoming around the grip of my helmet. I threw it on and buckled it.

"I thank you for your—"

"You still have not asked the right question," she said, her voice powerful and echoing once more.

"What is the right question?" I asked. She continued to wave her branch wand and ignored me. "Will Timoxenos return?"

"Wrong question," she whispered, "because you already know the answer in your heart. He will never breathe the Greek air again."

"Pythia, please…" I halted to lower my voice. If the gods were angry now I couldn't imagine their wrath if they overheard me yelling at Apollo's oracle. "Please help me to understand what question I most need to ask."

"What is it that consumes your mind?"

"My family," I replied without hesitation.

"And you have no questions about them?"

She knew I did, but I was afraid of the answers. "Will I be able to protect them?"

She opened her mouth wide and inhaled long and loud. "No."

I gritted my teeth and stood to my feet.

"You ask the wrong questions and therefore you receive the wrong answers. I am Apollo's voice, his shaking reed, his envoy. So I will tell you the answers to the questions you cannot ask."

"Go on," I said.

"War will beset you all the days of your life. Battles you do not seek, cannot win, and do not desire. You will feel the gods have cursed you, but in fact you are their chosen. Their tool, their sacrifice, their vessel."

My legs became weak and my breaths shortened, but I masked it adequately with anger. "Can a man not alter his fate?" I asked, knowing the answer a representative of the gods would likely give.

"Within the confines of your destiny. The day of your death and the manner in which it will take place is already inscribed on the pillars of Elysium. From now until then? Take care, lest you travel down a path of treachery and destruction."

I shook my head. She could make whatever prophecies she'd like, but she couldn't convince me I would pursue evil. "I will not travel down that path, whatever the Fates have in store for me."

She smiled then, her teeth white and sharp. "For a tree to grow tall enough to reach Mount Olympus it must have roots that descend down to Tartarus, and oh..." She moaned, closed her eyes, and rubbed at the flesh of her cheeks. "You have a foot in both."

I pursed my lips to stay my anger. "If you could relay a message to your god, inform him to send whatever trials my way they see fit. I'll not betray the path my father put me on. I will pursue righteousness and meaning above all else. Tell him that."

She said nothing and I thought for a moment she was done with me. I turned to leave. "Your loved ones will lie down in the bed of your enemies. Father will kill son, and brother will kill brother," she said. "Bones will be crushed on the Field of Mars and flesh will be split over the breaking of bread. And you'll be there for it all. The gods whisper perhaps you're even the cause."

"Pythia, please!" I turned around. She didn't seem to notice. "I came to ask about Cerberus and yet you only prophecy the evils that lurk in the distant future. I'm not yet concerned for the future, as I know not if I'll even make it there. What does this have to do with Cerberus?"

She smiled again and clicked her tongue rapidly. "Oh, my child. It has everything to do with Cerberus."

I was red-faced as I stomped out of Apollo's temple. The Pythia frustrated me. I shook my head and considered all the time I'd lost coming here.

"She's all yours, priest. May you learn something more valuable than I did," I said as I approached the wagon.

Kallias was standing with his head bowed and his arms crossed.

My posture softened when I placed a hand on his arm. "Did you not enjoy your stroll through Delphi's streets?"

"I did. Very much," he said without looking up. "But I was interrupted."

I flexed my arms and balled my hands into fists. "By whom? Point me toward them and they'll bother you no more."

He did not smile, but at last he looked up.

"I think you'd best have a talk with him." Kallias pointed to our driver, a young legionary not much older than Gavius.

He snapped to attention. Beads of sweat were forming on his ashen face. He looked like a blood-drained sacrifice.

"What has happened?" My jaw tensed.

"Sir, I thought you were going to be longer… and it's been a long time since—"

"Soldier." I placed a hand on his shoulder and forced him to relax. "You can speak plainly."

His eyes were watery as he looked up, and he seemed to shrink from me as if he expected to be struck. I was trying my best to be patient, but I was perplexed, and thus fearful.

"I decided to visit one of the brothels on the outskirts of the city. I haven't been with a woman since Rome, see, and—"

I smiled with familiarity. "No harm done, lad," I whispered so Kallias wouldn't overhear. I relaxed, realizing it was probably Kallias who had given the boy a hard time for revelry in this sacred place.

"Well, there's more than that, sir." He shuffled on his feet.

"Soldier. It doesn't appear to me that you've done anything wrong," I said. "but if you fail to finish this tale before I empty this skin of wine, I'll have you lashed." I brought the skin to my lips as he continued.

"I wasn't meaning to eavesdrop, I swear it," he stuttered trying to speed up. "I just couldn't help it, see. It was a boring ride. And I heard you mention the name Anaiah."

I sipped slow to allow him to finish. Now he had my attention. I nodded for him to continue.

"There was a girl at the brothel called Anaiah. And she had golden hair."

I dropped the wineskin and slammed my hand into his throat, throwing him back into the carriage. I roared, "Did you lie with her? Did you lie with her? Speak!"

"I didn't. I swear on the... Black Stone... I didn't," he managed to say. I released my grip. "Left as soon as I heard it. I didn't even get my coin back." He rubbed at his throat.

I grabbed him by the arm and pushed him toward the road. The meditating citizens of Delphi watched in stunned silence.

"Go, take me to her."

He ran on, both to reach the brothel quicker and escape my wrath. We'd almost escaped the traffic of frightened travelers when he stopped outside of a stucco hut. He lowered his gaze and pointed inside.

"Lead me," I said.

He held back the bead partition and I ducked to enter. The straw floor was covered in dried wine and the dirt tracked in by travelers. Light poured in through holes in the ceiling but there was nothing to reflect it save the mud walls and torn curtains which concealed each room.

"Back so soon?" the Phoenician proprietor said to the legionary with a coy grin. "Don't worry. Many of our guests are shy. And you've brought a friend?" He stroked his forked beard and dabbed sweat from under his wrapped head.

"Take me to her now." I pushed the legionary's shoulder and resisted the urge to assault the Phoenician.

He walked halfway down the hall and pointed to one of the

rooms. I burst through the curtain to find a girl huddled on a mat in the corner and a man standing over her. He was pulling the tunic from his head.

"Be off, she's mine," he said.

I ignored him and searched the girl's face for anything that resembled Apollonius' descriptions. Bright-eyed and always giggling. He always smiled when he recalled her, despite the distance and time between them. He remembered how she was always chasing him or being chased by her, yet this girl remained still.

She tucked a blue tunic over herself to protect what little modesty remained to her.

"Are you Anaiah?" I asked.

Could it really be her? She was too old. No, Apollonius remembered her as a small child, but the years had cascaded past us faster than we could keep track of them.

She gave only the faintest of nods.

"I said she's mine, Roman dog." He stepped forward.

I lunged in to meet him and sent him to the floor. With one hand on his throat and my legs pinning him to the ground I sent my fist crashing into him. I was going to scar him up worse than myself. At first I could see only red, but from the corner of my eye I glimpsed Anaiah. She was cowering and huddled at the wall, trying to pack herself into the smallest shape she could manage.

Her eyes were filled with terror, more even than when this boar of a man stood over her.

I rolled off the man and allowed him to spit up blood and what looked like a chipped tooth. "Go, get out of here," I said, catching my breath.

"What by Ba'al is going on in there?" The proprietor yelled from outside the room.

"Stall him," I said to the legionary as he saluted and complied. I turned to Anaiah and held out my hands in surrender. They were shaking and bloody, no wonder she tried to squirm away farther. "Please, I'm not going to hurt you." I took off my helmet and unbuckled my sword. I laid them at her feet and inched away. "I believe I know your uncle. His name is Apollonius."

Her delicate limbs continued to quiver like reeds in the wind. Her eyes continued to watch my every movement but didn't register when I said his name.

"He's been looking for you. For so long. Say that you are his niece. Say it and I will take you from this place."

Even if she was no kin to my friend, I hope she lied. I wanted to take her away regardless. No one's daughter should live like this.

"He told me to tell you... to tell you..." I searched my mind as I heard a bustle by the door. "That you are his moon and his stars, his light in the darkness."

Her trembling lips parted, and she leaned forward. Tears dripped over the black paint of her eyelashes.

"It's you."

I lowered my head and wept myself. What god arranged this? Or goddess rather, as only a woman could have such a tender heart to save one who could offer no sacrifices. What goddess sent the foolish legionary to this desolate place and brought Anaiah to our arms. She alone should sit atop Mount Olympus.

What god could have cursed us if this great blessing was allowed to happen?

Anaiah fell into my arms and I said a prayer to Diana, promising to serve her first and foremost for the rest of my life.

The proprietor burst in and laughed at what he saw.

"You'll be paying double now, Roman," he said. "for beating my visitor and for... whatever you're doing." He snickered.

I slowly let Anaiah down and gestured for the legionary to assist her. "Let's talk, you and I."

He smiled. "I think that's a good idea. I'll show you what you're doing wrong."

I followed him back to the table near the entrance and pulled out my coin purse. The gods bade me bring more denarii than I'd need, and now I knew why. "How much?"

He pointed to the wall where numbers were crudely etched. "Depends on what service you require." He cocked an eyebrow.

"No. To purchase her."

"What?" He soured. "No. Not for sale. She's my best *porne*."

"How much?" I dumped out my coin and spread them out to show him how much.

His eyes glistened with greed but then he pushed them away to avoid the temptation.

"No. She's young. Plump breasts and good teeth. She'll bring me a fortune before I'm done with her."

My limbs twitched with repressed rage. I controlled my breath to steel myself. "I am asking you to name a price."

"Release her!" He shouted at the legionary. "Just who do you think you are, by Ba'al? I'm sanctioned by the city of Delphi. You can't come in and—"

"I am willing to make a fair offer." I counted out the denarii.

The Phoenician slammed his fists on the table. "I said no deal!"

"Go on and take her to the cart," I told the legionary and the proprietor huffed in exasperation.

"You'll do no such thing!"

"Please, just give me a fair price," I said, still barely controlling myself. "I have no quarrel with you."

He struggled for the words to articulate his rage. "You'll have to kill me to part with her! She's my favorite slave."

I didn't mention that doing so was an option I was actively considering. I lowered my head and thought of everything I had that might sway him. My dagger might fetch a hefty price, but not likely enough. A legate's crest would be worth something substantial, but I would return to Athens in disgrace. A tear immediately flooded my eye when I felt the cold gold on my finger. I already knew what I was doing, and it broke me. I slid off the ring and placed it on the table between us. "My father's signet ring. Passed down my line for generations. Given to my ancestor by the Roman consul Dentatus after the war with the Sabines."

He picked it up and inspected it carefully. He tested the weight and tried to hide his delight.

"It's as precious to a jeweler as it is to me. And this is the last offer you'll receive."

He bit down on the ring and sucked his gums to taste it. "And if I refuse?"

I leaned across the table and put my hand on top of his so he couldn't move away. "I slaughter men because some old politician points his finger and tells me to. What do you think I'll do to a wretched specimen like yourself if you insult me again?"

He quivered and retreated the moment I released his hand. "Go. Take her." He nodded to the exit, and I gratefully complied.

When I made it back to the carriage, Kallias and the other legionary were already seated. We'd overstayed our welcome.

In the light I saw just how the years had worn on Anaiah. Still little more than a child, she'd experienced a lifetime of agony. The sadness in her eyes reflected it.

Now I was glad Apollonius hadn't come. But if Diana could save her, perhaps she could restore her. We could only pray and sacrifice, and hope the gods hadn't, in fact, cursed us.

PART III

SCROLL XX

Spurius Insteius
Written at the request of Quintus Sertorius

"The sun was a particular shade of orange... is that something I should include? I've never written something like this before...

The sun was a particular shade of orange, and I recall it reflecting off every helm and lorica of the legionaries behind us, creating a sea of light.

"It's truly something isn't it?" Aulus said with the smug grin for which he was famous.

"What is?" I replied.

Aulus gestured to the legion behind us. "This. All these men following us."

Of course it was Lucius at the forefront, eyes fixed on the distant city of Sparta.

Lucius said to himself, "We've a job to do, and we'll do it adequately."

"I mean it though. Watch this." Aulus wheeled

his horse around, and naturally Lucius and I did also. "Halt!" he shouted.

The centurions echoed the orders back as the legions snaked to a standstill. Lucius and I looked at my brother with confusion. He simply laughed.

"It feels like yesterday my wife was yelling at me for falling asleep in her poetry reading," he said. "Now I say one word and 5,000 men obey it."

Lucius chuckled and gave the order to continue the march. "The power's gone to your head, my friend." Lucius shook his head.

"*Gerrae*, you're the one in charge. The great mighty Hirtuleius is leading this army," Aulus said.

Lucius turned, his smile faded. Aulus lowered his gaze.

I said, "I might say it's irregular for you to be leading from the front, Lucius. As commander you should be surrounded by guards in the middle of this formation. That's what we were taught."

"I am no commander. I'm Lucius Hirtuleius. And if we're to be attacked, I'd like my sword to meet the enemy first. And if not, my eyes should be the first our gracious hosts meet."

That was just the sort of statement that concerned me.

Lucius led the way over the rolling green hills of Lakonia, yellow flowers wilting under our soldiers' sandals.

Aulus and I didn't know a thing about the legion, let alone leading it. We were so young then. Aulus was greener even than me. I'd seen his knees buckle the first time he spilt blood.

I didn't doubt Lucius' ability with a sword. He'd seen more battle and killed more men than any legionary should hope for. But could he lead?

Ever since we were boys, he took orders from his grandfather, from Sertorius, from us. He executed them to perfection and longed for nothing but admiration in return.

He was the kind of man you want at your side during a fight. No one was more reliable in the thick of battle. His presence encouraged others because despite his rank, he ate what they ate and drank what they drank. He said his old general Marius taught him that, and it was the most important thing he'd ever learned.

But that didn't mean he had a talent for stratagem. We still didn't know one way or the other. One thing was certain, however. Aulus and I, and all of our men, would have followed that man to Hades and back regardless.

"So there it is," Aulus said. "The city of soldiers. Doesn't look like much does it? I imagined from the tales our mother told us it'd be bigger."

"Unlike Rome and Athens, my dear friend," Lucius said. "Sparta didn't concern itself with constructing great buildings and expanding their city as far as possible. They focused on building the quality of their men."

"Sounds like a story you were told being tucked in at night," Aulus said with a wink.

Lucius sighed. "You know damn well my grandfather never 'tucked me in.'"

"Well, no matter. Why couldn't they at least build walls? What kind of city doesn't have walls?" Aulus balked. We began down a hill toward the city's barren entrance.

"They didn't need them," I said. "The shields of their warriors were their walls."

Aulus chuckled. "Where are those shielded warriors now?"

We said nothing.

As Lucius led us down the hill several individuals in the distance formed to greet us.

"This is the upper echelon of Spartan society. Don't carry on with all that blather in front of them," Lucius said, and we both knew to whom he was talking.

"The upper echelon of a conquered people? I saw a beggar in the forum once covered in his own piss who outranks them."

Lucius whipped around and shot Aulus a look that shut him up. We said nothing until we reached the nobles.

"Greetings, friends of Sparta!" one said. "We welcome you."

A halt was called and the cohorts stayed behind while Lucius, my brother, and I rode forward.

"Greetings, friends of Rome," Lucius said. "We salute you." Lucius offered the traditional Roman salute. Aulus and I would have both been laughing at their awkward response if not for fear of Lucius' reprisal.

"We do welcome you, most humbly to this place…" Another man, dark-skinned and sharp-jawed like a warrior, stepped forward. "Although we do not know what has brought you here." He leaned to get a better view of the men. "And why you have brought so many guests."

Lucius handed his reins to a single legionary and pounced from his steed gracefully. He approached and stuck out his hand to the man. The Spartan accepted, but I saw him wipe his own hand off with distaste the moment it was released.

"We've received word there is possible insurrection in Lakonia."

The nobles looked at one another, flabbergasted and afraid.

"I'm certain that's impossible," the oldest and most unshapely of them said. "That can't be. Sparta is ever an ally to Rome."

If the tone was different I might have reminded him that Sparta was not our ally, but our subject. I declined and allowed Lucius to continue.

"Let me rephrase myself. We've received word that there is *definitely* insurrection in Lakonia."

I smiled. Perhaps Lucius had the stuff about him after all.

The nobles squirmed.

"Well… we will assist you in your search then," the warrior said.

"We'll have a dinner in your honor, Roman," the old one said, and Lucius beamed.

Another warrior, tall and thick stepped forward. "We can discuss matters over wine and bread." I was stunned to hear the voice of a woman, until I noticed the shapely limbs and beautiful face which could only belong to a goddess.

"We… we'd be happy to," Lucius said, suddenly lacking authority.

"The lady will be joining us?" Aulus asked, equally smitten.

She lifted her chin. "This isn't a *sysstion*, but a meeting of peers. Spartan women are free women. Yes, I will be in attendance."

The Spartan nobles looked down and kicked the dirt but didn't say anything.

"Lead the way," Lucius said, not taking his eyes off her.

"What about your men?" The suntanned warrior said.

"They'll set up camp here."

"So close?" the old fat one said.

"Break for camp!" I shouted back at the centurions.

Lucius nodded. "For your protection."

 The legends were certainly right in at least one thing: the Spartans were austere.

They spoke with pride about their banquet hall, but I've never seen a more sparse and insignificant dining area. Unlike the plush Roman couches of the patrician villas, their hay-filled couches were little more than long stools. Aulus had a particular hard time bending his legs at a proper angle for comfort.

"We'll serve you a traditional Spartan meal," the oldest said, now identified as Patrobos.

"What might we expect?" Aulus said while squirming.

"Vinegar pig legs in black blood broth," the chiseled warrior called Meleagros answered.

"Oh, how lovely," Aulus said, "thank you." My brother was closest to me so I reached over and tugged at the long blonde hair of his leg to shut him up. If he upset Lucius during his first moment of leadership, I'd feel the wrath too. That's part of being a twin—we share the blame and the spoils evenly.

But Lucius was too busy pining over the warrior lady named Andromache.

Aulus and I both noticed it and my brother winked.

He leaned over to Lucius and whispered, "Stare any more intently and her tunic will come undone."

Lucius elbowed him and turned the color of his soldier's cloak.

"May we discuss in Greek?" Patrobos said.

I watched Lucius exhale. Aulus and I learned the basics as children, but Lucius was occupied toiling on his grandfather's farm. I knew he was thinking of Sertorius, who was as fluent in Greek as he was Latin.

"I prefer if we speak in the Roman tongue, if you don't mind," Lucius said. They nodded their consent.

Male servants with dark locks of hair brought out plates of simple bronze and doled them out. I kept waiting for more to be served, but the meager portions offered us would be all.

Lucius cleared his throat and tore his eyes away from Andromache. "Athens was attacked. I'm certain you've heard." He pretended he liked his food, but I knew better.

All the Spartan nobles looked to one another. Some of them looked afraid.

"We haven't heard," Patrobos said, particularly concerned.

I said, "Yes. Many lives were lost and many buildings were burned." I took a small bite.

Several of the nobles flushed and shifted in their seats.

"What cause did you have to attack Athens?" Meleagros said.

"No, you misunderstand," Aulus said with a mouthful of blood broth. "It was attacked by the same rebels we're now looking for."

Their posture seemed to relax.

"I'm certain the brigands you seek are not here. We'd have caught wind and executed them." Patrobos dabbed at his balding head with a napkin.

"I'm afraid we must be thorough," Lucius said. "The captives claimed they answered to a man in Lakonia called 'Polemarch'."

"Polemarch is a position, not a name," Meleagros said.

"Yes, of course." Lucius nodded.

"And that position has been vacant for over a century." Patrobos was quick to add. "How can you be certain the captives spoke truth?"

All eyes fell to Lucius while he stirred his untouched pig leg in the broth.

"Men have a habit of telling the truth when they've just watched all their companions die."

"Ah." Patrobos stared wide-eyed at the ground. "That may be true."

"What else did you learn?" Andromache spoke with more authority than anyone in the room, her sharp eyes watching Lucius like a hawk. "Do you have any description or background on the Polemarch?"

"Not much. The men who attacked us were little more than a band of poor farmers under the thumb of some oppressive force," Lucius said. "But we've reason to believe the man has a standing force of some size and ability."

"That's impossible." Meleagros shook his head and took a sip of watered wine. "Sparta hasn't had a standing force since the Roman conqueror Mummius burned Corinth."

I clicked my tongue. "I didn't notice many young men in the streets as you led us here. Where might they be?"

Boy servants refilled our cups and waved tropical leaves to cool us down.

"Sparta is a warrior society, you understand," Patrobos said. "And we can have no army, as per your laws. And Rome has needed so little auxiliary force... with there being no wars in the East, you see—"

"You can speak plainly, friend." Lucius set his bowl down and leaned forward on his couch.

"Many have joined the eastern armies as mercenaries." Patrobos rubbed at his flabby neck. "Shameful, of course, but I fear what barbarity young men might be inclined to without structured violence."

Aulus cocked his brow. "And what happens when they come back?"

"Most of them do not come back," Meleagros said with cold, unblinking eyes.

"Some of them do decide to remain in those desolate places." Patrobos nodded. "Others die."

"Certainly that can't be true of them all?" I asked. "None of them have families or love ones to return to?"

"Spartan men love only battle. There is no battle here so they don't wish to return." Meleagros shrugged.

"Then why are all of you here?" Lucius said.

For the first time the room grew silent save the swoosh of the feathered fans. All the noble men

204 | WHOM GODS DESTROY

hung their heads. Only the lady Andromache continued eye contact with us.

"They are correct that warriors couldn't be within the city," she said. "There is nowhere to hide under Spartan law. Lakonia is vast and wild though, and there could be armed men anywhere."

"Where would you suggest we begin our search?" Lucius said, waiting for her reply.

"What about the mountains of Arcadia or the coasts of Argolis?" Meleagros said.

I stated firmly, "We heard Lakonia."

"We also heard some of the rebels had gathered in the ruins of Corinth before the attack," Lucius added. "They could be using that as some sort of base."

"See? Not in Lakonia." Patrobos sat back with relief.

"We heard reports of activity in Corinth," Andromache said, eyeing the others. "There have been squatters there since Corinth's fall, but there's been more and more activity of late."

"Nothing more than lowlifes and bandits." Meleagros shook his head. "Certainly not the type of enemy the Romans are looking for."

"I think it's a good place to begin our search." Lucius stood.

Not a surprise to Aulus or me that he agreed with the attractive woman, but we also assumed she was right.

"Do you have scouts we could send out?" Aulus asked. "No sense in making the trek otherwise."

Patrobos huffed. "Certainly you passed by it yourself on the way from Athens?"

"We had orders and didn't deviate from our path." Lucius crossed his arms.

"Yes. I have riders," Andromache said. "I will send them out first thing in the morning. We'll know within a week."

"Thank you, ma'am." Lucius bowed low and awkwardly.

Aulus and I bit our lips and nodded to the offended guests before we left.

"I'll bet you fifty denarii I bed her before you," Aulus said as we exited into the evening Spartan air.

"She's not some merchant's daughter, Aulus," Lucius snapped. "She's a lady of dignity and... respect. Neither of us will be bedding her." He moved on ahead to avoid hearing any more.

"Speak for yourself," Aulus said under his breath with a laugh.

My brother and I were alike in almost all things, but I was in no mood for laughing.

Within a few days battle would be ringing in our ear again, and Sertorius wouldn't be around to save us this time.

SCROLL XXI

Quintus Sertorius

ANAIAH COULD BARELY WALK. Her body had been abused badly and I sensed they kept her wine drunk—or on something stronger—to dull her senses. I put her arm around my shoulder and helped her to Niarchos' doorstep.

My heart was torn. What would Apollonius think when he saw what became of the little girl he'd known? I could only imagine finding Gavius in this condition. Would I praise the gods to see him again, or would I rather live in the fantasy that he'd been well and happy all this time?

"You're going to be safe here. Your uncle will rejoice to see you," I said.

She blinked slowly without a word.

Niarchos' jaw dropped when he answered the door. He looked at me with too many emotions to express. "Come in," he said and stepped aside. He led us to the courtyard, attempting to speak several times but unable to do so.

Apollonius was playing with Kirrha when we arrived. He

was the last to look up. He let out a yelp from deep in his chest—one of pain, joy, terror, love. He struggled to his feet but then ran like a man half his age until he collapsed at Anaiah's feet.

He wrapped his arms around her legs and wept freely.

"My girl, oh, my girl," he repeated.

She reluctantly placed her hands on his back.

He took her small hands within his and pulled them to his face. He patted them. He turned them over to see every inch. He couldn't believe it was real. He searched her face for anything he could remember. At last he stood and embraced her, at last she embraced him back.

I stepped aside to give them a moment.

"You've done... you've done a good thing, Quintus Sertorius," Niarchos said.

"I've kept my vow." I looked to him. "No matter what fate awaits me I can say I kept my vow."

The girls led Anaiah to a bench where she could rest her bone-thin legs and drink some water.

Apollonius came to me but couldn't cease his crying. He wrapped me up with the uncharacteristic strength of the Python.

I said, "The gods have blessed you, Apollonius... sorry... your God has blessed you. Perhaps he is as powerful and loving as you say."

"The will of God would have... never come to pass... without your bravery and friendship." He struggled to speak. "Something I'm becoming accustomed to."

"You've saved my life many times over, Apollonius," I said. "I would have gone to the ends of the earth to bring her back."

"I know... I know you would." He looked back and forth between his niece and me, still trying to believe it. "I am just so happy she's back."

He hurried to her like a giddy child, but as I watched her eyes I wondered if she actually was back—if she would ever come back.

"See? What did I tell you?" Didius said to his several attendants when I entered his praetorium. "He traveled the same roads as I but bears not a scratch on him."

"Sir."

"How did you fare, Legate?"

"Well. The weather allowed for easy travel."

"Ha! Of course, it did." Didius clapped his hands. "I said the gods bless you, did I not?"

He rolled up the scroll he'd been working on and passed it to a legionary behind him. It wasn't until that moment I realized it was my shield bearer.

"Castor?" I said, but he didn't look up.

He folded the scroll into a crease and poured the hot red wax for Didius to stamp with his seal.

"Yes, he's been attending me since you were gone. I think you were on to something, Sertorius." Didius smiled. "He's more useful than I believed."

"Now that I've returned, he will return to his position as my shield bearer. Correct?"

Didius pursed his lips and considered it. "What do you think, legionary?" the commander asked.

Castor kept his eyes down. "I'll serve where I'm needed most, general."

"Well, he certainly can't be put back on the front lines." Didius shook his head. "He's spent far too much time being coddled by you to handle a blade properly."

Breath burst from my nostrils. "Go and ask any of my men if I coddle them."

Didius tired of the conversation and flicked his hand for his attendants to leave us. "What did the oracle tell you? Do we know which gods to appease?"

I remained at attention, waiting for him to order me to relax. I didn't receive it. "All of them."

Didius let out a belly laugh. "Of course. Did she say what we needed to do to avoid their wrath?" He spoke as if he didn't believe it, but he was the one who sent me on the mission in the first place.

"She did…"

"Speak then."

I looked at Castor, who still refused to meet my gaze. "She said only the willful shedding of innocent blood beneath the shield of mighty Athena."

"That shouldn't be so hard. Even after the attack, Athens is filled with more livestock than man."

"It's man that she said must die." I kept my eyes forward and back straight.

"Perhaps we should tell her my son's innocent blood was shed." His jaw twitched. "She forced Agamemnon to kill his own daughter. Does she know my child is already dead?"

"They say the Pythia knows everything, Proconsul."

He shifted with only a moment's rage, but then cooled. "I'll talk with Kallias. He can coordinate with our camp priests. We'll find a way to interpret this riddle. Won't we, legionary?" He turned to Castor, who waited a moment before nodding. "In your absence, however, we've received intelligence. Battle may yet be upon us."

"What have we discovered?" I said, unable to remain at attention with such news.

"The Archon has been busy."

I stepped toward the table. "What do we know?"

He raised one of his brows. "We know nothing. But someone here has news to report." "He says he'll only speak the rest to you."

"Why me?"

"I was wondering the same thing precisely." His gaze was fixed on me. I didn't know what this could be about, but I was aware it didn't look good. "He's back there." He pointed to a backroom covered by another tent flap.

"Did he give a name?"

"Oh, we all know his name," he said, "and it would be unwise to keep him waiting."

I saluted and approached the backroom. He stepped into my path. "And, Sertorius... you know what happens if I smell even a whiff of sedition?"

"Yes, Proconsul," I said with a gulp.

"You may only have one eye, but I have both eyes on you. Now figure out what this reprobate wants."

I pulled the flap back and stepped inside. A candelabrum flickered in the corner, illuminating only half the face of a cloaked man.

"Let me get a look at you," the man said. A voice that deep, gruff, and resounding could only belong to one man. Even before I could see him fully, I knew Gaius Marius was the man before me.

"General Marius," I said, remaining in place. He wasn't a general any longer, or even a consul. He was just a man with an illustrious career marred by too many errors to count. But some things would never change, and I'd never be able to address him as a peer.

He approached and placed both hands on my shoulders. "Legate Sertorius," he said, drawing the words out and savoring them. "I knew as sure as a prophet this day would come. You belong in that armor."

Little had changed in Marius since I last saw him. His jaw still strong, chin jutting. Despite his age his back was still straight and his muscles thick and defined. Perhaps there was less hair on his head, and his belly a bit rounder, but none could have mistaken Marius as the man whose statue lined every street in Rome.

"It's been a while," I said, uneasy and unsure why he was present.

"It has. While you've been following in my footsteps, I've been making my pilgrimage throughout the East. Savage country, to be certain, but it's lovely." He turned and poured wine into two pewter cups. He extended one in my direction. I gazed back to the thin tent partition and accepted.

"I tell you," he took a quick sip, "There is no place outside of Italy where a man can truly consider himself more than a beast. These desert people live by a code, but it's more like that of animals than learned men."

"Why have you come all this way? I'm sure you aren't here just to share stories of your travels."

He placed a hand on his chest and frowned. "You wound me. After so long, I assumed you'd be delighted to see me."

I wasn't. "I am, it's just that—"

"I have information for you." He drained his wine like a common soldier and quickly refilled his cup. "I considered informing your proconsul, but I don't quite like the man if you want to know the truth. It must have been disappointing to serve under a pissant like Didius after years on my staff."

I scratched my forehead to hide the look on my face.

"I've spent some time in the throne room of Mithridates."

"The debauched king of Pontus?"

He nodded. "We played a game of wits for the few days I remained there. He did all he could to both impress and intimidate me, but I made it clear Romans are superior to the eastern kingdoms in every way."

I waited for him to get to his point, but he'd been traveling for so long he was determined to draw it out.

He chuckled when he recalled something. "After all his displays of extravagance and excess I told him, 'Boy, either become stronger than Rome, or obey her commands in silence.' That got the point across."

I considered mentioning how reckless and foolish that was, but I was anxious to hear his news so only said, "Go on."

"Not interested in minding his place like a good boy-king, he decided to make his most grotesque display yet. He brought out slaves."

"Slaves?"

"Roman slaves. He had dozens, maybe even hundreds. He claimed to use them for sport, but I'm certain he was collecting as much intelligence on Rome as he could get from the poor wretches." He grimaced and I knew it wasn't the wine.

"We've already determined that Romans have been enslaved in Greece," I said. "That's what started this war."

"Well do you know where they're being auctioned off?"

I shook my head.

"That's what I've come to tell you. The rebels you're looking for are holding up in Plataea, and it's from here that they barter Roman lives like barbarian peasants. He blurted it out with all the arrogance you'd expect of an eastern king, as if I wouldn't use this to destroy those involved."

"Thank you for informing us, General Marius." I nodded, wanting to believe that my former commander was acting simply in Rome's best interests, but I knew better. I waited for him to state his desires.

"Now, seeing as I've come by this information and I have twice over the military experience than that senatorial puppet Didius, I'd like to conquer these rebels myself."

I nearly spit out a sip of wine. I couldn't help but laugh even as his face reddened. "Do you think that's a power I can bestow on you?"

He grunted and for a moment I saw the rage so prevalent during his last Consulship. It soon passed and he smiled. "That'd be nice, wouldn't it?" He poured himself a third cup of wine, his teeth now stained purple. "Intelligent, battle-hardened men like you and I making the decisions. But unfortunately, we must rely on the infinitely wise 'Senate and People of Rome'." He watched to see if I understood, but I failed to signal whatever acceptance he expected. "I've sent word to Rome asking for this commission. If the time comes and you are called on for your

SCROLL XXI | 213

testament, I'd ask that in return for this great favor, you speak to my military excellence and encourage them to make me commander here effective immediately."

I lowered my gaze and exhaled. I felt certain Didius was listening to every word. I needed to choose my words very carefully. "If the rebels are indeed at Plataea, we will wipe them out and the war will be over before the Senate can even meet on the issue."

He crossed his arms. "I considered that. But given the information I have about the size of their force, and my lack of regard for Didius' competence, I believe the battle will be lost and the glory of Didius' replacement will be even greater."

"If we lose that battle you can be certain I'll no longer be around to speak your praises," I said. "I will die on the battlefield with my men and my commander."

Marius grinned. "My boy." He patted my face and I bit my tongue. "Brave, just as I taught you to be. But the gods tell me you're destined for greater things, and my assumptions about you have always been correct."

"We shall see."

"*If* the time comes. Will you answer your call?" He stepped as close to me as he could, a tactic he often employed when he wanted to assure compliance.

"I will answer honestly and faithfully whatever the Senate and People of Rome ask of me."

That seemed to be enough for him. and putting his arm around my shoulder instead. "As I knew you would. I best be going then. I'm hastening to Rome to make my case. I shall see you again soon," Marius said.

We departed together to the praetorium proper, and the old general made a point to linger by my side and smile triumphantly in Didius' direction. As he departed, Marius held his back straight and chin raised to the heavens, as if his command was already secured.

"Proconsul, he's reported where the rebels are mustering," I said, struggling to compose myself and salute before his desk.

"I know. We listened to every word," Didius said, his eyes unblinking. Everyone omitted a collective exhale when the tent flap closed behind Marius. Everyone except Didius. "What did I say about whiffs of sedition?"

I was in an impossible situation. I felt my skin heating up and I turned to my commander. "Without insulting a former Consul and the Third Founder of Rome, I stood my ground. I couldn't risk offending him, or the information we sought could be lost."

In disgust, Didius said, "Could he really be so petty?"

"I assure you he can be."

"You understand how it looks for you to share private words and wine with him? You understand he is an enemy of mine?"

I set the still full cup of wine on Didius' desk. "And he is no ally of mine."

"Really?" His eyes narrowed.

"I have no allies. And no enemies, I hope. I fight for the Republic and the home of my birth, Nursia. If anyone is willing to fight alongside me, I call them friend. Anyone against me, I call them enemy."

He continued to stare deep into my eye, looking for any sign of fear. I was determined to display none.

"Good work on attaining this information, Legate Sertorius," he said, perhaps sarcastically.

"I serve your will, commander."

He returned to his seat. "You're right about that," he said beneath his breath. "Boy! Show your former master to his new quarters."

Castor nodded and led toward the doorway.

"New quarters?" I asked.

"Yes. Somewhere a bit closer to the praetorium. Somewhere I can keep an eye on you."

I saluted and followed my old shield bearer. To where, I did not know.

He walked faster than usual, and not by my side.

"Castor, would you not talk to me?" I called after him.

He stopped before a lowly tent just a few paces away from the praetorium. "This is where the commander wants you to stay." He did everything he could to avoid my eye.

"I don't care about that," I said, although I did. "I want to know why you won't speak to me."

"You didn't have to kill them all!" he shouted as legionaries perked up around the camp.

"Castor—"

"No! They were defenseless and unarmed and you had them all killed!" He wept.

"Part of being a leader is—"

"No! All those men..." He squeezed his eyes shut to hold back the tears, his fists trembling.

"There isn't a Roman officer in the legion that wouldn't have done the same. Most would've done worst."

He struggled to breathe. "I cannot believe you."

"Castor... you are my brother," I pleaded.

"My brother wouldn't do that." He turned from me and hurried away, the legionaries around us both shocked at the disrespect and finding his outburst humorous.

Niarchos popped his head from the tent.

"Sertorius?" he said, but I watched Castor hurry back to Didius tent.. I didn't even realize my Greek friend was present for a moment. "They told me this was your quarters. I've brought you some letters." He spoke tenderly.

"Thank you," I said, following him into my new tent, not half the size of a legate's typical quarters.

He attempted to be cheerful. "I hope they bring you good tidings."

"We'll share a cup of wine, if you'd like," I said.

"Of course. I'll always share a cup with you."

I took the letters from him. "I hope you don't mind if I read these first? It's been a difficult few days and I long to hear from my wife."

"Far be it from me to deny a man a moment with his loved ones." He smiled and found a simple chair by my cot.

Rather than the words of my wife, I was surprised to find the writing of my son.

Father,

I write with ill news. Arrea was going to write, but I believe it is my duty as your son and the leader of this house in your absence. There have been riots in Rome. The Tribune Drusus has followed in the footsteps of Saturninus and Glaucia, who others say were once your friends. He has created violence around the city to inact his measures. From my studies, I believe he is much like the Gracchi. Do you know of them? I've been reading.

I ramble. I wish we could speak plainly and in person.

The riots have led to widespread looting and burning—

I crumpled the letter and bowed my head, shaken to my core.

Niarchos placed a cup of wine on an oak table beside me. "Ill tidings?"

I did not reply but unfurled the letter and continued to read.

—and we have been at risk. Fortunately, your senatorial colleague Lucius Cornelius Sulla has sent men to protect us. He has been here several times himself and says he considers it an honor and a service to Rome to protect your family in your absence. We've continued to show him your gratitude, since you're unable to.

• • •

I bellowed, "No!" And threw the cup of wine across the room.

Niarchos kept his eyes to the ground out of respect. "I can leave if you'd like," he said as I fought for breath.

"No," I managed to say. I fought back tears; I fought back the urge to vomit.

Since I arrived in Greece, I'd seen a little girl clinging to a piece of wood. I was there to witness a lifeless prostitute who so recently carried the joy of a child. I'd seen the birthplace of democracy burn, witnessed sedition and treachery, and buried my men. All this made bearable by the knowledge that my family was safe.

Now I knew they weren't. Rome was just as violent and tumultuous as I'd left it. And to think my family had been driven into the arms of Sulla... my enemy. I knew the man. He carried with him an agenda as surely as his own lungs. He knew what he was doing. And he was a deceiver, a manipulator... a womanizer. The brief image of Arrea in his arms flashed before my mind, but I forced it out, unable to bear it.

"Niarchos." I swallowed hard. "I feel as if I'm being abandoned by everyone. I'm losing everything." I crumpled the paper into a ball and placed my head in my hands.

"I've felt the same once before." He shook his head at the memory. "When I received a wound that rendered me unable to have children... Anthea, she never cursed me for it, but I could see the disappointment in her eyes. There was more than a time or two when I held a dagger to my wrists."

"What stayed your hand?" I did all I could to preserve my dignity and keep the tears in my eye.

He came and placed a hand on my shoulder. "Knowing the gods had something left in store for me."

"I suppose they do," I said. "You're right, Niarchos. Thank you."

He poured me another cup and we sipped in silence together. The gods might have something in store for me indeed, but what that was exactly, I didn't know. If the Pythia spoke truth, it wasn't good.

SCROLL XXII

Lucius Hirtuleius

"Here I was, in my first position of command—an opportunity I'd been waiting for since I was a child. As a boy I'd lay awake at night dreaming about winning glory in battle; only I imagined my grandfather would still be around to tell me he was proud.

Now I finally had my chance, and I could think of nothing but a woman. I chastised myself for it. I'd always had a weakness for women. Not like Sertorius or the twins, who had been wooing young women in Nursia since we were old enough to shave. They chased women and women chased them, creating all sorts of drama when we were boys.

It was different for me. My weakness was only in the mind. I dwelled on them with a pining that made my soldier's heart stop, always from a respectful distance. I possessed enough confidence to get a woman, or at least I believed, but growing up without a mother left me inept at talking to them. I placed them on a pedestal. I revered the beauty of a woman nearly as much as I revered the gods. With a desire to treat them how I wished my mother had been treated, I considered myself too lowly to even enjoy their presence.

But Andromache latched onto my thoughts in a way few had before. How foolish? She could be the Polemarch for all I knew, but yet I lay awake that night considering her every feature, imagining what her dark locks must smell like.

So naturally when she invited me to attend the theater with her, I accepted. I ensured the twins remained in camp so they couldn't tease me, and I set off for the agora of Sparta.

I nervously paced while I awaited her arrival. Surrounded by monuments, statues, and war prizes of old, and yet I considered none of them. I brushed back my hair, licked my thumb and smoothed down my bushy brows.

"I'm surprised you found us," her sweet voice sounded from behind me. She approached with a smile and her hand resting on the hilt of her sword. "They say officers have a penchant for getting lost."

I grinned and searched for something to say but finding nothing I remained in awkward silence.

"Do you attend the theater much in Rome?"

"No. Not me. I've rarely been within the city since I joined the legion," I said , casting my gaze to the ancient stones beneath us.

"How strange," she said. "for you soldiers to fight for a city you so rarely see." She crossed her arms, her biceps as defined and sinewy as most of my legionaries.

"We don't fight for the city, ma'am," I said. "We fight for an idea. For prosperity and peace. For glory."

"Now you speak the language of the Spartans." She smiled. I caught myself staring at her bow shaped lips, and quickly looked away red-faced. "Do you enjoy the theater when you happen to attend it?"

"Me? Yes... certainly." I swallowed.

"I can't stand it," she said.

"By the gods, me either. It's nonsense." I sighed with relief.

"Just look at them up there." She pointed to the two actors on the makeshift stage, one playing the role of a woman with bright white powder covering his face. "It's silly. As if they don't know tragedy lurks in every corner behind them."

"Perhaps the people need their laughter," I said. "or to see the tragedy in the lives of others to make their own pale in comparison."

She investigated me with raised brows. "You speak as someone who enjoys the shows"

"I might, if I could only follow them." I shrugged. "Not smart enough."

The actors continued to trounce around the stage to the laughter of the crowd, the protagonist completely unaware he was being cuckolded right behind his back.

"My scouts should be back before the sun reaches the mountain." She pointed to the massive Mt. Taygetos behind the theater. If that was true they'd be there within the hour, if I estimated the sun's movements properly, which I rarely did.

"I hope they bring good news. I'm ready for battle."

"Aye." She nodded. "It's strange isn't it? Spartans and Romans fighting alongside one another? It was so recently we were at war. Now we're your subjects."

"We're all playthings for the gods, aren't we?" I said, raising my voice above the sound of the laughter.

"Some more than others. You Romans are noted for your cruelty. Especially toward Greeks." She kept her eyes on the stage and I kept my eyes on her.

"Remember it was the Greeks who started it all. Greece raised a fleet like the world had never seen before to destroy the city of Troy, our ancestors. Our conquest of the Aegean was simply cold revenge," I said tongue-in-cheek, and she seemed to realize it.

"The Romans must be a petty and patient people then, to remember crimes committed so long ago."

"You have no idea." I shook my head.

We turned our attention to the play and listened as the comedy reached its climax. I couldn't follow. I laughed when she did, but I realized then I hadn't heard a word, clueless about what was going on.

"Do you have no husband?" I said, immediately regretting it as the laughter made it the most inopportune time.

"What?"

I doubled down and repeated anyways.

She shook her head. "No. I've been used by men, both Greek and Roman alike. Now no man would want me, and I want no man."

I was stunned by the candor with which she

spoke, but she showed no sign of shame or malice. "I am sorry I asked."

She shook her head. "It's the way of the world. If only I'd been born a man, I would rule Greece."

I smiled. "I have no doubt," I said and meant it.

"Ma'am," two men said, approaching us from behind. They ignored me but bowed their heads before her. "We've returned from Corinth." She led them by the arm away from the crowd, so we might hear better. I followed.

"What news do you bring?" she said, something of her gait reminding me of a general like Marius.

"There are indeed armed men within. They believed us to be members of their rebellion and allowed us in with open arms."

"There are many of them," the other added.

"How many?" she asked.

"Thousands to be certain, all well-armed. They looked like men from the east."

Andromache and I exchanged a look.

"Can a Roman legion take them on?" I asked.

"Doubtless," one said, but kept his eyes on her.

"A Roman legion plus the Spartan guard. In good faith, our two hundred warriors will ride out with you," she said. The two men looked perplexed but said nothing.

"When can we move on them?" I said.

One of the scouts said, "They are about to celebrate the festival of Dionysia. For the next three days they'll be drunken, addled wrecks."

"Now is the time to strike," the other said.

I looked to Andromache for her thoughts.

She considered it, her eyes glossing over the way Marius' did when he considered all branching possibilities. "Yes. This is the best opportunity we'll be granted."

"I agree," I said quickly.

"We should leave tomorrow morning by cover of darkness. With a full army it will be three days march."

"We Romans move fast. My legion can cover thirty miles a day if need be."

"Then let us get our rest," she said. "Tomorrow we leave and earn our place in Elysium."

The scouts bowed and departed. She nodded and touched my arm when she left.

It was the kind of touch one friend gives to another, and yet the feeling lingered. What a fool I was, but at least the twins weren't around to see me blushing.

Put a sword in my hand though, I return to being a proud, manly Roman. And the sword was certainly about to be drawn.

Spurius Insteius

 The sky was blue like the Mediterranean's deepest waters as we gathered outside the walls of Corinth, the sun creeping behind the Achaean hills in the distance.

There was a nip in the air, but I knew it wasn't the chill causing the fresher legionaries to shiver and their chainmail to jingle.

Lucius, Aulus, and I marched to the front of the

formation of legionaries with only our tribune's crest to designate us as officers. Our oldest friend took the center, while my brother and I stood at his flanks.

Our forces waited in complete silence. The only sound was the carrion birds squawking above us.

"Are they waiting for our dead, or the enemy's?" Aulus asked.

Lucius said, "Sertorius told me crows circle above their own dead, crying out like that to honor them. Perhaps they honor us." He exhaled.

Sliding his gladius from its sheath, he took a knee and slammed the blade into the moist earth. We waited for him to speak, but for some time he remained silent, staring at the ground and rubbing his thumb over the hilt of his sword. "Break formation. Loose ranks on me," he said. The centurions echoed back the call as the legionaries encircled us.

My heart thud beneath my armor as I feared he couldn't find the right words to say, but I could tell he was serene even from behind him.

He remained on his knee as he unbuckled his helm and set it beside him. He looked up and scanned the faces of our men. "Some of you joined the legion to serve this Republic. Others for land, wealth, or glory. Others still because you had no other options. Some to honor your ancestors and the dead," he said. In one swift motion he pounced to his feet and freed his sword from the ground, pointing the tip toward Corinth. "But it matters not. All that matters now is how you conduct yourself beyond those walls!"

Some of the men cheered, but most remained silent, teeth grinding and knees shaking.

"Today you fight not for a politician or a

general, but for one who so recently wore the issued sandals now chafing your feet." He pounded his chest. Some of them smiled. "More importantly, regardless of why you joined—you fight not for any of that but for the man beside you. Protect him with your shield and he'll protect you with his."

The centurions, experienced enough to know what the men needed, unsheathed their swords and banged them against their shields.

"And it's a glorious thing we do today," Lucius said, squaring off with individual legionaries as if he were talking directly to them. "For Rome is under attack. Our great Republic and our way of life is threatened by the cowards within these walls. Will you follow me to stop them?"

"We'll follow you!" they shouted.

The centurions added in a stomp and some of the men joined in.

"Then look!" Lucius shouted. He pointed his sword to the heavens and looked up with it. "I see there our fathers and grandfathers!"

He looked to me with wide and wild eyes, so I added, "And our brothers, too!"

Aulus chimed in "All our people, all of Rome's warriors, back to the beginning."

"They call to us!" Lucius said. "They beckon us to join them in Elysium. Can you hear them?"

All the men joined the centurions now, stomping and beating their shields rhythmically with our words.

Lucius cried, "They call us to Elysium, where the brave may live forever!"

"Will we join them?" I shouted in tune.

"Will we honor them?" Aulus said.

"Is today not as good a day to die as any?"

Even the greenest amongst them stood taller. Nothing was shaking now save our shields as we drummed.

"Some of us will not live to see the sun rise," Lucius said.

"But we will live on in glory!" I shouted.

"On the green fields of Elysium, with the heroes of old," Aulus roared.

"And if we fall this day," Lucius said, donning his helm and picking up his shield. "at least we're going to send these bastards to Tartarus with us!"

"Let them hear you!" I bellowed as the men grew frenzied.

"To war!" Lucius cried, leading the charge.

Lucius Hirtuleius

 Corinth's southern wall had never been repaired after Rome burned the city, so we didn't need siege equipment. No battering rams, ladders, or towers. Just shield and steel.

Six men abreast could enter at a time, so I called for the legion to form a column as we marched quick-time to the city.

Commanding officer or not, I was no general. I was no coward either, so I placed myself within the first century to enter, my shield locked with theirs. The Insteius twins followed suit in the centuries behind me.

This was my chance. The one I'd been waiting for all my life.

And yet, my heartbeat was still, my mind clear. Perhaps this is what Sertorius was always talking about with that stoicism philosophy he so loved. Live or die, I would go down in history as a Roman. A *Roman*. I felt my grandfather's pride shining down on me despite the sky darkening.

We reached the opening in the walls, slowing down so we could stay in formation as each rank took turns stepping over the rubble.

I braced for the arrows and the javelins barrage. Nothing came.

"Wake them up!" I shouted as our men echoed a war cry like hungry wolves. Between the outbursts I listened for the enemy but heard nothing.

When we reached an open courtyard, we stopped the march. Still no foes were upon us.

"Shields down," I ordered. I lifted my head and gazed around. There was nothing but burnt ruins. Blackened trees with neither leaves nor branches. Temples with columns toppled to bits and dust.

If we were assaulted by the most powerful army in Greece, I might have kept my composure. But with no enemy at all, I began to panic. I'd be remembered as a fool now, and nothing more.

"Andromache!" I hollered, and the men assisted by sending the call back.

She rushed through the line, and I broke formation to meet her.

"Roman," she said, the strands of her hair darkened by sweat.

"Where are they? Your scouts said they would be drunk and celebrating Bacchus," I said. I could hardly be angry with someone who had the face of a goddess, but panic and rage were setting in.

"They must have run. Word must have reached them of our plans."

"Not possible," I said. "My legion moved faster than Zephyr's wind."

The Insteius twins joined us.

"The scouts must have been telling the truth. Look," Spurius said, "barrels of ale and wine, fires still smoldering."

I huffed and rubbed at my eyes. I was twice dishonored: first for believing the word of a Greek, and second for encouraging the men to embrace their deaths when no enemy awaited us. I was like them recently enough. I knew the jokes that'd be made at my expense. I continued to rub at my eyes until bright spots developed beneath my lids. What was I to do? Send out trackers and scouts? Perhaps dogs could sniff them out, but we had none. No, we'd need horses too, and left those in the Spartan stables.

The whistle of an arrow sounded.

I looked up and found it through the center of my bicep, the head clean through. For whatever reason I looked at Andromache and burst into hysterical laughter.

All was still for a moment. No one moved, no sound rang out but my laughter.

When a second arrow flew and cracked into my shield, I returned to reality. "Back to formation!" I bellowed as I ran to the ranks and the hole they opened up for me.

Arrows, javelins and slingers rocks came from the shadows all around us.

"Testudo!" I shouted and the centurions echoed me.

Through the small gaps in our shield wall, I searched for the enemy. On top of ruined temples, crouched in the hundred-year overgrown shrubbery.

A young legionary in front of me cried out when a javelin splintered through his shield and wedged into his cheekbone. He collapsed as the men struggled to fill the gap he created.

"Orders, tribune?" the first spear centurion asked.

My mind was blank. I spilled over all my training and the battles I'd fought in, searching for some gem of wisdom Marius might have left me. Before I could answer the earth shook beneath us. A blood curdling war cry sounded as a horde of heavily armed spearmen charged us.

"Brace, brace, brace!" I shouted. They crashed into us, the first ranks stumbling and rolled up like a carpet as the long spears slithered through the shield wall like snakes.

"Attack," I bellowed, barely audible through the screams and war cries.

The centuries behind us rushed to our aid, along with the Spartan guard with Andromache at their helm.

Missiles continued to pelt us from all sides. It felt a little bit like the storm at sea, tossed about by the will of angry gods, defenseless.

I pushed my way to the front rank. My panic had dissipated but my torrent of rage sustained. I wanted to whet my blade. The moment I reached the battle line a spear struck my shield. It fell easily from my hand as I realized I was unable to grip from the arrow in my arm. The spear jabbed at me again, and with all the strength left in my injured arm I grabbed hold of it and severed it in the middle with my sword. I grabbed on to the broken end and pulled the hoplite warrior to me. He struggled back but was pushed forward by his bloodthirsty brethren. My blade punctured his jugular and blood and phlegm sprayed over me.

I started the tally in my head. I would need to remember the exact number of deaths so I could make the proper sacrifice after the battle. And I knew this was the first of many.

But I realized the men beside me were wavering. Beams of light poured through their shields where arrows and javelins pierced them. As we learned on the Field of Mars, we pushed back against the attackers, marching forward one step at a time. Our progress was impeded though by the number of Roman bodies piling at our feet.

Even as I lurched forward with a stab at my next foe I prayed. *Mars guide our blades. Neptune ride out on your four-horse chariot. Jupiter strike them down with lightening and flame.*

The second rank pulled us back and took our place.

A brief reprieve, I looked over at Andromache. Her warriors were faring well, their long spears matching that of the rebels. Blood was splattered over the silken skin of her face and neck, and I prayed it wasn't hers.

I strained to find the twins. I feared for them. The only warfare they'd seen was chasing down a few stragglers after the attack on Athens. If something happened to them, I would never forgive myself and Sertorius wouldn't forgive me either. I couldn't see them.

"Protect the tribunes!" I cried out. Several legionaries hunkered closer to me. "Not me, fools!" I pushed them away and snapped the arrow in my arm. I ground my teeth and pulled both sides clear. What began as a dull ache was now searing like a burn, engulfing the left side of my body.

Before I could whine any further a spear wedged through the belly and out the back of the legionary in front of me. He cried out, fell, and again I was on the front line.

A round studded shield bashed into my chest, driving the wind from my lungs. The spear was next. I had no choice but to sidestep and charge the warrior, breaking rank like an undisciplined recruit. But it was that or die, and I wasn't ready to visit my ancestors in Elysium just yet.

The rebel snarled at me with bloodstained teeth. I slammed my head into his nose and then cracked him over the head with the hilt of my gladius. Straining for room, I wedged my gladius into the exposed flesh under his arm.

"Rally to the tribune! Protect the tribune!" the first-spear centurion cried out as the men pushed harder to reach my side.

The enemy moved forward to meet us. They fought like beasts, clearly veterans of innumerable campaigns. But their numbers were waning, and for a brief moment I thought the day was ours. Before I could celebrate, I heard the most dreadful thing to ever fill my ears: the screams of charging horses.

"Turn, turn!" I cried to our back ranks. Too late. The horsemen shattered our back wall, some pouncing over and crashing down on top of our legionaries with the bloodcurdling sound of crunching bone. Panicked, our men lowered their shields. The arrow volleys increased and screams soon followed them.

All was lost.

Swords clattered to the earth as legionaries ran.

"Stand fast, stand fast!" The centurion's cry echoed in my helm, but a haze was overcoming me.

To die in battle, a dream I'd always held dear. But while leading our men into a crushing defeat? My ancestors were ashamed. My heart cried out for my friend. Sertorius would have known what to do.

The horses screamed out and flailed as Andromache's warriors rushed to our aid, their spears lancing the beasts and sending their riders through the air.

Honor and legacy be damned. A disgrace or not, I didn't want to die with any more blood on my hands.

"Retreat!" I shouted. "Retreat!"

SCROLL XXIII

Quintus Sertorius

I began with Anthea.

"Take care of your old husband. I'm afraid he'd be lost without you," I said.

She smiled and shaded her eyes from the sunlight on the terrace. "I always do. I'm afraid he'd be lost without you, though. You best visit when this campaign of yours is over."

"I'll do that." I kissed either of her cheeks.

"How are your ribs?" she said.

I shrugged. "All better now. Only notice it when I run or lift something heavy," I said. "But for whatever reason my arm is throbbing." I grabbed my left bicep.

"Let me take a look." She took my arm and turned it over.

"I see nothing. Maybe the pain is being transferred from your side? A healer once told me that happens."

"Perhaps. Or maybe I fell while I was drinking with your husband."

I smiled and she did too, the same sadness in her eyes that

were in mine. I took the stairs back into the home. I needed to say goodbye to the girls as well.

They were in the courtyard, seated across from one another. They were playing a game of marbles with some walnuts they'd scrounged from the kitchen. Kirrha was trying to teach her the rules, and Anaiah only stared blankly.

"Girls, I am leaving," I said. "Battle calls."

Anaiah remained seated but young Kirrha sprang to her feet and wrapped her fragile arms around my waist. She'd grown so much since we pulled her from the depths of the sea.

My chest tightened. Proof of perhaps the only two good things I'd done in my life were there before me. If Charon was preparing for my voyage across the River Styx, at least these girls were safe. And if the gods had in fact cursed us for our rescue of Kirrha, then gods be damned.

"I don't want you to go, Quintus," she said with her cheek smushed up against my breastplate.

I smiled. "I will return before you've realized I'm gone."

She pulled away and looked at me. "But you said sometimes soldiers don't return."

I pinched her cheek. "But this time I believe I will." I knelt beside Anaiah and waited until she cast her sad eyes in my direction. "I'll bring you both a flower from Plataea. They say the soil there is rich and the fauna is beautiful," I said, leaving out that the reason for this was the number of bodies that had decomposed there after a great battle three hundred years before.

"I want a yellow one." Kirrha smiled and clapped her hands.

"And what color for you?" I asked Anaiah.

She paused for so long I thought she might ignore me. "You don't have to bring me a flower."

"I'd like too." I smiled but she kept her gaze averted.

"Red then," she said, barely audible.

"Done. I'll return safely with the two most beautiful flowers in Greece, for the two most beautiful girls in Greece." I kissed

Anaiah's head and consented to another of Kirrha's hugs before I turned to leave.

"Quintus," Kirrha hurried after me. She whispered, "I don't like her. She's strange and she doesn't wash."

My shoulders sagged. I exhaled. "You must be kind to her, Kirrha."

"But she is not kind. She doesn't even speak!" she said. "She sleeps on the ground instead of a bed and doesn't eat her dinner."

I knelt and placed my two hands on her tiny shoulders. "Consider that she isn't kind because no one has ever been kind to her."

She squinted for a moment but then nodded. "I've never thought of it like that."

I stood. "She's been in the dark for a very long time. And you can be a light."

She perched up on her tiptoes and kissed my cheek. I departed quickly so she couldn't see the tears in my eye.

Niarchos was next. I found him in his workshop, his hands caked in clay as he kneaded it into fine form. "Is it time already?" he asked.

"It is," I said. "We're departing at the seventh hour."

He sucked air though his teeth and nodded. "And where are you going exactly?"

"The enemy is at Plataea, or so we've heard. We aren't wasting any time."

He tried and failed to dry his hands on a stained rag. "Could you not wait till the legion in the south returns?"

I pursed my lips. "My commander is not a patient man."

He stepped around his potters' lathe and threw his burly arms around my neck.

"As long as you make it back," he said. "You've become like a brother to me... or a son... or nephew... A fine friend."

I could tell he was unused to displays of affection for other men, so I took it to heart. I slapped his back roughly to keep his confidence.

"Don't grow soft on me, old boy," I said with a grin. "I'll be back to eat your food and drink your wine. No question." We laughed until we remembered what was about to happen. Then I left.

Apollonius was the last member of the household I needed to address. I searched most of the house until I found him in his own quarters, on his knees with his hands folded.

He was whispering something in a strange tongue I didn't understand. I stood in the doorway watching him for some time. I considered leaving. Maybe that would be easier? But before I made a decision, he patted the bed beside him. I took a knee at his side and mimicked his posture. "Shall I pray to your god or mine?" I said. He ignored me and continued his prayer. When he paused, I asked, "What are you saying?"

He smiled. "Surely he will save you from the fowler's snare and from the deadly pestilence. He will cover you with his feathers, and under his wings you will find refuge; his faithfulness will be your shield and rampart."

"You pray this for me?"

He continued, "You will not fear the terror of night, nor the arrow that flies by day, nor the pestilence that stalks in the darkness, nor the plague that destroys at midday."

"I fear many things."

"A thousand may fall at your side, ten thousand at your right hand, but it will not come near."

To avoid melancholy, I attempted at humor. "If I kill ten thousand men, then I would surely deserve a crown."

"You will only observe with your eyes, and see the punishment of the wicked." He spoke with such serenity, the words spilling out over his lips like honeyed wine. Then he smiled. "Or *eye* in your case."

I wrapped my arm around his shoulder. "You know what you must do if I fall in battle."

"You speak of death far too much for a man so young," he said.

"Romans are born dwelling on how to die."

"Why should this battle be different than any other?"

"We're at a disadvantage. We've been complacent and weak, our enemy active and strong. An army of warriors materialized out of darkness, and we don't have time to muster more legions."

"You speak almost as if you seek defeat."

I exhaled. "It's easier that way. Now tell me you know what to do."

"I will send the letter, Quintus." He looked at me with a level of frustration that was usually foreign to him. "I prithee don't make me."

I squeezed his neck. "If you stay here in Greece, you should call on my family. They'll be safer with you than in Rome, I fear. Take care of them."

"I do not like how you're talking."

"Just tell me you've listened."

He huffed then nodded. "I hear you."

"Good." I kissed his head. "That gives me peace beyond measure, like you talk about in those prayers." I stood and adjusted the sword on my hip. I stopped at the doorway and turned back to him. "If I die, do you think your God would let you visit me in Elysium?"

He nodded, smiled, and blinked a tear from his eye. "I do."

"Good," I said. "Good."

He returned to prayer and I returned to camp. The men were forming up for departure.

One way or another, I would be leaving Greece soon. By ship or by sword, either way I was going to annihilate my enemy first. And nothing—not even the fury of the gods—would stop me.

Forty miles lie between us and Plataea. Forty miles between stillness and chaos, between safety and bloodshed.

We departed first thing that morning, before the sun rose. With Greece's hills, crags, and valleys, it was a difficult land to traverse, so the legions were drawn up into tight formation. The five thousand men stretched back and extended forward as far as the eye could see.

I was assigned somewhere in the middle, atop a new horse and riding with three hundred horses beside me. I didn't mind fighting in the cavalry—I was as natural on the back of a horse as I was walking—but I preferred to know the beast I rode to death with. I missed Sura just as I missed everything else back in Italy, and the horse beneath me was little more than a foal, anxious and stubborn. I ran my fingers through his hair and patted his mane. Perhaps he could sense the pending battle as well as any of us. If one listens to their beasts, they'll find they're generally more perceptive than we are.

The slow pace of formation was as intolerable to him as it was to me. He needed to move. To calm him, I broke formation. "Stay in line," I called to my men.

I kicked both his haunches and he gratefully charged ahead. The scarlet cloaks and plumes of the men blurred as we zoomed past them. To the vexation of my beast, I tightened the reins when I reached the first century. I said, "Centurion Herennius. How are you?" My horse—who I now dubbed Ajax—clopped along beside the men as if he were marching.

"As good as any Roman can be. Right men?" he said as the men cheered. This is what made him the finest centurion in the legion. "And what of you? Ready to whet your blade again?"

"I'm ready to return home," I said. "If bloodshed will expedite my departure, I'm happy to be the one to shed it."

He smiled. "What are you looking forward to most?"

We passed underneath the shade of ancient poplars to the morning sunlight, a golden field lush with Greek sage before us.

"I'm looking forward to a woman who isn't hairier than a Gaul," one of the men said to the humor of his friends.

"What about wine that doesn't taste like minotaur's piss?" another said.

"Shut up, Dex. You're not going home after the campaign unless you cut off one of your fingers like you've talked about."

"Let's hear what the legate says, boys." Herennius hushed them. "Maybe you'll learn something."

I smiled at opportunity to rib the men at least. "I'm looking forward to a hairy Gaul. My wife."

They all laughed except the legionary who spoke first, who instead hung his head and blushed.

"What a thing to return to," Herennius said. "The gods bless you."

"A more fortunate man might still be with his wife."

Herennius pushed a few of the men from his path and came closer to my side. "You look grave."

"My wife is my homeland. My standard and eagle, the flag I'd gladly die in a rainstorm of arrows to defend. Without her I'm nothing."

"She's waiting on you, legate. You still fight for her."

"Things aren't going well in Rome," I said, quietly enough I hoped only he would hear.

"I can't say I'm surprised. I do my best to avoid talk of politics while I'm on campaign. It makes the fighting much harder," he said. "Better to pretend Rome is the city of heroes we were told it was as children."

"And that's why you're the smarter of the two of us, Herennius," I said. "I haven't quite learned that yet. Perhaps I'll grow up to be like you."

He smiled and shook his head.

"Legate," one of the soldiers said. "Do you think the war'll be over if we win this battle?"

I considered how to respond. This was the sort of question leaders learn to avoid, but I hadn't yet converted tenets to actions. "If the seventeenth legion is successful in the south. Yes," I said. "I do believe we'll quash this conspiracy and be ready to leave this place." I hoped that was true. If it was a lie, I only hoped it would inspire them to fight harder.

Everyone considered what it might feel like for all the fear mongering and whispers of sedition to cease. We marched on in silence as the terrain declined sharply toward a ravine. I pushed Ajax to the water to allow him a quick drink before rejoining the men.

"Four hundred years ago, the Greeks fought the Persians at Plataea to keep their homeland safe from invasion," I said.

Herennius placed a hand on the brim of his helm to shield out the sun, waiting for me to make a point.

"Now we are the invaders. The conquerors."

"Greece is ours now by sacred oath."

"You speak true," I said. "But in their stories, they are the liberators. The heir to those noble ancestors. They believe the gods fight for them."

He sighed. "It's my belief that the gods care little for who wins in battle. Seems to me—after twenty some years with sword in my hand—that the strongest army wins."

Some of the men's eyes widened, but this sort of sacrilege wasn't uncommon in the legion.

"It matters not. The belief is the only thing that matters. We must be prepared to fight with the same determination," I said.

One of the men said, "We won't let you down, legate!" The others shouted in agreement.

"And I won't let any of you down," I said. "We will win this battle and those that follow at any cost. I'll ensure all of you grow old enough to marry a hairy Gaul of your own."

Their laughter was disrupted by the sound of water sloshing

in the distance. At first I believed we were coming to a waterfall or rapids, but instead it was two black stallions charging at us.

Herennius called the formation to a halt.

Even from a distance I could see the panic in the eyes of the scouts, the mud of hard riding stained on their face.

I wheeled about to find Didius charging furiously to the front of the formation. "What is it?"

"Sir," one said, giving a pitiful salute as he struggled for air.

"Get on with it," Didius said. "Report."

"There is an army on the move."

Didius inhaled and cracked his neck. "How many?"

The scouts looked to one another.

"Thousands."

"How many thousands, you fools? That does not help me," the Proconsul said. The scouts shook their heads. "More than the legion?"

They nodded. "Easily."

"They have at least a thousand head of horse," the other added.

"Sons of *Dis*!" Didius swore. He closed his eyes and bit his knuckle.

"How could they have this many men?" Herennius asked, slack-jawed.

"More are arriving from the east. They must have come by sea and beached at Marathon," the scout said, still fighting for air.

"They must be the mercenaries from the east," I said to myself.

"If we fight them in open battle…" Herennius shook his head. "We'll lose too many men to take their fortifications at Plataea… if we can win at all."

Didius still hadn't opened his eyes. I knew this feeling well.

"Commander," I said. "I have an idea." I scanned the river and the lush forests on either side of it.

"What is it?" Herennius asked when Didius said nothing.

"Do we have rope in the baggage train?" I asked.

Herennius shrugged. "Of course."

"Commander…" I reached over and patted his leg.

His eyes were bloodshot and violent when he looked up. "I've got a damned plan too. We wait here and kill them all!" he roared, his voice echoing along the treetops.

The men shifted their weight and kept their eyes on their sandals.

"We'll sustain too many losses," I risked to say.

I thought he was about to erupt once again, but instead he said, "And what would you propose, legate?"

"Follow my plan to the letter, and if I fail I'll resign my commission. I'll stand before the senate and people of Rome and accept full responsibility for our losses," I said. "I vow it on my honor."

He inspected me for any doubts. Finding none he said, "Aye."

A bold claim on my part, but if we were defeated, I knew none of us would be alive long enough for it to happen.

There are moments in a man's life that he can look back at in his old age and wonder how differently they might have played out. This was one such moment.

Twelve men abreast, ten cohorts deep. We'd formed our own little Thermopylae. Their best fighters against ours, Herennius at the front. I only feared their phalanx formation—with its sixteen-foot spears and heavy shields—would be too much for our men to resist.

Ajax and I waited on the high bank to the left of our line; the only three hundred allied horsemen we had at our backs.

The men waded in water almost up to their knees. Despite

the sun's heat the water was cold. I knew from experience the feeling in their feet was leaving them. Remaining balanced would be even more difficult, and I only hoped our enemy would struggle the same.

What must the fish have thought? Or the frogs, eels, turtles? I saw red deer as large as our horses in the distance; so used to friendly travelers they spectated our fate with apathy.

I observed the men and knew their lives were about to change forever if they survived at all. Some would bask in the ecstasy and power of taking life. They'd pursue that feeling until the end of their own lives, unable to experience the same thrill any other way. Others would be haunted—seeing the dismembered corpses, tasting the blood, hearing the screams—every time they closed their eyes.

One thing was certain, none of them would be the same. Killing has that effect on young men.

My pondering was interrupted by the rumble of the earth below us. Ajax snorted and whipped his head against his restraints. They were here.

The low beat of a drum carried over the misty waters, each beat matched by their thousands stomping through the water and mud. The birds on the trees above and around us abandoned their branches and scurried off squawking. The red deer vanished. We remained still and the world around us did too. Only our enemy continued to creep forward.

Not so bad, I thought when I first saw them. They looked smaller in stature, and not as numerous as the scouts led us to believe. But they just continued to appear. Their line seemed to never end. And they got larger as they drew near, the scars of their many battles becoming visible on their exposed arms.

I felt almost like I was watching the moment from above, from outside myself. The marching Greeks looked exactly how I imagined the three hundred Spartans at Thermopylae had, or Alexander's world conquerors. The stuff of myth and legend,

Greek's warriors like this were supposed to be extinct with the gorgons and cyclopes.

But this was not the plan. Where was the damn cavalry? If they flanked us, my stratagem failed before it'd began. But what could we do with only three hundred horsemen of our own?

Bile collected at the back of my throat and I threw my head around looking for any movement in the forest on either side of the river.

Then it began.

Massive and muscular horses of the Thessalian strain flooded from the woods on either side of the river, the riders' lances aimed at our front ranks and their voices lifted high.

"Legate?" one of our allied horsemen asked, his hands shaking on the reins of his steed.

"Wait," I said.

If it were possible, the horses increased their speed. The water flew up around them like an angry whirlpool in one of Odysseus' adventures.

"Now!" I raised my fist and the bugle blew.

On either side of the river, the legionaries placed there did as they were instructed. With all their strength they lifted the rope, pulling it taut as it rose from the waters.

Their horsemen crashed into it, their riders flying through the air like an arrow volley into the ranks of our men and their swords. Those behind them tried to skid, but it was too late. Chaos ensued, murky water flying so high and the horses screaming so loud one could barely make sense of it. Stallions were charging in every direction but the one they intended.

I thanked the goddess Diana.

The few horsemen who remained on their steeds wheeled about and bolted off to regroup. But the phalanx still marched on, unperturbed but angry.

"*Pila!*" the faint voice of Herennius cried out from the front ranks.

They let loose a volley and then hunkered down as the

bodies of the struck foe collapsed with them. The second rank stepped up and launched their *pila*. More Greeks collapsed and the water quickly reddened.

The third and forth took their turns, but the rebels marched on. Silent as shades of Hades they filled in the gaps left by their dead, one step at a time to the slow beat of their drummer.

"Sir?" the horsemen beside me asked again.

"Not yet."

Gaia's earth shook as the two lines crashed into one another, an eruption as when a torch is tossed on pitch.

The legions pushed forward; the front ranks batting away their spears to reach them when they could. My eyes locked on Herennius; only his horizontal horsehair plume was visible from the distance. I didn't want to lose another friend, but there was nothing I could do to stop it.

At least Castor was safe with Didius. Perhaps it was the protection of the gods that he'd scorned me. They'd be the most likely to retreat and survive if this went badly. Perhaps he'd forgive me in time and tell my story after I fell.

"Sir, the front ranks are crumbling," the legionary said.

Herennius was a veteran and contained the prowess to protect himself. The recruits beside him were not. Line after line joined him at the front and fell beside him as the first cohort was slowly pushed back.

It was a marvel that Rome was ever able to conquer the phalanx. It was by superior cavalry that we were able to do so, and if my commander had planned better, we might have had more horsemen at our command. But we had three hundred, and three hundred we would use.

Ajax resisted at first, but eventually he followed my orders and moved a few paces forward and wheeled about to face my horsemen.

"Soldiers of Rome," I said. "Live or die this day, we're unlikely to find our names in the annals of history." The wounded continued to cry out for their mothers or for death in increasing measure. "But we'll live or die knowing we served something greater than ourselves. That we gave our lives so that others may live. Your families will honor you and sacrifice on your behalf." Their eyes darted between me and the battle line. "And your ancestors will rejoice at your coming." I unsheathed my sword, the sound so familiar to my ears. I held tight to his mane as Ajax kicked and reared on cue. "For Rome!"

The bugle blew again and I whipped around and charged through the forest.

The two cohorts in reserve split and climbed the riverbank.

I ducked under branches as Ajax swiveled around stumps and jumped over logs.

The standards waved and centurions roared. The cohorts formed up on either side of the river and crashed into the side of the phalanx wall.

We burst into a sunlit glade, and I jerked to the right to see we'd passed the enemy line. I swung my gladius round my head as the cavalry wheeled about, myself at the helm. Ajax pounced into the water, the enemy flank so close down the river.

"Charge!" I bellowed, and my men repeated it.

That stretch of water seemed to last a lifetime. I thought of leaving Nursia, swearing my oath, watching my brother die. I remembered Arrea stitching me up and our wedding, the first time I held Gavius and when I adopted him as my son.

And despite the speed of my heart, I was at peace.

The Greeks spun and cried out to warn their brothers as Ajax crashed into them. I cleaved through a man's helmet beneath me while horses raced through and over bodies on either side of me.

A horn blew again and more ranks of legionaries poured through the forest and fell onto the encircled phalanx.

"Cut them down, kill them all!" I shouted like Mars possessed with the rest of my men.

Spears and shields dropped with the bodies while some scrambled to retreat. They found no mercy, for they met sword tips on the riverbanks rather than freedom.

Ajax cried out and I toppled over him. And crashed into the water, my face colliding with a jagged rock. I rolled over just in time to catch a spear plunging toward my chest.

The battle faded around us. Regardless of defeat or victory, my life only came down to these next few moments.

I pushed back against the spear as the dark-haired Greek put all his weight into it. The water rushed over my head and filled my nose. The spear tip reached my chest.

Fishing with Gavius. On the balcony with Arrea. Drinking with Lucius and Equus.

Not yet.

I heard Diana's voice and obeyed.

In a final surge of power, I wrapped my leg behind his and he slipped on the muddy rocks beneath him. I rose, gasping for air, but wasted no time climbing over him. My fist split his lips, blood mixing with the water like a potion. I pushed him under the water. I looked for my sword. I couldn't find it. I heard the crack first as my head whipped back at the end of his fist. Blood drained from my nose. I shook the cobwebs from my eye and put both hands on his throat. Bubbles ripped from his lips as he gasped, his dark eyes staring from underneath the red water, enraptured.

He threw a thumb into my only eye and dug in hard with untrimmed nails.

I cried out and released my grip. He lifted his head from the water while I struggled to free myself, but Mars came over me then. I struck him in a torrent before he could regain balance and sent him back into the water.

No memories came to mind, no maxims of philosophy or ethics, no hopes and dreams. Only survival.

I kept him submerged with one hand and struggled for the dagger on my calf with the other. Just as my grasp weakened, I freed the blade and jammed it through his bruised throat. The breath driven out from his body, his eyes rolled back into nothing but whiteness and his body jerked.

I gasped for air and looked up to find the phalanx packed in so close they could hardly move their arms. There was nowhere to run. They could only wait to die. I dropped to my knee, my chest tight and throbbing from the exertion. Out of the corner of my eye, I saw cavalry riding. And it wasn't mine.

They'd returned. Most of my men rode on farther, carving up anyone in their path. I was nearly alone. They couldn't change the tide of battle, the brave fools, but they would certainly kill me.

I stood and composed myself. I said a final prayer for protection over my family and tightened my grip around my *pugio* dagger.

They let out war cries as their frightened horses jerked back and forth. I raised the dagger and let it fly.

Rather than taking out the rider I aimed for, they all dropped. Horses flipped and riders flailed to their deaths in a storm of *pila*. I turned quickly to find Herennius standing there, bloody but smiling.

"Take heart, legate! The gods still watch over you!"

The men were exultant, as if we'd won the war and Plataea was already ours. While they cheered and sang songs, I searched for Ajax.

He was on his side, a spear lanced clean through one of his haunches. He was neighing in agony, struggling with all his incredible strength to stand. He quieted when I crouched beside him. His large, longing, wet eyes searched my face for comfort.

I ran my blood-soaked hands over his head. "It's all right, boy." I took off my helmet and sat beside him.

He laid his head in my lap.

I exhaled and stroked behind his ears. "I did not know you

long, Ajax. But you can tell Neptune or whatever awaits you that you died with a friend. And you died bravely." I held the young stallion until the current carried away the last of his lifeblood. I whispered, "Thank you."

Didius spotted me from a distance and came running when I stood. "My boy!" He grabbed me by the shoulders and kissed my cheek. "You've more schemes in that head of yours than even I knew. Well done!"

Blood from my nose dripped onto his cheek, but he already wore plenty of his own.

"It was your leadership, commander—"

"Nonsense," he said. "I don't want to hear it. If I hadn't already given you the grass crown, perhaps I'd give you one now. If I gave you two, though, all of Rome would think I favored you as a lover!" He burst out laughing, joyful and manic in a way I'd not seen him.

"Thank you, sir."

He grabbed my neck, not knowing how bad it was hurting me, and kissed me again on the cheek. "We set out on this voyage together with the shared goal of a triumph. By the gods, we've earned it now!"

I nodded, although we both likely knew a triumph was never my desire.

Castor joined us, his eyes curiously and emotionlessly watching the bodies being dragged from the water around us. He didn't look sad or conflicted. Only empty.

I grabbed his arm. "You did well today, Castor."

He looked up—almost like he didn't know me—his mind elsewhere. "Thank you, legate."

"We still have to take Plataea," Herennius spoke sense, sheathing his blade.

"Yes, yes… of course. Onwards and upwards and so forth," Didius said, unable to stop smiling or take his eyes off me.

"We lost some good men," I reminded him.

He nodded, his mood only slightly affected. "Yes. But we still have the best of us."

Herennius and I exchanged a look, and I lowered my gaze.

Didius peered over my shoulder. "It looks like you'll be needing a new horse. We'll find one with a fallen rider. The best in the legion!"

"Actually, sir," I said. "I have another plan for how we take Plataea. And if we utilize it, I won't be needing a horse."

He shrugged. "I'm not foolish enough to refuse you now." He slapped my shoulder and returned to celebrating with his legion.

I hung my head. I wasn't sure he'd like this plan, though. And I didn't like it either.

SCROLL XXIV

Spurius Insteius

"My feet bled not from the battle but from running. My legs were swollen and throbbing, my back aching and my arms too sore to move properly. My lungs felt like they were full of sand, each breath of the cool night air stung.

"Here, let me take him," Aulus said.

I passed Lucius onto my brother's shoulders, and they promptly continued running as I collapsed. This couldn't be how it all ended. As I lay there in a Lakonian field of poppies, I thought about our speech before the battle. Death seemed so courageous then, so easy to accept. So glorious. But watching Lucius slowly die since the moment we began our retreat stripped away the illusion. *This couldn't be how it all ended*. I ignored my body's groaning and rolled over and pushed myself up.

"Come, Roman, we're almost there," Andro-mache said, helping me to my feet.

What remained of our legion split off for our camp outside the city, to prepare for whatever came next and to heal the wounded. Andromache, however, insisted we get Lucius back to Sparta, where the best doctors in Greece could tend to his wound.

Despite the stories she told us of their medical prowess, I was beginning to doubt even the gods could save Lucius now. If there had ever been a tougher or more robust man than Lucius, I've not met him. He was the symbol of health and virility, eating and drinking only what fueled his body for warfare. How could a single arrow—to the arm no less—be the end of him?

At first we believed he was simply overcome by our tragic defeat. He could barely talk when we made camp the first night. He lay awake, sweating profusely and complaining of an unquenchable thirst.

Andromache and I hurried to Aulus' side, and she gratefully took Lucius onto her own shoulders.

By the morning after the battle, he was changing for the worst. I hadn't seen battle before, and the only death I'd witnessed was the slaughter of our sheep and fowl back in Nursia. I didn't understand the signs, but Andromache did.

"His body is fighting itself," she had said as we watched the color of his skin evaporate and his limbs tremble. She demanded we find horses and get him back to Greece. But even in his haze Lucius refused to abandon his men; so instead we marched on together, resolute and unwilling to break for camp again.

And for the past two days we ran, legs weighed down by exhaustion and dread. We might have stopped if Andromache didn't warn us that his hours were fading.

His breath began to smell of death. Perhaps it was just the battlefield—the stench of battle has a way of clinging to the hair in your nose—but she said this was common of battlefield injuries. Lucius's chest heaved as his heart beat with the power and speed of Hephaestus's hammer. His skin as pale as Nursia snow, only the wound of his arm was swollen and discolored.

It'd been hours since he last spoke or looked up at any of us. Periodically we'd check the pulse in his neck. It was weak despite the throbbing of his heart, but he was still with us, and that was enough to beckon us on.

Andromache moved like a woman possessed, even with Lucius on her back. Aulus and I struggled to keep up as we passed Sparta's threshold.

We passed underneath the giant statues of Castor and Pollux, the ancient protectors of the city. Something about that was ominous rather than comforting, but we followed on until she reached a dilapidated old temple filled with old priests either blind or dull-witted.

Aulus said, "These are the men who will restore him?" He gasped for air.

"Just one of them," she said.

She laid him down underneath an altar to Artemis Orthia.

I knelt beside him and laid my head on his chest. His heart still beat furiously, angrily like a small boat fighting an angrier sea. His flesh put off heat like a pyre.

"Hold on, my friend."

"Diodorus!" she shouted. "Diodorus, we need you!"

Some of the mortified priests echoed the call until a small, frail, unassuming man stepped forward. Despite his unimpressive stature, his eyes shone with courage. When he saw Lucius he rushed to his side and managed to push me from his path.

I said, "This is Lucius Hirtuleius, tribune of the—"

"Nevermind who he is." He turned over Lucius' arm and inspected the wound. His eyes were grave. He lowered his head and exhaled once, deep and long, before snapping back. "I need honey, vinegar, olive oil, and mother's milk," he said. "Leaf bandages sown with wool. Go!" he shouted at anyone listening. "And soak those bandages in unwatered wine!"

"What is happening to him?" I asked, the reality of it all flooding over me as I awoke from what felt like the fever dream of the past two days.

"If only we had tree-nuts. Tree-nut juice would be useful." He brandished a small iron tool and poked at the flesh around the wound, inspecting the color it left.

Aulus said, "No, Lucius breaks out in welts anytime he touches tree-nuts. Has been since we were boys."

"It matters not. We don't have the time," Diodorus said under his breath.

I stomped my foot to gain his attention. "I ask again: what is happening to him?"

"The Greeks call it gangrene."

"What does it mean? Will he live?" I asked.

"He won't if he hears you sniveling like a

coward," the doctor replied. Strange to hear such words from a man his size, but it had the desired effect and I remained quiet.

"The wound has grown infected," Andromache answered for him. "Infection is much more lethal than an arrow."

"Was it poisoned?" Aulus gasped.

"No," the doctor said. "Now be quiet so I may think." One of the old priests brought the requested materials. "Have we any frankincense or myrrh?" he asked.

We shook our heads until he turned to the priests.

The fat old priest looked stunned. "Our offerings here are for the gods."

Diodorus turned back to Lucius and drenched the wound in honey. "The gods would look unkindly on you if you let a supplicant die in your presence."

"Whether he dies or not is out of our control," the old priest said. "It's in the hands of the gods now."

Diodorus turned, his eyes flashing the kind of fury that usually belonged to a much larger man, like a dog who didn't know his size. "Bring me the frankincense and myrrh," he said. "Or the next time one of you fine priests is needing medical attention you might find me unavailable."

The priest bowed his head as if struck with a whip and hurried to oblige.

"Diodorus, thank you. I owe you a great deal," Andromache said, folding her hands together.

"You already did," he said with raised brow. "I'll add this to my ledger."

She smiled but I saw her eyes shimmering when she looked down on Lucius. She felt the heat of his forehead and then ran her fingers through his dusty hair.

"We'll give you some space," I said, nodding for Aulus to follow me.

The air outside was colder and damper than before. If possible, my knees were even weaker too.

"Aulus," I said, "when we go back in we need to prepare our goodbyes."

With a burst he took hold of my breastplate and shook me, teeth grinding and veins bulging. "He would not give up on us! We cannot give up on him."

"I'm not giving up." I considered my words carefully. "But if he falls, we will want him to know how much we…"

"We'll see him again if that's the case." He released me and crossed his arms. "Besides, the gods won't let him die."

"I thought you didn't believe in the gods?"

He looked at me, tears welling up, and threw his arms around my neck. "I'm glad I have you here, brother."

I heard shouting from the *Dromos,* near the statue of Herakles. When I looked up I saw the criers wore Roman armor. I placed my hands around my mouth and bellowed, "Jupiter Optimus!"

They spotted me and charged up Sparta's natural hills to meet us.

"Sir." They both saluted.

"What is it?" Aulus said, blinking his eyes dry. "We told you to prepare the camp."

"Tribune, the... the scouts have returned."

"The rebels are on the move."

Aulus turned to me, and we shared a moment of acceptance. Our fates awaited us.

"How far away?" I said, far calmer than I was inside.

"They took only enough time to lick their wounds," the legionary said. "They'll be here by morning."

I exhaled, pausing to allow this to set in.

"Go to the stables. Gather several carriages for the wounded to be brought to the city. The healthy must prepare themselves," Aulus said. I was surprised to hear him so composed. I was rather expecting him to wretch and his skin to turn green as it had before.

"Moving, sir." They saluted and charged off.

"Let us say our goodbyes," Aulus said, but this time we meant it not for Lucius' pending departure, but our own.

When we returned Diodorus was working diligently on the wound. Andromache sat holding Lucius' head in her lap.

The Greek doctor looked up, his hands covered in our companion's blood. "I have leeches in my quarters. If I could, I'd go and retrieve them, but I'm afraid he'd be traveling the river Styx by the time I return." The doctor scratched his forehead, unaware or unconcerned by the blood he left there.

"Andromache, the rebels have followed us," I said.

Aulus nodded. "They smell our blood in the water and mean to annihilate us before we can receive reinforcements from the north."

She took her own moment to accept this, looking down at Lucius's still and peaceful face, combing back his brows with her thumbs.

"We won't need reinforcements from the north," she said. "I'll muster every warrior in this city. They'll answer my call and rally in our defense."

"How many men?"

"Three thousand will answer my calls. Men and women both," she said with pride.

"How long do you need?" I asked.

"This requires time. The city is sleeping, unaware of what's happening."

"Time is the one thing we don't have." I shook my head.

Aulus placed a hand on my shoulder. He met my eyes, his own filled with resolve. "We will ride out to meet them."

"No, Aulus, no," I said. "We should remain within our fortifications and—"

"We must bide our time. If they reach the city then…" He didn't need to finish his thought. He took hold of me and forced me to look at him. "I understand now. Why we fight, why we kill." A single tear spilled over his eyelid. "Lo there, I see my fathers!" He smiled, with acceptance rather than mischief for once.

I grabbed him by the neck and placed my forehead against his. "Let us go then."

We both knelt by Lucius.

"If we'd had a sister, we'd have let you marry her, Lucius," Aulus said. "Even though you are an ugly bastard." He chuckled, more to his character. "You're a damned good man, a good friend, and a good Roman. I'm no soldier and never will be, but it was an honor fighting alongside you." He stood and turned away before his composure broke.

"Lucius..." My lips quivered as I looked down on his ashen face, Diodorus continuing to work diligently. "The greatest treasure of my life... is... was... your friendship."

His hand slowly reached for mine, and he squeezed it. His eyes, purple rimmed, looked into mine. He said nothing, but he didn't have to.

I kissed his head and stood. We nodded to Andromache and she nodded back. We knew she'd take care of him if we didn't return and weren't likely to.

"Let's go," Aulus whispered.

We took one last look at our oldest friend and rode out to meet our fate.

Lucius Hirtuleius

The sensation of living between two worlds caused me both pain and awe. Sometimes I felt myself, pain radiating from my arm or an itch on my foot. Sometimes I'd wake and see a strange Greek huddled over me, and I wondered what he was about. But at least Andromache was there. Even fading I felt my stomach leap and peace reside.

Then I'd be standing in green fields. Was it Elysium? If so, it was more beautiful than I'd imagined. But it looked a lot like Nursia. And Sertorius and the twins were there too, and I knew they still strode the land of the living.

I saw my arms and legs and they were younger than I remembered, missing all the scars I'd earned over the last decade. We'd play in a crystal blue river and Sertorius wasn't scared of the water. There were deer there and they were friendly as dogs, kneeling by our side and chasing after the sticks we threw. My grandfather Manius was there, his arms folded but a smile on his face, watching us. My little brother Aius was there too, but he was far younger than I knew he was. It'd be so long since I'd seen him, I couldn't imagine what he looked like now.

As we ran and played together, fish swimming to the banks of the river to follow us, everyone I'd ever known appeared on the hillside. They watched us like a play in the forum, and when we did something spectacular, they'd clap and sing our praises. We laughed and cheered with them, but then I woke.

"He's waking!" Andromache's sweet voice whispered, and it nearly put me back to sleep. I nestled my head further into her lap and basked in the rose-pedal scent of her hair.

"If you have something to say to him, I'd say it now," the Greek man said, or so I believed. Perhaps I knew more of their language than I gave myself credit for.

"Can you hear me, Roman?" she said.

"Always." I closed my eyes but felt myself smiling.

"You have an infection. Your body is failing. You must fight."

My eyes split open and I struggled against their

restraint as memories of the battle flooded back to
me. "No!" I shouted as more bystanders rushed to
hold me down. I stopped struggling. "No…" I said,
a few vivid memories of dying legionaries flashing
before my eyes.

"You took an arrow through the arm," she said.
"It has not healed well."

I looked over. Black black leeches were
burrowing their way into a wound much larger
than an arrowhead. They hadn't been there before,
and I couldn't feel them. "Am I going to die?" I
asked, surprised to find that I was at peace with
whatever answer awaited me.

"I won't let that happen," Andromache said,
and I felt her hand brushing through my hair. They
were as rough and callused as a man's, but gentle
and tender nonetheless.

"I'm not sure you'll be able to stop it, my lady,"
I said, briefly fading between worlds again.

"At least he still has his mind," the doctor said.

"Are the leeches not working?" I asked.

"They're eating away the dead flesh as they
ought. Hungry little buggers," the doctor said. "But
we won't know for a few days if they've cleared
away what's ailing you."

I released all the tension in my body and looked
up at the crumbling ceiling of whatever Spartan
building I was in. I always imagined dying would
be more… interesting. I'd always secretly hoped I
would be the first of my companions to go. Not for
contempt of life, but for the love of my friends.
Death had been a part of me since my mother and
father died before I could even shave. Yet I couldn't
lose Sertorius and the twins. I knew it'd break me.

Sertorius would suffer the most. He'd blame

himself… my heart hurt for him. I ached as I recalled the words I last spoke to him. No one on Gaia's earth was ever a truer friend or more dutiful companion. What a fool I'd been. I hoped he'd be able to forget me in time, ignore the empty promises of wine, and enjoy his family as he ought.

"Is there anything we can do, Diodorus?" Andromache asked. "Anything we can do to save him?"

"If we cut off his arm we'd increase his odds exponentially, but even then it's not—"

"Do it," I heard myself say.

They became silent and looked down on me.

"You soldiers tend to value your extremities," the doctor said.

"It serves no purpose to me if I'm dead." I managed to open my eyes and look at him to ensure he understood I was of clear mind. He looked to Andromache.

"Lucius," she struggled to say, "how will you fight and—"

"There are too many words left unspoken to allow myself to die without a fight. To live is to fight, right?" I said. "Sacrifice. And this is my sacrifice."

"Bring us blade and flame," the doctor said.

"Please, use my sword." I pat the gladius with my good hand.

"You could still live, Roman," Andromache said, holding onto me tighter.

"And I could still die if I do this." I craned my head to look back at her. "But we must try."

She swallowed and nodded. "Do it," she told the Greek man.

The cracking of a flame appeared close to me,

the warmth comforting on my sweating but freezing skin.

He pulled my blade from its sheath. I breathed in deep and collected my thoughts. Sertorius would tell me to accept my suffering with dignity. At least I could honor him in this way.

I felt them tie a band beneath my shoulder, and they whispered to each other about holding me down.

"Give me something to bite on," I said. "And I won't fight you." I spoke with confidence as if I knew, but the fever made me feel very assured. I wanted to live but dying in Andromache's embrace wasn't the worst the Fates could have in store for me.

They placed a wooden peg within my teeth and I felt more gatherers huddling around me, their hands grabbing on to my legs and shoulders.

The doctor raised my blade.

My eyes shot open. Spit out the peg. Shouted, , "Hold!" I looked over my shoulder and found Andromache's eyes. "I've lived my whole life as a coward, unable to say what I truly ought. I won't die that way. Andromache, I love you." I waited for her to laugh or gasp, but she did neither. "I know you have no need of a man, but perhaps you might enjoy one... I don't mean... well..." My mind faded again until I realized what I was saying and snapped to. "If I don't survive, I wanted you to know. From the moment I saw you, too... the stuff of myth." My voice faded. "And if I don't... then perhaps we could..." My mind played out all the different endings to that sentence I might have mustered, but I spoke none of them.

Instead a deep, searing pain developed in the

arm I so recently couldn't feel. I bit hard on that wooden peg and screamed through it. My eyes fluttered and I could see nothing. I felt heat like I imagined one might in Hephaestus' forge, and I smelled roasting flesh.

Then I saw the green fields again, and I ran along with my friends some more.

SCROLL XXV

Quintus Sertorius

THEIR ARMOR SMELT AWFUL. But what could one expect from something stripped from those who'd just voided their bowels, bladder, and life blood?

The forward contingent and I marched the way we imagined our living enemy had before we dispatched them. We found their drums and gave them to our bugle players as if they'd know the proper rhythm.

I couldn't imagine we looked like the highly-trained, proficient rebels we'd just fought. Fortunately, we'd had several miles to perfect it before we reached the enemy camp. We had it as good as we ever would, but it still wasn't great. I could only hope those waiting within Plataea were too drunk on wine and victory to notice.

"This armor is chafing me," one of the legionaries said behind me.

"Shut up," I said.

I heard someone empty their stomach behind me.

"Finally, something more pleasant to smell than their armor," another said.

"Quiet. All of you," I said, keeping my eyes fixed on the fortification in the distance.

They must have been strong men, our foe. Those spears were difficult to balance properly, for their length.

I said, "You know your orders?"

"Pretend to be ravenous, treasonous bastards."

"I think we can manage that," another legionary said and his companions laughed.

"We attack on my orders," I said, "and keep the gates open until our legionaries arrive."

It sounded more foolish when I said it aloud than in my head. At the very least, we would be a distraction until Didius arrived over the hill with the bulk of our forces. Whether this was stupidity or bravery, no one could say for certain. The newsreaders in Rome would decide based on our success.

The cheering began as soon as we could see their fortifications in the distance. Horns blew but the rapturous cries still overcame them. It must have been exhilarating to think you'd won a battle against the Roman forces who oppressed you. If only they knew.

"March like you just defeated the world's greatest military force, boys," I said.

"Perhaps we did."

They laughed, but I knew they wouldn't be laughing long. None of us would.

The cheering intensified the nearer we drew. The men marched with swagger as if we were actually returning heroes rather than wolves in sheep's clothing.

Their fortification was not made of walls but of logs sharpened to a point and facing out. Cavalry would be useless here, but we had little left. There was something of a spiked gate at the center, and their guards pulled long ropes to part it.

We marched to the arrhythmic beat, thinning out to enter the gates properly. I swore under my breath, hoping we'd had the formation spaced properly. If we hadn't, the rebels didn't seem to notice.

I remained fixed forward, but my eyes darted back and forth beneath the shadow of my Corinthian helmet. I tried to get a sense of their numbers. There were plenty of them, but I was unafraid. What concerned me was the women and children I spotted spread out amongst them.

That wasn't part of our plan.

When the drums stopped and I called us to a halt, the rebels within rushed to shower us with flower pedals and grain seeds.

If there was some way for me to call it off now, I would've. But there was nothing to be done.

Victory or death—the only two paths left open to us.

A man in white robes and a golden breast plate approached from before us, his arms outstretched and a smile on his face. "Victory, my brothers," he said. "Greece is one step closer to liberation!"

So, this was the Archon. I knew it the moment I saw him. If I was attempting to play the role of an antiquated Greek magistracy, I'd have worn the same thing. His hair was grey and his face chiseled like a statue. Perhaps he already imagined himself as one.

I broke from the formation and felt calmer when I did. *Death waits for no man.* That's what my father said. If this was it, I'd not go without achieving what we set out to do.

A *buccina* sounded. That was the signal. Didius would be charging forward with the bulk of our forces. I turned to ensure our men still blocked the gate. They did.

The Archon was still grinning when he approached. He leaned in to kiss my cheek, but I thrust my spear into his belly instead.

I roared like a Carthiginian lion and weighed down the end until he rose into the air, his intestines spilling out freely. "Attack!" I shouted.

The men dropped their spears and brandished their swords, splitting in every way to meet the closest assailants. None of them had to go far. There were enemies on all sides of us.

I dropped the Archon and he crumbled to the ground twitching like a headless chicken. Cerberus would be howling less now. I pulled out my sword, river water still dripping from the tip.

My eye darted all about, my mind trying to decide what was relevant. Women and children were screeching like harpies, running about in a blur. I stepped back into line with my rounded Greek shield hoisted in front of me as indigent rebels rushed from all sides.

Their haste was their downfall. The first raised his *xiphos* and left his body exposed to my thirsty gladius. His chest split. I made out his cries even in the tumult. I managed to block a club strike from my left, my arm throbbing more than ever. The deflection gave me just enough time to cleave through the man's exposed chest. He convulsed and fell underneath the stomping feet of his companions.

I placed my blade in the divot along the top of the Greek shield, comforted by the presence of the men on either side of me. "Let's end this here, Romans!" I bellowed as I ducked underneath my shield to impede the next assailant.

Our bugles played, and I'd never been so relieved to hear war's call. Didius was arriving. I stabbed through the belly of the man before me and turned to find our legions pouring through the open gate behind us.

I exhaled with relief again. Defeat and death were part of war, but for it to happen as a result of my "plan" was something I'd like to avoid at all costs. They say Fortuna favors the bold; otherwise I might not have spoken about such reckless plans.

A two-handed axe wielded by a beast of a man cleaved my shield from my grasp.

"Legate!" some of the men shouted.

My head whipped against my shield as I crashed into the

270 | WHOM GODS DESTROY

ground. I tasted the iron of blood and felt the jagged tip of a
broken tooth.

A shadow descending over me. As if the gods stole my will
and controlled me themselves I rolled without considering it.
The axe cleaved the earth where I'd been, clumps of dirt bursting
up like sparks from a fire. I didn't hesitate. My head still hazy
and my ears ringing, my blade ripped through the man's leg.

For a moment he stood still and I imagined I was dreaming.
But then the slit appeared beneath the knee, and he cried out as
he fell forward and the rest of his leg went the other way.

I stood and plunged my sword through his burley chest. His
dark, warrior eyes still raged as the blood spilled over his lips
and his grip around my arms fell limp.

The men rushed around me, their shields forming a barrier
like our fortifications outside Athens. I'd never been so proud of
these recruits. I dared not say it, but the nod I extended to them
as I struggled to my feet was enough. They knew what I meant.

"Roma sovereign, Roma victrix!" I heard Didius' voice faint
in the distance.

I felt pride then. I hoped he was proud of me. I prayed he'd
accept me now, even if I didn't know why I cared. I straightened
and let out a war cry that was echoed by all my men. Those that
railed against us stood no chance now. Mars had descended
upon us. "For your Republic, for your families!" I roared. "For
your brothers, and your ancestors!"

They fought like wild dogs. No... like Romans. If there was
quarter to be given, we might have given it to hasten the end of
battle. But there was none. They couldn't escape without passing
through both our pseudo-Greek army and our legionaries. They
knew they couldn't, so they fought to a respectable death as best
as traitors can.

Didius—bold and inspiring as I'd always hoped he'd be—
rushed to the center of the Plataea fortifications when the rebels
were defeated and scrambling. "Legions of Rome!" he said,
smiling with blood on his pearl-white teeth, his eyes stark white

against the scarlet drenching his face. "We have won a great victory!"

The men let back their heads and roared with abandon.

"Now let's secure it!" he said. "Kill them all! Every man, woman, and child!"

The smile dropped from my face as the men broke from their ranks and took off in a frenzy. I lowered my head. Is this what we fought for?

When I looked up, everyone around me was gone, left for their plunder. I sheathed my sword and crashed to my knees on the earth of Plataea. I pulled the Greek helmet from my head. I was sweating and itching awfully. I'd never wanted to sleep so bad in my life.

Pain was pulsating from my left arm throughout my entire body. Still no cause presented itself.

Screams echoed around me, but I kept my eyes on Plataea's soil.

I stayed there for some time. There's no telling how long. I didn't want to look up and see legionaries I respected doing something I abhorred. But they'd been given orders, after all. Just like I'd given orders after the attack on Athens.

I wondered how my father would have acted. I saw his face, his dark hair and the stubble of his beard. I heard the whisper of his voice, repeating maxims of Stoic philosophy, of how a man should live and conduct himself, even in moments like this. He'd served in the legions. Was he ever in a moment like this? How did he conduct himself then, if he was?

Interrupting my thoughts was a singular cry. It cut through all the noise. As if everything else faded to silence I only heard one voice, and it was one I was familiar with.

Castor.

I sprang to my feet and charged toward it, brandishing my sword again whether I'd need it or not.

There was a sunbaked mud hut toward the back of the camp. As if Mercury himself guided me, I knew where to go.

When I entered I found two legionaries restraining him, grins on their faces. Another had a dark-skinned woman pushed over a table with some of her tunic ripped off and the rest of it bunched up to her belly.

"Stop," I said. My grip tightened.

"Don't hurt her!" Castor cried.

"Shut up, pig boy," one of the legionaries shouted.

The Roman standing over the woman turned to me with a twisted grin.

"We have orders don't we, legate?"

"I'm giving you orders to desist," I said. "Now."

The three legionaries looked to each other. They weren't men I knew, and they were emboldened by that fact.

The legionary who was to be first in the deplorable act read-justed himself and turned to me. "She's a whore, see? Her husband was a traitor," he said. "A rebel. A dog. This is what happens to the women of such men. Surely you know that. Right, legate?"

I stole a glance at the woman. She was eastern, Parthian perhaps. She must have come back with one of the mercenaries.

But her eyes contained the same fear as any cornered human I'd ever know. I noticed the small boy in the corner. He was crouched behind a wooden table. His mother's eyes locked on him and her head was shaking. He wasn't properly concealed, but the lust of my legionaries had obscured their awareness.

"She did as any good woman might. She followed her husband where he went," I said. "Now stand down."

"Want her for yourself, legate?" one of the men holding Castor said. "I can't blame you. She's a tasty piece. I'd fault you for being greedy if I thought you didn't deserve it."

I stole a glance at Castor, whose eyes were wet and fixed on the sobbing woman.

A cruel world it was that a boy like Castor was forced to see such things.

I pushed away the thought before I hurt these men more than I ought. "Step away," I said. "Now. Get out of here, or I will hurt you."

They released Castor and approached me. One of them shook his head and clicked his tongue.

"That's not very Roman of you, Legate," he said. "Should we tell the Proconsul you're disobeying his orders?"

"You can tell him what you'd like," I said, pretending that threat didn't worry me. "But if you continue to disobey me, I'll kill you where you stand."

They looked at one another with mock fright, but I saw sweat develop on their foreheads.

Castor, now freed, rushed to the woman. She fought him as if he was an assailant like the rest, but he quickly covered her up with his scarlet cloak.

I watched their eyes bounce from my face to my sword. I knew they were balancing their options.

The woman's face looked eerily like Kirrha's then. I shook my head slightly to break the image, but the feeling in my chest remained.

"Go on then." I heard the Pythia's words then, *Who now greets me? The one covered in the blood of his countrymen.* But it didn't disturb me. If that's what she meant I'd gladly fulfill my destiny.

They tried to laugh, but there was uncertainty in their eyes. If they felt confident they could kill me, I believe they would've. But I stood resolute, my jaw flexing and my sword arm ready to strike. If my status as legate wasn't enough to stay their arm, my superior fighting skill was.

"We hear you, sir. We'll be going on then," the calmest of them said, tugging at his friends to avoid a confrontation.

When they were gone, I exhaled a breath I didn't know I'd been holding in.

"Can you speak Greek?" I asked the woman. Reluctantly she nodded. I looked to Castor. Eventually he looked at me. "We're going to get you and your son out of here."

She seemed surprised that we'd noticed him but asked him to come out when she accepted it.

Castor and I walked out before them to ensure no one had their eyes on us. Everyone was too focused on the pillaging to care. Even the legionaries from the hut had moved on to new targets.

There were stables in the distance, and luckily they hadn't been lit on fire yet with the rest of the fort.

I offered the woman assistance onto a brown Boeotian horse, and Castor helped the child up behind her.

She looked at me as if I had horns or one eye... well, one eye like a Cyclops. With a thick accent, she said, "Thank you."

"Go and do not look back," I said, and slapped the rear of her horse, sending it flying from the stables and through the gate of the fort.

Castor and I stood there alone.

He met my eye for the first time in a while. He didn't have much to say, but then again neither did I. He nodded. And that was all I needed.

I walked a few paces and plopped down on the ground. As if the gods led me to just that spot, red and yellow flowers rose up from the weeds beside me. I plucked them and tucked them safely into my belt.

Then I lay back. And despite the chaos, I fell asleep.

SCROLL XXVI

Spurius Insteius

"We lined the men up in full battle array, a little more than half of what we had when we entered Corinth. Those who marched out with us were battered and bloody too, but if they could carry a sword and stand in a shield wall they joined us.

Aulus and I had no mind for stratagem outside of the very obvious, but Lucius and Sertorius had taught us the basics of terrain before we departed Rome. We positioned ourselves with our left flank at a small body of water. A man could wade through it if he had a mind to, but it would be enough to slow their phalanx and that was all we could hope for. Behind us was a hill. We considered fighting from the high ground atop it, but we chose this terrain to make retreat nearly impossible, and I prayed that would make our men fight harder.

A few horses were drawn up, no more than

thirty. A vanguard at best, not large enough to function as a real tactical unit.

Aulus' eyes were bloodshot from exhaustion and fatigue, but his wily smile spread across his face as he thought of something mischievous.

"One of us should lead the horse. It'll give us the ability to charge from flank to flank where the men are faltering. The other should stand at the front lines," he said.

"What would you propose?" I asked.

His grin grew. "I know it might be crass..." He pulled out a pair of bone dice.

"Leaving it to the gods. Nothing crass about that."

"Highest number takes the front, and the glory it deserves."

He rolled, and I followed him. My number was higher, six to four.

"I guess that settles it then." He threw on his helm and buckled it beneath his chin. He placed his forehead on mine again. "I'll see you on the other side," he said. I didn't know if he meant on the other side of battle, or on the other side of death.

He swung himself on top of a horse and nodded for the cavalry to follow him. I took a moment to compose myself before squaring up before the legion.

"Legionaries of Rome," I said. All were silent, the only sound was our muddy standards flapping in the wind. "You all know why we're here. The rebels have come to annihilate us. They have us trapped here in southern Greece. There is nowhere to go, and there are none coming to our rescue."

Their eyes glazed over as the truth settled in their hearts. I could see in their eyes the sorrow and knowledge that they'd never see their families again, never love another woman, never drink another cup of wine.

I shook my head. "There is no retreat. If we try, they'll flood into Sparta and butcher us all. We must stand and fight, to the grave if it's what the gods require of us. But even now our brave allies within the city are rallying a defense. We must hold out until the morning light."

"Where is Tribune Hirtuleius?" one of the legionaries asked, and several others nodded.

I hung my head. "He is wounded badly. But he fights for life as he would implore us to. We fight for him today. He believes in us. Let us make him proud!"

Bruised and bloody, they still beat their shields and lifted their voices. We would need whatever inspiration we could muster.

Finding nothing more to say I walked to the front ranks and stepped into the space opened for me. I placed my shield along theirs. A few of them looked my way and nodded, knowing if they died, I would die with them. None of us would be going to Elysium alone.

We perked up our ears when we heard a dull thud in the distance. It grew nearer. The sound of a drum, four thousand feet stomping on each beat.

"They cannot surprise us this time, men!" Aulus shouted from his horse behind us. "No shadows for them to hide in. They face us in the open now. We are Romans. We've beat the Greeks before and we'll do so here!"

"No mercy shown, no quarter given!" I screamed.

A blur of armor and spear tips appeared along

the horizon. They marched in perfect unison, one cohesive unit. I hoped they fought with less discipline.

Our eyes were locked on the enemy, each man's teeth grinding and knees shaking. Some urinated, others wretched. Some whistled in an effort to stave off the reality of their fear.

"Jupiter!" I shouted.

"Optimus!"

"Jupiter!"

"Maximus!"

They lifted their voices higher. I raised my sword above the shield wall, the tip gleaming in the moonlight.

"Jupiter!"

"Optimus!"

They would hear us, and I prayed fear struck their hearts.

"They march slower than patricians run, don't they?" one of the men said.

"Don't stop, let them hear you! Let them know your name, let them fear you. Jupiter!"

They outnumbered us. But I saw no cavalry. That was good—or bad, if they were moving to flank us. Nothing to do now.

"Let loose!" I shouted, and our first ranks sent their *pila* volley. The rebels cast aside their splintered shields and reformed. The next rank stepped up, but most of our supply had been spent in Corinth.

"Out sword," I bellowed as three thousand blades sang from their scabbards. "Brace!"

The force of their spears crashing into our wooden scuta sent us back, our sandals digging into the damp Lakonian soil. The men grunted. There was no time for war cries now.

The line broke. Some of our men charged their ranks, and others broke into ours. They smelled our blood, and we could smell theirs too.

"Stand in formation, stand in formation!" I shouted but couldn't even hear myself. The din of arms was already overwhelming, dizzying.

The battle before us was as close to our training as the corruption of Roman politics was to Plato's Republic. Not a man amongst us fought as he was trained, the chaos stripping away whatever discipline we'd formed.

I stepped back into the second ranks and scanned the legion as best I could. I could see nothing but swords shimmering in the starlight, hear nothing but smashing shields and agonizing cries. I hoped the flanks were faring better, but how could I tell?

"Protect your standards! Protect your brother!" I heard Aulus' voice come and go as the small cavalry unit flew behind us toward the right flank. I took a deep breath. Had they been flanked?

A spear tip flashed before my eyes, striking the man beside me. I stopped thinking and turned to push my way back to the front. There was nothing I could do about the others. Nothing I could do to save my brother. All I could do was fight and hope my men would fight and die with me.

I lifted my shield and bore my weight against it, charging into spears and deflecting them from my path. "On me!" I shouted and they pushed up beside me.

As we battered into their line, the front ranks dropped their spears and brandished the sharpened *kopis*, the only blade to conquer the world except the one we wielded. And these Greeks knew how to wield it like their ancestors.

The wood of our shields splintered as the curved blade hacked away at us. I lurched forward with my gladius. Ducked so low beneath my shield, I couldn't even see the rebel, but I heard his screams and felt the warm blood traveling down my blade and onto my hand.

"To the tribune!" some men behind me shouted.

Beside me a legionary stood straight, with neither sword nor shield in hand. His head was bloody and his helmet missing. He looked at everything around him as if it were merely curious, like a dream.

"Legionary!" I shouted.

But he did not move. A kopis ripped through his shoulder blades and exited beneath his sternum. He crumbled without crying out.

I crossed to the assailant and bashed my shield into his nose. His head whipped back but his resolve was strong. Before I regained balance he was hacking away at my shield. I stumbled back, trying to find solid ground between the bodies of the dying and corpses of the dead. Agile like an athlete, he kicked my shield away.

His own shield, circular and gilded, slashed across my face, crushing my cheek and two teeth cascading from my lips.

Cassia will curse me for that, I thought. Her image appeared before my eyes as clear as the snarling Greek. How easy it was to forget home when you suppose you'll never return. But that blow and my own vanity reminded me.

He stabbed forward as I dropped my shield. I

stepped to the side as the blade sliced through my breastplate. I felt no pain. He stumbled on the legionary he'd killed, and I wrapped my arm around his. I brought my blade up, Cassia's bright eyes still flashing before mine. I butted my head into his nose; then I severed his arm beneath the shoulder.

I dropped the severed limb and stabbed through his chest, pushing with all my weight until the bones of his ribcage snapped and it slid easily to the hilt. I wedged the gladius free and kicked him back into the ranks of his men. "Reform! Reform!" I cried as the men did what they could to rejoin their shields.

Diana's moon had disappeared. The sky was turning blue. But our ranks were thin and our men faltering. We couldn't last much longer, even without retreating.

I heard a familiar voice on the other side of the rebels. A rebel leading from a single chariot, shouting out encouragement to his men. Even with the Corinthian helm covering most of his face, I could tell it was Meleagros, his bronze skin and thick jaw unmistakable.

Aulus must have seen him too, for he let out a cry and led the cavalry straight toward him.

I watched them descend past the right flank. There were few horsemen remaining, but I kept my eyes on the purple tribune's plume of my brother's helm.

A horse's scream broke through the tumult. The beast reared up on its hind legs, and I saw my brother fall into a swarm of rebels.

The breath was driven from my lungs. I felt the pain of the fall myself. My twin, the Castor to my

Pollux, my dearest friend. Life was impossible to imagine without him, so I chose not to do so.

"Fight, fight to your deaths!" I shouted, picking up my shield. "To death!" The men repeated my cry.

I wouldn't live if my brother died. He was always a greedy bastard. Of course he meant to leave me here—he to glory and I to agony and regret. We'd followed each other everywhere our entire lives. This was no day to stop.

A pike ripped through my shield, the wood caving in. It missed my forearm by a frog's hair. I lifted it high and charged to impale the defenseless spearmen. He dropped the spear and I dropped my shield. He wrapped his arms around me with their waning strength while I twisted the hilt. He almost embraced me as his legs gave out.

A *kopis* sliced down through my forearm from somewhere in the tumult. Exposed bone was stark white against the blood which poured out in pulses. At least I wouldn't live long enough to develop an infection like Lucius.

Horns blew far behind us. They'd flanked. Their cavalry had flanked us, and this was the end.

All our eyes—on both sides of the battlefield—looked up to the hill. One lone rider looked down on us, dark and shrouded. For a moment I thought I was envisioning a god.

To reinforce the theory, Athena herself appeared by his side, atop a strong white horse like Pegasus. A cloud broke and the twilight illuminated Andromache's face.

The rider lifted his sword with one arm, and I saw he was missing the other.

Horns sounded again, and riders appeared all around the hilltop, enveloping it.

"Charge!" the rider roared, and the voice was unmistakably that of my friend, Lucius.

"Fight on, men, fight on!" I shouted.

The rebels, stunned by the thunder of horsemen charging down the hill, stumbled back and broke ranks. Our legions parted, the wind of the cavalry flying past us nearly toppling us over. They pounced over the faltering shield wall and down onto the rebels. Lucius slashed and stabbed wildly with a longsword, the reins wound tight around his shoulder. His flesh ghostly pale like a shade of Hades but his eyes full of fire like Vesta's flame.

"Roma victrix!" the men shouted.

I fell to one knee and bore my weight on my sword. Tearing a scrap from the tunic of a dead legionary I dressed my wound. I still couldn't feel it. There was only the throbbing in my head, and the ache in my heart.

Pluto had denied me.

But at least Sertorius wouldn't. Sertorius would be proud.

 It took some time before all the rebels could be butchered. But there was nowhere to run. Lucius, Andromache, and their Spartan cavalry would have chased them to the ends of the earth.

Andromache herself cut the head from the treacherous Polemarch, bringing Meleagros' head to Lucius like a present. He held it up by a tuft of hair, then frowned and threw it into a pile of the rebel corpses.

I approached him. His eyes were glazed over now, and I knew the last of his stamina was wasting away by the moment. I wept when I saw his missing arm. He wept when he saw I was amongst the living. We found no words to share, so we embraced again.

He pulled away and said, "Men of Rome." The legionaries set down the bodies of the legionaries they'd been gathering and listened in. "We're going home. We're going home."

Their grateful cries lifted to the heavens, and it must have touched the gods for their tears soon filled the battlefield in a rain shower.

Lucius clapped me on the back of the neck. He shook his head, still struggling to believe it all.

"You bastards sure do have a habit of forgetting about me."

I turned to find my brother standing there, blood-covered but still wearing his infamous smile.

"Aulus!" I shouted as we both ran to him.

His eyes flooded with tears, but the moment I opened my mouth he burst out into laughter. He doubled over and placed his hands on his knees, barely containing himself.

"Why, by all the gods, are you laughing?" I asked, incredulous.

He reached out and pinched my cheeks to see my missing teeth.

"*Now* who's the handsome brother?"

I pushed his arm away and wrapped him up. "You fool. I saw you fall."

He shrugged. "If I widowed Balbina, there's

nothing the Polemarch or anyone else in Greece could do to match her fury."

"Surely the gods have made a mistake," Lucius said, matching Aulus' furtive grin. "How could such a poor swordsman as yourself survive a battle like that?"

Aulus clapped his shoulder. "If you had trouble pleasing a woman with two arms, I fear you'll have no chance with just the one."

We collected wood and the bodies of our fallen. Priests from the city came and offered rites, praising their heroism I knew the rest of the Republic would not.

It took all the pitch in Sparta to light the fire in that downpour, but once lit the flame roared with the force of each spirit it carried to the river Styx.

We each approached the pyre and said our farewells to so many men we loved like brothers but barely knew. One by one we departed and did not look back.

Lucius was right. We were going home after all.

Lucius Hirtuleius

 I remember so little of that battle, or the immediate aftermath. I remember even less of losing my arm or the pain I'm sure it caused. It was a wonder I was up and walking. If it hadn't been for some concoction of the tiny Greek doctor's, I'm not sure I'd have been able to stand. But it would take more than a missing extremity to keep me from fighting with my men. When I learned they were fighting, I demanded in my haze that they give me whatever I required to go out and fight. Andromache disapproved, but she understood—she was a warrior herself.

When the battle was over and the bodies were burned, we deconstructed our camp and gathered what little we had with us. The Spartan elders graciously offered a carriage to bear me home, for they rightfully assumed I wouldn't be able to remain atop a horse for three days, regardless of the potions I drank.

A legionary opened the carriage door for me.

I clapped him on the shoulder to show my thanks for what he and all the men had done. I sat on the edge for a moment. I was ready to return home. I was even more anxious to see Sertorius. To say the things I feared I wouldn't be able to say.

But there was something keeping me in Sparta, and I feared to leave. Then that reason approached before me, her smile making my stomach leap as it had the first time I saw her.

"You won a great battle today, Roman," she said.

I shook my head. "I have you to thank for that." My mind flooded with all sorts of things I'd like to say. I reddened when I remembered actually saying some of them. "I recall saying some strange things in my haze... I... I ..."

She leaned in and kissed me. I felt her pull away, but she couldn't yet. Her breath so fragrant, her touch so warming, I could no longer feel the pain of my amputation. With the only hand I had left I ran my fingers through her hair. My callused fingers etched the lines of her soft face.

Her eyelashes batted bashfully when we parted.

"I didn't know you felt the same way."

"I didn't either." She looked down. "Eros—or Cupid as you call him—abandoned me after being treated the way I was," she said. "I did not know to look for his arrow."

"If I could go back and kill them all, I would," I said and meant it.

"I know you would. And I would too. But the damage has been done."

"So you cannot love again?"

A sad smile parted her pink lips. "Perhaps I already have."

I stood and took one of her hands within my own. "So then you'll return with me to Rome?"

She blinked a few tears but they clang to her lashes. "This is my home. These are my people, and they need me," she said. "now more than ever."

"Andromache... I..."

"I wish I could." A tear fell freely now.

I pulled her in closer. "In another life then?"

"In another life..."

I squeezed her hand and kissed the tear from her cheek. "I will never forget you, Andromache."

"Stay with me," she said.

I stammered, "My ... people..."

She nodded. She understood.

The few centurions still remaining called for the men to line up. It was time to leave.

"There will always be a home for you in Sparta."

I wrapped her up in my arm, finding her more fragile and delicate than I'd imagined. I smelt the fragrance of her hair, and for a moment all slowed down around us.

"In another life," I said.

"In another life."

I kissed her once more, and savored it till the last moment.

The buccinae sounded and the legions started their march. I closed the carriage door behind me and my driver whipped the reins.

I watched her until she faded back into the city of warriors, knowing a piece of my heart remained with her.

SCROLL XXVII

Quintus Sertorius

I WAS FAR TOO familiar a presence to need to knock at Niarchos'
now. Besides, I hoped to surprise them. I gently pushed open the
unlocked doors and crept through on cat's paws, hoping I might
find Kirrha in the hallway and jump out to give her a fright. I
followed the sound of a harp to the courtyard and leaned up
against the doorway to look in before anyone could see me.

Kirrha was the one playing, and Anthea stood beside her
tossing seed to the house birds while listening intently. Niarchos
had brought his potter's lathe in from his workshop, and Anaiah
was working on it while he stood behind her.

"If you add a little more water the clay will be more pliable,"
he said, leaning down and assisting.

Then I saw Anaiah smile. The first time I'd seen it—so sweet
and innocent—unmarred by the cruel machinations of evil men.

"It's a good thing to see, isn't it?" Apollonius said quietly
behind me.

I jumped with a start, finding myself the victim to my own schemes. "Did you miss me?"

He shrugged. "We hardly noticed you were gone." He grinned and embraced me. "I'm so thankful you've returned to us."

I looked back to the courtyard where the lathe started spinning out of control, muddy clay flying about. But Anaiah and Niarchos were laughing.

"I'm glad I've returned as well. I'm ready to go home."

"You know I'm coming with you?" Apollonius' grey eyes became serious.

I swallowed, relieved but somehow sad as well. "I did not know that. I'm thankful to hear it though. There will always be room for you and Anaiah in my home."

He shook his head. "No... I think Anaiah will be staying here."

"What?"

He nodded to the room. "Look. They have a family. Niarchos and Anthea were made to raise children. Kirrha and Anaiah both need a sister. My God or your gods have orchestrated this arrangement, and I'll not be the one to disturb it," he said. "Besides, I go wherever you go. And where we go isn't pleasant. No place for a sweet young girl."

"Where do we go exactly?" I said, facetiously.

"Back to Rome." He exhaled. "I debated on telling you this... but in your absence I opened your mail as instructed." He waited for me to signal for him to continue.

"Go on."

"The Tribune Marcus Drusus was assassinated in Rome, and the city has fallen into chaos." He slowed now and I could tell he was struggling to finish. "Gavius writes that he and Arrea have taken up in the home of Sulla, under his protection."

My heart sank, but I stayed my panic. Fear and anger could do nothing for me now, so I swallowed them down for a time when they might be more useful.

I forced a smile. "We need to return home quickly then." I entered the garden but then stopped and turned again to my friend. "You've just found Anaiah after all this time. I'll hate myself for separating you again."

His eyes stared past me at Niarchos and his niece as they had begun throwing clay at one another. "I'll say again: I go where you go. To battle, to your Hades, or to my Gehenna. Like it or not, we're one now. And besides," he said. "I'd rather know that she's here—safe and in the arms of a loving family. This is all I could've ever wanted."

I could find no words to express my unending gratitude, so I embraced him firmly instead.

"Look who has returned," I said when I entered. "just as I promised."

"Quintus!" Kirrha shouted as she and Anaiah ran to greet me.

I embraced each in their turn and then knelt to dig through my satchel. "And at your request I've brought you..." I pulled out red and yellow flowers to find them smushed in my bag. The pedals were still attached, but they drooped like a frown. I was probably more upset than the girls. "I apologize. I thought I'd protected them."

The girls both took them from me and pretended they loved them regardless.

"It matches the color of my eyes," Kirrha said. "I'll use mine as a bookmark in one of Apollonius's scrolls." She twirled with delight.

"You'll have to learn to read first, dearest." Apollonius chuckled.

"I think it's perfect." Anaiah placed hers behind her ear, and under a curl of golden hair. "Thank you, Quintus," she said.

"Unfortunately there's not much else from the battlefield you'd find of use." I turned to Niarchos and Anthea, "You two however..." I tossed a bag of coins that struck Niarchos in his chest.

"Now, do not insult me." Niarchos huffed like he usually did.

I shook my head. "The spoils of war. Certainly it should be shared with my gracious hosts?"

He stepped forward and held out the purse. "I cannot accept this. I am your friend and duty binds me to—"

"Oh, that's not for you," I said. "That's for her." I pointed to Anthea as everyone chuckled. "Someone should pay the woman for putting up with you."

A tear slid down Anthea's face as she hugged me again.

"Thank you, Quintus," she said, better at accepting kindness than her husband.

"It's I who should be grateful," I said. "You deserve all the gold in the world for the love you've shown these girls."

Niarchos managed a smile and placed a meaty hand on the girls' shoulders.

"We're grateful you brought them into our home. The gods have truly blessed us," Anthea said, smiling but with a tinge of sadness in her eyes.

I grinned, knowing how delighted they'd be when Apollonius and I told them of our plan. They'd be the consummate family, the kind poets write about and tutors encourage young children to pursue. Their names would be lost to the sands of time, but they'd never have to suffer the brutality of warfare, sedition, or political violence.

And for that, I was grateful. Another sacrifice needed to be made to Diana.

The camp was still being constructed when I returned. The men were moving slowly, both as a result of our depleted ranks and the fact that the rest of them were hungover from the wine of celebration.

"Look like you're happy to be serving, boys," I said as they groaned. "We'll be leaving soon."

Didius' praetorium was only partially constructed in the center of camp, but I knew I'd still find him within.

"There he is," Didius said as I entered. "The man of the hour."

He ignored my salute and embraced me as a dear friend.

Kallias was beside him, smiling. "Your commander has been regaling me with stories of your brilliance."

"All exaggerated, I'm sure," I said, kissing the priest's cheek.

Didius rolled his eyes. "Nonsense. I stand nothing to gain by exaggerating the exploits of anyone but myself. We'll just see if I'm still feeling as gracious when I stand before the senate." Didius winked and poured me a cup of wine.

We all lifted our cups and took a sip.

"It's quite amazing what a man can do when he's anxious to return home," I said. "That's all there was to it."

"You give yourself too little credit," Didius said. "But I'll be happy to collect for myself the credit you leave on the table."

We laughed. It finally felt like this nightmare had concluded, like waking from the dream of the woman in the forest. It was behind me now, and difficult to imagine that it was even all real.

"So much for the gods' curse," Didius said.

"Perhaps we've done enough to assuage them." I shrugged.

Kallias nodded. "The gods are quick to forgive courageous men," he said. "Still, I think you should sacrifice in their honor."

"Agreed," Didius said. "To whom should we pay restitutions, legate?"

"We're in the city of Athena," I said. "To whom else should we sacrifice?"

"Very well. We should sacrifice to Athena Parthenos. Perhaps we can do so this evening."

Kallias shook his head. "I'm afraid the Acropolis is shut down to visitors for the evening." He smiled. "Even visitors as illustrious as yourselves. Tomorrow perhaps?"

"I was planning to march out with the men in the morning," Didius said.

"To assist the men in the south?" I asked.

"Gods no. Have you not heard? The seventeenth legion won a major victory over the rebels in Lakonia. They've found and assassinated the Polemarch and are on route to join us presently."

I nearly spilled my drink with relief, so I took a sip instead.

"I guess you're ready to move on then?" Kallias said, a tinge of sadness in his voice. "I'm glad there are no more battles to be fought, but I'm disappointed to see you go."

"What about the third member of Cerberus? The guardian of Hades is said to have three heads, does he not?" I asked.

Didius waved it off. "No matter. Let the bastard cling to the shadows. The gods will see him to justice soon enough. But for now, their armies are crushed. They are a ship at sea with a torn sail. We've won and they know it," he said. "All those who seek to defy Rome have a shining example of why they shouldn't. The Archon's severed head should be proof of that."

"So we really are ready to leave then?" I said, still struggling to believe it.

"We should be back in Rome before month's end. I've sent word for the ships to prepare for boarding on the western banks of Megaris."

A beam of light stretched throughout the tent when a flap opened. Castor stepped inside.

When he saw me, he didn't look away, but met my eye and nodded. I saw a bashful smile develop as mine grew as well. "Have you any need of me, Proconsul?"

"I do have a final order," Didius said, straightening like he was about to give some grave and arduous task. "I release you back into the command of your legate. May you continue to bear his shield with courage and excellence."

He let his smile shine now, and I reached my hand out to clasp his.

"Thank you, sir," he said. He turned to me and whispered, "I've been making some new wood carvings. I think you'll really like them. One of them is supposed to be a dog from your missing friend's house."

"I'll get my coin ready." I smiled and was as relieved to have Castor back at my side as I was to leave Greece. It's difficult to explain why, but some people just have a way of bringing peace into your life. Castor was such a person, and even then I knew those people were too important to let go. There isn't enough of them.

"Back to the sacrifice," Didius said. "I could leave you behind with a contingent of men to perform the ceremony. After you've concluded you can meet us on the path to Megaris. Acceptable?"

"What do you say, legionary Castor? Would you like to sacrifice to the gods with me? We can earn cleansing for all the bad things we've done and pray for their protection on the journey home."

He grinned his boyish grin and nodded. "I'd like that."

"Who else should stay behind?" I asked.

Didius shrugged. "You can ask the men yourself if you'd like. I doubt many of them will volunteer for double the marching and standing through a religious ceremony for hours on end."

I chuckled. "You may be right about that." I turned to Kallias. "Can we go in full kit?"

He shook his head. "If you go armed and in armor you might risk offending the gods. Better to go as civilians, if you can manage it."

I stretched and tugged at my chainmail. "I'm ready to get this damned thing off anyhow."

"Will you join us, Kallias?" Castor asked, sheepishly.

The old priest smiled and placed a wrinkly hand on Castor's shoulder. "No, my boy. These past few years have weighed heavily on my old bones," he said. "and my wine cellar has remained woefully neglected throughout. I believe I'll retire to my quarters and sip in my own little ceremony to the gods." He smiled and turned to me. "But something tells me the gods will be smiling on you."

"That would be a welcome change," I said.

We laughed, free from care and concern for the first time in as long as I could remember.

SCROLL XXVIII

Quintus Sertorius

THE KNIFE CUT DEEP, and the victim made no sound of resistance with his dying breath. Blood seeped out and ran through the cracks of the marble altar.

I waited patiently for awhile, but Didius was right in his prediction that the ceremony would last several hours.

We were ready to go home. The men were restless and moving at attention far more than they were supposed to. I would have chastised them if I didn't feel the same way.

I gestured for Castor and the rest of the fifty or so odd men who joined us to remain in place. I scaled the steps to the altar of Athena Polias and the two young priests as they directed the blood into a pewter cup. "What does it look like?"

One of the young priests smiled and pulled down his hood. "The gods demand more sacrifice," he said. "but they favor you."

I smiled and exhaled. All I needed was to receive another bad omen before we got back on those damned boats.

"We'll let you tell them," the other priest said as they stepped down from the altar.

I knelt before the sacrifice for a moment and placed my hands on the cold stone. The simple offerings of Athenians were strewn about all around the goat, everything from apples to burnt offerings. I prayed they received Athena's blessing as well. I stood and turned to the men.

They waited, praying their own prayers that the gods favored us, and we could travel back to Italy in safety.

"Men of Rome." I paused for the theatrics of it all, determined to keep them waiting as long as I could. "The gods favored us!"

The fifty men yelled like they were five hundred, breaking ranks and throwing their arms around one another in mutual joy.

"You can now approach the altar, one by one, to say your individual prayers. When we've concluded, as Athena dines on the fumes of our sacrifice, we shall dine on the meat." They cheered again. Like me, they were ready for something more substantial than the slop they gave us in camp. The priest tapped me on my arm to remind me. "Oh... yes. You may purchase turtle doves from the priests if you'd like to make a sacrifice of your own."

"At a discount," one of the priests added.

I strolled back down to the men as a few of them hurried up to get their prayers out of the way.

"Do you think the gods have forgiven us?" Castor asked.

I smiled. "I don't think you have anything to ask forgiveness for, my boy," I said. "but I hope they've forgiven me."

He shrugged, unsure of himself. "I think they've forgiven you. I have."

"You have?" I said, throwing my arm around his shoulders and leading him away from the formation.

We passed by the Erecthyion where Athena and Poseidon were said to have fought over the patronage of Athens. Poseidon struck water from the ground by throwing his trident from the heavens. Athena raised the first olive tree from the ground. We all know who won.

Castor didn't know the history of it all but was fascinated nonetheless. We'd spent all this time in Greece, and spent so little time here, in this sacred place.

I led him around the precipice, past the sanctuary of Zeus, and looked out over the city with him. Breathtaking. We could see the Areopagus, beneath which we stormed the slave quarters. We could see the neighborhoods of the cloth dyers, and across from it the neighborhood of the potters, where I'd been living with Niarchos all this time. We could see the unfinished temple of Zeus as well, the one which had remained unfinished for centuries as a rebellion against tyranny.

"You see that mountain?" I said. "That's Mount Pentelicus. All the marble used to construct these temples were brought from there."

"Really?" He squinted his eyes. "It's awfully silly for them to go so far. What about these mountains here?"

I laughed. "They wanted to make sure the marble was of perfect quality—a testament to the human spirit which will carry on through all time."

He appeared lost. "How do you know so much?"

"I read a lot of old books."

"I'd like to learn how," he said.

I patted his shoulder. "And I'll teach you if I'm given the chance."

We walked farther down the line, spotting more and more of the city, places we remembered, and places we couldn't recall at all.

"So you'll be returning to Rome?" He looked downcast.

I exhaled. "That's correct. Legates only serve for the duration of the campaign. Now I've been called back."

He swallowed. "What will happen with me then? Will I be another legate's shield bearer?"

That was a question impossible to answer. The truth was it was extremely unlikely another legate would give such a position to a random legionary like Castor—even less likely that they'd put up with his childlike ideations and peculiar behaviors. The next legate would curry favor with a powerful family by giving the position to one of their sons. Castor would probably be sent back to the front lines. The thought made my stomach churn. What use did Rome have in making a simple young man like Castor take life? He could serve far better anywhere else… caring for the horses in the *Veterinarium* or working with a needle and bandages in the *valetudinarium*.

"Don't talk about that now," I said. "You'll make me jealous."

He laughed and rolled his eyes. "He probably wouldn't even like my carvings."

"Like it or not, we're both men of the legion now." I stopped and stared out over the city, the people busying about like ants, safe because we'd fought to ensure it. "I plan to return to my family and take a long holiday," I said. "But after that, I'll be back in full kit. And when I am, I'll write to your commander and request your transfer to my command."

He looked at me with his big, wet, unassuming eyes. "Really?"

"You can count on it. On Jupiter's Black Stone," I said. "Who else can I trust to watch my back? Apollonius? I'd wind up with a spear through it while he's reading Aristotle."

"Roman," a voice sounded from behind me. I turned to find a Greek man with his head bowed low.

I approached, still full of humor. "What can I do for you, Greek?"

"I have a message." He extended a carefully sealed scroll.

I flexed my jaw. "Who sent it?"

He shook his head. "Please don't make me say."

I turned back to Castor and nodded for him to rejoin the men. The moment I took the scroll, the messenger sprinted off like he wore Hermes wings. I unfurled the letter and began to read.

> *Greetings, Son of Rome,*
> *In this moment there are likely many you would seek to blame. Your enemy, your commander, your gods. But no, Roman, it is your own hubris and folly which have brought you to this pass.*
> *You have only two options: you may either die like a man or die like a coward. Either way, I do you a curtesy by sending this letter. Prepare yourself for the afterlife. The spawn of Cerberus are ascending upon you as we speak.*
> *The Martyr*

I rolled up the scroll, still trying to make sense of it all. So the third member of Ceberus, this Martyr, was still at large. And he sought our doom.

"Legate?" one of the men said, noticing my expression.

I pushed the letter into his hands and ran toward the Propylaia, the Acropolis' monumental gateway. There I looked out over the entire city of Athens, and the odeon of Herodes Atticus. Those ant-like people were massing up, just as the letter described. And they were moving up the winding path toward us.

"Legate, what is it?" Some of the men had followed after me.

"Rally the men before the Parthenon," I said. "Go!"

I watched the gathering horde, trying to assess their numbers and their armament. I couldn't get a clear description or a clear count, but I knew we were vastly outnumbered. With Didius' army halfway to Megaris, and my men stuck on this sacred rock, there was nowhere for us to go. I assume the Martyr and I had little in common, but at least there was one thing we could agree on. The only option left to us was to die like men or die like cowards.

It was an easy choice for me.

"We've been betrayed, men." I paced before them, acting as if I had a plan but all the while trying to devise it. "Someone whom we trusted has betrayed us. They knew we would be here while the rest of the army left. They knew we would be unarmed and without protection." I hung my head. "But believe me when I say this: justice will be served." I looked around us.

The Acropolis was deserted. The priests were nowhere to be found. Even the animals which had been scurrying about seemed to have disappeared. But the altar where we'd sacrificed contained a roaring flame.

I considered the meaning, but I was no priest or augur, so I turned back to my men. "The only way to leave this place is down that hill—through the Propylaea—where our enemy are now ascending." I met each of their eyes. They still searched mine for hope and answers. I wished I had more to offer them. "All we can hope to do now is die well. How would you like to be remembered? I know I'd like to be remembered as a hero."

Their stoic composure collapsed. Some of them shouted, "Me too," but others wept and turned to their brothers for comfort. It was one thing to fight an open battle which might lead to death. It was another to stand firm while certain death slowly crept upon you.

As they shouted amongst themselves, I spotted something.

Behind the formation was the Parthenon. Within, shields, spears, and swords adorned the walls.

Contrary to conventional wisdom, I laughed. *The gods will*

certainly curse me now. But it was a good idea that came to me, and I was determined to follow it. "About face," I ordered.

Despite their trepidations, they obeyed as their instructions had taught them.

"Forward." I marched them back into the Parthenon. I called a halt. They looked at me mystified. "Hear me now, men," I said, "I believe those who fight to the death for their country are heroes. Don't you?"

They looked to one another and shrugged.

"They certainly are," I continued. "Like Jason, Achilles, Ajax… like Theseus, Pericles, and Alexander. You are heroes just the same as them. Don't you agree?" Some nodded or mumbled their consent. "I said, don't you agree?" They shouted now. "Then claim what is yours. You are heroes now and these now belong to you. Arm yourselves. We'll not go down without a weapon in hand!"

They broke off in a frenzy, ripping the most famous weapons in Athens down from the wall. Here the supposed club of Ajax, there the xiphon of Alexander.

"I don't know what to take," Castor said, standing idly while the others ripped the place apart.

"That's easy," I said. "What kind of hero do you think you are?"

"I'm no hero, not like you," he said. "though I'd like to become one."

"Which kind of hero, Castor?"

"The kind that's good to animals."

"Good. What about here then." I led him to the far wall. "This is Bellerophon's spear. He tamed Pegasus and became companions with it, just as you tamed your Pollux."

He smiled, and I think he stifled a tear, but was quick to reach for the spear and shield. "I'll carry them proudly."

"Now it's time to become heroes." I nodded to the men as they formed up by the exit. I spent a few moments looking for my own weapons, determined to ensure my men were armed first. I settled on the kopis of Eumenes of Cardia, one of Alexander's successors who fought many battles he didn't seek, something to which I could relate. "Here it is then, gentlemen. For death and glory."

"It's something to tell my children at least," Castor said. "that I fought with Quintus Sertorius, Hero of the North." He chuckled.

"So you have children I've never heard of?"

We were sitting with our backs to the Parthenon walls, quietly awaiting whatever fate prepared for us.

"No. Of course not," he said. "But I like to think ahead."

"That's a good quality." I nodded.

Silence developed while we listened for the approach of our enemy.

"I am ready to die though," he said.

I looked to him with furrowed brows. "What? Why would you say that?"

If any of the other men said the same thing I would've applauded them and told them they were right to do so. I wasn't ready to lose Castor to the underworld though, even if I was gone.

"I've already done everything I need to do in life." He was rather matter-of-fact.

I burst out laughing despite my best efforts to resist. "How can you say such a thing while you're still so young? There is so much left for you to experience."

"For instance?"

"A wife and child for starters." I laid my head back against the wall, my ears still perked up to the rumbling out in the city.

"I've loved a woman... the one I told you gave me a good price. That's almost like a wife." The other men began to listen in. "I've had a child…" He thought about it for a moment, "Well something *like* a child. Pollux, my dog," he said. "Had to feed him and all."

I managed to smile, watching the men listening. Despite how they mocked him when we first arrived in Greece, they now found the same comfort in him I did.

"I'd rather stay here, but if I must go at least I can say I experienced that."

I patted his knee and shook my head. "You're too good for this world, Castor. That's why we can't afford to lose you."

"I think we need a new nickname for him, boys," one of the legionaries said.

"What's wrong with pig boy?" another spoke up but was quickly elbowed into silence.

"What about 'war hog'?" said the legionary.

Castor lit up, his white cheeks blushing as they cheered for him.

"War hog." I rustled his hair.

A horn blew outside. From the direction I knew it was coming from the base of the hill. They were about to ascent to the Acropolis.

The men heard too. I saw several of them try to swallow. But the courage in their eyes still gives me courage today.

I stood. "They're nearly upon us men. There is no shield wall we can form with these… but we carry the arms of heroes. And their strength flows through our veins today," I said. They nodded along with me. "No, I said *the strength of heroes* flows through your veins. Let them hear you."

Several of them pounced to their feet and beat their shields to amplify their cries.

The Republic would be worse off without these men, but I could think of none better to die for a just cause. I was proud to be among them. "Gather your strength men. We fight our last battle now." I marched to the exit and the men lined up beside me.

We stood in formation as they flooded through the Propylaia. They were armed citizens like those who attacked us before, not the armed forces we met near Plataea. Still, they outnumbered us three to one. No, six to one. And we didn't have the armor or weapons we trained in. Yet I felt the strength of the men beside me, and I knew we'd take many of them with us before we fell.

They charged us with a fury I knew belong only to men who are filled with either hate or fear. But we had both too.

"Fight like heroes men!" I shouted as they crashed into us.

Natural light was beginning to fade. The torches behind us helped to illuminate as best they could, but they truly only served to glisten on the tips of sword and spears, nearly blinding our eyes.

With some much going on, I could only focus on the man before me.

Bovine face, thick shoulders, strong jaw. I imagined he was a butcher, or perhaps a farm hand.

No matter.

He thrust his sword for my jugular, but we were both surprised that Eumenes' shield was still very much functional. Not only did I block the attack, but his sword wedged within the wood and refused to be withdrawn.

I leapt and thrust my kopis down into the cavity of his chest.

One more wife widowed, another child orphaned. And it was his fault.

They flooded to us like high tide on sharp rock. We fought the best we could but were being pushed back. Before we knew it, the Parthenon had engulfed us again. It gave us strategic advantage: their best versus our best, but we couldn't retreat much further.

Another Greek lunged over the partial shield wall, his sword slashing through my tunic. Any closer and he might have severed something vital. But as it was, it only served to anger me.

I brought the kopis up and cleaved into his head. The sickening thud of bone cracking resulted. He twisted to the side and collapsed. "Fight hard, men," I said, trying to provide the consummate example.

The Greeks screamed encouragements in their own language, with far more voices to echo.

Another warrior thrust a spear at me. I lifted the shield and blocked it. When he recoiled, he took the shield with him, but I also swung my blade and connected with the exposed flesh of his neck. He buckled and collapsed.

I took the moment of reprieve to look for Castor. He was fighting strong in the second rank. There were a few droplets of blood on his cheek, but his hands were clean. That comforted me. If we were all about to die, I wanted him to go with a clean conscience. No legionary should feel guilt for bloodshed, but Castor was a special lad.

"Jupiter!" I bellowed, and they echoed with 'Optimus' as they had during training.

A few legionaries cried out and dropped on either side of me. I might have stopped and checked on them if I was able. The second line might have pushed up and taken our place if they were able. But they weren't.

"Roma!" I shouted. The men struggled to answer with "victrix." I continued the cry as more legionaries fell beside me. I took up the shield of a dead man and hoisted it before me as I checked our ranks. We were losing men fast, and the enemy onslaught continued. "Fight on," I said, or at least I meant to. More young legionaries fell beside me. In the fog of my eye, they wore Gavius' face. They died like heroes, like I'd asked them to. But I didn't want them to die.

It was much more heroic to lay your own life down. At least there was some redemptive quality to it. There was nothing pleasing about watching your own men die. Ask any commander, if he's brave enough to answer honestly.

Even as I fought and considered the nature of death, I did not want them to die. *Live, live.* But we had nowhere else to go. We were halfway to the center of the Parthenon now.

"Your fathers are watching over you!" I shouted, but I was out of breath. I'd been fighting harder than I knew. I hoped they heard me. Regardless, more of them fell.

We stepped back farther into the Parthenon.

The sun had all but faded. The only light from outside left afforded to us only illuminated endless scores of bodies. Bodies belonging to those who wished for nothing at the moment but our deaths.

The Martyr's name rang out in my head. So did Rabirius' words, and the slaver Hyrkanos too. We'd been so close.

One of the Greeks cracked into the shield I'd picked up with a club. I barely deflected the blow and felt the pain ricochet up my arm. There wasn't a place on my body that didn't feel a tinge of that pain.

As the left side of my body recoiled from the pain, I hacked Eumenes' kopis into his shoulder. The warrior batted it away, and someone managed to butt his head into my own. I stumbled back but the remaining soldiers by my side held the line.

I came to just as the club was about to crash down to my exposed head. I lifted my shield. Barely deflecting the blow and feeling the pain of its force again. But his body was exposed. My training took over and I forgot to hack and slash as the Greeks do. Instead I stabbed as if it were a gladius in my hands. Regardless the blade slid through the flesh of his belly. He roared out like a Carthaginian lion but toppled onto one of his men.

We'd lost nearly half.

So this really was it? We'd taken a good bit of them then. That's worth it, right? I guess I'd just never believed it, even as we waited for them to ascend the hill. In my heart I expected the gods to offer some divine escape route. Finding none, I shouted, "I'll meet you in the green fields of Elysium, brothers!"

More men fell beside me. Here's another I'll see in the green fields, there's another. That's all I could think. But I knew the

Fates would cut my cord soon; so it was becoming less frightening, less hurtful.

Another horn sounded. We didn't react to it. We continued fighting. There were no more than fifteen of us left, and we were nearly to the back wall.

But the enemy turned. It wasn't their horn.

Slowly they retreated from our line and rushed back out toward the Propylaia. We gathered ourselves the best we could and rushed out to follow them.

"Castor?" I shouted.

"I'm here," he said.

"War hog is fine," one of the men replied as we ran, slapping Castor on the back.

"Is it over?" Castor asked.

"Not yet," I said.

The enemy reached the gateway and looking through it they saw something they didn't like. They turned back to us with the fires of Vesta in their eyes.

"Keep ranks!" I shouted.

They came back with all the force they could muster. Regardless of momentum, steel still punctures deep. Of the four men to my left and right, two of them dropped.

I had no indication about who might be coming up to our aid . I knew it wasn't Didius . But it didn't matter.

"Fight till the last," I said as they crashed into us. With my kopis I cut through the calf of one of the assailants. Another quickly took his place. I don't know what happened, but my shield was quickly removed from my grasp. Something took over then. Perhaps it was the gods. I rushed forward. I swung my kopis left and right, taking out rebels as I went.

Someone was coming to our aid. Someone. And they'd find me in a heap of bodies when they got there.

All seemed to fall silent then. The only thing I could hear was the javelin whistling toward me.

I turned. My eye fixed on the iron tip streaking to side. *This is it.'* And I wasn't afraid. I closed my eye and lowered my head. But I felt no pain. I opened my eye and discovered nothing had impaled my flesh.

By my feet lay Castor, the javelin wedged in his chest.

"No," I cried.

"For war hog!" the legionaries shouted.

I fell to my knees by my shield bearer. "Hold on, my friend. We've won. You just have to hold on."

He said nothing, but those eyes stared up at me, searching.

I looked down and knew his wound was mortal. I wanted to keep fighting, but I realized he probably wanted me to stay as I would want others to stay. I stopped and put both of my hands —on top of one another—over the free flow of blood. I met his eyes. He was still very much present, even if he couldn't speak. "You've been the greatest friend I've known, Castor," I said. "This world doesn't deserve you. Never has."

His eyes continued to watch me, wide but not frantic.

"You've seen far too much turmoil and tragedy for a man so young. But now you can have peace. If there is something after this, you'll get the best of it."

He continued to struggle, trying to say something. But the words were unavailable to him.

I did my best to calm him, as if his words meant something to us, as if we knew. Part of that was true, but I would have loved to hear it if he were able.

When his head fell back and the blood flowed freely from the corners of his lips, I knew it was time.

I stood and brandished the kopis again. But when I turned, I saw the seventeenth legion charged through the Acropolis gateway with Aulus at their helm.

"Charge!" he bellowed.

And I hurried back into the fray.

SCROLL XXIX

WHEN THE LAST sword was sheathed, I turned to look behind me. Thirty-seven of my men in total lay there. None of the wounded survived.

I stepped over some of them, whispering a silent prayer as I did, to find Castor. He was still now, his flesh pale and his lips a blueish hue. Yet his eyes were still wide, and they stared out in amazement at whatever he saw last. I sat beside him and took his hand within mine. I had no tears to shed now; they're often stifled in the aftermath of a battle. But my soul wept. I closed his eyes with the back of my bloody thumb, fixing in place whatever it was that brought him joy in his final breath. Perhaps it was Pollux waiting for him on the River Styx, barking and leading him to the green fields and honey river of Elysium.

"Orders, legate?" one of my men asked, still clutching tight to the legendary shield and *sarissa* with which he'd fought.

"Gather carts for the men," I said. "And shrouds to cover them properly."

"Yes, legate."

"You wait for me there, Castor," I said. "We'll share a drink then. Perhaps you can meet my family." As I whispered the tears finally welled up in his eye. "And I can meet Pollux. We'll ride horses and tell stories about our time in Greece... but only the pleasant ones." I dried my nose. "Tell the gods this brutish one-eyed legate is coming. And I'll see you there." I blinked until I could see again and stared up at the Greek sky.

Above us stood the towering statue of Athena Promachos, one golden hand on her spear and the other on her massive shield.

The oracles words returned to me: *"Nothing but the willful shedding of innocent blood beneath the mighty shield of Athena can stay the gods wrath."* She'd been right. If only I'd have known... put the pieces of the mosaic together... I would have shed my own blood. But if the gods base the worth of a sacrifice on the heart of their offering, the Republic should be safe for a long time.

I struggled to my feet as my knees cried out in resistance. Turning I found the one man who had the capacity to make me smile even amidst such tragedy.

Aulus shook his head and wagged a finger at me. "Don't you say it, Quintus Sertorius."

"What do you mean?"

He huffed and threw up his arms. "You know exactly what I mean. I know how this is going to go. You're wondering why we found ourselves back in Athens."

My cracked lips managed a grin as I approached him. "I was wondering that, yes. Weren't you supposed to be heading straight for Megaris?"

"See? Here we go." He crossed his arms.

"Was it the gods?"

"No, it wasn't the gods." He attempted to pout but I stared at him until he continued. "I came back for my ornamental vase." He balled his hands into fists to prepare for the mocking.

I couldn't help but chuckle. He cursed me while I doubled over and grabbed at my splitting sides. "You marched three thousand men back to Athens for a vase?"

He grunted. "I sure did."

"And Lucius and Spurius let you do this?" I asked, suspiciously.

He looked up, a smirk on his face. "They were ... asleep in the carriage. So no one was there to stop me."

"Asleep in the carriage?" I asked, perplexed.

His face suddenly became serious. "You should come with me."

Aulus led me through the city we'd spent so long defending to the rest of his force by the postern gate, a cortege of our men following for protection. As we went, citizens appeared in windows and doorways.

Crying out like only the liberated can, they showered us with grain and flowers they ripped up from their own gardens—our own impromptu triumph.

We waved and smiled. Young girls ran up to kiss us, not deterred by the blood still covering us head to toe. If only Castor could've seen this. He'd think he was in Elysium still.

The crowds followed us as we exited to the Achaean countryside. I spotted the remainder of the seventeenth legion in the distance and a carriage there. The moment I spotted the bull-like frame of my old friend Lucius I lost all sense of dignity and sprinted to him like a child.

"Lucius!" I shouted, I clung to him.

"We're back, brother." He managed to embrace me with the strength of a two-armed man, although now he had only one.

"What has happened?" I said, turning and throwing an arm around Spurius' shoulder.

"It's a long story," Spurius said, shaking his head.

"Perhaps one to distract us on the voyage home." Lucius smiled as I clasped his one hand.

I meant to let go, but he pulled me in and forced me to meet his gaze.

"Wherever you fight, I fight. My sword is yours, Sertorius. I don't want to be parted from you again."

I clapped his neck. "My glory is yours, Lucius. Always."

"This really is something," Aulus said with crossed arms and a tapping foot. "A one-eyed legate and a one-armed tribune. Between the two of you, you almost make up a whole man."

"And still twice the lot of you," Lucius said, charging him. He still managed to out wrestle Aulus even with his wounds.

"We thought we'd never make it back," Spurius said, more sober now. "We're lucky to be here."

"That's all that matters now," I said. "We're all still here."

He dropped his gaze and nodded, still making sense of it all as any man does after his first real taste of war.

"We almost lost you again today. How is this possible?" he said. "How could they know the perfect time to strike?"

We shook our heads at our friends as Aulus cried out for release from the chokehold Lucius had managed to pin him in.

"That's the only mystery still unraveled," I said. "I can't make sense of it."

"Could… Didius be the traitor?"

My eyes widened as I considered it. "He always did want to ensure he received his triumph."

"And perhaps he wanted you gone before returning so all the glory would belong to him." Spurius grimaced.

"No. No, that can't be." I shook my head. "Didius is many things, more so since the death of his son… but he's no traitor. And he's no coward either. If he wanted me dead, he'd create a charge against me and do it himself."

"Who else could it possibly be? Who else could have known all this, from the moment we arrived? Apollonius?" He laughed at his own suggestion. "Paullus seemed the most likely source at one point, but now he's in Hades and the treachery continues."

"I think it's Apollonius," Aulus said. "Never did like the old bastard." He winked.

Lucius joined us, scratching at his chin. "The traitor knew the last night we'd be quartered. They knew you'd be defenseless on the Acropolis today."

"And they knew we were marching on Plataea," I said. "Whoever it is must have sent a messenger. The enemy rode out to meet us before even their scouts could have spotted our advance."

My stomach churned. My vision tunneled. I bit my lip, knowing who it was.

I found him exactly where I expected. Seated in his courtyard and sipping a cup of vintage wine, surrounded by his servants.

"Tell them to leave," I said. "They won't want to watch this."

He looked up and smiled, completely unperturbed by my bloody appearance or the sword in my hand.

"Please, by all means. Join me for a moment," he said.

I struggled to swallow. "What should I call you now?" I said, my voice betraying my pain. "Priest? Kallias? … the Martyr?"

He only continued to smile as he nodded for his servants to leave. Only the two of us remained in that silent, empty courtyard.

"You may call me whatever you like."

"I am going to kill you, Kallias."

"Of course, of course," he said. "But you can sit with me for a moment, can't you? I'm a dying old man. I'm not going to outrun or outfight you. You've already won, my boy."

I weighed out my options. The scale refused to tip in either direction, but there was still part of me that didn't want to kill the kindly old priest. I sat on a bench across from him, hand still on the hilt of my sword.

"Do you know why I've done what I have?"

"Because you're a coward," I said. "and a liar. And a traitor."

He lifted a glass cup and twirled it so the light ran along its edge. "You're right, of course. In a manner of speaking. But there are many frames through which we can perceive the world."

"There is no god, no nation, no culture which would exonerate you now." My breath became heavy. "You betrayed those who called you friend. Your actions resulted in the deaths of men who looked up to you." Castor's smile flashed before my eyes and it took all the power left within me not to tear him apart in that moment.

"I was never your friend, Quintus Sertorius," he said without malice. "Although I do think fondly of you. We simply believe different things fundamentally, you and I. We could never be reconciled."

"We agree on this one thing at least," I said. "So tell me. What is it that I believe? That you find untenable?"

He gestured to a vase of wine beside him. I shook my head. "Well, Rome of course," he said.

"What?"

"You and the rest of your men. You fight for something I find deplorable. Wretched. Evil."

I ground my teeth. "And explain to me why." I said. "Have we not been gentle masters? Are your people not free to come and go as they please? Are you not sharing in the wealth of the Republic? Not benefiting from the safety our men buy for you with their blood?"

He nodded along as I spoke. He took a sip of wine and smacked his lips to savor the taste. "You're a reader of history, aren't you?"

"I am." I leaned forward on the bench.

"Rome defeated Hannibal at Zama. Ninety-eight years passed between that victory and your general Marius's defeat of

Jugurtha. Over that span, sixty-eight triumphs were held for the governors of Africa alone. Sixty-eight triumphs in ninety-eight. A triumph requires five thousand dead enemies, correct?"

I glared in his direction but could only nod.

He balked. "Five thousand dead boys, sixty-eight years over that past century. And for what? For peace and prosperity? For civilization? For protection? And if so, protection for whom?" He spoke without malice or ill intent, calm and kind with his ancient voice as if he only wanted to show me the way. "Your glory is a myth. It exists only to fuel the ambitions of ambitious men."

"What of myself?" I said. "Am I here only for advancement, for ambition? Have I left my family for these long years for power and wealth?"

He smiled and took another sip of wine. "I've already said I admire you. I've served as an advisor to the Roman governors for as long as I can remember, and I've found so few men who care for anything outside of themselves the way you do." He became serious, but softened. "I did not want to see you die. But your death, if it served some role in diminishing Rome's stranglehold of the world… it would have been worth it."

"What of our governor then? What of Didius? Was he not your friend? He has served honorably here and stamped out a rebellion that could have sown the seeds of death throughout all Greece. Was he here only for glory?"

He smiled sadly. "My boy, I was there when he told you of his desire to kill five thousand men, his desire to parade about Rome like a god for stealing the lives of young men. He was going to butcher regardless, so all I did was give the Greek people something for which to die."

I couldn't stop blinking, couldn't stop shifting. I almost accepted that cup of wine—I wanted to—but to share a cup with a man saying such things was tantamount to treason. "You've not hurt rich old politicians. You've not harmed Didius' political career, or stolen sleep from the senate," I said, my voice beginning to shake. "You've done nothing but take the lives of men who only wanted to serve, to give themselves a better life than the poverty into which they were born."

He nodded and his eyes glossed over. "And yet how many more would they have killed if they'd grown to be grizzled old veterans? How many more young maidens would they have left widowed, or children they would have orphaned?"

I stood and slowly drew my sword. He watched the blade, but with nothing but mere curiosity. "You have failed, Kallias."

"You cannot begin to comprehend what we've accomplished, my boy," he said.

"Your 'polemarch' and 'archon' are dead."

He nodded. "Yes. As we intended."

"So I guess that leaves you. The 'martyr.'" I stepped across the courtyard, my legs heavy. "And you'll die here. You have *failed*, Kallias."

He finished his cup of wine and poured another, continuing to inspect the light on the glass. "We called ourselves Cerberus. But what could three old Greeks do to bring down an empire?" He chuckled. Perhaps he was beginning to understand, I thought. "But the real Cerberus is still out there, and its three heads are howling. From the East, from Italy … from within Rome itself. All we ever sought was to delay you until they could strike. And we've done that. In a manner of speaking, we have won."

"You speak nonsense, old man. There are no wars to be fought. No one is 'striking,'" I said.

His eyebrows raised. "Oh, have you not heard?"

"Heard what?" I said through gritted teeth.

"Kill me now, my boy, and go find out."

I struggled to say, "I should take you back to Rome for trial, for execution."

He lifted his cup. "I couldn't risk that. There's hemlock in the wine."

I straightened my sword before me. So death it was then. I stood before him and brought back the sword. But Castor's voice whispered in my ear. He was unarmed, he was defenseless, I didn't *have* to kill him. I sheathed my blade. "No. I'll not make a martyr of you," I said. "You're not a hero. You're nothing, and you'll die like it." I turned to leave.

"What?" he said. "No. You must kill me. They'll want my head."

"They'll hear of your treachery and your death." I continued walking. "But they'll not be tales told of your defiance. Only of your fitful, wretched death."

"No. Come back here and finish this," he said.

"You'll grow cold and rigid. You'll lose the feeling in your feet and it will creep up till it reaches your heart."

"No!"

"You'll vomit and shake. You'll void yourself."

"Roman!" He shouted after me.

I turned and looked at him for the last time. "You haven't made a martyr of yourself. You've made a martyr of your people, Kallias."

"Please." He stretched out to me.

"You're no hero."

"Roman… please…"

His voice trailed into silence as I left his home and left Athens.

SCROLL XXX

"THE THIRD HEAD of Cerberus is dead," I told Didius when I caught up to the legion on their march to Megaris. I was still unwashed, covered in dried, cracking blood.

"And you're certain?" he asked, calling for a halt.

"Yes," I said. "It was Kallias."

His eyes flickered as the realization flooded over him. Shock, rage, shame, disappointment, pain… he felt them all. He cracked his neck and cleared his throat. "It appears I've been wrong about many things," he said. "And that's difficult for a man like me to admit."

He pounced from his horse and squared up to me.

"I've gravely misjudged two men. The one I held as an ally and companion. I embraced him even as he stabbed my back. The other," he said, meeting my eye. "I've treated with contempt and suspicion. I've held him responsible for everything from the death of my son to every headache I've had on campaign… and I was wrong." He cleared his throat again and straightened to preserve his dignity. "Quintus Sertorius is a good man. Good Roman. And I'd be honored if you'd serve with me in the war in Italy."

"What?" I said before I could process what I was hearing.

He squinted. "No one has told you?"

"I've done nothing but sacrifice and fight since the moment you departed from Athens."

He rubbed at the stubble of his chin. "The Italians have rebelled. We're going to war." He pounced back on his horse. "We must make haste for Italy."

I felt numb from the news, but managed to say, "There's one thing left we need to do, sir."

Both of our legions pulled off the road when we reached Timoxenos's vineyard. A few squatters lingered within, but they quickly scurried off when they heard us approach.

"This is a good spot," I said.

Didius nodded. "I'm inclined to agree."

Timoxenos's gardens were untended and overgrown, but nothing could mar the beauty of this spot. The sun was large and gold on the horizon, and the wildflowers were blooming in every color in fields as far as the eye could see.

We split the legions on either side of the dirt path, while the carriages bearing our dead passed between us. The other officers and I helped unload them as the men gathered wood. We built a pyre that would have honored a king and laid them each beside one another with coins on their eyes.

I bore Castor myself and sat him on the edge. He'd carved two wooden figures for me. I placed one in his hands and closed them around it. The other I've kept amongst my personal effects all these years.

One of the men lit a torch and passed it to me.

"Until we meet again, my brother," I said and lit the pyre.

I walked back slowly and joined the ranks of Lucius, the twins, Apollonius, and Herennius.

When the fires died down, we silently mixed their ashes with wine and buried them under the shade of an ancient oak.

I patted the soil level and stood. I jumped with a fright when I felt something wet tickling my leg. I turned to find one of Timoxenos' dogs. He was shaggy with a long pink tongue and big floppy ears. Of all Timoxenos' canine companions, it seemed this fellow was the only one to remain. "Hello there, boy."

Without my invitation he jumped up and threw both of his paws on my stomach. His tail was wagging, and he tapped his feet with ecstasy when I scratched behind his ears.

"We're preparing for movement, legate," one of the men said.

"Moving," I replied.

I turned to Castor's mound and smiled. He'd sent me "a Pollux" from his golden fields to keep me company.

"Would you like to come with me, boy?" I said. Whether he could understand or not, he continued to wiggle with excitement and followed my every step as I made it back for the line.

When I set out for Greece, I was afraid I would return as someone else. I feared I would come back scarred and burdened, as I had before. I was afraid I would turn back to drink, that I might scare my wife and child.

But despite my efforts I had changed. Castor made sure of that. I'd changed for the better. And Rome would need my absolute best with war waiting for us within our own borders.

Arrea and Gavius needed my best too, though. And they needed it more.

When we stepped onto the ship, not even my seasickness could deter my excitement. I was going to get my family back. I had many stories to tell them. Of a little girl in the water, another saved from torment... of a simple young man who liked dogs and making wood carvings.

I could leave out the stories of treachery, war, and turmoil. The past was past, and those other stories are vastly more important to me.

Join the Legion to receive Vincent's spinoff series "The Marius Scrolls" for FREE! Just scan the QR code below!

GLOSSARY

- *Ab urbe condita—Roman phrase and dating system "from the founding of the city." The Ancient Romans believed Rome was founded in 753 BC, and therefore this year is AUC 1. As such, 107–106 BC would correspond to 647–648 AUC.*
- *Aedile—Magistrates who were tasked with maintaining and improving the city's infrastructure. There were four, elected annually: two plebeian aediles and two curule aediles.*
- *Agnomen—A form of nickname given to men for traits or accomplishments unique to them. Many conquering generals received agnomen to designate the nation they had conquered, such as Africanus, Macedonicus, and Numidicus.*
- *Amicus (f. Amica)—Latin for friend.*
- *Appian Way (via Appia)—the oldest and most important of Rome's roads, linking Italy with farther areas of Italy.*
- *Aqua Marcia—the most important of Rome's aqueducts at this time. Built in 144-140 B.C.*
- *Arausio—the location of a battle in which Rome suffered a great loss. Numbers were reported as high as 90,000 Roman casualties. Sertorius and Lucius Hirtuleius barely escaped*

with their lives, and Sertorius' brother Titus died upon the battlefield.

- *Argiletum* — a route leading direction to the Roman forum.
- *Asclepius* — The Greek god of medicine. There was a temple to Asclepius overlooking the Tiber River, and this is where Rabirius and many other wounded veterans congregate.
- *Augur* — A priest and official who interpreted the will of the gods by studying the flight of birds.
- *Auxiliary* — Legionaries without citizenship. At this time, most auxiliaries were of Italian origin, but later encompassed many different cultures.
- *Ave* — Latin for hail, or hello.
- *Basilica Porcia* — the first named basilica in Rome, built by Cato the Censor in 184 B.C., it was the home of the ten tribunes of the plebs.
- *Basilica Sempronia* — built in 170 B.C. by the father of Tiberius and Gaius Gracchus. It was a place often used for commerce.
- *Bellona* — The Roman goddess of war and the consort of Mars (see also **Mars**). She was also a favored patron goddess of the Roman legion.
- *Bona Dea* — "Good goddess." The term was occasionally used as an exclamation.
- *Boni* — Literally "good men." They were a political party prevalent in the Late Roman Republic. They desired to restrict the power of the popular assembly and the tribune of the plebs, while extending the power of the Senate. The title "Optimates" was more common at the time, but these aristocrats often referred to themselves favorably as the boni. They were natural enemies of the populares.
- *Caepiones* — A powerful aristocratic family, and the former patrons of Sertorius.
- *Caldarium* — hot bathes.

- *Carcer*—*a small prison, the only one in Rome. It typically held war captives awaiting execution or held those deemed as threats by those in political power.*
- *Centuriate Assembly*—*one of the three Roman assemblies. It met on the Field of Mars and elected the Consuls and Praetors. It could also pass laws and acted as a court of appeals in certain capital cases. It was based initially on 198 centuries, and was structured in a way that favored the rich over the poor, and the aged over the young.*
- *Centurion*—*An officer in the Roman legion. By the time Marius's reforms were ushered in, there were six in every cohort, one for every century. They typically led eighty to one hundred men. The most senior centurion in the legion was the "primus pilus," or first-spear centurion.*
- *Century*—*Roman tactical unit made of eighty to one hundred men.*
- *Cimbri*—*a tribe of northern invaders with uncertain origins that fought Rome for over a decade. Sertorius began his career by fighting them.*
- *Circus Maximus*—*a massive public stadium which hosted chariot races and other forms of entertainment. It's speculated that the stadium could have held as many as 150,000 spectators.*
- *Client*—*A man who pledged himself to a patron (see also* **patron***) in return for protection or favors.*
- *Cloaca Maxima*—*the massive sewer system beneath Rome.*
- *Cocina*—*Kitchen.*
- *Cohort*—*Roman tactical unit made of six centuries (see also* **century***), or 480–600 men. The introduction of the cohort as the standard tactical unit of the legion is attributed to Marius's reforms.*
- *Collegium(a)*—*Any association or body of men with something in common. Some functioned as guilds or social clubs, others were criminal in nature.*

- *Comitiatus (pl. Comitia)*—*a public assembly that made decisions, held elections, and passed legislation or judicial verdicts.*
- *Comitium*—*a meeting area outside of the Curia Hostilia. The rosta speaking platform stood at its helm.*
- *Consul*—*The highest magistrate in the Roman Republic. Two were elected annually to a one-year term. The required age for entry was forty, although exceptions were occasionally (and hesitantly) made.*
- *Contiones (pl. Contio)*—*a public assembly that did not handle official matters. Discussions could be held on almost anything, and debates were a regular cause for a contiones to be called, but they did not pass legislation or pass down verdicts.*
- *Contubernalis(es)*—*A military cadet assigned to the commander specifically. They were generally considered officers, but held little authority.*
- *Contubernium*—*The smallest unit in the Roman legion. It was led by the decanus (see also **decanus**).*
- *Curia*—*The Senate House. The Curia Hostilia was built in the 7th century B.C. and held most of the senatorial meetings throughout the Republic, even in Sertorius' day.*
- *Decanus*—*"Chief of ten," he was in a position of authority over his contubernium, a group of eight to ten men who shared his tent.*
- *Dis Pater*—*god of the Roman underworld, at times subsumed by Plato or Hades.*
- *Dignitas*—*A word that represents a Roman man's reputation and his entitlement to respect. Dignitas correlated with personal achievements and honor.*
- *Dis Pater*—*The Roman god of death. He was often associated with fertility, wealth, and prosperity. His name was often shortened to Dis. He was nearly synonymous with the Roman god Pluto or the Greek god Hades.*

- *Dominus(a)—Latin for "master." A term most often used by slaves when interacting with their owner, but it could also be used to convey reverence or submission by others.*
- *Domus- the type of home owned by the upper class and the wealthy in Ancient Rome.*
- *Equestrian—Sometimes considered the lesser of the two aristocratic classes (see also **patrician**) and other times considered the higher of the two lower-class citizens (see also **plebeian**). Those in the equestrian order had to maintain a certain amount of wealth or property, or otherwise would be removed from the class.*
- *Evocati—An honorary term given to soldiers who served out their terms and volunteered to serve again. Evocati were generally spared a large portion of common military duties.*
- *Faex—Latin for "shit."*
- *Falernian wine—The most renowned and sought-after wine in Rome at this time.*
- *Field of Mars—"Campus martius" in Latin. This was where armies trained and waited to deploy or to enter the city limits for a Triumph.*
- *Flamen Dialis—Priest of Jupiter Optimus Maximus.*
- *Forum—The teeming heart of Ancient Rome. There were many different forums, in various cities, but most commonly the Forum refers to the center of the city itself, where most political, public, and religious dealings took place.*
- *Gerrae—"Nonsense!" An exclamation.*
- *Gladius(i)—The standard short-sword used in the Roman legion.*
- *Gracchi—Tiberius and Gaius Gracchus were brothers who held the rank of tribune of the plebs at various times throughout the second century BC. They were political revolutionaries whose attempts at reforms eventually led to their murder (or in one case, forced suicide). Tiberius and Gaius were still fresh in the minds of Romans in Sertorius's*

day. The boni feared that another politician might rise in their image, and the populares were searching for Gracchi to rally around.

- *Hastati* — Common front line soldiers in the Roman legion. As a result of the Marian Reforms, by Sertorius's times, the term hastati was being phased out and would soon be obsolete.
- *Imperator* — A Roman commander with imperium (see also **imperium**). Typically, the commander would have to be given imperium by his men.
- *Impluvium* — A cistern or tank in the atrium of the domus that collects rainfall water from a hole in the ceiling above.
- *Insula(e)* — Apartment complexes. They varied in size and accommodations, but generally became less desirable the higher up the insula one went.
- *Jupiter* — The Roman king of the gods. He was the god of the sky and thunder. All political and military activity was sanctioned by Jupiter. He was often referred to as Jupiter Capitolinus for his role in leading the Roman state, or Jupiter Optimus Maximus (literally, "the best and greatest").
- *Jupiter's Stone* — A stone on which oaths were sworn.
- *Kalends* — The first day of the Ancient Roman month.
- *Latrunculi* — (lit. Game of Brigands) a popular board game of sorts played by the Romans. It shares similarities with games like chess or checkers.
- *Legate* — The senior-most officer in the Roman legion. A legate generally was in command of one legion and answered only to the general.
- *Mars* — The Roman god of war. He was the favored patron of many legionaries and commanders.
- *Medicus* — The field doctor for injured legionaries.
- *Military tribune* — Senior officer of the Roman legions. They were, in theory, elected by the popular assembly, and there were six assigned to every legion. By late second century

BC, however, it was not uncommon to see military tribunes appointed directly by the commander.

- *Nursia — Sertorius' home, located in the Apennines mountains, and within the Sabine Tribes. It was famous for their turnips and little else until Sertorius came along.*
- *October Horse — A festival that took place on October 15th. An animal was sacrificed to Mars, which designated the end of the agricultural and military campaigning season.*
- *Optimates — (see **boni**).*
- *Ostia — Rome's port city, it lay at the mouth of the river Tiber.*
- *Patron — A person who offers protection and favors to his clients (see also **clients**), in favor of services of varying degrees.*
- *Peristylum — An open courtyard containing a garden within the Roman domus.*
- *Pilum(a) — The throwing javelin used by the Roman legion. Gaius Marius changed the design of the pilum in his reforms. Each legionary carried two, and typically launched them at the enemy to begin a conflict.*
- *Plebeian — Lower-born Roman citizens, commoners. Plebeians were born into their social class, so the term designated both wealth and ancestry. They typically had fewer assets and less land than equestrians, but more than the proletariat. Some, like the Metelli, were able to ascend to nobility and wealth despite their plebeian roots. These were known as "noble plebeians" and were not restricted from any power in the Roman political system.*
- *Pontifex Maximus — The highest priest in the College of Pontiffs. By Sertorius's time, the position had been highly politicized.*
- *Pontiff — A priest and member of the College of Pontiffs.*
- *Popular assembly — A legislative assembly that allowed plebeians to elect magistrates, try judicial cases, and pass laws.*

- *Praetor*—*The second-most senior magistrate in the Roman Republic. There were typically six elected annually, but some have speculated that there were eight elected annually by this time.*
- *Prefect*—*A high ranking military official in the Roman legion.*
- *Princeps Senatus*—*"Father of the Senate," or the first among fellow senators. It was an informal position, but came with immense respect and prestige.*
- *Proconsul*—*A Roman magistrate who had previously been a consul. Often, when a consul was in the midst of a military campaign at the end of his term, the Senate would appoint him as proconsul for the remainder of the war.*
- *Publicani*—*Those responsible for collective public revenue. They made their fortunes through this process. By Sertorius's time, the Senate and censors carefully scrutinized their activities, making it difficult for them to amass the wealth they intended.*
- *Quaestor*—*An elected public official and the junior-most member of the political course of offices. They served various purposes but often supervised the state treasury and performed audits. Quaestors were also used in the military and managed the finances of the legions on campaign.*
- *Res Publica*—*"Republic," the sacred word that encompassed everything Rome was at the time. More than just a political system, res publica represented Rome's authority and power. The Republic was founded in 509 BC, when Lucius Brutus and his fellow patriots overthrew the kings.*
- *Rex sacrorum*—*A senatorial priesthood, the "king of the sacred." Unlike the Pontifex Maximus, the rex sacrorum was barred from military and political life. In theory, he held the religious responsibility that was once reserved for the kings, while the consuls performed the military and political functions.*

- *Rostra—A speaking platform in the Forum made of the ships of conquered foes.*
- *Salve—Latin for hail, or hello.*
- *Sancrosanctitas—a level of religious protection offered to certain political figures and religious officials.*
- *Saturnalia—A festival held on December 17 in honor the Roman deity Saturn.*
- *Senaculum—a meeting area for senators outside of the senate house, where they would gather before a meeting began.*
- *Scutum(a)—Standard shield issued to Roman legionaries.*
- *Subura—a rough neighborhood near the Viminal and Quirinal hills. It was known for violence and thievery, as well as for the fires that spread because of the close proximity of its insulae.*
- *Taberna(e)—Could be translated as "tavern," but tabernae served several different functions in Ancient Rome. They served as hostels for travelers, occasionally operated as brothels, and offered a place for people to congregate and enjoy food and wine.*
- *Tablinum—A form of study or office for the head of a household. This is where he would generally greet his clients at his morning levy.*
- *Tarpeian Rock—a place where executions were held. Criminals of the highest degree and political threats were thrown from this cliff to their inevitable deaths.*
- *Tata—Roman term for father, closer to the modern "daddy".*
- *Tecombre—The military order to break from the testudo formation and revert to their previous formation.*
- *Temple of Ascelpius—located on the Tiber island, it was a temple of healing. The sick and ailing made pilgrimages here in hope of healing.*
- *Temple of Bellona—dedicated to the consort of Mars and goddess of war, this was a temple often used for meetings of the Senate when they needed to host foreign emmisaries or*

    meet with returning generals awaiting a triumph. It lay
    outside the city limits, but close to the Servian wall.

- *Temple of Castor and Pollux—often times referred simply to
  "Temple of Castor", it remained at the entrance of the
  Forum by the via sacra. It was often used for meetings of the
  senate, as it was actually larger than the Curia. Speeches
  were often given from the temple steps as well.*
- *Temple of Concordia (Concord)—a temple devoted to peace
  and reunification in the Roman Forum. It often held
  meetings of the senate.*
- *Temple of Jupiter Capitolinus (Optimus Maximus)—a
  temple devoted to Rome's patron God, which resided on the
  Capitoline hill. It was sometimes referred to as the
  "Capitol".*
- *Temple of Saturn—a temple of deep religious significance
  which lay at the foot of the Capitoline hill in the Roman
  Forum. Sacrifices were often held here following a triumph,
  if the generals didn't surpass it to sacrifice at the
  aformentioned Temple of Jupiter.*
- *Testudo—The "tortoise" formation. The command was used
  to provide additional protection by linking their scuta
  together.*
- *Teutones—a tribe of northern invaders with uncertain
  origins which fought Rome for over a decade. Along with
  the Cimbri, they nearly defeated Rome. Sertorius began his
  career by fighting these tribes.*
- *Tiber River—a body of water which connected to the
  Tyrrhenian sea and flowed along the western boarder of
  Rome. The victims of political assassinations were
  unceremoniously dumped here rather than receive proper
  burial.*
- *Tiberinus—the god of the Tiber river.*
- *Toga virilis—Literally "toga of manhood." It was a plain
  white toga worn by adult male citizens who were not*

magistrates. The donning of the toga virilis represented the coming of age of a young Roman male.

- *Tribe*—Political grouping of Roman citizens. By Sertorius's time, there were thirty-six tribes, thirty-two of which were rural, four of which were urban.
- *Tribune of plebs*—Elected magistrates who were designed to represent the interests of the people.
- *Triclinium*—The dining room, which often had three couches set up in the shape of a U.
- *Triumph*—A parade and festival given to celebrate a victorious general and his accomplishments. He must first be hailed as imperator by his legions and then petition the Senate to grant him the Triumph.
- *Valetudinarium*—a hospital, typically present in Roman military camps.
- *Via(e)*—"Road," typically a major path large enough to travel on horseback or by carriage.
- *Via Appia*- (see **Appian Way**).
- *Via Latina*—"Latin road", led from Rome southeast.
- *Via Sacra*—the main road of ancient Rome, leading from the Capitoline hill through the forum, with all of the major religious and political buildings on either side.
- *Via Salaria*—"Salt Road" led northeast from Rome. This was the path Sertorius would have taken to and from his home in Nursia.
- *Zeno*—The founder of Stoic philosophy. Sertorius was a devoted reader of Zeno's works.

ACKNOWLEDGMENTS

I'm going to do something a bit unorthodox for the acknowledgements of this book. Although there are so many to thank (family, friends, editors, designers, beta readers, reviewers, supporters, those who studied and wrote the incredible research which makes a book like this possible, and my readers), I want to use this space for something special.

This book is dedicated to a good friend of mine who was unjustly taken from this world by an unidentified shooter on December 1, 2020. It's been difficult to mourn during this time where there is already so much pain and turmoil, but as the months have dragged on I've continued to think about Andre and the legacy he left behind.

I want to use this space to tell his story. It makes me smile to think that anyone still reading might be willing to hear about my friend Andre, and perhaps be inspired by his life.

I wrote this shortly after his death and would like to share it with the world now. This is more personal than I would typically share in this space, but I'm willing to be vulnerable for his story to be told.

Andre was my brother.

I still remember the first time we met. Andrew was the one who introduced us, we met at his apartment downtown. We found out we shared a similar passion for business, and we both had big dreams. We believed in motivation.

The two of us really clicked. We talked constantly about what we would one day accomplish, about all the future might hold in store for us if we only worked hard enough to take hold of it. We'd sit in my car with the engine on in the church parking lot and talk about going into business together and starting a hedge fund. His passion inspired me and we pushed each other. Sometimes we'd argue. Sometimes we'd cry when things got hard and we didn't know how we were going to make it.

We came to know Christ together. We served in soup kitchens together. We "got swole" together (our way of saying we put on three pounds of muscle). We kicked our feet up and wasted Saturdays together. It seemed like my whole Freshmen year Andre, Andrew and I were together—pursuing Christ, our dreams, and laughter.

We loved football. One day we'd split ownership of an NFL team, that's what we decided. I always had my doubts, but Andre believed. He always believed that you could get what you wanted if you were willing to sacrifice for it. And it was so exciting to just hear him talk. The world seemed larger when he was around, possibilities endless. The inspiration and excitement of youth was never choked out of him by everyday life.

Even after time passed and he moved away, he'd still call and tell me again about all the amazing things we were going to achieve.

When Addison died—even from half the country away—he was one of the firsts to reach out. I was so devastated I couldn't bring myself to talk to anyone, so I didn't reply. He gave me some space and reached out again the next week. He said, "Brother I'm always watching over you like a hawk". That's the kind of guy he was. When you were one of his people, you stayed that way no matter how far away you were or how rarely you talked.

He loved everyone he met, and they loved him. He kept everybody laughing just being himself. He was made for comedy.

I never saw him treat someone poorly. He had this persistent habit of making everyone around him feel like a giant (and not just because of *his lack of height!). He built everyone up. By the time I published my first book he was telling everyone I was a famous author. When I joined the army, you would have thought I was a Medal of Honor recipient to hear him tell it.*

He loved his family. He talked about his momma and grandparents all the time. He wanted to achieve big things so he could give them big things. And up until his last day he was still fighting to achieve the impossible. And he would have too.

It's a sad, sad world when a guy like that... who lived to make everyone smile... is taken away from us so young.

I'm sorry, brother. I would have visited or called more like we talked about if I had known. I always thought there was more time.

I'll miss you, brother. But I'll see you again. Enjoy your mansion in the sky and get mine ready. We'll buy a football team when I get there.

Thank you so much for reading. I'll be back with more scrolls soon!

Always keep fighting,
    Vincent B. Davis II

ABOUT THE AUTHOR

Vincent B. Davis II writes historical fiction books to keep the past alive through the power of storytelling. He is also an entrepreneur, speaker, and veteran who is a proud graduate of East Tennessee State University and was honorably discharged from the US Army in 2022. Armed with a pen and an entrepreneurial spirit, Vincent quit his day job and decided it was as good a time as any to follow his dream. He went on to publish six historical fiction novels, four of which have now become Amazon International Best Sellers.

Vincent is also a devoted and depressed Carolina Panthers fan and a proud pet parent to his rescue pups, Buddy and Jenny. Join Vincent in celebrating the past through the pages of his books. His newsletter, The Legion, is more than just another author email list. It's a community of readers who enjoy free additional content to enhance their reading experience—HD Maps, family trees, Latin glossaries, free eBooks, and more. You can join the community and snag your freebies here.

Vincent also loves connecting with his readers through social media. Find him on social media at the links below, or email him at Vincent@thirteenthpress.com.